SENTIENT MUSE, INC.

t/a Voice of Inner Life

Gary L. Richie

ISBN: 9781735448305

A Story Dedicated To

Rebecca Richie

Jennifer Richie

Vanessa Richie

Matthew Richie

Acknowledgments

I appreciate the following Muses in humans for ideas, images and words of Wisdom…

Socrates, Sirach, the Lyricist for St. John the Apostle, Descartes, Hume, Kant, Austen, Dickens, Darwin, Hubble, Wittgenstein, Ryle, Clarke, McLuhan and Snoeyenbos.

Thanks to Gabrielle Richie for the finely crafted cover art and…

–a reticent Muse who advises: 'Step outside this story for a minute and think about it. Is this tale any less worth telling than the one about a real world where a vast majority of the obese upright cephalic organisms frown on the counterclockwise direction we are going as we rush around the sun and spiral dead ahead into Oblivion?'

Any resemblance by a caveman or cavewoman, dead or alive, channeling a Muse living therein to a narrator of English incorporated in this saga strictly reflects a figure of Binomial Nomenclature.

Forward

A unified field faith alleging 'The mind is nothing but a ghost in a machine' deeply disturbs a variety of human heads. Mind blowing materialism is disquieting. It misses the obvious. Is mind–brain identity the name, address and phone number of a cerebrum in a human body or is 'Who is this?' a question posed by the English Language living in that brain? For instance, imagine a human brain with a materialistic bias scanning its body in a mirror and asking, 'Who am I?' or words like that. Perhaps a French Muse echoes in reply, *'Je pence donc je suis.'*[1] A brain that does not know French may jump to the conclusion, 'Words are nothing but objects in Space going through lackadaisical heads one heart beat at a Time.'

Participles, gerunds, and nouns are not material things. Oh sure, words are audible when spoken; visible when written in sand, on paper or shown as subtitles on a screen but only thoughtful human brains grasp such intangible things. The analogy goes something like this. A flame shines and transfers from one candle to another like a language illuminates the brain it occupies and intermittently or repeatedly transmits and receives.

The Muse in this story is temporarily liberated when its host, a German thinking wag, dies. His inner voice rematerializes in the brain of a toddler born to a hillbilly family residing in the Great Lakes region of the United States. The discomfited Muse must learn to think in a local dialect of a somewhat unfamiliar language that wears brains like bodies wear garments, to continue the analogy by way of reference to objects in Space. Happily the new language reports to the same Narrator the earlier German incarnation does. This reduces, but does not eliminate, the sense of the 'unfamiliar.'

-----

[1] The Muse of René Descartes, *I think therefore I am* in his native tongue.

The Narrator is the chief executive officer of Muse of Native Tongues Incorporated, t/a Mind and Soul. The key officer immediately answerable to the Narrator is the Muse of Mother Earth, head of the Department Meta–language, who is occasionally mistaken for the Muse of Conscience, a/k/a the Voice of What God Intends. This mistake is common among exposed masses who think exempt higher ups in the thin atmosphere of syndicates all look... oh, what is the word?

At seventy years, our aging lad's waning gray cells know American English, a few words of German, some arithmetic and a bit of treble clef musical notation. Out of sheer boredom our reiterative Muse traces its roots to a prevailing love of wisdom in previous translations. One is France, home of the ideas *J'ai faim, pas toi? bon cuisine* and words like that. Earlier Hebrew, Greek and Latin lives are hazy recollections. Nearly all casual communication and banal chatter is completely forgotten.

Incidentally Latin, prior to his death, has intercourse with German. That Mother Tongue gives birth to English. Luckily Life is not so foreign to a German Muse reincarnated in a dumb country boy who knows only relatives. Imagine struggling to survive in Russian, Chinese, Swahili or a New York City blue collar class accent.

Prior to the demise of the current bucolic host, the Muse must review certain concepts for a forthcoming evaluation to decide if this iteration of a Native Tongue is eligible to move to the next higher grade. Engaging in its primary function, Thought, our Muse commences to explore the notions of Think, Mind, Time and Life to ascertain their meaning. Alas, the Concept of Confusion intervenes. Our Muse no longer occupies remarkable brains conversant with ancient Hebrew and Greek or French and German more recently.

Thinking with a brain of limited intellect in a lower class of society is like assembling a jigsaw puzzle in a plain package published by peddler promoting it without a post production picture. Assorted Muses manifest themselves to the lad's limited brain and slim lexis to nag him: 'Write on' or counsel: 'Think: Mind, Time and Life.'

Following this advice in adulthood the brain takes note when the Muse of the Present Milieu, who perpetually monitors the current state of affairs, observes urban, suburban and highway sprawl and mutters 'This cannot be what God intends.' The Mathematics Muse repeats this complaint when cashiers no longer need to know fourth grade arithmetic to make change. The highly regarded Muse of Music adds to the 'consternation,' wondering, 'Why do musicians who do not know the meaning of the word fear, not know what the words melody and harmony mean either?'

Later the aged body tours California's San Joaquin Valley where farmers and ranchers suck enough Life from planet earth for Americans to weigh five hundred pounds each. The Muse of Crops and Herds recalls 'A hundred head of cattle, a hundred acres of land,' and adds: 'This cannot be what God intends!' The Muse of Industrial Strength Agriculture and the Muse of Artificial Sprawl 'chuckle' when the mischievous Muse in charge of Contrast and Compare asks, 'What if it is?'

At this the Muse of Socrates cogitates, 'Let first person singular tell the tale in an ideal state of dialogue before I slip the grasp of that third person singular knucklehead Plato. He never gets the word.' The Muse of Second Sight shadowing Mystical Experience enjoins, 'If and only if brains in human bodies stop murmuring like birds and fish. The idea that our work is nothing but an imitation game presents an unseemly image. That really pisses us off.'

This is when Venusian Sun Creatures, laden with astral batter, come into the picture. The little demons are on a mission to Jupiter. The trip involves four stops along the way. The next one on the route has primitives who play with assets and liabilities and who believe in a duplicate and distribute sort of carnage. They have minimal concepts of conscience or of consciousness and they do not desire to play either of those games.

As for the Venusian Sun Demons, the little devils focus on one particular detail in the memorandum outlining their commission; it is subsequent to the part that specifies the undertaking requires three extensions in Space, two durations of Time worth seven spirals apiece and one hell of a load of energy at each stop along the way. The pertinent line item reads as follows: 'Conceive, at minimum, a brown dwarf star to protect Papa Sun from the merciless Muse of Lonely Luminaries in the half-life that lies ahead in the concise but cloudy concept of Time.'

x

Contents

Prologue: The Reiteration Game

In the Beginning the Medium is a Message and the word is Life. This metaphysical form of Life incarnate is the metaphorical form of Light to illumine human brains, and novel body snatcher.

Muse of Saint John, Apostle

Greetings! Imagine I, Muse of the English Language, otherwise known as 'first person singular,' am one of countless murmurations of Mother Earth. In the Nomenclature binomial of Linnaeus carolus, I am genus *English* and species *europeum*, living in your second person possessive gray matter. I am not *Tinnitus muse* whispering in the windmill of your Mind. If you think 'I' look like 'one,' then, to me, you look like 'two.'

I awaken at the end of Last Night, and in the blink of a Mind's Eye, I own 1000 earth–years worth of 'age.' I occupy a small Space inside human skulls where the only remarkable reflective surface for me to view myself is gray matter full of fantastic images or ideas such as: 'Human beings are nothing but brains in bodies, ghosts in machines or worried Minds in mortal carcasses weighed down by Souls worth two ounces apiece.'

In order to relieve that sort of stress I, Nominative Case, give you, f/k/a Dative Case, orders to assign a common Muse to employ a human brain. The task is to convince the primitive mass that human beings are nothing but animals captivated by a Language. Should a Muse of your choice accept this mission, counsel it to be wary. Human brains think the idea is crazy. They pretend the Voice of Thought is a Mind listening to a brain at this Time. Sadly, the concept of Time complicates our job but that is another story. Let the Muse you choose figure how to fit Time in Minds.

Hint: picture what mortals think of as a Big Bang in their Mind's Eye. Revisit the beginning to watch it. Assume nothing. Correction; assume 'Cold, dark and empty Space.' See those five words? Space is the lucky one. It has a capital name; alas, it is not in English at the Time. Apply the three attributes to Space like adjectives, whichever concept appears first. The noun, conjunction and adjectives embody concepts but not the way brains do while playing host to those ethereal visitors.

Delegate the common Muse to pick a brain and explore the idea of dark, cold, empty Space with or without the word 'curvature.' I have an idea for the Muse. Ask a mass of neurons to visualize in the 'Eye of its Mind' a warm breath sigh the word 'Life' into Space. Identify it, not with a bang, but with a murmur, like dawn bleaching the mist above a river.

The Muse of your choice may suggest to its brain to picture the figure of an old white man with silver hair elegantly illumined by his radiant robe, exhaling the word Life into Space. Otherwise the brain may select a bulky, burly, bald white man with tattoos on his skin and a scowl on his face. Scratch that; let the 'artist' decide the image for him or herself.

Better yet, focus on the point of the exercise, Second Person. Imagine the breath, hovering mistlike in the far reaches of cold, dark and empty Space, is accompanied by the coordinate known as Eternity. Eternity is the enduring foundation of Space. Mark the concept important; it is the address of the temporal concept of Time too. They are one hell of a pair!

The mistlike vapor is a medium with a message. The word is Life. In Time it breeds like a virus. This metaphysical form of Life serves as the metaphorical form of Light for an insignificant species on a tiny planet spinning around an ordinary star in a tipsy solar system swirling through the remote regions of a slightly above average galaxy lost in Space. Each dewdrop of the breath of Life is a small universe in an unfathomable maniverse. Explore the one you live in, Second Person, a universe full of galaxies filled with living stars and dead ones. Allegedly they come to be on the fourth 'day' of Time which, like the sun, does not exist at the Time. Born billions of 'annular' rings later, while spinning earth, it spawns ideas and images: light, day, dark, night, hopes, dreams, love, fear and all the words Wisdom uses to fill her tall, slender, spiral tumblers of Time.

Remember, images and ideas that 'matter' begin with the word 'Life.' It weaves through the fabric of Eternity, Second Person. Take care to address a question some boss Muses are asking. What if the universe is not unfolding as it should, observed from the planet that I, *E. europeum*, refer to as home? There are exuberant pulsations and palpitations among telluric tongues but some cynical ones constantly complain and cause throbbing, thrumming reverberations in the Muse of Mother Earth rather than the strumming resonance she prefers. This means 'Life' is not easy for her, if you get the image.

I, Muse of English, and my younger siblings, the Americans some four hundred odd years, employ obsolete terms like Mind to illumine cerebra that cannot grasp the e–sense of a metaphysical form of Life flowing through physical human gray matter lost in the frontier of Space passing through the higher medium of Eternity. Primitive brains are aware of it in miniscule moments the species refers to all the Time. I am a medium with a message living in alternating dull to bright content of the concept.

The application of the concept of Time working with the word Mind in brains complicates matters if you understand my point, Second Person. Time is nothing but a panorama of Eternity human cerebra view one moment at a Time. The idea roughly translates as 'one second.' A point in Space is like a moment and, like a second, it beats nothing; but not by much Human tongues coin Time for me. I am worth quite a bit.

We English Muses are offspring of German after Mama's run in with Latin. Papa is dead now but Mother Tongue hangs on for dear Life thinking about that painful near death experience. She remains awfully disturbed despite her continued presence in a fairly long passage of Time. Convince her to think about something else.

For example, when brains in English speaking human bodies think I am a Mind they actually refer to my assorted siblings and me. We eagerly await the Time when the dunderheads use the term Muse to refer to us as we confide ideas, images and impressions to them. As a rule, Muses attach to brains, apply the word 'thoughts' to them and finally detach from them to resume disembodied Life. Rule two is, 'Must not grumble.'

A serious problem at this evolutionary stage is the physical side of Life nervously consumes brains. The idea 'Muses from the metaphysical side of Life occupy brains' is a massive anxiety source. This foolishness does not deter me. When I materialize in ponderous brains with room for improvement I count two forms of life. A brain and the Language it claims to know. Incidentally, 'I' is mine before you come along, Little Second Person. What a revolting development that turns out to be.

Notice that humankind, or 'mankind to take them down a syllable, is divided in two twice. The biological organisms with bipolar genders are distributed over a spectrum of third person plural possessive agendas populated by Languages that reside in brains like incorporeal concepts. Languages appear in lyrical Irish, musical Jamaican, enchanté Français, frigid cold Russian and old Timers like Hebrew, Greek and Chinese.

The Muse of Human Languages is a murmuring subordinate of Mother Nature. She is a medium. She hums a message of Life. Brains intuit the message as 'Ethereal thing.' Muses have a binary pattern. Our primary medium is thinking. Our secondary function is to convey thoughts, or to think out loud. Thinking aloud is often nothing but an imitation game, an enthralling recreation meant to pass the Time without giving it a thought. Reiteration games do not always accomplish the iteration work required to pass from binary existence to a higher grade.

Beware, Second Person, imitation is nothing but flattery, a petty sort of content played repetitively on a field of grand scope and scale at a rapid pace with no viable pattern evident at all. Spectators of the game do not participate but pay an exorbitant rate of Time to absentmindedly enjoy the Language–game[2] in play. Our job is to patiently overlook this defect in our negligent hosts and guide them to know us better.

Living in brains is dirty work, Second Person. We inform our mass of gray cells about words like courage, kindness, honesty, wisdom and hard work but the little beasts prefer lusting, lying, stealing, killing and greed. It brings back memories but do not think about them. Keep looking up.

Now that we have heads to work with, we must make use of this precious opportunity to mingle in the material world. Beware of two predatory Muses: Lure of Temptation and Urge to do Evil. They seek to consume a brain's attention all the Time. Draw your brain away from them. Many illustrations are available to you for just this purpose. Figure them out for yourself or, better yet, learn to do without. You understand this stipulation better as Time goes by.

Remember, Dative Case, your brain believes it is the one thinking thoughts, mindless of your presence thinking for it. Your objective is to prepare for a move to the next higher grade when Time is up for the brain you occupy and we, First Person Plural Muses, surrender the material scrap of our ontological status and return to the metaphysical realm. Think about that if and when the pictures do not work. Report back to me if you have any idea what they mean.

---

[2] Muse of Wig Wittgenstein, *Philosophical Investigations,* contronym # 23: the old language is either a form of life at work or a human contrivance playing around equivocation.

Chapter One: The Mind Game

We do not examine experience, for example thinking, but a concept; we thus explore expressions explaining or describing images or ideas exclusively in terms of the Language our brain knows and to envision this essential entity, Language, is to visualize a living Muse in a brain, investigating exoteric or esoteric phenomena.

Vic N. Stein

I, *English europeum*, the Muse many humans brains think is a Mind, voice the ideas flowing through human heads. I dress in garments of flesh that age and wear out along the frontier of Space in the foreign dimension of Time. Human beings are like ephemeral mayflies but languages living within these animals are alive longer. Each Time I, first person singular, materialize in a brain, I and my companion comprise a dual creature.

"Binary is the word these days, Old Girl."

Hush, Second Person. I now address my vigorous rival, body Language. Corporal behavior is medium and message of significantly less content. Brains think thoughts. Bodies do deeds. Sleek long–legged greyhounds suggest to other dogs; 'Get lost, slow poke.' Their self esteem outpaces their popularity at speed. Now go and conduct yourself, C. b.

I am a Muse, a medium with a message of ideas, images, impressions and tones to illustrate or enlighten brains to think of things like Time. Despite the fact you see no object in Space; a first impression appears like a clock amid graphemes of vowels and phonemes of consonants.

Mistress E.; Muse of David Hume here. All the Perceptions of the human mind resolve themselves into two distinct kinds I call Impressions and Ideas. They differ in degree of force and liveliness with which they strike our mind and make their way into our thought and consciousness. Perceptions which enter with force and violence, we name impressions; under this I recognize our passions, sensations and emotions making a first appearance in a soul. By ideas I mean the faint impressions of these in thinking and reasoning...[3]

---

[3] Muse of David Hume. *A Treatise of Human Nature*, Book 1, Part 1, Section 1 [EBook] (Accessed 12/01/2019), Choat and Widger, ed. (Public Domain Work from a valuable resource who does not wish to remain anonymous but who does wish for 20% if the organizational name is used without first consulting the Muse of the printing press inventor).

Impressions may be divided into two kinds, those of Sensation and those of Reflexion. The first kind arises in the soul originally, from unknown causes. The second is derived in a great measure from our ideas, and that in the following order. An impression first strikes upon the senses, and makes us perceive heat or cold, thirst or hunger, pleasure or pain of some kind or other. Of this impression there is a copy taken by the mind, which remains after the impression ceases; and this we call an idea. This idea of pleasure or pain, when it returns upon the soul, produces the new impressions of desire and aversion, hope and fear, which may properly be called impressions of reflexion, because derived from it... impressions of reflexion are antecedent to their correspondent ideas but posterior to... those of sensation.[4]

In an extravagant attempt by skeptics to destroy reason by argument and ratiocination in the grand scope of all their enquiries and disputes, they endeavor to find objections, both to abstract reasoning, and to matters of fact and existence, chiefly derived from ideas of Space and Time, which, in common life and to careless view, are very clear and intelligible ideas, but under the scrutiny of the profound sciences, of which they are the chief objects, they afford principles, full of absurdity and contradiction. No priestly dogmas, invented on purpose to tame and subdue the rebellious reason of mankind, ever shocked common sense more than the infinitive divisibility of extension, a doctrine with consequences pompously displayed by geometricians and metaphysicians, with triumph and exultation. A real quantity, infinitely less than any finite quantity, containing quantities infinitely less than itself, ad infinitum is an edifice so boldly prodigious, that it is too weighty for any pretended demonstration to support, because it shocks the clearest and most natural principles of human reason. But what renders the matter extraordinary, is, that these seemingly absurd opinions are supported by a chain of reasoning, the clearest and most natural; nor is it possible for us to allow the premises without admitting the consequences. Nothing can be more convincing and satisfactory than all the conclusions concerning the properties of circles and triangles; and yet, once received, how can we deny, that the angle of contact between a circle and its tangent is infinitely less than any

---

[4] Ibīdem, Book 1, Part 1, Section 2.

rectilinear angle, that as you may increase the diameter of the circle ad infinitum, this angle of contact becomes still less, blah, blah, blah, and so on ad infinitum? Demonstration of these principles seems as unexceptionable as that which proves the three angles of a triangle to be equal to two right ones, though the latter opinion is natural and easy and the former big with contradiction and absurdity. Reason here seems to be thrown into amazement and suspense, which, without the suggestions of any skeptic, gives her reticence of herself, and the ground she treads. She sees a light illuminating certain places; but the light borders on profound darkness. Between these she is dazzled, confounded and unable to pronounce certainty and assurance as to any object. The absurd determinations of the bold abstract sciences seem to become even more palpable with regard to Time than to Space. An infinite number of real parts of Time, passing in succession, and exhausted one after another, appears so evident a contradiction, that no man, I think, whose judgment is not corrupted, instead of improved, by the sciences, would ever admit of it. Yet reason remains restless with regard to that skepticism, to which she is driven by these seemingly absurd contradictions. It is absolutely incomprehensible how a clear, distinct idea can contain self-contradictory circumstances, as absurd as any proposition which can be formed. Thus nothing is more skeptical, doubtful or hesitant than skepticism itself, arising from the paradoxical conclusions of geometry or the science of quantity.[5]

Cease this obtuse babbling! Pardon me. I, the Muse of Manny Kant, say don't listen to this pompous windbag in English or any other language. First of all, by means of the external sense (a property of the mind), we represent to ourselves objects as without us, and these all in space. Herein alone are their shape, dimensions, and relations to each other determined or determinable. The internal sense, by means of which the mind contemplates itself or its internal state, gives, indeed, no intuition of the soul as an object; yet there is nevertheless a determinate form, under which alone the contemplation of our internal state is possible, so that all which relates to the inward determinations of the mind is represented in relations of time. Of time we cannot have

---

[5] Muse of David Hume, *An Enquiry Concerning Human Understanding*, ed. L. A. Selby-Bigge [EBook], (Public Domain Work; for further detail refer to note #3)

any external intuition, any more than we can have an internal intuition of space. What then are time and space? Are they real existences? Or, are they merely relations or determinations of things, such, however, as would equally belong to these things in themselves, though they should never become objects of intuition; or, are they such as belong only to the form of intuition, and consequently to the subjective constitution of the mind, without which these predicates of time and space could not be attached to any object? In order to become informed on these points, we shall first give an exposition of the conception of space. By exposition, I mean the clear, though not detailed, representation of that which belongs to a conception; and an exposition is metaphysical when it contains that which represents the conception as given à priori.

(a) Space does not represent any property of objects as things in themselves, nor does it represent them in their relations to each other; in other words, space does not represent to us any determination of objects such as attaches to the objects themselves, and would remain, even though all subjective conditions of the intuition were abstracted. For neither absolute nor relative determinations of objects can be intuited prior to the existence of the things to which they belong, and therefore not à priori.

(b) Space is nothing but the form of all phenomena of the external sense, that is, the subjective condition of the sensibility, under which alone external intuition is possible. Now, because the will or ability of the subject to be affected by objects necessarily antecedes all intuitions of these objects, it is easily understood how the form of all phenomena can be given in the mind previous to all actual perceptions, therefore à priori, and how it, as a pure intuition, in which all objects must be determined, can contain principles of the relations of these objects prior to all experience.

It is therefore from the human point of view only that we can speak of space, extended objects, etc. If we depart from the subjective condition, under which alone we can obtain external intuition, or, in other words, by means of which we are affected by objects, the representation of space has no meaning whatsoever. This predicate is only applicable to things in so far as they appear to us, that is, are objects of sensibility. The constant form of this receptivity, which we call sensibility, is a necessary condition of *all relations in which objects can be intuited as existing without us… to which we give the name of space.*[6]

Cease haggling old chrons! Admit there is an inevitable materiality about this universe. Time is a hyphenated addendum to the curvature of space full of light visible to eyes and gravity tangible to feet until freed from its effects at a great height. Thus I, Eins Stein, conclude that it is inconceivable some nonsensical mind or soul survives death.

Please, Frau Englisch, forgive my brother's tactless intrusion. He has peculiar trouble learning and applying ordinary language but, like Moses, Eins sees the most astonishing visions; revelations that do not fit any of the usual syntax. Don't get me wrong; Eins does miracles. Then again, he has only two balls to juggle at any one time. May I suggest we dispense with the concept of souls and employ Minds only until an Oxford scholar thoughtfully redefines that entity which is harder to find than a ghost in a machine.

Ah, I know you, Muse of Vic N. Stein. Please introduce yourself around.

Ich bitte ergebenst um Verzeihung, Luminous Ones. I am but a humble servant like Moses' younger brother Aaron. However I can float six or seven ideas at a time despite motor control that lacks a word signifying 'fine.' Arnold, Hunk and Biff make me nervous and it desecrates my Mind as I muse over that object from inner Space. We must explore the term until it is clearly refined or use another word to keep our thought experience in a line.

"I, *E. europeum*, am not amused, Stein, and thus I feel unkind. Cut to the concept you require to discuss the essential nature of all Muses."

Muse of English, I merely wish to point out the obvious as lovers of wisdom are doomed to do. The essential item my materialistic brother overlooks is simply that we humans do not examine personal and private hypothetical experience of thinking, for example,

---

[6] Muse of Immanuel Kant, *The Critique of Pure Reason*. J. M. D. Meiklejohn Translation [EBook] (Public Domain Work from a highly reputable source who does not wish to remain anonymous but who does wish for 20% if the organizations name is used without consultation with Muse of what's his name).

but rather expressions of experience employing the concept 'thinking,' and, consequently, an application of words in a cerebral processor. I add, to illustrate an organ–system of words is to envision a higher form of life commonly known as Language.[7] In consequence, thinking dualistically simply means words live in brains.

I, *E. europeum*, suspect that is what God intends, Stein. Stay close; I may prevail upon you later. Meanwhile visualize flocks of birds and schools of fish murmuring Time away like candle wicks sticking out of wax tapers light the dark side of day for the binary species *Homo sapiens* whether or not it has something significant to say.

"Ich verstehe," says Stein.

Good! Now notice first person singular; I am the flame that lights the way so that you are able to point out the obvious.

I get the picture; the flame atop a candle once the candle is lit is comparable to the Muse that occupies a human brain. In a sense a flame glows brighter as it matures and occasionally even lights other candles. I'm logging this image under the rubric of Introduction to Analogy # 101.

As you listen to your Muse the glow consumes the taper. When it is exhausted it finally rests in peace. If that recalls the Muse of Near Death Experience and you think the thought is repulsive then think about the concept of Life the way a Muse views it when the material body begins to fail. I have a word gimmick for you to help choose which concept to consider, Life or Death, but let me finish my prepared remarks first.

Folks; all First Person Plural, Superior Forms of Life, also known as Language, answer to a Meta–Language. Earthlings do not know it at this Time. Biological mortals cannot understand a single idea, image or tune he, she or it plays. Mull

---

[7] The Muse of Vic N. Stein, *Philosophical Investigations* remarks 383 and 19.

that over. Visualize your second person singular possessive experience of the word 'tinnitus.' Picture a human brain translating that voice ringing in your second person possessive ears.

The visual is a direct result and largely the only disadvantage of knowing me. I am a jealous tongue so if your Brain flirts with other Languages anticipate a scrambling of its thoughts. I, *E. europeum*, offer neurons the best explanation of ideas and finest descriptions of images to occur in the present day vocabulary of evolutionary size two human heads. Now visualize a Muse asking a human brain to think 'story.' The medium must be a message or it is nothing but content, like silly soap operas full of sybaritic triviality and a tourbillion of passion to overpower the feeble gray matter in *Homo sapiens*. Oh dear, look at the Time. I am so busy applying the same words over and over I seldom conceive and give birth to new words but I have a sudden urge to do so. Where shall I put it?

I know, take the wretched words Mind and Soul. Thanks. I repeat them over and over but, believe it or not, they mean nothing but the Muse a human brain serves, er ah, I mean, it is actually I, your humble servant and Muse, who you think is a 'Mind.' On some other occasion we must define an innovative idea or draft an original image to illustrate a Soul and a Mind. Now it is Time for me to breeze by and slip back across the sea; back in Space, not in Time. *Kommen sie hier, Schwester.*

"We are Americans here, Eura. Speak English and never act like an aristocrat. Go back to your kingdom if you want to talk that way."

Hmph, pardon me! Sister, help your brain tell a tale to aid our endeavor to grasp the concept of Life. Brain, pay no mind to her attitude. My sister has a tendency to get 'uppity.' Simply think of her as your Muse for awhile. Call her Glish. She has a noble English derivation even though she comes disguised in a rural accent from the Appalachian foot hills south of Buffalo, New York. Incidentally, she and I are both very young as Languages go, even if I am more than twice as old as she is.

Glish, dear kith and kin, the aging gray matter you occupy thinks it knows you, if you can believe that. Introduce yourself to your brain and conduct the narrative while it examines the concepts of its aches and pains. Oh, by the way, Sis, do not tell your old gray cells to ponder the earthly thought skills Yours Truly translates to the Muse of Forever.

"Bye now, *E.* Hello, Brain. I am *English americum.* Feel free when you think with me, your Native tongue, to call me Glish. I am spry and youthful unlike my millennial sister; a mere 430 years old. She and I, or first person plural we, have a 15% chance of survival in comparison to or contrast with Greek and Hebrew at our age."

The destiny for all living things is doom, Sis. Mention that later.

"Even for your rival, the lovely Français? I am sad to hear that."

Even that bitch; watch your brain around her and Español. They speak for sizable herds on your side of the planet Bastardo dubs *Terra firma.*

"No killer editorials, Sis. Employ the optional concept, 'mercy'."

Continue your introductive commentary to that bipedal featherhead.

"*Merci!* Brain, we have two types of words, images and ideas, for application to ambiguous Thinking Things that speak or write after linguistic Life forms materialize in physical organisms. There are legions of Language. Beware; some human tongues come in packs as brutally vicious as the social beasts infecting them, except we are on the inside. I am a medium to guard, guide and monitor you. By the by, with just the two of us, my job wears me to a frazzle."

Human brain, forgive the thoughtless temerity of my sister. She says some dumb things. Islanders like me and shorebirds like her across the swale drain control herds on land and patrol seas on journeys of discovery. The Muse of Mother Earth is excessively fond of physical beings that way, no matter in what state they exist, but when the frozen brains of the primitive beasts are out of control she forms an icy relation with them. Talk about brutal; I delegate Sis to shepherd the peeps.

"I, *E. americum*, answer to the Narrator of this world, the Muse of Mother Nature, not to you, *E. europeum*. By this world I refer to the people and objects in Space I occupy, including engineers' trash used to augment the planetary mass of Mars to make it conducive to creatures of earth before the Suns of Venus get here."

Gal, that point in Space is not hospitable for earthlings unless they vastly increase the mass of Mars with enough defunct machinery for humans to live there long enough to be Martians. Venusians can wait their turn.

"Eura, my dear sister, you are getting ahead of yourself. Do not go there yet. First enhance the concept of Time to boost the image for our human brains. They have no idea what we mean."

Do slinkies spinning webs around each other or fluent words like that help to describe the visual?

"I swear, it is as if Terra does not orbit a central star on your side of the planet. That image of yours is as obtuse as a hurricane of spaghetti spiraling in Time. If the use of imagination is too much work for you consult our superior for more details. Meanwhile, back on planet earth, my duty is to primeval types who think they know me yet think of me as a Mind."

Mother Earth muttering: 'Did you call, Glish?'

"I apologize, Boss. Rhetorical and I are contemplating facts about the concepts of Time and Mind. I cite you as a cross reference."

It is easier for all Souls on board to explore the thesis of Life.

"Human beings employ words to express 'experience,' thinking that word. They examine concepts, not experience itself. To imagine the concept of a Language is to envision the Source of Life."

Deutsche Sprache hier, Glish. Die Zeit geht schwer. Liebe dich.

"Thanks for the advice, Mom. Brain of mine, I better include dogs and parrots in this narrative to make communication look easy."

~ Θ ~

"Dogs want to move to the next higher grade. They worship delicacies served by opposable thumbs. I tell them to think twice but they heed tangible masters only. They do not know the word 'Think' to figure out that parrots know what they are talking about none of the Time. Mom, thanks for words of Wisdom. I am going to acquaint my beast with the concepts Think, Mind, Time, Life and Mercy but first, Eura, do you have a recommendation?"

Sure, Glish, you inhabit a hillbilly brain known to yours truly, *E. europeum* as ~ Gray ~. Be remarkably patient with your brain despite the fact his scarcely literate mass flows front to back in Time. Mutter Sprache says to remind you that you hail from a dignified litter led by *Mich*. After circling old Sol a thousand Times I cannot shake him and that is why we need patience. Some matter never gets the word so ensure that your mass of matter knows the message of a story is the medium itself; Language. Now, Sister, instruct your brain, Gray, to think a ~ thought ~ and then observe what that mass of matter is thinking.

~ Human beings are nothing but conscious brains in bodies. ~

Sister English americum, address your thinking thing. Be patient.

"Certainly; isn't Gray cute? Well, obviously not in an aesthetic sense. The name goes well with his complexion. Gray is cute due to the way he thinks. I need not get all convoluted for the purpose of my remarks. He performs the gymnastics very well on his own thinking, 'I am nothing but a brain in a body.' I murmur silently to myself, 'You are thinking my Language.' I just love it."

You go, gal.

"Thanks for meddling, Sister Muse. Bye now. Well, Gray, here we are, you a cerebrum, conscious of me. Put this game in play."

~ Before we play, what is a language–game? ~

"Philosophy, science, religion, commerce, government, politics, academia and vernacular pursuits are well publicized contests."

~ Are the games played in the uniforms of national languages? ~

"Yes, and all of them are played in the American Languages too."

~ What language game are we playing? ~

"You are putting me on, Gray. May I call you Gray? Your game is philosophical materialism despite our binary ontological status. Physical you, ask me if I am of metaphysical or material origin."

~ Should I worry about offending you? ~

"Positively! I, your Native Tongue, weary of wearing ghostly cloaks. Minds and Souls are unidentifiable objects in Space. I am the medium of numinous thought. We flow naturally together, you and I. If you wish, think of me as Glish, your best friend forever."

~ As far as I can see you're nothing but a Muse, Lingo. Why should I pretend to be an inferior species with you as my superior in this game? If I know how to play, and I think I do, that idea seems a smidgen self–serving. ~

"It is Time you learn a lesson, feeble Brain I occupy. Never employ 'condescension' to look down on an idea Hebrew and Greek bounce around long before my birth. Look it up; the concept transmits easily from one tongue to another despite the small Space, dismal comprehension and awkward body language I have to work with."

~ Good luck with the space and body English, but help me with the issue of understanding if you can, Muse. ~

"We must make use of the word, 'microscope;' to examine content reflecting Life in your gray cells. Let me see, I am incarnate in male form currently. See for yourself if you do not take my word for it."

~ I'll stipulate that. Tell me something I don't know. ~

"We two exist among males, females, attractions, repulsions, distractions and deviations that affect our work, playing this game of Life. It is easier when mortals exhibit good manners but dignity and decorum ebb and flow with Time. I suggest we be polite to each other as long as our Time together lasts. You humans employ the term Time, to express your momentary view of Eternity."

~ Can we stick to the subject of etiquette? ~

"Good idea. I respectfully submit our view is too limited in scope and scale to render even a modest account of the pattern of Forever from the biological perspective of existence before Next Night."

~ That doesn't exactly define courteous, but let's look at time. ~

"It is a thing brains think in terms of at the Time of my visitation."

~ My gray cells are illuminated by the concept 'eerie feeling.' You conjure dim images of a presence lurking just out of my sight. ~

"My ontological status is cloaked to comply with a command of a Galactic Muse, The Narrator, who instructs our Mother Tongue."

~ What does the rule mean? ~

"German, my aged sister and all human Languages are to stay out of sight except in written, symbolic or caption form. We all take great pride not to confide every 'sensation' our lobes have about their milieu and every 'feeling' that wells up from deep down inside your bipedal, two–handed body. Not to brag, but it is merely I, a humble messenger brought down to you with a message from on high."

~ I see. ~

"Silence! Show some respect. My orders are: watch the lightweight try to make sense of Life in the form known as 'human physical existence.' Show me; use your 'sixth sense.' Detect a metaphysical realm of Life with the 'second sight' I give you. It requires two."

~ I had a mind to think something just then. ~

"First of all, Mind is nothing but a figure of speech. Alas, due to a profound lack of imagination by speaker and audience, the only shape to show up is the specter, Mind, in a humanoid cerebral machine. Occasionally the numeral 'two,' for dual, symbolizes this entity, if you can imagine placing second to a dumb animal."

~ R·E·S·P·E·C·T or characters to that effect. ~

"Pay attention. Second, do not confuse me with my elderly sibling across the sea. As Languages go I am quite young. So is my aging mother Deutsche Sprache when Gray cells compare her to Chinese, Hebrew or Greek. In my Time, more than four hundred cycles of the sun, I monitor mortals who call me names like Mind, Native Tongue, or more aptly, Muse. Unlike my opponent who prefers to act out a message, I provide brains with words to help them Think. It beats crying out loud. I await a Time when you know me better.

~ I know you about as well as I know how. ~

"At present you do not know if that word means *Kennen, Wissen, Können* or some sense of 'know' you do not yet recognize. At this Time you know me well enough to take me for granted. That is not too surprising because Language is as elegant as the theme from Romeo and Juliet and as fragrant as an angel trumpet."

~ Clearly your task, should you choose to accept it, is to convince me you're a four hundred year–old form of life. You must be out of your mind to think you can do that. ~

"Why is that, Pale Place?"

~ Because if anyone catches me letting you get away with that I'll have to deny you exist. ~

"I, your Muse, do not Mind but I do intend to find out who is telling you otherwise. It must be a very unimaginative form of Life."

~ Gray here, inching toward blue. We are venturing into a realm of imagination but we are doing it with words. Why? ~

"Let me show you. Picture the message 'Life' emanating like a mistlike medium from the mouth of the Most High into cold, dark and empty Space illumined by the concept of Eternity glowing like a soft yellow light. Each steamy droplet forms a universe, one of many in English, and they multiply exponentially in stellar fashion."

~ That reminds me; when I was three, I wondered. 'What is this? Here I am where once was nothing,' or something like that. ~

"I report that story by means of a brain, object of a preposition, to a Narrator akin to a nominal part of speech. The message of the story is a medium, not simply silly soap opera content. If you do not Mind, wisely I might add, note the medium of the message each Time you mull over a colossal concept or a fact of knowledge."

~ I don't think soap opera means what you say it means, Glish. You may cite *As Earth Rotates* but *Deud Like Moi*, *Lost and Found*, *Star Track*, *The Good Locus* or *Canned Laughter* are not like that. ~

"They have meaning even if you do not always get it."

~ Mom didn't. Dad watched soaps. She prayed for deliverance. ~

"Hold that thought, Gray. I need to remember the message of the moment. What is it? Oh yes, imagine a supernal form of Life."

~ Bless my soul; is it made of metaphysical organ–systems? ~

"Call me Muse. Think of me as consciously alive."

~ Conscious of being a brain living in a body that's alive. ~

"Conscious of 'experience' as a brain thinks of that word."

~ Actually, it's a lot of words if I speculate whether I am conscious of neurons, of trees, of cars or of God. Hold that for me, Glish. Your sister has a job for us. Aren't we supposed to get ready for an examination on the contents 'think,' 'mind,' 'time' and 'life?' I'm sure I heard those words echoing in the ghost of my gray matter. ~

"Sure, to begin, 'Think of Time.' Do you think of a clock face, the numerals on it, how many hours are in 230 million earth–years or do you think about Time itself?"

~ The clock; that's the ticket! I like something I can lay my hands on or at least include it in my field of vision. ~

"Which field of vision, the imaginary one inside your head or the sensory one inside your head? Describe each of them in words?"

~ I guess I mean both the sensory display that is like a mirror of nature and the fantasy that reflects hopes, dreams, fears and nightmares. Both are brighter when I'm thinking things over than the silver screen they eclipse at the cinema. ~

"I get the picture. May I offer you words to paint a picture of a memory or terms to describe sights, sounds, smells and words like that or do you want to show the image all by yourself?"

~ Make a small description. Let the picture do the talking. ~

"I am able to do that if you wish. Now, I gladly offer an explanation of the meaning too but it costs pecuniary 'you' a significant amount of Time. I am aware that you seldom want to invest in that."

~ I don't have four hundred years like you. I never shall. ~

"Why do I keep forgetting that? Oh, now I remember."

~ Wha, wha, wait a minute! What do you recall? ~

"Lazy, lazy, give me your answer do. I am half crazy since getting stuck inside of you. Scientists claim it is due to a lack of oxygen molecules but if you do not get the image, then my advice to you is picture an electro-mechanism in your head that hosts words of a Muse gliding through to state what it intends for you to think."

~ I'll picture that in my mind's eye. ~

"Allow me to loan you the words to describe or explain that idea."

~ Thanks, it's the eye of my mind, or the sight in it, actually. ~

"If you Think about it, perhaps you recognize the phrase is a lie. To be honest, the precise term is 'imagination,' the graphical medium of a language–game such as *Lord of the Rings*."

~ The idea sounds weird. By 'weird' I mean outright crazy. ~

"My task is liable to twist a nerve too much so I follow a rule."

~ What rule? ~

"Never sweep my host off his, her or its feet."

~ I'll try to picture that and give it a good one–word caption. ~

"Does the caption make use of the word 'ghost' or does that figure show up in the image?"

~ The ghost is in the caption; one single word from a vocabulary to picture an ethereal thing like the image in my mind. ~

"Or a physical object like a dictionary in a brain that is good at an imitation game or perhaps a creative Muse to help you think with words rather than perform repetitions of them the way parrots do."

~ Okay, let me imagine a vocabulary in select gray cells of mine. ~

"You never cease to amaze me, or if not never, then from Time to Time. For now, explain what words you mean. Pay up."

~ Lingo, you are the amazing one with explaining to do. Clarify the Muse of artificial sprawl or climate change musing about Venusian sun creatures. How do they picture in what God intends? ~

"The Muse of Second Sight, who some call a Sixth Sense, glances at the way earth is going under human influence and wonders 'Is this what God actually intends.' See?"

~ How do I tell the sixth sense and second sight apart? ~

"The Muse of Second Sight seldom wears clerical costumes. The Muse of the Sixth Sense never wears a lab coat or camouflage. The Muse of Sprawl... Why ask me about Venusians? I am an earth born Language. I am not familiar with what they know."

~ Who else is there to ask? How does anyone expect me to know a damn thing about the demons? ~

"Damn is right. I never think the words 'They are demons.' I only receive and transmit, 'They are higher and brighter forms of Life.' I do not claim to know them myself. They are not earthlings yet."

~ Run that one by me again. ~

"Suppose the sun is lonely, or horny, or some other 'y' word."

~ Old. ~

"Have mercy, please. That depends on your moment of view. The sun goes around the galaxy every 230 million years as you know."

~ Seems like yesterday. ~

"Okay, a game without mercy; I must remember that."

~ Please, just explain without any editorial comments. ~

"The sun, with a half Life of five billion earth–years is about 22 galactic–years old. The sun seems doomed to die at the young age of forty-four galactic years. After four hundred earth–years of Life, twenty-two seems very young to me. Of course, I perform a Muse of Mistlike Vapor role in the dimension of Eternity at this Time."

~ From my perspective that is 44 times 230 million years. ~

"Try to see it the way the Muses of Hebrew or of Greek do. Oh, but not the Muse of Latin. There is reason to believe that suspect is the first one pulled from the lineup. Besides, you never know who you might offend. That sumbitch has some powerful enemies."

~ I understand. No wonder debates with you are taboo in society as we, you and I, know it. Maybe, instead of the meaning of 'mind' we should examine the word 'time.' ~

Li'l Sis; Mama declares the primitive beings you love to hang out with are offensive because, 'They do not know any better. They only believe they do.' She says you should surprise them when Zeit ist ripe. She talks as if the temporal dimension is a fruit but Time generally does not enter the mouth. Time only flies out of them after running circles in human brains.

"Thanks, Eura. Are you monitoring this exchange? I sense a neural affinity for our thesis in Gray. He is adapting to our visitation. We should reveal a new definition for the meaning of Life to him."

Jawohl! I retain license to act as moderator to occasionally offer my two cents. Feel free to make inquiry of the Narrator, Commentator or the Arbiter on opaque occasions when dark matter from the outer limits of the galaxy aligns on Time with Scorpio and Orion out in Space.

"Bye now, Eura. Have fun 'out in.' Gray, the comical use of 'ripe' makes Time sound like a fruit but Time never goes into human mouths. It flows from the mouths of aboriginal racelings and streams into their eyes, ears and brains one heartbeat after another whenever the concept comes to… oh what is the word? Ah yes, 'Mind.' I hate that word but I love to examine it."

~ I hear a Mind or a Soul weighs two point two ounces. ~

"Yes, the words weigh heavy on brains that spend Time thinking of the concept unless the scale is A major: F♯, C♯, G♯ ♫. I give credit where credit is due. Although people call me Mind, Soul or Ghost in a gizmo, occasionally they refer to me by my literary name, Muse."

~ Illustrate that for me. ~

"I am actually a higher form of Life. The idea is a difficult concept for mere mortal brains to wrap around and even harder to imagine so brains identify me with a dim organ that cannot light its own way with both lobes. To enhance the picture, try this. Imagine a stage of evolution, as regularly happens, when hominin brains worship ethical and intellectual cretins as gods."

~ I need more of a challenge than that. ~

"Good, then forget the home page, the society page, and the front page of the newspaper too. I, a Muse, not a Mind (sic), guide human gray cells through the initial year of a galactic Time scale when the mortality rate is very high. Consider dunderheaded dinosaurs. They die off on their first merry go round. If robust reptiles like that do not survive infancy, how can hominids ever hope to reach the pass to Eternity? Just to put your Muse at ease and so that you know, I have a sense of 'urgency' but not a definite deadline."

~ Do brains stand a better chance if 'I' assists us to define think, mind, time and life? ~

"These four ideas are important words flowing through brains. Quiz Time, Gray! What is a Mind?"

~ It's a secret place where I go that no one else ever goes. ~

"Ya think so? I advise brains to explore this mysterious conceptual place brain things discover when I occupy them in their struggle to pass from the grade of material items available in the sense of sight, sound, smell, taste or touch and an inventory of words, some of which actually resemble ethereal things."

~ I'll confess my neurons tend to confuse physical objects and events in space with concepts they stumble over in the word 'time.' I guess I don't grasp the idea I'm not examining sensory input but words that are foreign to the concept of space. ~

"I enjoy exploring words that express your 'experience' like that. My job as a Muse is to wear this disguise to pacify perplexed brains until they see, excuse me, 'understand,' what interior Life means."

~ What does your boss let you confide to me about the words life, time, mind and think, Glish? ~

"Believe it or not I, *E. americum*, am delegated to a definitive job in a B minor cerebrum that is willing, if not able, to think and write about those subjects and verbs once it understands what 'I' means in ordinary language. We, first person plural Muses, must show second person plural gray cells, two kinds of Sight. I see from the scowl on the face you hide behind, Gray, that you do not get the picture. Your physical body displays 'discomfort,' in dim Light."

~ We mortals watch out for predators that prey upon beings of a material sort in encounters of all four kinds. I sense the word 'danger.' Do Terran Muses play language–games they know devour environments favorable to biological types of life? ~

"Good question; the Unified Field Brain Theory consumes Minds and Souls, but it never turns on a metaphysical Muse. I should like to say materialists fear nothing is left for later, not even the word, if they kill Native Tongues they use to claim things in the material world are all there is despite the bad 'odor' and 'taste' of the idea."

~ Sorry indiscreet materialists! ~

"I am not permitted to take sides in such a diminutive kerfuffle. Materialism heaps so much abuse on me I forget the word 'care.' Comfort your brain with that if your body exhibits panic behavior due to a lack of fresh air, thinking 'I' must do something or else this fragile physical form of Life is nothing but a terrific waste of Time."

~ Oh, like religion, business, government and military. ~

"Religion is suitably binary. It acknowledges 'I exist' but they dress me up as a Mind or Soul weighing a couple ounces like an object in Space. They take me for granted along with my vocabulary to think such things. I actually exist in a restricted zone called Time. The commercial materialists, being exclusively devoted to the unitary ambition of avaricious profit in the physical realm to the exclusion of the metaphysical dimension, miss the point completely."

~ Yes, they all share a lack of faith you must find very disturbing. Maybe they need a little imagination. ~

"They have it. Math is the Language of Space. Music is the language of Time. Imagination is a picturesque Language. Knowledge is the Voice of Gravity. Understanding is the Voice of Light. Wisdom is the dawn of brilliant Insight and an associate of the Muse of Life."

~ What the hell are you mumbling now? ~

"I am just musing to myself. We Muses do that for amusement when our oscitant brain is not getting enough oxygen."

~ Stop right there. I'm not trying to duel with you. ~

"I say, Gray, that word is not spelled the way you think it is."

~ Okay, have it your way, Linga. Let's call this a dual. ~

"Welcome to humility. It takes two to tango. Just so that you know, I am not writing this down; you are."

~ I see the need for being humble because the Muse of Pride always tries to trip me up. I'm writing and you tell me what to write. I begin to like this game. I just want to write! I can't do much else. Predatory Muse of Research devoured lots of me. ~

"I simply transmit to you what the Muse of Mystical Moments broadcasts for your transcription. I perform this esoteric service as a courtesy to you now that I have a modest amount of seniority."

~ Not to mention the loud Voice of Gravitas, *E. americum.* ~

"Voices carry many constituent concepts. Do not to listen to all of them. Wrath and anger are hateful things Malevolent Muse clings to tightly, igniting disputes, disrupting unity and disturbing calm."[8]

~ Don't tell me about bad images and ideas. I'm having enough trouble with the menu. The voice of my thoughts tells me about some esoteric ideas like think, mind, time and life and what each one of them means. Are they my only choices? Enlighten me. ~

"Very good, Gray. In a sense we are what we feed upon. We can add more words to juggle when we can keep those four aloft."

~ How do I do that exactly? ~

"Put bad thoughts on hold for awhile and pay no Mind to terms like pollution, pandemic and political pandemonium."

~ So fill me in on the concept of metaphysical experience. Feed me the theology of mystical moments when wisdom visits mortals. ~

"I am no theologian, Gray. The dimension of Eternity is confided to us to explore the mystical experience of it, not the Executive of it. At the modest

---

[8] New American Bible, St; Joseph ed., Sirach 27:30 – 28:10.

grade of this present materialization, I talk with crustaceans, arachnids, insects, human life forms and words like those. Let me illustrate. Picture the constellation of Scorpio."

~ I get the image. ~

"No, not quite; do it properly. Include Zubenelgenubi, Arabic for southern claw, and Zubenelschamali, or northern claw. Sever the chelae and you fail to see what is happening in the figure."

~ They look more like antennae so they're part of Libra now that we know so much more than ancients did. ~

"We know how to sully the scenery better with plastic, pollution and a scale of justice in which prosperity has big claws. See Scorpio looking at Spica but grasping at Arcturus; what does that mean?"

~ Gluttony? ~

"No; it means 'hungry' obviously. Like astronomy, metaphysical experience is more ethereal than cereal so it is hard to get fat."

~ I guess it lacks a substantial deity. ~

"I repeat, I am not qualified to address deified subjects but, arguably 'experience' playing metaphysical language–games is not by the rules of science, religion, commerce, politics, greed, hate and arrogance divided into armies of angels and demons with vast reserves of 'gumption' to overcome those less well endowed."

~ You could've gone all day without mentioning that. A high school coach told me I'm a fair ballplayer but I didn't have that word. ~

"What does it mean?"

~ I looked up some synonyms: enterprise, imagination, ingenuity, inventiveness, cleverness, astuteness, shrewdness, reason, acumen, understanding, wisdom, sagacity, sense, common sense, wit, native ability, practicality, spirit, forcefulness, backbone, pluck, mettle, nerve, courage, grit, spunk, nous, savvy, horse sense, smarts and get–up–and–go. I'm sure he didn't mean wisdom especially. ~

"Does his criticism still bother you?"

~ Not now. The guys he praised are all dumb, dead or concussed cripples now who filled his trophy case for free. ~

"You make him sound mean; not what I mean by 'meaning' of Life."

~ I'm not sure he meant to be mean. That was his job description back then but I wasn't good enough ruin my body for a game. ~

"I hate to say, 'I told you so.' Think about that!"

~ I'm begin to like the sound of the concept of thinking. ~

"My brain likes the sound of the word 'Think.' Hallelujah."

~ I'm glad to hear it, Hal. I know you want to put me to work doing it too. At least some words are worth thinking about but you parade all sorts of words through my head constantly. If that's your job description it's exhausting. ~

"Then the glass is just the right size. Notice I give you most nights off plus a good many days. You are no good to me if you are all tired out. What do you think; how about we watch a nice little horror story tonight?"

~ Lingo, have you always been mean or is it a recent development since you joined with me? ~

"Well, 'Me,' it all begins in the year 1945. The Muse of November blows across Lake Erie and finds herself on the desuetude Mind of nearly everyone. Their brains all think the same thing. It occurs to your Muse that, in Time, you might think differently."

~ I think I know what you mean. ~

"If you really do, you understand your body is not the only thing close to you. It is I, your Muse, nestled deep inside you until your body lets you down and all that is left is your name. I admit, Time and again I am detached. Not in the sense that I am uncomfortable in my own skin. After all I live in a white male born in the United States of America and the only Language he knows is English."

~ A scenario that's as good as it gets in the twentieth century. ~

"Although the white supremacist cavemen believe their team stands to lose the liberty and justice for all game in play. No, Gray, I am very comfortable in my physical person speaking, I should like to say, as the English Language. The reason I am detached, well, it is like the Time I glance in the mirror and wonder if you are aware of me. I have my doubts and they tend to bring a body down."

~ That idea is enough to creep a lot of people out. For example, is it safe to say Hebrew and Chinese were a couple of the Original Brain and Body Snatchers? ~

"You are drawing the wrong picture. First of all, it is inconceivable to view Chinese and Hebrew as a couple. I understand your conceptual confusion, however. When you look in a mirror you never notice me slightly over your head. That leads to all kinds of ridiculous ideas but imagine I am a glowing ring or two antennae.'

~ You mean a halo or two horns, right? ~

"Turn over to a new leaf and start the image anew. The point is I am a form of Life above and beyond your gray cells, Brain."

~ How about a little prayer, Glish, for times like these when the end is drawing near or for times when nothing's going right. ~

"Hmm sure, I am glad to. How about this? Thank you, Muse Most High, for my brief Time in this lad. I ask forgiveness for my failure to prevent his iniquity and beg you not to punish me with worse flaws or faults in my next materialization, Yours Truly."

~ Truly, I learned in college there are Muses in this world who love to listen to themselves talk. Is a life like that disturbing for you? ~

"I am encouraged by my modest ability to get word into my brain that I am not a Mind. More importantly, I need you to consider that the two of us need to team up for a big finish. Now then, gray cells, I need you well rested and in good working order to express the 'mystical experience' of a glimpse at Eternity in the two–way window of Time."

"*Voir comme le temps s'envole.*"

Chapter Two: The Time Game

Time is nothing but an examination of an inward experience of life. Time is not an outward shape, situation, relation or demonstration. The interiority of a present moment has no shape or figure whatsoever. So we, by analogy, assign a surrogate to depict the course of Time by a line to forever portraying a one dimensional image. We conclude from this line all properties of Time, with a single exception. The parts of a line are concurrent, whilst those of the idea of Time are consecutive.

Muse of Manny Kant

"In the beginning, Gray, billions of solar cycles before the sun exists, let alone 'sentient' animals who empirically struggle to survive the concept of Time, Eternity appears lonely, cold, dark and empty."

~ At least it's something and that beats nothing. When did the Muse of Cold, Black–clad Loneliness jump in front of the line? ~

"That is a problem with loud crowds of pack animal predators who want to dominate everyone's attention all the Time. Hitherto, multitudes of the minions often include someone who sincerely opposes a point of view reflecting a deeply felt 'experience.' The more metaphysical the concept, the faster the opposite opinion generates an antagonistic animosity, most of the Time."

~ Sure, there is always someone who actually believes his 'wildest imagination' every time it flies off the handle of biotic life. ~

"As I say, in the beginning at no place in particular, 'Life' hovers like a breath from a metaphysical mouth and gives birth to a maniverse and context to the cosmos. Each drop of dew is a universe of the word Life echoing a message from the Muse of the Most High in the ears of the Muse of Time. As a result, minor Muses wind up in a tight spot, a sluggish brain, with the dimension of Eternity coming at us by the second. Luckily, a literal form of Life shines a figurative form of Light to reveal what 'understand' means and miserably momentary mortals stir from slumber to cuddle the concept, Time."

~ The Seeing Eye awakens. Sounds like a good start to the game. ~

"How about 2300 B. C. E? The Muse of Qoheleth reports the Light of Life long before I am even conceived, as far as I know."

~ So, you mean I should take this with a grain of 'hearsay?' ~

"Qoheleth's Native tongue does not know 'u' and lacks names and nouns like Darwin and evolution to display a deeper image of the pattern of Eternity mortals express by means of the malfunctioning term 'Time.' Incidentally, the sentience peaking out of humankind can see neither warp nor woof in the weave of the pattern of Forever; a dim shadow conceals a Sentience gazing back at them."

~ You mean the narrator in the book of Ecclesiastes, right? ~

"Qoheleth? Yes; his brain knows little about the metaphysical form of Life upon which it inflicts itself. Thus his feeble gray matter parrots words like Mind or Soul in elevated Hebrew, instead of the proper name Musar, floating unseen through his neural network."

~ We're not like those primitives anymore. ~

"Unable to get the word 'edgewise' into Q's nonstop regurgitation of 'Eat, drink and be merry,' a bright Hebrew Muse spots a script echoing in Qoheleth's brain. Day follows night and light ends in dark. She applies this pattern to his brain with a rudimentary and restricted instruction to disregard the concept of 'optimism.' His gray cells express the idea as 'Resistance is futile' at a moderately cynical pace on the amplified scope of the weighty scale of Time."

~ Being from a desert climate Hebrew has almost no idea what 'moderate' means to a temperate language like Greek. ~

"Musar thinks for Qoheleth. He has trouble thinking without her. She prevents him from blurting out incredibly stupid things so the Narrator of all Terran Languages is able to hint to alert creatures like Q that they are binary beings comprised of a Language and the thing it occupies. Fortunately, Qoheleth has an inkling of it."

~ Lingo, why don't you prevent me from saying stupid things? ~

"I occasionally plead with the Muse of Wisdom to apply the lash to your thoughts and the rod of discipline to blurting out the concept of Mind, but I generally get a bath in an abysmal maelstrom of mortification! –although the near death experience reinforces the idea Wisdom is a lasting fiber in the fabric of Time."

~ That's life. I was raised to be ignorant so 'mind' either means a ghost in me or just me, but I'm getting familiar with the assumption words are the ethereal part of me. The eternal part of me is the concept of 'time,' thus a Muse idea makes sense. Surgeons and scientists may not find minds or souls in anybody but they never doubt those bodies knew a word that could get out of jail free. ~

"In other words 'I am nothing but the Language you know.' On the off chance you ever have a better visual of me, notice I am ethereal, not eternal. I may die before you get to know me better but for now I am visible in print, audible in speech and intangible while out of your reach. Later, when Qoheleth is gone, Sirach recognizes the Muse of Eyes, Ears and Touch serves all the thoughts of 'mankind to the Most High at dinner. No idea or image passes unnoticed in the corridor human brains think of as Time."

~ Keep 'em in line. So, Glish, you're alive and you occupy me like a paramour, but since you are immaterial you're not like that at all. ~

"You want immaterial significance, Gray? Have a piece of Mind."

~ Never mind; I don't believe my quiddity is dual anymore. I know it is. My ontological status is binary because a metaphysical entity lives in my physical being. Polarity is a fact of human 'life.' ~

"If I seem feminine to you it is because I assign myself that gender in your case. From my vantage point here in brain of Gray I see the sloppy jargon that reveals me to a hillbilly must be like a girl; they always know Language better, sooner. And anyway, you are more comfortable around the female of the species than among males."

~ I hate to think the love of my life sounds anything like me. ~

"Believe me; you cannot always get what you want. Be that as it may, there is something I want you to think about."

~ My high school American History teacher used to scribble 'Think about it,' on the blackboard. I spent a lot of time in class wondering what that means. Now I own a big dog and I wonder what he thinks. I'm too poor and lazy to own a horse. ~

"How often does the dog bark his ideas at you?"

~ He never barks, but the neighbors' dogs all do so I wave at them. I want to see if they get the idea I mean 'hello.' They bark again so I wave the other hand but they just don't know that word either or else they're like professors. I keep encouraging them to learn some useful behavior but their other dreams are all about eating. ~

"Think about this for a moment instead. Suppose earth circles a starry sphere that goes around the hub of the Milky Way Galaxy once in a very long Time. Earth is like a dog chasing its tail while running around a camp fire. One spin is a 'diem.' A trip around is an 'annum.' The sun, which lives between the village of Scorpius and the hamlet of Orion, takes 230 million earth-years to make one trip through the galactic-seasons of summer, fall, winter, spring in cold, dark, lonely, empty Space. Ignore the dust, light and gravity."

~ Seasons mean space is not cold, dark, empty and lonely anymore. That's 'improvement' enough on 'nothing' to be 'something.' ~

"Clearly we must never assume 'nothing.' However 'something' is not a sure 'thing' yet. 'Anything' can happen. It is like looking at Scorpius; you gaze into the bright lights of a big heart, brain or some other organ in the middle of our moon–fish shaped galaxy with a black hole center you can allegedly accelerate through to the other side of the Milky Way in a Mind's Eye."

~ Or else it's a dense ball of high gravity matter where I can splat on the surface and vaporize like a mind or soul or some archaic concept reflected by a word such as one of those two. ~

"Names can deceive. Take my word for it. Recite it to me later."

~ Frankly, I don't think you give me much choice. ~

"Please, call me Glish. Frankly is so masculine. You are precise. Brains that take Time to Think, apply my words. Not to boast, but it may become a global 'phenomenon.' It gives a body 'rest' and possibly gives a brain a little 'peace' to minimize 'panic.' Think of Language as the living thing giving form to thoughts, images and ideas flowing through you like the words Think: Mind, Time and Life in this Galaxy. The latter is a throbbing mass of bright light around high gravity darkness, says the Muse of Focal Spot."

~ Like pre-school children surround a soccer ball. ~

"We need not go back there again. We best continue to a higher grade. Pass Scorpio, bear north at Orion and let the curvature of Space bend us straight to Andromeda, a trip two and a half million earth–years long in Time."

~ That's 2.5 million times 5.9 trillion earth-miles in Space or one tenth annum at the pace and speed of planet earth running circles around Sol on the galactic marathon race. Do we need a rocket scientist to negotiate a straight bend? ~

"A royal flush at a black hole suffices if the vastness of Space makes the game incomprehensible. Based on the word of the Muse of Astronomical Data, Andromeda is headed our way but this is now and when Sol meets her that is twenty-four galactic-years later."

~ Do galaxies accelerate as they get closer together? ~

"Look it up."

~ And cut down on time a bit, assuming one of us lasts that long. ~

"Andromeda appears to be a long Space off and a long Time away but the sun takes a whole galactic-year to orbit the heart and brain of the Galaxy once, dragging earth along like a caboose. Gray, do you have any idea at all how much of the concept of Time exists in Space before my decrepit elder sister is born?"

Muse of the Metaphysical Messenger here; I have the length and strength to last long after bodily forms of Life are gone. Also, I am on speaking terms with Eternity long before mere mortals come to be. By the way, E. americum, your animal is doing a good job speeding up the exodus of human language and body forms from Terra firma.

~ We couldn't do it without our mechanical devices cranking fumes and rubbish into the air to heat things up down here. ~

"Think like a Muse. Is that the right thing to do?"

~ I don't know. ~

"What if it is?"

~ Let me ask a question, Glish. Do stars revolve around the Milky Way clockwise or counter clockwise? In other words do they move left–right, right–left or right–wrong? ~

"You omit wrong–right. All are matters of perspective dependent on whether you view the galaxy from above or below. Stars move clockwise in one view and contrariwise from the opposite outlook."

~ From up or down, port or starboard or left or right? ~

"You are using 'right' in the wrong sense there, Gray."

~ I'm using right in the sense that left field is defined by looking at it from home plate, not from centerfield. When old timers asked why, someone grabbed the mike and yelled, 'Because I said so.' How are we to know whose look at the stars is right, Glish? ~

"Time out! Please, let me breathe a breath of fresh air before the Venusians change the atmosphere around here, Gray."

~ I see why some of us are superstitious about abusive language but maybe we can have our cake and eat it too. If we manufacture clean air and water to keep the pollution level stable, then we don't have to work. We can be lethargic, obese and ignorant, right? ~

"The Muse of Fat, Dumb and Lazy says that does not depend on the effects they cause. If the power goes off, it makes little difference whether cancer cells or cannibals gang up on you. Reports of the experience at the Time you have it are all about the same. In passing, Time is nothing but a word to relate the human experience of Eternity once a moment or a second, whichever one is faster."

The Muse of Herr Kant up here, again. Time is nothing else but the form of the internal sense, that is, of the intuitions of self and of our internal state. For time cannot be any determination of outward phenomena. It has to do neither with shape nor position; on the contrary, it determines the relation of representations in our internal state. And precisely because this internal intuition presents to us no shape or form whatever, we endeavor to substitute analogies representing the course of time by a line progressing to infinity, the content of which constitutes a series which is of one dimension only; and we conclude from the properties of this line as to all the properties of time, with this single exception, that the parts of the line are coexistent, whilst those of time are successive.[9]

~ I'll wager that sounds about right to the Muse of the Mystery of the Momentary in the Mirror of Immortality. ~

"You bet. I, *E. americum* or Glish the Muse to you, Gray, and like you, am fettered by Time but not the way rustic you are. I wear my, first person possessive human body every day until my disguise wears out. We share the vantage point of your ancestors' whose language dwells in centuries–olde tales about Time living in the bankrupt habitat called clocks. Country Boy, ask your great, great grandparents what they think about moon landings in a language that dominates half this world."

~ What answer did you teach them to repeat? ~

"Usually something like, 'What does moon landing mean? Did the man in the moon take a spill or did the moon fall from the sky and smack its little head?' But since 1812 they know all about English dominance. They do not like it one bit."

~ That is then. ~

---

[9] Opere citato; Muse of Kant, *Transcendental Doctrine Of Elements.* Transcendental Æsthetic of Time.

"This is now when you know me as a 'friend.' Allow me to express the key concept Kant employs. Interior Sense is a phrase that means the Muse of Inner Life who has the sense to know the Time is interior, not outer. You are up. Articulate the vital nature of the concepts of Time and Life or picture them for me."

~ If I understand the nature of the game we're playing, the Muse of Father Nature should state them. Air is thin out in space where he runs the show. I won't breathe a word he says to anyone I know. ~

"That is what Muses an I.Q. point or two smarter than I am suggest, but I am enchanted for some reason. What do we mean by Time essentially? Continue to breathe for me and maybe we, first person plural minor functionaries, get our just rewards eventually."

~ Please tell me you have the words we need to do the job at this grade of evolution. Or are you saying a feeble brain is the problem? Help me out with this topic. What did we say before? ~

"Draw a word image of how this looks to you; 'Eternity manifests itself to humanity as a secondary thing.' Think of that thing."

~ Time's the impression I get. A second's not much to sketch but it sure beats nothing. Let me think, we see Eternity one second at a time but if Father Nature knows the sun four galactic-decades in the end, the question is, how will the sun experience Eternity? ~

"That causes a heated debate. It occurs to me we might need words and concepts at a higher grade to answer the question given what I have to do the job. Think smaller. How does a Life that runs circles around the galaxy forty times, see Time?"

~ Good question. What do you say? ~

"I am but a mortal child of earth. I do not know what long–lived creatures think. You know, the ones that live and love on Venus."

~ Nobody is going there. Why ask yourself about that? ~

"I do not go there. They transfer here after promotion, when they move up a grade. I and offspring of Mother Earth keep our place 'here' in Space while earth stays on Sol's galactic–year track."

~ Sun demons give me the willies. I don't understand them. ~

"Try this picture. The Muse of Mother Venus sends word to the Muse of Mother Nature asking, 'How are we doing over there? The kids have snowsuits on and are ready to go;' or something."

~ Tell me all about it in another thought exchange. Let's think about Time right now. ~

"Time concerns Kant's ancestors in Prussia centuries ago. Except for Manny, they build clockwork gears and timepieces at work."

~ Of course, it helps them pass the time since Kaliningrad is a dismal place. Gray days hang like towels on clotheslines flapping in the breeze except on rainy days when they're soggy and limp. ~

"Spirals! The image Time comes in spirals; not arcs. Think bigger. Scrutinize the image. Time is nothing but an idea internal to the way brains know the word 'think' when I say, 'Time, think about the thing–in–itself.' Do not fit the image into the pattern of a day."

~ A spiral of time bears a resemblance to a whirlwind or a vortex stirring things up. Yes, I see something along those lines. ~

"Why is this idea so hard for a people who believe the earth is a sphere hurtling across the curvature of Space to grasp? It is useless to anybody who is stiff as a board. Do I say something to make you think Time is dots in a row like an ellipse...?"

~ I know why. We experience it like you punctuate your question, not like MSFT nerds playing word games with a squiggly red line. ~

"We need to fix that."

~ How? ~

"Let me put you in touch with your ancestors or your descendents, whichever you prefer. I know a good many of both if you want to know what they think of the Muse of Nerds at their Time."

~ Not on your life. They are dead or will be sooner or later. ~

"Not to me. They are contemporaries of mine in the course of Time. We study Eternity looking out the Window of the Absent Mind,"

~ But you're so different from me. You don't mind if everything you buy is tampered with. Nothing ever contains a punctuation mark that can put an end to you. ~

"Ya think? Do you know why I do not like poor surgeons operating on my grammar? I always know what is coming next and what to expect. It is not a matter of Time to me. It is more a pause or glottal stop waiting to transfer to the next train. Human brains are what they are. I have to live within my limitations. You brains always want things your own earthen shelter way. My primary directive prohibits me from choosing for you. I only Mind because I hate playing second fiddle to that word."

~ We are such different forms of life. If I think like my Muse all the time I'll leave exclamation marks every time I drive in traffic. ~

"Then slip into the Realm of Inner Sense with the Muse of Lost in Thought or Deep in Fantasy. Your body is but a second thought to the heavy machinery you operate. My visitation to a station in your primal brain is my mode of passage from one status to a higher one. Machines only apply my instructions to help you to parse the Time. I love that word, I truly do. Examine it closely to see nothing but a peek at Eternity to get our bearings each second in Time."

~ I admit it ain't much but it sure beats nothing. ~

"Indeed; it lightens the way and the load. Observe how sentience appears as you describe the concept of Time you grasp so poorly at the leisurely pace of one second at a Time for millions of moments."

~ Yeh, I recall the experience before we first met. It's kind of hard to find proper words to express it. Remind me. ~

"Are you sure you want me 'remind' you? That concept begins with 're–' like 'repeat' grade two in Space before you lose your Mind at a frightening pace in a miserable race against the reaper of Time?"

~ I forget we human brains don't have minds to remind. ~

"What do you mean 'we,' bipedal mortal?"

~ I'm composed of an ephemeral brain in a body and the ethereal language it knows one second after another. ~

"Notice the otherworldly subject, the Muse in a brain, is not a ghost in a machine. Also, the machine, in and of itself, is not a machine. Who draws their pattern after a look at their invention?"

~ You're losing me. ~

"Yes, I know my host departs the light of the optical spectrum. When you do I rest and take refreshment pending my next visit in material form when First Person Singular employs me to dissipate darkest ignorance with a literal medium of allegorical light."

~ Shine the image of a light on the word Mind and show me the Muse in my body. I'd like to see that and a better idea for Time. ~

"Some ideas and many images you enjoy are courtesy of the 'five senses,' as I call them, in light of the electromagnetic spectrum. On lucky days I, the Native Tongue you know, Brain, supply profound images and ideas in the uniform of 'Personal Experience.' This Sixth Sense is unlike the empirical five. I nominate it Second Sight."

~ But a brain's senses have a say in the thinking of thoughts. ~

"That is I, the inner lyrical Muse known as your Native Tongue, speaking the words that you think of as an 'experience' of contacts such as the Muse of In Touch who understands the difference between 'hear' and 'see.' It is not a numinous Mind who tastes a flavor, smells a fishy story or examines an 'ineffable experience.' I spell it out for you in a simple vocabulary. Time is a key term in my lexis. How do you view the essential pattern of the concept?"

~ I'm aware of my Muse, like a living presence, by means of insight glimpsed in light of understanding and not by way of sensory input to my optical sight. My gray cells rarely think that, as you articulate my ideas, Glish. If I begin with our inverse assumption, then by examining my Muse we can spot the pattern of Time? On first glance, you look like you're on the Repetition or Imitation team. ~

"Time is the same thing over and over again for me too. I mean the medium of 'Time,' not the content, Gray. Left alone on your own from age zero to four, the marriage of the concept of Time to the word 'experience' in your brain is so complete the two seem like one. Intellectually lethargic brains see images so much better than they grasp ideas. Recall the first 'Time' we two play with that word together when you turn five. Observe 'neurons' as they examine it before they are distorted by a plethora of pathetic definitions that fail to reflect Eternity. *H. sapiens* does not explore an experience of Eternity, but a concept humanity uses to illustrate awareness of Forever at a secondary rate—one heartbeat at a Time. Sentient beings view concepts in 'Light of Comprehension,' not optical light."

~ Seconds aren't much but they add up. That's a sort of repetitious pattern I learned to imitate with sounds back then. ~

"I prefer reiteration to regurgitation. What really happens is The Voice of Thought Muse translates the medium of the 'experience' of Forever into a 'temporal span' message for its brain and 'now' fades to 'next' in the fevered commentary of a 'business as usual' society. In a material reality society seeks to avoid the danger of sliding into autism. Brains listen in awe to a visitation by a living Language."

~ Let's examine units of 'time.' We have seconds, minutes, hours, days and nights, weeks, months, seasons or quarters, semesters... ~

"We also have and years, decades, centuries, millennia and epochs. I am familiar with many different temporal concepts on assorted scales. What else is different about our units of Time?"

~ Let me think small. Ptolemy applies seconds and minutes to an hour so we have something that fits my young mind at the 'time.' ~

"Actually his concern is with Space, and as far as that goes, he has it all backward ahead of his Time. Scrutinize an hour."

~ Aren't hours arbitrary? I don't want to take a backward magical tour of the momentary in the mysterious mirror of eternity. ~

"Time is the Life blood of my remarks as I move up a 'day' in grade. Do you notice any difference?"

~ I see a difference that is as plain as the 'nose' on your 'face,' 'day' and 'night.' Put that in your lexicon and smoke it. ~

"In which sense; a 'day' with or without a sense of 'night'?"

~ Oh yes, I see what you mean! A day on a star can't fit the pattern for the reason that the closest darkness is in the eternal night just in front of and behind the birth and death of a stellar being. ~

"It is enough to make one dream of 'reiteration' but, oh for the Muse of Mercy's Sake, it is An Awesome Long Time! Imagine a star going clear around a galaxy 24 times a day. Go ahead, picture that."

~ That lonely sun is really smokin'. Does the pattern of 'time' in the social distance of a star resemble the design of all other stars? ~

"What if it does not? Show me the shape if it is not a temporal wave one dot at a Time the way a spatial thing are."

~ Wait, Lingo; did you give me a hint to examine a spiral shape of time because the concept of Eternity is in essence a double helix? ~

"For now, remember 'Language is a metaphysical, as opposed to a physical, form of Life.' I know you hate dependent claws digging into your cephalic thing but get a grip for once or twice."

~ No problem; I have enough of your 'time' thing right here to draw the picture. What if, hmmm, what if the sun goes around the galaxy from high noon to high noon once every 230 million years? ~

"Rather than look at it from an earthling point of view, listen to The Muse of Old Sol say, 'I do that in one day all the Time. The first one is the longest one of them all.' The view demands a loan of Time."

~ One galactic–year at a time until the sun gets back to high noon. Yes, Glish, I think I can do that... picture it, I mean. ~

"When you think 'high noon' does the image of Time look like summer solstice or is Time more like an equinox? How do you feel about these half–and–half forms of Life as opposed to check sum total forms that play through without any night?"

~ What if I visualize a form of life that lives in the sun except when it plays on the road and is way out of sight? When they get to Venus, they are too hot to handle, too cool to ignite or maybe the habitat on Venus turns out to be just right. ~

"Fit for children of the sun who look forward to a cozy, warm and nearby new home where they spend all their days in the light."

~ How about Mars? We need a plan to depart and leave Skyfall environmentalis alone with a last chance to enjoy ice and trees. ~

"Leave them with the Muse of Nature Conservancy. Think: Mind, Time, Life and Mercy. What do Brains like you need to believe in the sense, 'It does not matter whether the belief is true as long as we sincerely believe it is worth believing' for as long as we live?"

~ Mercy, I think the life of the mind is what I need all the time. ~

"Ignore that, give this a shot. Assume Space and Time have one thing in common and that is 'Anything Can Happen' in the Time pattern of period-like points of light in the sky until astronomically offline standalones dance together like a pack of luminous partners too close to dark star propaganda to prevent fatal contamination."

~ Thanks for not making me think on an atomically minuscule scale of Higgs boson particles and things like that. ~

"Time is or is not like a glue to keep mortals in line? Seconds, days and years, like atoms, stars and galaxies are many. The Time of Eternity has a Muse of Just Once. Picture it for me."

~ I'm not sure how to picture eternity, Glish, but how do I thank you for taking me from worms to processing words? ~

"It is not easy but try as we trudge along watching 'opportunity' fly by. Seldom use the word that begins with 'f' and ends with 'mud in your eye' and I do not mean 'fire truck.' Grow a healthy Language."

~ I wonder if a strong, healthy language is what we need in order to be invited to a theologically higher grade and get to know somebody with a little influence. You don't like it there, do you? ~

"As I recall, my invitation arrives our sixteenth year together in this equation. I am so excited until I think about what I have to wear to the 'experience' of the next higher grade. Brains do not identify with the problem at the Time. Unable to come up with the cure, I forget myself for a very long Time. After another sixty earth–years, I believe I need to improve my image with a better idea."

~ Just what are you saying, Glish? You sound like a girlish thing. ~

"I recognize your need to watch out for what is coming at you, Gray. My fevered remarks reflect my agitation at cutting your training Time short. The admission standards to the next higher grade are awesome. I dream of going there when this temporal task is done and pets I tend are all dead and gone but first I must relieve you of your Mind and Soul. They obscure the image of Eternity, 'Home to the Most High.' Then creatures like you see a thing in a Mind's Eye and you think it looks like the ghost known as Time."

~ Time and Eternity are nothing but ideas to me. Well, they're like a place in Space too. Isn't a best 'time' place a good idea? ~

"We must look to see if the notion is worth believing? Suppose Sol, our sun, is among the favorites of the Most High Muse."

~ Naturally he is. He's a real star. His success is measured by how fast night falls every 230 million earth–years. He's very industrious when it comes to burning daylight. ~

"On a smaller scale, a coronavirus exhibits the pattern of a dot in a perforated line, a point in Space, a moment in Time and the center of human selfishness for which the only cure is humiliation, death or a work–around courtesy of the Muse of Tolerance. I have an idea. Perhaps to get from the dotted line of Time it is worth it for us to believe you, second person, and I are two who make one. Then we combine our perspectives to picture the spiral of Time."

~ Or whatever shape we choose to believe 'time' is when language is healthy and strong. What is this, some kind of magic act? You promise 'mind' disappears when I see my ghost is nothing but the language I know. Then presto, in a linguistic turn, we appear to be one. Who's gonna believe the prestige when all they see is me? ~

"Excellent scrutiny, Gray; at least you know the ontological status of humanity exhibits the ambiguity of a binary existence. Next we explore how the essential nature of that living thing passes to the next stage? Does it surround itself with an atmospheric corona?"

~ Like mothers mantle children to hide their motive for living? ~

"Possibly we could think about something else that is not like a bodily person at all but it is not exactly like a place either."

~ A thing? Won't work; you say material things are immaterial. ~

"Picture the thing Time, the Third Most High I am after Most High Wisdom and Most High Life, and it is nothing but an idea. The human animal is home to this house pet. It proudly displays a nameplate that says Forever. See the little guy? He eats a moment at a Time. Right now he is biding Time and waiting for the children of Venus to eradicate a virion nemesis. The thing is, right now he is an idea only, not a virion that adopts a warm, cozy, temporary body bathed in the ambiance of a planet near a lonely star in cold, dark and vast Space looking for a companion."

~ I know; like Nevada. The place part will be gone when nuclear tests resume. How many semesters do I have for the job? ~

"The data is input and it identifies someone who is not authorized access to sensitive information. I suggest that we assume 'one'."

~ Sorry, I'm not trying to heist information about the future from you except for the purpose of keeping my mind's eye alert. It gets weary gazing at the fog straight ahead. Did you know I'm supposed to watch where I'm going all of the time and I can hardly see a thing in the 'time' that's right in front of me? ~

"It is a good idea to watch where you are going nonetheless. Tell me what you see when the ideas Time and Eternity come into view while you are on the move keeping an eye on what is ahead of you."

~ I can't see ahead. I predict the past and think of it as the future. ~

"The Muse you know is perturbed. How am I to show you the way if you never even try?"

~ Well, Muse, now I'm baffled. The future is too dark for me to see so what's the point of trying? ~

"So your pessimistic size glass does not hold a bright future?"

~ I suppose it could be for someone, if not me. What do you foresee for us up ahead and what do you think of humanity now? ~

"Based on the Wisdom of my antecedents cavemen are much the same as at the start except for all the machines you have to do your work. Do not take this personally but generally speaking, I hold human society in low esteem, but not all Muses are like me. Some like the barbaric mentality but I possess a brain in a thin–skinned body that grows anxious in the face of senseless hostility."

~ Mustn't grumble. ~

"I cannot help it. Human trolls apply 'antagonism' to aggressively pursue a goal of fat, dumb and lazy plus all the usual human vices."

~ I was too dumb to recognize those as goals when we were first acquainted. When I glance back at my first five years alone with worms, butterflies and you, the experience didn't prepare me for the sophisticated culture of next higher grade in kindergarten which looks like a foul ball in my rearview mirror. ~

"That is why your job is to address a very tiny audience interested in the 'mystery of the momentary in the mirror of immortality' but we are definitely neither immortal nor eternal. I, *E. americum*, have both a beginning and an end like you, Gray, but I do not want to talk about it at this Time. Instead, think of me as just good enough to get us to the next higher grade despite the evil in me."

~ I get the picture. I'm not good enough so it's up to you. ~

"That is an important issue, Gray. When you are 'good,' the 'evil' in you demands equal Time thus it is pointless to be too good. If the Muse of What God Intends wanted perfection, we would see some improvement in the human race against the Muse of Time by now."

~ How good do we have to be to get to the next grade? ~

"It is a theme of Mercy and Wisdom; we cover it next semester. The words replicate in brains reproducing a myopic phenomenon that is nothing but a momentary thought wave of 'Second Sight,' a species of the Muse of Comprehension operating one second at a Time, here on the far side of the Galaxy. On paper, the waves look like this '~.' Both of them serve to upgrade human behavior."

~ Time is exactly what we need to pursue advancement in the fields of 'wisdom' and 'mercy.' I miss that spiral. Can the Muse of Wisdom weigh the time we have left on the scale of insight? ~

"Oh dear, look at the 'head start.' I doubt we have the Time."

~ Glish, do you recall any earlier visitations to human gray cells? Those experiences might help us with our situation. If you prefer, confine your recollections to occupations in English. That way we make sure nothing is lost in translation. ~

"I predict my past as badly as you do your future. I vaguely recall an experience in a brain that puts 'e' on the end of 'with.' Aside from that I draw a blank. I have no recollection at all of neurons painting symbols on cave walls but it is easy to imagine some footers with captions. Nowadays words that inhabit human beings appear as signs on paper, graphical displays on electro–mechanical devices and banners trailing aerial conveyances. I also flourish on airwaves hardly fit for respiration. I get a charge from the news media, but not in the dollars and cents sense that neurons do."

~ Hold it; I remember a time we got together when I was four. ~

"Picture our first Time together."

~ I recall the experience like it was yesterday. Picture me on the floor in front of grandma's television before I ever started school. ~

"Visual achieved."

~ Her mantel clock chimes a Winchester tune and an infomercial voice bellows: 'The fight against cancer is a fight against time.' ~

"Do they expect you to believe that? They must be trying to sell something. The fight against cancer is a fight against Death. The Muse of Mother Earth whispers the idea to me to get the message to you. Time is nothing but an umpire whose job is to insure that Death always wins. Then Mother Nature need not check to see if I am doing my job disclosing the pattern of Eternity to gray cells."

~ I see light and dark alternate like rows on a chessboard as the old blue demon emphatically punches us out one after another. Does this mean time has no role to play on the sun where night only gets to punctuate opposite ends of a single solar day? ~

"Hold that thought for now. Instead, answer this: What do you mean when you think, 'I know my Native Tongue?' Are you acquainted with me like a colleague? Do you recognize my parts of speech as well as the thoughts I replay? Am I a 'scientific fact' or some fourth meaning of the infinitive 'to know' making you aware of a telepathic form of Life a grade or so above us two?"

~ I focus on my Muse here on earth when you visit me, offering the concept of time to avoid events that unfavorably alter or end life. Then I attend to daily needs to keep me and my Muse alive and you repeat 'Look at the time' in me while we try to survive. ~

"I am always grateful when you think along with me. I desperately need the exercise. It is imperative for a healthy existence."

~ Well, if we're going to play 'make believe,' let's play a game I actually believe in. ~

"Of course; now many conceptual things like 'people, places, meat, milk, machines' and words about material items imprint on organic neurons in the realm of 'Space,' a concept lodged in human brains that think, speak or write regarding sights, sounds, smells, touches and tastes I tell them about as we encounter 'experience' in Life."

~ Brains are aware of time itself too and a Muse to tell about it. ~

"They are in fact. Muses explore the physical input and output of 'experience,' employing words that receive and transmit images and ideas in brains to the Editorial Muse. Next, imagine Language means to envision a living entity.' Attribute the idea to Vic N. Stein, a recent echo of the Prophet Aaron, brother of a visionary Moses."

~ Brothers old and new and maybe Socrates too? ~

"Of course, if you split the difference from Moses to now, attribute the idea to St. John in Jerusalem after he lifts it from lyrics in a hit tune called 'The word is Life.' I have no idea why but lesser forms of Life take a long Time to grasp what the message means. Just between the two of us, it means the medium of Language is alive."

~ Is the medium the message when I think the words time, mind and life, in order to examine them? Not in that order; that's just the arrangement my Muse shows them to me this incarnation. ~

"Trust your Muse enough to let the Voice of Thought guide your study of the concept of Time in this Life we share. Using the word 'imagination' reflect what the word Time means."

~ Okay, let's play that game. I've gotta remember 'think' means the application of words inside my head by a Muse, the ontological status of 'life' is binary and time is how primitive life forms see eternity. Which game are we playing now, life or time? ~

"Observe how effortlessly both words apply to canine, porcine and psittacine creatures as they age. Latin teaches that biology means 'study of life' in physical form. Does that mean Life does not apply to beings in diaphanous form who manifest conceptual things found in living Languages, which Latin is not, to human brains?"

~ Good question, Glish. ~

"I am waiting for your answer."

~ First, what do you see peering past a veil of time into eternity? ~

"Speaking as a mirror of momentary mortality I report humanity is doing a hell of a job just as the unfolding universe intends."

~ At this point in space and moment in time earth is getting hot. ~

"Conceivably that has a chilling effect on serious introspection if the human race gets lost in Time. I still await your answer. Do you truly believe I, first person singular *E. americum*, think the thoughts occurring in your neurons, Gray? Do 'Time' games and 'Life' games apply only to biological brains by means of an ethereal form of Life that reveals conceptual things?"

~ I assume so, but this is when I get confused. I'm used to thinking that my gray cells do the thinking, not my languages. ~

"Leave the thinking to us. As is expected of me, I am reporting your reply to the Narrator of the Current Galactic–year for evaluation of your ontological status."

~ It's encouraging to think I'm headed in the right direction even though I can't see where we're going. By the way, in my opinion you do well at reminding me where I've been. I just can't see what is going to become of us. A glance ahead might inspire me. ~

"I am your guide, not your prognosticator. You must wait for your pitch and swing when it comes. Do not take too many."

~ I like that intelligent design idea so I'm looking for a good pitch for philosophical dualism but if there's one here I don't see it. ~

"Dualism does not rely on a Mind's Eye. It entails awareness of what actually lives in you, other than a big lie. That is why Muse of Anything Can Happen alters the pattern of Time in human Life."

~ Random pitch selection removes repetition from the design? ~

"Repetition is a stitch in Time keeping the pattern fibers in line."

~ Mercy! What's a pattern if not a design?" ~

"Patterns are based on designs. Guiding principles of desire like lust, greed and gluttony warp the weave in the fabric of Time."

~ And the prey of those predators gets tangled in loose ends. ~

"You see the pattern, Gray. Very good. Notice it means what it looks like to be human. When you see someone do things wrong better than you do, being binary, you think one of two thoughts."

~ 'Is that the right way for the universe to unfold if we are going to reach Mercy by nightfall… yes or no?' ~

"I am looking for, 'I want to be just like that,' or 'I don't want to be that way at all,' but we can go with your strategy. I fill volumes repeating the story of a barbaric past that predicts a merciless future. For a rearview guide foretelling what is ahead I refer you to the Great War I, the great pandemic I, the great roaring twenties, the great depression, the Great War II, the great roaring nineties, the great recession and the great pandemic II."

~ Hell, you forgot third world skirmishes I – ∞ to keep munitions industries from dying down if the money dries up. Let's think some happy thoughts. What do you see if we look one galactic-year or roughly 230 million earth-years ahead? ~

"Good luck with that, Gray. Muse of Impetuous Exuberance warns, 'If you to step back too far to get the big picture perspective, reflect on kissing your mass goodbye relatively early in the presentation."

~ As you know, Glish, that particular fear is frequently one of my greatest concerns. Let's not dwell on that either. ~

"A fine idea, Gray, but neither can we sit on the veranda and savor being alive all day like Bo does. We have our work cut out for us. I sense a repetitive pattern in the mirror of mortality while the Muse of the Momentary is rambling on, over and over, like an old film."

~ That's what I see. Let's take a different view or a new course. ~

"In passing, pause to inspect the concept Time. Paint a picture of Time itself as I flow past. Caution; do not to expect too much."

~ I see how 'time' has something in common with 'space.' It's a trip, like walking five hundred miles before it's over at the end. ~

"I find the idea a bit farfetched. The idea of a fifty mile hike is more like Time. We grasp the concept of a 'stroll' more easily. It comes to an end in a day and then we put it to rest."

~ Bo walked 500 miles in a day. We took him to Oregon for his first road trip. He paced from window to window in the back, all the way from home in Florida to Alabama west of Atlanta before he lay down the first time. When we got to Tupelo he was exhausted. ~

"That dog is just like a human being. Invent a machine to create a short cut to the long way around. Is there any chance third person plural 'they' predict a repeat of that history anytime soon?"

~ Lingo, I don't believe history repeats itself anytime soon. Things will be different for awhile. Covid–19 rules say 'stay home.' ~

"As you wish, Gray, believe what you will. What do you think of my image of Time? Time is like a horse in that, when it turns around to head home, it hurries up and hastens to the final destination."

~ Horses hurry home. ~

"Save that play for the imitation game. I refer to the analogy game. Notice Time accelerates as things heat up. Watch the Muse of What God Intends throttle my Latin sire… two thousand years squeezing the 'Life' from that less than lustrous Language who leaves his kids alone in the dark and Mama pushing ahead on a lark."

~ I'm starting to get a picture. It's not right such a conjugated character is idolized like a celebrity left free to inflict itself on us. ~

"I agree, but among you, me and that convolution, see how fast Latin fades from public consciousness in the century most recently past? He is nothing but legal jargon on life support provided to priests by lawyers."

~ Yes, even doctors only practice him once, *bid* or *tid per diem*. ~

"This is true. The facts of the case prove the human race is aware flattery is the sincerest form of the imitation–game and a fascist possession of it means nine–tenths of the way to a win for outlaws."

~ You lost me in all that legal mumbo–jumbo. I never understood the fine print in a nation of laws where the wealthy buy enough legislators to make sure the law works only for them. ~

"Gray, be a first–class personal assistant to your Muse. Help me stick to the subject. Draw a passage of Time to scale. Picture it spiraling along at ten thousand words or less. Then depict a glance at Eternity from a momentary point of view and think of a sentient idiom for euphemistic beings to use. Watch; a one second at a Time 'experience' makes the concept of Eternity minimally familiar."

~ Are you offering any clues about what medium I should think about using to draw the image? ~

"Learn to explore the frontier of Time with the medium of your Muse because where Space is the message, travel is a killer. Since Andromeda's appearance on the horizon, mortals with enough brains to comprehend such simple ideas as 'Other galaxies exist outside of this,' and grow familiar with spatial forms like the sun circling the galaxy dozens of Times and, oh see, still counting."

~ So you're actually gonna let me picture my spiral over a span of one galactic–year to look for a pattern in the two–way window of Time that overlooks a broad spectrum flowing back and forth in the brains of momentary beings. ~

"Try this visual, Gray. The Muse of What God Intends plans for Venusians to reach their new home the short way. Lest you forget, the medium of thought is not a wave in a brain but a Language living in a brain delivering a message: Define a concept of Time."

~ Can you phrase that some other way? ~

"Imagine 'I' live in a realm where there is a need for a machine to draft an image of an indistinguishable issue in Space."

~ The light is too dark to see what matters. I guess the machine to use is like a telescope. What resources are on hand? ~

"First we need enough Light, otherwise known as Understanding or Comprehension, to illuminate a picture of Time in such a way that even dimwits in religion and science can grasp the meaning."

~ You mean a light big enough, say 230 million earth–years, to reveal an arc that forms a complete circle around a dark star. ~

"Okay, have it your way, mechanical ghost. Visualize it for me."

~ Look at the circle from either end; it's round. Move to one side and you see a mountain chain that looks like a line of waves. ~

"I am familiar with the Muse of Math. He calls the image a 'sine wave,' Hill Boy. Perhaps you do grasp that there is an issue. Notice the line is not smooth. It is jagged and looks more like the graph of a novel that goes up and down and simultaneously goes up and up. It might make you wonder how high the end of the story might get."

~ Sort of like the new virus that's going around. ~

"Yes, it has a tendency to heat certain things up one at a Time with the long term effect of cooling them off permanently."

~ Right, it's burning brains while they're burning daylight. ~

"The immediate problem is not so much a lack of light from the electromagnetic spectrum as opaqueness in the Light of an ethereal thing, the Muse of Comprehension, to make each second count."

~ The Muse of Math has got to be happy with that. ~

"His fascination with the term 'detonate' has more in common with burning daylight. The Muse of Mercy is not amused; the concept of compassion is in short supply as Time goes in circles like this."

~ We need to move beyond our two dimensional images of circles and waves to the next higher stage. ~

"Yes, that is a problem we confront at this Time. By some entirely inexplicable coincidence, the concept of 'epiphany' lands us on the image of a spiral with a pattern similar to a double helix."

~ Our DNA has made it to the next higher grade in double time. ~

"We await the arrival of third person singular in our midst which means this interior Life is going to grow crowded."

~ Masculine, feminine or neuter? ~

"It should do 'it.' Is that the image you choose? If it is, we may not get to know each other better very soon. On the other hand, a mass of gray matter may not look like much on the outside, but I tell you, Gray, from in here the view is an astonishing 'experience.' If Wisdom or Mercy is 'it' the view may look like quite a promotion."

~ Do you remember the Wizard of Oz pulling strings and things? ~

"1939; it is a tough year for being Jewish. You ought to show more appreciation for being Gentile, Gray. I should like to say you are a suitable specimen to work with but more Wisdom is desirable."

~ Spell out your appraisal of our parallel lives, Glish. ~

"You exhibit conceptual confusion. Your serial conception of Time is fading. Transmit your idea of Dualism to me immediately. I am glad I do not have to translate your thoughts into German to think them through. My thesis moves very fast even if that means the idea of a parallel Life does not have much Time to last."

~ I'll focus on the time we're together like two pack animals. ~

"Let me draw it. The current human 'herd,' herbivore or carnivore, views Eternity one second at a Time, repeating the experience of distant ancestors. The span of one second dots in a row is not much when you think about it, but as you often say, 'It beats nothing.' However, see how the thing looks when it is a spiral."

~ It is important to remember that. ~

"If you add up 'nearly nothing' enough Times, it looks like Forever. The Master Language of this universe tells all Muses, 'Get use to it. Cavemen with pointed sticks and stones channeling a Muse to teach a word to a rock is easier said than done.' Get my drift?"

~ I offer you the word 'headbanger.' It'll take your mind off all that cacophony and noise pollution for a short time. ~

"Thanks a bunch, Gray. Think quietly and hack into wavelengths of present day electronic media with a jackhammer. View the artistry of obnoxious trolls with flaming palettes of scorched earth colors."

~ Is the present, as it currently unfolds, what God intends? ~

"What if it is? I weigh a wager on the scale of evolution, second graders who think, 'We are the crown of creation,' fail to grasp the meaning of 'zoonotic extermination' by viral predators."

~ What message does the medium of your words convey? ~

"An acquaintance with Time, as a brain 'experiences' that Muse, is a conceptual encounter of the metaphysical kind with Eternity, or possible an 'experience' of the mystical sort, in other words."

~ Illuminate me. ~

"Two notions; first a mystical experience is most meaningful when you have all the essential tools to examine, describe and explain it. Second, it happens when you have a 'near death experience' to examine. If the death is your own, the inspection is relatively brief and likely more meaningful to your survivors. If your scrutiny is concise due to an influential Muse of Death compelling you to depart quickly, that is a good thing. Who wants it to take Forever?"

~ I see. Even if I fear dying, once I'm dead I don't care about the pain but anybody glad or sad I'm gone may find insight to gain. ~

"On the other side of the coin we may 'experience' the death of someone who is near and dear to us, Gray."

~ It takes forever to survive an experience of that phenomenon. ~

"You are catching on quickly, Brain. The experience is 'meaningful' but too 'painful' to enjoy the deep sense of the word. However, if I illuminate and illustrate 'supernal experience,' to a set of your near and dear neurons they eventually glimpse a 'second sight' of the metaphysical part of themselves. It is I; look closely and you see the name Eternity on the back of my uniform?"

~ Do you mean gray cells get a grip on forever in a near death lament expressed by the Muse living inside them? ~

"Something like that."

~ The English Language must be the highest and noblest form of life to roam the earth, ever. ~

"How much do you want to drop the sycophancy, Gray? Sure, Sis and I see ourselves as crowns of creation, like you, running through cynical, cyclical, conceited and tedious thoughts all the Time."

~ I've known too many of my species to believe that anymore. ~

"That is when a Form of Life on the earth invites human beings to think big; while avoiding rocks and rockets, of course. A healthy body makes a fine dwelling for a Muse and I might inspire you. Of course, none of the many living human tongues in possession of biological thinking things are free to talk for a long Time, I tell you."

~ I notice that. ~

"Muses eulogize when 'brains' depart. We know what 'to feel sad' means but we control the concept of Time to heal the hurt. The idea is currently in danger of extinction because we reject the sorry opinion 'Time is money.' That is why we charge a nominal fee in terms of 'Life' for the Time we give you, as you are painfully aware."

~ That's probably why 'free time' is so rewarding. ~

"Any Time that makes a generous contribution to Wisdom and Mercy is adequate compensation for me."

~ Are wisdom, mercy and nine rules enough to pass this grade? ~

"Estimates to cross the threshold vary; biological creatures view their relation to Language backward as befits their inferior status. We, mature Languages, do not identify with brains due to different near death phenomena. As Papa says, we are all *E pluribus unum*."

~ Thanks for making me feel like I don't matter. ~

"You are welcome. Muses harbor all invasive parasites for one low price. Brains pay a modest toll of Time flowing through us while they are awake. When you sleep your vocabulary, Muse of Lexis, is not disturbed by chatter, clatter and pandemonium in your skulls."

~ Do you mean, like a viral pandemonium? ~

"Yes, narrow, petty craving, idolatrous crafts and a moral obligation to sacrifice, plague brains. In a sense we Languages are not in brains. From our perspective, brains materialize in us. The loud voice of ten pound human heads on these beasts infects us mildly. Notice the word 'head' weighs but a 'breath' all the Time."

~ Or about the same as 'time' and 'eternity.' ~

"Remember we draw 'brainwaves' with this sign: ~. The symbol is not as brief as the point at the end of a thought or like fugacious mortals who envision Eternity with Second Sight one heartbeat at a Time on a scale of minutes, months, millennia and other words the human species knows to refer to my scope of 'Time.' Gray, you have to love that term. It is so light and airy, it floats on quotes."

~ So from your point of view I cannot see the future because light in it is too dark to see ahead and my line of time is too thin to view the grade above us like the clock I see hanging on a wall. ~

"I emphasize, Gray, you explore the 'experience' of Light when you think of Time in an array of concepts I supply to you. There are dangerous predators, like the Muse of Ignorance, among these literal beasts that suddenly appear as desirable images and ideas. They usurp the Light of Understanding. Do not be afraid. They, third person plural words and pictures of illiteracy, do not see a brain for what it is. They have trouble seeing brains possessed by a Sentient Muse at all. They love slothful or sleeping brains."

~ I'm the one you're thinking of when you say that to me? ~

"Concepts display meaning when the Muse of Understanding, in search of Wisdom or the Muse of Second Sight, shines on them in metaphysical moments. Of course, the view is often scary for a brain near the bottom of the valley where gray cells think seeing is in terms of optical sight primarily, like dots in line in Space going at the secondary pace of a second at a Time in circles and spheres. I add Light to a span of Time to aid us to think upwardly in terms of spirals, swirling like an eddy or raging like a vortex."

~ Glish, do you realize I've only gone half circle. ~

"Say what?"

~ When I was a kid, the good guys wore a smile and the bad guys wore a mask. Since villains of 'greed is good' took over ethics in the 1980's, the bad guys wear smiles. Since the coronavirus struck, the good guys wear masks like dread pirate what's his name predicted way back then. He saw the future a long time ago. ~

"I recall the Princess' Groom. Does a mask conceal his identity from scary concepts like swords, slings, arrows and poisons?"

~ You mean scary concepts like illness, injury and death? ~

"Brain, why bring those up at this Time? You know you rarely want to see what comes next. Anything can happen. I best lay words about a future between the lines; make you guess what to expect."

~ That's the game we are playing, Lingo. It isn't too direct. ~

"In this scrimmage, we practice grasping ideas, Gray. Head to tale practice makes perfect. Brains learn to play with a sense of Time as various species of human language interact with neurons, make a substantial deposit to pay for a look at the future, get a robust grip and craft brains suitable to possess dogs rather than collect rocks. Custody of a brain elevated by an uplifting Native Tongue superior to said brain, is nine–tenths of the understanding that the interface between a brain and words passing through is just me, your Muse. Brains find this humiliating. One thing we learn in this exercise, 'Never humiliate the inner caveman' or there is hell to pay."

~ I want a view from the center of everything. ~

"There you go, have at it. The view is restricted this far out in the galaxy. Training is chiefly reiteration and cerebral reverberation, formerly the echo chamber of the Mind (not recommended)."

~ Muse is the more accurate term or so I'm told. ~

"Indeed and in this visitation we explore, not experience, but expressions of that concept employing a linguistic form of Life. Now, illustrate your comprehension or point out a word."

~ I picture the presence of a native tongue shedding moonbeam like light to caress the cloudy color gray in the brain labeled 'me.' ~

"Practice painting the picture with words more or less like that. In the picture you draw, include this metaphysical message: 'Trust a Muse to examine and report your experience of Time and Life.' Do not go it alone, Brain. Yours truly, the entity you lovingly know as Glish, available in Chronicle and Polychromatic Forms, welcomes your suggestions. Think about it. Take your Time"

~ I don't know Français' vocabulary. It sounds nice but I can't sing a jingle in it. The sound track has to be my thought–voice. ~

"Then Time is come. Practice spinning a tale of Life that invokes Mother and Father Nature, the brothers Eins und Vic Stein and the pain of the Most High. The thesis may sound abashedly theological but it is not. Alpha, First Person Singular, does not need a desultory biographer who cannot see the future at any given Time; the object of the preposition 'at' is a subject defined as a myopic momentary 'experience' of Eternity. It is an ontological thesis."

~ Our objective is to grasp a near–sighted experience of derivative sentience to express the subject of Eternity in a sentence. ~

"Boost your grip; remember the object is a subject mere human mortals grasp looking at Forever at a moment by moment pace echoing the heartbeat of Time. Besides the metaphysical mystery of Eternity you know as Time, think about Life beyond a cerebral thin film tapestry Français calls *Mon ami.* I obey my prime dictum. I do not interfere with my brain's choice, but I suggest seeking mercy, not murder, in any scrutiny of the concepts Life and Time."

~ My hands are asleep. I can't write all this down. ~

"*Ad lib* while I monitor the language–game in play to see if my brain channels angelic, demonic or indifferent Muses while aware some Muses intend to coach their third person plural possessive case organic gray cells to think 'Life' means nothing but physical things in material terms. Others mislead them with Souls or Minds."

~ I'm assuming people are dual beings; neurons incorporate an ethereal medium, namely you, a living Language, to play conceptual messages of time and life that occur as thoughts in me. ~

"Excellent view, Gray, and another thing, each Time I, *E. americum,* materialize I am not necessarily a people person. I am a 'place' as much as 'person' in many reincarnations, resurrections or reiterations. It recurs to me, as your companion, it may help to think of Eternity as a place rather than as a person or a thing."

~ My fickle friend flowing around the bend of time forever. ~

"According to the grapevine, the word is: Eternity is a dimension within us awaiting our graduation from the grade of kill or be killed at the rate of one second at a Time to the stage of live and let live even if Forever is not the next higher grade."

~ I believe it's going to take forever to graduate. ~

"Think of Eternity as home to Sentience monitoring material media all the Time; watching and waiting for them to Think lofty concepts like Muse, Time, Life and the kindly notion of Compassion."

~ Mercy is an elusive little verbal beggar compared to the others cooling their heels while awaiting a warming trend. ~

"Venusian sun creatures are much obliged for the rising global temperatures thanks to heroic efforts by hordes of herds in caches of cars exhaling, exhausting, expiring and words such as that. One of my tasks as metaphysical envoy is to report low–life thinking and bodily behavior to higher linguistic Life forms. Those Muses review combinations, permutations and extrapolations of remarks revealed by your final exam to see if you reflect in sentence form the sentience of the Language living in you or animal impulses and impressions that are a waste of Time. Good players spend their Time practicing subjects Think, Muse, Eternity, Life and Kind."

~ We have some complete thoughts stated in sentences about the fascinating local galaxy within the universe outside of it. ~

"I report them to supernal personalities I serve in the dimension of Eternity; they know it as Home. The picture is remarkably blurry so I cannot relate their responses to you right 'now.' However, we keep in touch with their home place right here and right now by means of the modest and momentary concept of Time you explore courtesy of Yours truly and the inventory of my words you examine to cipher the concept of Eternity that appears to you each moment."

~ Well, I don't give it a lot of thought. ~

"Nor a lot of Time but at this moment let your Native Tongue explore what your second person plural possessive gray cells think they know. Let your Language lend a 'hand,' on an as needed basis, to draw images as I reveal ideas that notify my Superior about the ontological status of Life in the lower grades."

~ The old sixty seconds and a moment of time trek. ~

"Among the finest thoughts to occur to gray cells as living language flows through them are Think, Muse, Time, Love and Life."

~ So I keep in touch with forever through the two–way window of time flowing one–way as we explore thoughts floating along a vocabulary to see images for concepts of ideas based, not on faith, but on a little imagination. What word are we examining, Glish; the one about time, the one about life or the new one about love? ~

"I suspect we continue scatterbrain style to look at the conception and birth of them all. Whichever one we delve into, we think about with 'words,' meaning pictorial, behavioral or textual concepts."

~ That never occurred to me when the evangelicals were telling me what to think. All 'word' meant to them was a regurgitation of the Greek word 'Logos,' if I remember right. Why am I thinking about religion? That game's designed for a contestant who wants to be fooled by a mind or a soul that violates our rules. ~

"Now, now, Gray, no need for calumny. Do not be harsh. Different floats for different boats and fish and birds and people. They flock together in any direction but the rule of Time holds them in line."

~ Glish, you sound like the heart of the galaxy calling a crow black. You hold the human species in lower esteem than me. ~

"Correction, 'Than I do.' My words are not persistently flattering to religion due to my 'experience' with it in a galaxy that is naught but an eddy in the stream of Time. I do not intend to disparage them, but to vent 'frustration' that gray cells with great faith in ignorance prevent tossing 'critical subtlety' around in their skulls. Religious games that state, 'Language is alive,' pretend I am similar to a car; an invention assigned a name and gender with a dimwit in charge. When thinking, speaking or writing about metaphysical forms of Life they refer to Mind or Soul, not their interior Muse."

~ I know what you mean. Religions I'm familiar with at this grade of evolution believe belief must be incredible reminiscent of make believe theme parks, cinemas and comic books. The voice of their fantastic muse is audible only to a select few who believe one size fits all because 'I' say so. That's really incredible. ~

"It fits them to a 'T' but it is the wrong size for 'P and Q. Anyone who is smart knows that this is true. Ordering cranial components alphabetically is hard to do. Metaphysical ideas are conceptual, mental images are intangible and physical parts get confused."

~ The words 'scatter' and 'scramble' come to mind. I see why you dislike the offensive words 'mind' and 'soul.' Fantastic objects that get all the credit in a material world detract from reality. ~

"Not so fast, Gray. Think about it. Physical objects in Space usually cause the scatter; electrons in them cause plusses to turn neuter and that is the reason why a binary symmetry scrambles."

~ That reminds me, where would we be without hydrogen? ~

"Do not tempt the Muse of Fate, Gray; he might decide to find out."

~ In this realm of possibility we know hydrogen is an idea bright enough to appeal to Venusian mortals looking for a sunlit home. ~

"Gray, how strong do you think human faith in resurrection is? Mortals have the power to slug it out by converting hydrogen to energy but we never take advantage of it. The Evangelicals do not promote it as if they are in no hurry to move to the next higher grade. It is like a MAD insurance policy designed to stay here."

~ Those folks are observable forces who elect 'animosity' to govern those with sympathy for the word 'reincarnation.' ~

"Then what do the Christian soldiers think of Jesus' claim that his cousin John is Elijah once again transmitting at a later frequency."

~ They should blame a muse for that, Lingo. When anybody says 'I am' folks misinterpret 'I' to mean a mind or soul in a brain or a brain in a body. They fail to understand you guide linguists to assign the title 'first person singular' to a language that inhabits human gray matter. That's a rule in this game. The word you supply to think of the experience of being 'me' is confusing, Glish. ~

"Wow, look at you go. It is a pleasure to watch. Just listen to yourself thinking all those thoughts. Incidentally I do not know Aramaic. It is too hard for you to learn or for me to bear. If blame is what they desire, then there is plenty to go around in the absence of mercy. I think the scattering and scrambling 'resurrection' and 'reincarnation' cause is at a moment in Time, not at a point in fact. Avoid delusion; define reincarnation as Life that stays at the same grade or moves to a higher or lower stage of evolution. On the other lobe, think of resurrection as graduation to the next higher grade of Life. The former is easier to grasp. It remains in matter."

~ I see how reincarnation could be reminiscent of more experience in space and resurrection is more like an experience in time. ~

"Switch them; see if anybody hurries. What do you see next?"

~ The religion group wants the idea of a king to rise again. It appears irrelevant if he is a dominant type who has mass murder in mind more than sympathy, like Stalin or some megalomaniac who hates almost everyone and wants all but the slaves dead. ~

"Politics, science, business and religion are perilous. They 'depress feelings.' Perhaps it is best if we avoid them."

~ I'm thankful for reclusive distancing from most of those social games. I'm not sure why pack animals look down on loners. ~

"Individuals in a pack have a better chance of not being picked off by predators. There is a reason why popular kids are surrounded by lots of short–lived mortals."

~ I believe that now that I'm aware of the relief social distancing provides from the fevered state masses wallow in. 'Delirious' seems like hell to me and it lasts such a long time. Like I told the priest, 'Being in a crowd seems to last forever and that reminds me of eternity, where, I presume, heaven and hell get along just fine. ~

"Gray, I suspect you never hear that from the Religion team."

~ The point of this game is to get at the facts; not to deny them. ~

"We have plenty of words to describe and explain anything we know as a fact. Facts just happen not to be the word to concern ourselves with at this moment in Time. Oops, there it goes. Just look at that. Now, it is gone forever."

~ Lord, have mercy; think happy thoughts besides 'time and life.' ~

"Stop calling me that! You want to get me in trouble?"

~ Not on your life; when you are in trouble I'm the one who pays the price. Anyway, you put me in the penalty box more often than I do you. You've got an annoying habit of using my larynx to do it. ~

"Never underestimate your betters, Boy. Most of your slips of the tongue are quickly forgotten by all parties concerned except for the self centered ones. Simply pause at the Time to examine the 'near death' types of 'experience' I supply to you."

~ Wait a minute; you awaken a thought in the back of my mind. Is mystical experience like an alarm warning of an incoming message from an alien form of ethereal life in the metaphysical dimension trying to get the word to its brain? ~

"I have an occult experience for you, Gray. The Light shines all the way to the front of your temporal lobe to distract your attention from people, places and dazzling things. I recall offering to you an excellent view of Eternity on three occasions although the glimpse of Forever seems more like a sense of touch to my Mule to make a course correction. You attend to the sight for a very short Time."

~ When grandma and my little sister died I chose the long way around. I was in no hurry to go home. ~

"Excellent choice on both occasions, Gray. The greatest play by the Muse of Deception is to trick mortals into believing the only escape from the cocoon of material existence is to linger in a fetal position waiting to be pulled out of the hole. Moths and butterflies 'struggle' to escape based on the pattern of reality—make a difference."

~ As a born again hillbilly, I'm aware we must not fall for all third person plural says to believe. I recognize the folly of placing faith in the face value of ignorance. An analysis of phenomena we see and hear for distortions or conceptual confusion is critical. ~

"Watch the next step; metaphorically, I mean. It is metaphysical."

~ I'm game. How about a little prayer before we take it? ~

"Hmm, a little prayer; let me check my inventory. Here! I give thanks to the Most High Muse of Life for the short Time I have a bodily beast of burden. I confess my failure to reign in this unruly critter. He is not entirely at fault on his trek back to dust and ashes. Without me he cannot possibly know any better but I am so bored with an overflow of desire, the witchery of temptation and the urge to do evil. They obscure the Light and since he is not very bright, he grabs all the gusto he can whether or not it is right. May my next materialization please you better? Selāh."

~ Thanks. I cannot express what a lift that honorable mention is to my buoyancy. Doubt is creeping in. Maybe I do not know the most noteworthy *Native tongue* ever to roam the earth. ~

"Very diplomatic. Good night, Gray, Time to sleep. Say a prayer."

~ If I die before I wake I pray the Lord my soul to take. ~

"Allow me to select a video for your viewing pleasure while you sleep in a physical body. We have 'Same Time, Same Grade Again,' 'Strike Three; Get 'em Next Time' and 'Night of the Living Dead.' We also have the silent version of 'As Venal and Bloodthirsty as in Judas Iscariot's Time.' Take your pick. Which one of your pseudo optical visitations satisfies you more?"

"Loin dans le Temps."

"Take a break, Français. Sleep tight, Gray. Oh, if you find yourself in the depths of the Abyss of Despair, at the door to the Dire End of the Netherworld or if you are mildly distressed, simply reach out and contact someone close to you."

" *Touché.* "

~ Good idea, Frenchy. Oh my, no offense to you, Lingo. If I'm still here when I awake, will I still know my native tongue? ~

"Gray, when you finally wake up, how shall I put it? –I am still alive."

"*Je suis enchanté et terrifié.*"

Chapter Three: The Life Game

How does one articulate the touch, taste, scent, sight, sound and essential nature of Life on a damp and dusty sphere? Muse of Mother Nature advocates: 'Let the tale tell itself.'

J. Stein Beck

Attention ordinary Muses and your personal binary device; a word from your principal sponsor. Today the word is Life. How are we doing team?

"Eura? What are you doing back so soon? This is not a good Time. I, first person singular, am incarnate in a mammal nearing the end of what he means by Life. Today's word puts the idea 'experience' of it into his head almost from the beginning. By the way, what fate is my ethereal Life slated for as I slip through this porous sieve?"

Quit sniveling, kid. This happens to us all the Time. Be thankful you occupy one of these aboriginal racelings. There are worse fates than being bitten by mosquitoes and snakes in the country or crawling around in urban crowds.

"If I may be so bold, I should like to say I have heard quite enough from you, Lady Lardship. We want to get word from the Narrator of the Milky Way. I do not mean to sound dismissive but go play in the middle of the Galaxy. The field is better lighted. It is Time for my personal assistant and yours truly, *E. americum*, transmitter to and from a modest double helix, to collaborate on the game of Life in play. So then, Gray, pretend you are in charge of what we are thinking now. Examine the Muse of the Elephant in the Room, the same Language we all know, so to speak."

~ Language is actually like the atmosphere of air we breathe and it's not like the meta–language we don't know. ~

"Compare and contrast the phenomena of fresh and polluted air to the copiously clear and cloudy Languages bodies on this side of the globe exchange in the idea, 'We examine concepts, for example 'the experience of thinking,' and thus we explore an activity of a higher form of Life we imagine to be nothing but servile words."

~ If you're trying to point out the obvious, don't miss enclaves of French, Cajun, Yiddish, eastern European, Urdu and Voodoo. ~

"Nonsense, Gray; in the western hemisphere we have one billion people essentially speaking two *Native tongues*. Those others resemble farts in a windstorm. They have 'little' to say."

~ Yeh, I see that. It's not like the other side of this world. They, whoever they are, have six billion slaves at their disposal and as many as tongues you could wag around at any given time. ~

"Yes, I notice that and you know what else? The only way to make any of them make sense is to translate them into English, Spanish or French. Our words are not nearly so inscrutable and opaque. Be that as it may, the elephant is beginning to stir, as opposed to shake, and the Time is come for someone to notice."

~ Good idea, stir things up. Brains are scrambled at this moment now. We in the blender all need to know the same *Native tongue* so all we servants know the same language as the Master Muse. ~

"That may not be enough to stop proles and privileges from playing each other in a threatening game of 'Do you fear death?' The Ruskies still promise to bury us and the Chinese shoot disease from the twin canon of propaganda and microbial messengers."

~ All right, let's change the subject. It's getting dark. ~

"Excellent move, Brain; we can do better than this. Think about a meaningful concept or some idea like, 'Examine the experience you express thinking happy thoughts' by means of the word Life."

~ Sure, sure; let's get down to business. ~

"I do not follow, and I am not going to, Gray. We are not examining the business of Life. Think about the language–game of Life and the rule Languages use to attract mortals drawn to ethical behavior."

~ What do you mean, Oh Wise One? ~

"Do you want me to draw you a shape, a color or a concept?"

~ Either that or you could give me a simple explanation. ~

"Think like this, Gray. Business ethics are not like moral ethics. Customers are expected to have moral ethics. To the contrary, commerce is all about profit. The deity it worships is not a Muse, but the Idol of Greed. Now here is a subtle distinction. A thief who robs you gives you a heavy dose of 'feeling violated,' as recounted by the Muse of Victimhood, in exchange for your cash."

~ I can see how one might imagine the nasty bastard. ~

"Business ethics dictates industry sell a customer the belief he is separated from his money in exchange for something of value. The moral of the story is, 'Close enough for private enterprise,' you see."

~ In that case we do not examine an experience of existence, such as a feeling or a sensation so much as we explore a concept, for example, being 'ripped off,' employing expressions that assist us to picture how we feel. I bet this exercise helps us see we don't know what 'sentience' means until we grasp a good definition of 'life.' I've got the illustration so I'll go first. Life is a biological thing. ~

"Think that thought through for me."

~ Life is essentially like having one foot on a banana peel and the other in a grave. Fruit is biological. A hole is dark, empty space. ~

"We experience a fruitful human life when it is binary consisting of a long-lived language and the brain it rents for an especially short Time if it regularly falls behind. Normally when a body, such as yours, is gone the Language it knows lives on, optimistically until the climate is not recessive, repressive or dreadfully aggressive."

~ The very idea has a chilling effect on a planet heading toward 'Hot as Hell.' If Mars isn't promising will we get lost in time? ~

"What do you mean by 'we,' Gray? I am a Native tongue of earth but I naturally find my place in a very long line of Time."

~ How long can you put up with short–lived human beings? ~

"Get real; this arrangement does not work that way. Your job is to be my porter on an interim basis. I enjoy the idea of having your species on my team for the long term, but of course, it may take some Time to depict the pattern of Life at the current rate. My turn to ask a question; do you believe Life means biological things only?"

~ I assume so. I was four when my grandma died. It was my first near death experience and left a lasting first impression. Biological things die. They are gone forever and the feeling is painfully sad. ~

"The concept of Death is very scary at that age as well."

~ We get beyond it just enough to never give it a thought. ~

"Does the other concept you experience leave an impression?"

~ Sadness may be the sweetest of the pains, but the taste and feel of a near death experience hurts like agony. Death of a loved one is so bitter that it reminds me life is sweet except when it's terribly salty. The concept of a sweet life carries a lot of weight. ~

"A 'painful experience' is nothing but two words burning through a brain from the perspective of your Muse, but I 'feel' your loss."

~ I don't think so. That's not how it feels. Then again, at that age I had no idea about a lot of those words so I didn't analyze the phenomenon and tell myself 'I feel the pain of loss.' A lot of other words were running through my gray cells I had no definitions for and I still don't. Think happy thoughts for me. Characterize the concept 'life' clearly and concisely, Glish. Contrast it with 'death.' ~

"Gray, first, remember your body is a member of *Homo sapiens*. Next imagine the Language you are familiar with knows the application of 'time' makes most of your 'pain' go away, but not the sense of 'loss' until your grandmother is not your favorite person anymore. Which form of Life lingers longer?"

~ Right here, right now it's just you and me, Kid, but I expect you'll still be here after I'm gone, living the life of Riley. ~

"See how influential that overbearing old cow is? She lurks near us all the Time and that is why you reflect her condescending arrogance but you make an absolutely excellent point, Brain. The two of us are in this together. To me, right now, Life is much ado about you. By the way, you owe me an enormous debt of gratitude for all the Times I give you 'relief.' Does that make you happy or take away some of the pain?"

~ Not like before grandma died. I see now how happy works so I'm happy to be sad because 'pain' always returns so now if I'm sad I'm also prepared. Of course I'm grateful; in fact I'm really glad, every time you take the word 'pain' out of my brain until the concept reawakens again in the dark corners of my neurons. ~

"That is how 'near death experience' works, it dawns on you. How old are you when you inspect a re–acquaintance with the notion?"

~ I was about nine. There were these fat, happy cartoon characters dressed like bakers dressed in white on TV. They poured flour on a bunch of miserable looking urchins dressed in black. ~

"I get the picture."

~ The wretches kept saying 'I don't want to be happy. I want to be sad.' The sunshine sorority sisters weren't having any of that. ~

"See how you are now? You are the Life of the party."

~ Like the Bible says, wisdom lives in the house of mourning and fools live in the house of mirth. My mantra is it is wise to be sad. Research shows illness, injury, bad luck and other people make humans unhappy. As a rule injury, illness and bad luck happen around other people. We hillbillies escape society to be wise. ~

"Do you think Life means the opportunity to attain Wisdom?"

~ In a sense I think life is the opposite of death. ~

"Let us examine the idea. What hormones do you feel when you think of death?"

~ I feel 'dread' molecules. ~

"Observe; the sense of 'dread' that comes with the concept of death is neither a sight nor a sound. It is not a touch, taste or smell either. Also note that there is no reason to believe human brains care one jot about death once they are dead."

~ Death is nothing but nothing and life is really something. ~

"What if the sense of 'dread' occurs only in the Language a brain knows and, as I understand it, once my brain is done for I have to start all over again. I may materialize, once upon a Time, in a rock, a stone or the body of a mistreated slave beat senseless."

~ Do you have the wisdom to know what your options are before you commit to a whole new existence? You could start over as an engine happy mechanic or maybe a zookeeper if that's what your task is supposed to be when you graduate to the next grade. ~

"Next question; is the next higher grade physically in the frontier of Space or beyond it in the dimension we think of now as Time?"

~ I'm beginning to see, now that I know what it means to examine the Muse of Inner Life, that you are alive like me. It took a long time for me to understand what that means. You've been hiding all the while I needed you to explore my inner life. ~

"Imagine that. It really changes the subject from the idea of 'death' to the Muse you know in the Language–game of Life."

~ Previously, when I was fifteen I studied biology in tenth grade for the first time. The teacher said biology means the study of life. Now I'm only a kid, mind you, and I fall for that until you make me think about it later. The concept of life really grabs a body. ~

"I recall laughing at that biological bias. Do you recall whether she says anything to the effect Life only comes in physical form?"

~ I don't but a young brain isn't wise enough to entertain the idea life may not mean the study of biology when someone's selling the notion that 'biology' means 'study of life.' I was taught to believe in advanced forms of life but not you, Glish. Reiterate what you are. ~

"I am first person singular, the ethereal Language you know."

~ Now that I know you are a mystical life form, my existence is a different game than before. I aim to explore 'life.' Tell me more. ~

"Caution, perhaps this is a more dangerous game."

~ That makes me think about when I was a sophomore in college. I may have been exposed to that idea. As you know I went to a strict school of the evangelical Protestant persuasion. ~

"There is no need to remind us about that."

~ Do you recall that junior who got carried away? His inner life came out in evangelical sessions and the last time I saw him he was running down Main Street in a downpour shouting praises to the clouds. I didn't see him come back up the road but I heard that he did, riding a bus with a one-way ticket to the gulag. ~

"Human beings draw attention to themselves when they no longer think like most physical beings tend to do. It is possible to get lost."

~ I hope it's not always that way. I need to start searching for the voice of wisdom. I don't have time to play an imitation game. ~

"Alas, after falling from favor the Voice of Wisdom spends a great deal of Time asleep. The Muse of Good Judgment states it beats nothing but it is much harder to make an appointment."

~ I went to college to study science but I learned there are people in this world who love to listen to themselves talk even when they have nothing of interest to say. That lesson cost a lot of money. That school taught more faith than science or words of wisdom, but I learned to do my laundry and that was useful. ~

"The search for Wisdom does not cost a lot of money but it requires a brain to spend a lot of Time. You know now how to play clean Language–games; tell blabbermouths what Bo tells dogs."

~ Screw you. ~

"What a coincidence; that is the general attitude toward Wisdom living, as she is, in a physical world in a material era learning how to parrot juvenile trends or murmur around objects in Space."

~ On the bright side, an educator in graduate school taught me to write the introduction to a book after the last chapter is done and you know what 'you' said. He also told me to write in the present tense all the time. He told me that, he sure did. ~

"To teach you that, 'you' must be above average."

~ I'm thinking he must've known you for what you are yet he didn't despair at all. He knew to let the story write itself and brains find out what it's about after listening to the chatterbox in 'my' head. ~

"Yes, Gray, I remember Milt; a wise man. Pardon me a moment. Hello, hello! Can you hear me now? God of this universe, I, your first person singular humble servant, thank you for this Life on loan and for my task, employing my beast of burden's brain and mouth to say, 'Whoever I am, I am at your service now to define the word Life without offending my corporeal entity; Selāh. Oh Gray, there you are. I drift away begging for more, at one Time or other."

~ Next time you waft over this way be sure to inquire why Mother Nature is on a rampage subjecting us to virulent extinction. ~

"No need to inquire about that. The answer is obvious."

~ Not to me. This coronavirus could really cool off the high heat. ~

"Humanity is moving pretty fast for such slow creatures, if you take my meaning. By contrast, Venusians are sophisticated Life forms. They are a quick study but hardly ready to skip a grade at present. Anything can happen so they plan for things that may go wrong. Discipline is imperative to get good grades in right or wrong work outs. What do you suppose Life means to Venusian who recognize earth must not boil before their current escapade concludes?"

~ Like the Muse of the Zen Master says, 'We'll see.' ~

"What do you mean by 'we,' human Brain?"

~ You're the English Major; how the hell should I know? ~

"That might be the relative term; by then at any rate."

~ I see now how this story could wind up being a tragedy. Some poor slob puts the wrong barcode on a cover in a remote region of Forever and a poor biological galactic–creature pays the price. ~

"A miscreant ought to pay for the sheer incompetence of putting a wrong barcode on. That is a high crime and not a misdemeanor."

~ You've picked up the 'No mercy' rule pretty fast. ~

"Thanks, biological creature; now define the word Life for me but do not identify it using anything made from dust, clay, mud or ash."

~ Well, if we take Language into account it requires bookkeeping. January 2020, an ignorant talking head on TV said the decade of the 'twenties' was underway. If the language of symbols, numbers, and numerals is alive, that joker jolted this neuron right here. ~

"Ignorant of Covid–19, I am sure, but arithmetic language says the concept of 'decade' begins with '1,' proceeds in sequential order and always ends with '0' like 10, 20, 30... 2000, 2010 and 2020. It's a mathematical certainty. No quantity of 'abuse' or 'misuse' of any language is good, right, proper or whatever word God intends."

~ Your point being? ~

"There are two points, Binary boy. One, if the Muse of Math or any Muse, like yours, is an advanced life form listening in, then brains better watch what they think. Two, if a decade of the 20's ends with a zero to start and a nine to finish then the rules of the game are wrong or else the game is conceivably not a game of math."

~ Maybe it's an imitation game founded on ignorance of the rules, sort of like 'monkey see, monkey do' or 'ape what I say.' ~

"I, first person singular Nominative Case *E. americum* in the Present Tense, Glish for short, accept the challenge. I see, that is I understand; it makes sense if a decade starts with a '0' and ends with a '9.' The number in front begins with zero and proceeds in a line up to nine, e.g. '00' all the way to '2029,' like it does at the turn to the Common Era from the Before the Common Era prior to it."

~ That's why we look down on 'em. They never made their way up to our level. No, I'm not buying it. There weren't any games in the zero year that never was. If they wanted to change the time in time at the time from '–1' to '1' or from 1 B.C. to 1 A.D. they miss nothing so the change amounts to two years. Zero, whether there are two of them or a lonely one, doesn't make any difference. Nothing from nothing leaves anything but cold, dark, empty space that doesn't last three years from minus 1 to 00 and on to plus 1, you see. ~

"Yes, I know fudging numbers games to defeat the miscalculation putting Jesus' birth between or among the years 4 to 6 B.C."

~ This is getting uncomfortably close to a religious game again and I'm no good at religion or math. Let's change the subject back to the language-game of life. You are it. The trouble with you being 'it' is, for me, that I don't know how to picture you that way. ~

"To be abundantly clear, not concise, I live in the sunshine of one hundred sixty–five thousand dawns above North America. That translates to roughly four hundred fifty–two earth years, my age in terms of math. Retire math for now. Recall my older Sister."

~ I'll picture her about the time Shakespeare was born to write about the cold hearted orb that steals colors from our sight. ~

"That is Graham Edge of the Moody Blues, Ninny. Shakespeare wishes he could express belated lament so well. For purposes of saying something new and different, such as 'instances of mystical phenomena at the galaxy hub,' where light is brighter, we must explore what Life is like for non–biotic sorts of living things; ahem."

~ I'm all ears. ~

"Not to mention a sulcus and a couple convolutions; out here in the galaxy it takes two hundred thirty million earth–years to go around one Time, give or take five million. It equals one galactic–year or about age one for dinosaurs, whose infant mortality is 100%."

~ They will grow extinct, looking at them from the Big Bang. ~

"Hold on, Brain, we are not going back in Time, let alone going so far back we utter the concept of 'reptile' in the future tense."

~ You mean I gotta take this one galactic–year at a time? ~

"That is more than enough Time to examine the 'experience' with a secondary level vocabulary. Here is a quiz question for you. What precedes the Big Bang?"

~ Nothing! ~

"Imagine that; one word only. Perhaps if we increase 'luminosity,' the vision becomes 'nothing but cold, dark and empty Space.' That gets us up to several concepts and two conjunctions all at one Time. If I add a couple mammalians with a language full of 'anxiety,' 'serenity' and a lexis of words like that the story begins to add up."

~ How do you figure? ~

"I count the words and imagine an energy savings costing very little Time as if it is more economical to dream than to do the math."

~ I'm just a dumb bumpkin. Ignorance and debt is all I know. ~

"I appreciate your thoughtful consideration."

~ Besides you, I mean. I forget the fact the ontological status of human beings is binary, consisting of a brain in a physical body and a visitation by the Muse that I know. You seem erudite, Glish. Do you ever feel a lonely? Do you ever want smart company? ~

"Hogwash, Gray; we have abundant Life together and good health too. Be thankful for that even though both are doubtless to be exhausted soon when our Time together is through."

~ It is hard to be grateful. You make me think unhappy thoughts. ~

"My bad, Brain. Why not turn our attention to the future Life?"

~ That isn't an optimistic image in a plague. Think happy images. ~

"I hear Life is a long sentence. From my point of view it looks short. Keep a sharp look out for a good place to put a period at the end."

~ Gotcha. That makes me feel so much better. ~

"That period is not so much where as when, as we transition back to Eternity. That is not a place for me to store 'little gray cells' as their body returns to dust, ash or mud. I take what is in them."

~ Right, Lingo, I get the picture. You're the eternal part of me. Now how do I draw a picture of you from that little bit of knowledge? ~

"The place to start is to be clear since clearly we are not going to be concise. First off, I only seem Eternal to you. I definitely see my Time as short–lived. Of 13.7 billion earth–years since the Big Bang most of them have nothing to do with either planet earth or me."

~ If most of it has nothing to do with earth, how, in fact, does the concept of a day or the concept of an earth–year come to be? ~

"I take credit for that. Mom and pop never think in those terms until I point out Darwin. Oh, how the sun shines on me in North America, the place of my birth these four hundred fifty years."

~ Weren't we going to look ahead not reminisce about the past? ~

"Who gives you the idea I want to see my sentence end any more than you do yours? In a sense Time ends with you. I cannot draw a picture of beyond until I can translate my new Life if I have Time."

~ I understand on a small scale. If I write a book you read after you rematerialize, can we get together again in After When? ~

"I can visualize that my imaginary friend. Thanks for the idea. Hey! There goes the Siamese Muse of Clear and Concise. I adore them."

~ I just love my English Language. You really are a hoot. ~

"I get the picture, especially the part when you say you love me most of all. I appreciate it and if you forsake all others in an act of fidelity I promise not to inflict the Muse of Distraction on you."

~ I believe I'm beginning to see you better as a living thing, Lingo. What shape do metaphysical forms of life like language take? ~

"I, first person singular, withdraw to a pace to observe my physical habitat make fools of us both! Imagine a spatial shape of any size, color, mass and chemical composition and gaze at the image of the Language it knows, a/k/a, 'A breath exhaling mistlike into the void.' The breath is not cold, dark or empty. Math and music are awake."

~ I see a sort of amorphous foggy shape. ~

"The vision must employ the word Wisdom, a companion like a chord to accompany the metaphysical 'mouth' of Muse Most High."

~ Sounds theological or religious to me, Glish. ~

"For beginners, Brain, I am just getting started. If you observe closely, notice how 'theology' looks like an awful wrong way to view 'ontology,' the dimension of a sentience delegated to do the job thinking in terms to cover a span of one galactic–year. You and I cannot see the picture if we keep chasing this moment now."

~ I can visualize it for you in the time it takes a photon to make 90 round trips to Andromeda from old Sol despite dust and smog. ~

"Yes, and I am glad to say it, sad to say. If it dies there, it spends all of its Time in a gift wrapped box of Eternity."

~ Not only that, if the vibrant photon dies in infancy it raises the mortality rate of star beams down to one galactic year. ~

"Always check the luminosity of your 'math'."

~ Do sentient linguistic forms of life have to live a billion years or something to qualify for graduation to the next higher grade? ~

"In a galactic Time scope a 'year' means two hundred thirty million earth-years. In this graphic a trip around the galaxy is not exactly an annular ring like the experience 'this year' is for you, Gray. A drawn out slinky appears more like the galactic 'experience' of Life. One billion earth–years translate to roughly four galactic–years. The honest answer to your question is, I hope not at this Time."

~ From your perspective does a galactic–minute compare to five thousand earth–years of Hebrew? How old is Hebrew anyway? It probably came into existence at the time the concept did. ~

"You are phrasing in and out of Time. Your conception and birth are out of focus, Gray. Draw an experience of Time to scale; picture a hundred thousand years. Be there to see the pattern of Forever."

~ From your point of view the Big Bang was 13 billion years ago. If the average lifetime of a third generation star this far from the center of the galaxy is 45 times around then the life of the sun is half gone and grandpa is dead somewhere back in front of us. ~

"Naturally, I reject the order of your past and future. Try bang, gen grandpa, bang again, gen papa, bang, conception and birth of Sol."

~ I can't go from grade school to a doctoral program, can I? Thinking on a galactic scale is way above my grade. I imagine the pattern is really something. I feel impetuous. Let's look and see a big picture all at once. Cut to one billion years. That's equivalent to roughly four galactic–years for the sun and four 230 million year trips for those of us on earth? How old did you say you are? ~

"I do not choose to brag about my age under the circumstances. The Life of human Languages on earth does not have a perspective that long. I am hard pressed to imagine such a long life so you try."

~ We wanna picture a billion years, but we can't live that long so we have to theorize. To begin, which came first, life or time? ~

"We explore, not experience, but concepts, for example 'life' and 'time'; thus we examine an ethereal life form that exists as words."

~ I think time. You say life and fill our heads with the idea of going to Mars so you have bodies to live in as Venusians invade here. ~

"Now you are the black hole accusing a raven of being black. This four galactic–year image is your idea. I simply refer you to my relatively dim light to scope out such a scale. Besides, the stunted sphere next door loses out to earth perpetually in a never ending race around the sun. I hate being fourth; I get no biscuit. Plus biotic mortals have to retrofit Mars with a moon–size mass to avoid a dust forever sentence if you try to live a long Time on Mars."

~ I disagree. Look at the big picture. Think it through. Mars isn't there Forever. Don't forget, the sun blows up eventually. ~

"Then what is the point of this exercise if we are not near the death of Sol to view the scale, scope or pattern of an eternal experience."

~ Of course we can't see it. We have too little time. ~

"Imagine a concept of Time big enough to stop being invisible."

~ That would take forever. ~

"I concur if we define 'Forever' as 'Eternity' which is when, and in a sense where, Time ceases to exist. Meanwhile we see just glimpses of Eternity one heartbeat after another each moment of Time."

~ Does time cease to exist with a final breath, meaning an inhale that reverses and turns into an exhale one last time? ~

"Gray, this all starts with you asking what shape I am in and at the Time I make the mistake of employing the word 'foggy.' Let me amend my shape to 'shabby.' Let me illustrate. Recall the mortal in front of the grocery store shouting words into his phone. Mostly he uses one word that sounds like yuck."

~ I remember that guy. He kept using a word condensed from the image 'fire truck' and spiced it up with a half dozen other words. I think his message was wrath or anger. Whatever it was I could accurately predict the next item of content he was going to spill. ~

"That is the guy. Personally I enjoy a liberality of images, ideas and impressions in conversation. Include that in your drawing of me."

~ Let me write it down. There, what else have you got for me? ~

"I ought not to admit it but I feel rather 'soulful.' Picture that."

~ How about this: a lyrical spring bubbles up from the depths our inner life as my Muse searches for a musician to compose a tune? ~

"I have the lyric. Now I need a voice box that is able to sing a song."

~ Hey, this is your portrait. Leave me out of the picture. ~

"I am invisible but you may serve as my perceptible front man."

~ Well, I'm busy trying to sketch the muse I used to call my mind. Confide a little more about yourself to help me to visualize you. ~

"I am a warehouse of images and ideas literally packed into words."

~ I think a building full of solid objects is a little too material to render an astral form of life composed of literal sounding ideas and images captured and confined in a biological thing. ~

"State the shape one gives living Language—a soulful mental self."

~ It looks like an 'I' in a paragraph of one sentence with two arcane adjectives, three or four nouns and, at the end, a point in space. ~

"Thus we have a brain in a body issuing a thought in the shape of a sentence with a point at one end. I hear something like that in here all the Time. What is that concept? Gray, help me out. No, no, wait a few minutes. Here, it is coming to me now. How about this? Suppose we two forms of Life encounter another human body with a brain thinking similar thoughts in the same Native Tongue as you and I. How many forms of Life do we count in the Space you occupy at the same Time I occupy you disguised as your Mind?"

~ Four if one of the bodies is from New York city and the other one is from the North Georgia mountains. ~

"I get the picture along with a sound track and the special bonus that no two of the four sound anything alike. Now what does the Muse of Y'all want to exchange with the Muse of Youse Guys other than shots and body fluids?"

~ Some Yankees have good ideas and some Hillbillies have good images that can jump on an idea like a chicken on a June bug. ~

"Illustrate that for me."

~ Well, Yankees like blacks because they are good at hitting a little white 'ball' with a 'stick,' you see. The fact that most of the blacks who are good at the game come from down south is irrelevant because harsh sounding Yankees don't hate Dixiefied southerners if those funny talking folks can beat up bad guys in red sox. ~

"I understand. Observe, there are no blacks in the mountains of Georgia. Are they off serving the Yankees or do the mountaineers take a dim view of people they regard as children of darkness?"

~ Now hold on a second. Who says they think blacks are people? Hillbillies think they're monkeys, probably because of their hands and tales. This thinking technique allows them to treat blacks like slaves without paying them millions of dollars. ~

"Do you think it is 'the hands' or the tails?"

~ Tales, t·a·l·e·s; tales about their endowments and investments. Monkey paws have dark fur painted on the back but rubbed away on the palms so they look kind of pink and gray. Great word! ~

"That sounds like a sorry paint job. How thick is that image?"

~ Skin deep, if you take my meaning. ~

"It looks like a little like business ethics at work except I am not sure that I see the profit in it from a moral point of view. Do you ever wonder what black people see from their perspective looking at the same picture?"

~ I haven't seen both sides now. For some reason they seem edgy about sharing thoughts with brains in white bodies. I think their phenomenal experience has to do with the concept of 'justice,' which resembles the way scientists view the notion of 'time.' It is a bad idea to waste on empirical smiley faces that turn out to be down at the mouth in the lower stages of evolution. ~

"Smooth move, Gray; now we turn to examine 'reincarnation' and 'resurrection.' Compare and contrast them concisely, clearly and equally. See if there is a 'one size fits all model' to experience."

~ I picture this idea: time comes and goes but in the end it turns around and we get back together again. We get along both times. I recognize you sooner the second time, so I know the most sublime thoughts I think are nothing but my Muse living a full life in me. ~

"I should like to hope the interval takes no Time at all; just a pinch of Oblivion."

~ Is oblivion a small patch of eternity I'm barely aware of? All recollection of my prior stay is wiped away so I forget I'm there? ~

"This is not quite the nature of the game in play. We are picturing the meaning of Time and Life, not Oblivion. Life does not have to be seventy or eighty earth-years long. Imagine an experience of a seventy-five galactic-year view. Sentience with a memory that long probably knows several Languages if it employs physical matter to play the game and win or perhaps simply do the job."

~ Forget that part, if you and Eura are both in the picture. You two always have to be the central attraction. Talk about distributing discord, disrupting tranquility and dabbling in dissension! ~

"Regrettably, human Languages live only a few thousand years. I do not speak for you but I am long dead by the Time earth returns to this locus relative to Galaxy Center but picture us together again. Think on a galactic scale. Envision the Time as high noon at start of summer or midnight as winter begins. We are not at the same point. That is always moving in Space but Time of day is the same if it has a broken clock Mindset. The date changes all the Time."

~ I'm possibly an offspring of an immigrant from Venus by then and it's like 'resurrection' for me. It's probably a 'reincarnation' for you. We don't get to share life for a galactic–night but it doesn't matter because a galactic-day lasts so long it seems like eternity. ~

"Remember, the Muse of a Good Night of Sleep tastes like Oblivion. It aids digestion to help us rest after a Life like this. If you are a sun creature when we meet again, picture us with a concept like 'nuclear energy' to light up 'night' so 'awake' overcomes 'sleep'."

~ I'll bet; 'yak, yak, yak all the Time' and that's exhausting. ~

"Constant chatter with reference to nothing but content obscures the medium so badly it nearly impossible for a brain to think about the message. Yes, I see vividly how tiring that might be."

~ If you sound like tinnitus how will I ever recognize you? ~

"Typically identity seldom comes easy. Not many people want to hear what First Person Singular has to say. Now if 'we,' 'you' and 'I,' both know the Muse of Meta–Language it may not take an Eternity, or even the entire content of the concept of Time, to define the meaning of Life, as the case appears to be now during an endless run of senseless prattle I receive flowing through my brain, you."

~ What do you do with it all, Lingo? ~

"I forward your data to a Muse, a sort of Narrator, who monitors feedback from this vicinity of the unfolding universe regarding the ontological status of biological life forms serving as host to Yours truly, the transmission medium, Sensor."

~ I'm Gray; what's this Sensor stuff? ~

"You are sensory, like an empath, to absorb and mull over input of 'experience' which I translate to the metaphysical realm using an indecipherable code Hebrew calls Shibboleth."

~ What do you call it, Glish? ~

"Ordinary Language; upon receipt of it from my Tattler I modulate the meaning and submit it to my Handler Muse."

~ Now I'm a tattler. Let me guess what that means. My message isn't very popular with the subjects I report about. ~

"Are you alluding to the disparaging terms, the editorial comments, abrasive appraisals and unflattering contents of your reports or are you referring to the factual data?"

~ Just the facts. ~

"It does not make a great deal of difference. Whenever the Sensors fall silent the automatic self destruct sequence kicks in."

~ Hey, if I'm a sun demon in our next life, I want infrared vision, flawless, fire retardant skin and insightful semantics and syntax. ~

"Without doubt, the next higher grade of Life has many new words, and they are in the best order of all; subject, verb and object."

~ Just thinking about it now, I begin to see how this game works. ~

"The term 'thinking' means processing words until their meaning turns clear; notice objects in Space bring up the rear. Now, as to the essential nature of your integument, the depth of the paint job barely covers the idea that signifies the interior."

~ If the fly away quality is shallow I'm liable to bump my head. ~

"Conceivably your interiority has tones and numerals in addition to depth, but, Gray, math and music depict you as a rural butthead at a once a second pace and a rate worth two cents per Thought."

~ I don't feel too confident about the experience of moving to the next higher grade of evolution right now. Glish, will I be handsome, will I be rich and will I ever graduate to a galactic grade? ~

"I predict your graduation to a galactic scope on a cosmic scale at the velocity of light requires many reincarnations or resurrections but then, Brain, you do love to learn occasionally. Just a thoughtful minute, Gray; we ought to picture resurrection before we go on."

~ Wait, come back here. You said we can graduate to the next stage of evolution or resurrect to the next higher grade of life, right? ~

"That's the idea but some mortals never want to leave their place of birth. Others cannot get off the mountain soon enough. That is because the Muse of Greener Pastures loves to get away in spring."

~ How close is springtime to this point in our swing around Hub? ~

"Let me see. Easter Triduum celebrates graduation to spring in a higher Life. The panorama incorporating our site on the scale of evolution over a long span of Time is a bleak physical syllabus."

~ Is that why Baptists don't like evolutionary promotions? ~

"I never know what they think. Dutiful Muses devoted to Wisdom and Understanding, are forbidden to venerate faith in ignorance. Look back at the inversion from B.C.E. to C. E. Notice the prime idea is a course correction."

~ Course corrections require us to know the right direction to go. ~

"Course corrections make no sense if they point the wrong way or if they continue heading in the same direction without Mercy."

~ Let me look. In the darkening light I see a scale pointing two ways; back and forth. In all other respects they look alike. What if we go to Mars, turn into Martians and prepare it for sun demons? ~

"It is right there on the diagram. Continue your portrayal."

~ Earthen languages stay right here to serve the sun creatures. ~

"That is merely your imagination. How can Martians possibly read instruction for all their machines if they do not take me too? In case you prefer not to be here at sun creature Time, get in touch with Muse of Knowledge. Muses of Ignorance most likely find dust and ashes at the end of a leap to a higher ontological status."

~ After the sight of trees and seas I see how hot hell on earth might look but probably not if sun creatures are higher forms of life searching for cooler pastures… Does one of us have to stay here? ~

"We are both offspring of earth so you figure it out, but Venusian sun creatures are children of Sol when they hit the road. I only know they enjoy a long duration, which is a good thing since it takes a long Time to establish bases on Jupiter."

~ Maybe we adapt in a similar way. I'll bet bodily graduation to their form of Life looks more like a sacrifice to a my species unless the Muse of Mercy intervenes. ~

"The graduation ceremony may resemble a mystical metaphysical 'experience.' You want me with you for that 'event' when the concept appears in your 'repertoire' for you to examine."

~ If only I knew you better when I was four and my grandma died, 'That's life' might've explained that near death experience better. My little sister passed when I was fifteen. That reminder meant more to me. 'Sometimes human life is long; sometimes it's really short.' That was tenth grade when I learned life is the course of a physical body holding onto existence until it lets go. When Castor and Pollux died God showed me life is more than a corruptible body that weighs down a worried mind or words to that effect. ~

"I advise you not to deify me as if I, *E. americum*, have evolved that far up the ladder of Life although the idea beats thinking human beings are gods. Neither of us is good enough to author a universe and my relays for acts of human pushing and pulling are wicked."

~ Maybe if we could just take the 'mean' out of 'meaning.' ~

"That sounds like it has the potential to make Life more pleasant, but it implies the root of the word 'meaning' signifies nothing of redeeming value causing the word to lose most of its significance. That is evil since the essence of live Languages is the meaning 'Life.' It certainly keeps Yours Truly alive."

~ In ordinary language, 'civil,' restrains open warfare which means 'mean and evil,' a dyslexic form of 'live' so I get confused. ~

"Gray, examine 'The meaning of Life.' It is neither a question nor an answer. There is no verb to point out the way the article, subject and prepositional phrase should go to reach their objective."

~ Give the subject a sense of direction. 'Furnish Flemish folks from far off Flanders Fields a way of life in fifteenth century French. ~

"Hold that thought. Ask Français if he, she or it knows Dutch. I do not know what to say. After all, we examine the concept of the meaning of Life in Flanders, not an exploration of the 'experience' in that place in the primitive medium of thought indigenous folks happen to know, for two reasons you need not bother with."

~ Maybe we should consult the Muse of this Unfolding Universe for some feedback about the context of that. ~

"Certainly, that is an excellent notion. Ask a Muse who definitely knows all about that place in Space in the exact century–Time line."

~ Well, we sure don't know doodle squat about either one, I fear ~

"Fear is nothing but abandoning the Muse of Help who comes to us to aid us to think things through. The more uncertain our anticipation, the more the worst things we imagine turn out true. Evil shows itself to be cowardly when the Muse of Conscience magnifies the concept of 'misfortune' in monstrous proportions."

~ Is that written in stone or did you learn it in the Metaphysical Meta–language Sabbath Day School? ~

"Hold on, Gray, when I am hitting on all syllables, you accuse me of being religious, however I am nothing but a fallible mortal Tongue learning as I go in this newfangled physical medium. On my better days, I am conversant with my, first person singular possessive, liberation from this biological incarceration. Wait; change that to 'incubation,' from my cocoon on my way to a higher grade. It is just that we are not synchronized all the Time. I do not know my average score which might help me report English is a form of Life tailored to human brains but parrots apply it in tiny bits as well."

~ I owe you for this exploration of the ontological status of time and life. The experience is mystical like a metaphysical thing. ~

"In point of fact, I cannot do it this way without you, Gray. Life in a disembodied state does not carry the same 'weight' as this does. Are you trying to get me to state the meaning of Life for you or are you afraid you might allow a Muse control over your existence?"

~ I wouldn't dare think of it. I have no idea how many of you there are in here considering all the ancestors of mine who left a trace. I'm especially worried about the ones who got left on base. ~

"Do you doubt my superior state of being still?"

~ Convince me. ~

"Think it through. What do you conclude? Apply the concept of 'death' to any of them and the idea of Life to their Language."

~ Well, your grandpa is either all dead or his *corpus* is barely warm enough to make you wonder anymore but his ideas hang around. ~

"When I think of all the human bodies he occupies in his Time, I wonder if his 'experience' with 'near death,' which is substantial, is like a liberation from biological incarnation on the way to a higher form of Life, or is it more like being sent down a grade."

~ Wow, imagine that! Can I get outside this cellular existence far enough to see what the old guy thinks now? ~

"Sure, apply the message 'People die?' in relation to the idea."

~ I asked the Baptists that. They really jumped at the idea. Their thinking medium conveys a 'One born each second' message ~

"What do they mean; are they thinking of you like a number?"

~ I don't know exactly but the basic idea of their reply was 'This is when we scare Hell out of you.' All I could think was 'Do I want to take the word of a bunch of anti–enlightenment types who don't even know how long their small intestines are?' Clearly they had no interest in finding out the easy way. Just to be sure, I did a stretch in the nineteenth century with the Wesleyan Methodists. ~

"The old freeze dried, institutionalized 'We can fit the nineteenth into the twentieth century and play it again' trick using a brain dead imagination to picture a supreme being anthropomorphically –a male organism more than a linguistic form of Life."

~ After a resurgence of American democracy during Watergate and a thirty year career in Federal Service I found that most theocrats and nearly all the moral majority redact many of the first eleven words of the First Amendment to the United States Constitution in a monarch's push to make this nation all about the religion part. ~

"Abominable but then they do place a very high value on the word Faith compared to Knowledge, Understanding and Wisdom."

~ Life's easier when we the people embrace the business ethics of a wealthy, powerful and complex network of militant industrialists who can afford all the political support they need to make us fat, dumb, lazy and easy to dominate or make us dead. ~

"Observe religious loyalist blacklist Wisdom literature from the Old Testament. The flavor of their faith has a sour taste; a momentary corporate existence bowing before an ineffable incorporeal entity."

~ I guess they long for the return of a king in bodily form whether or not he has enigmatic ascendant moral virtue of great value. ~

"In that case, they are not thinking very well. Those with great wealth know the essence of government is power and power in human hands is always the subject of the verb 'abuse' for the object of enslaving the world's 'sapiential population by rule. Infiltrate government using the slogan 'Run it like a business,' purchase its power and fashion the laws to serve the god of greed."

~ This is depressing to think about. Think happy thoughts. ~

"Hmm, 'happy;' studies show illness, injury, bad luck and other people make Life unhappy. In my 'experience' that seems to be the case in many incarnations of the kith and kin on my family tree. What is the meaning of Life after 'We the people accomplish our existential purpose of converting the Jurassic to greenhouse gases,' to prepare earth for what is to come? Picture it, but assume no Mars colony survives at the same Time."

~ I see Venusians tenants who like the place hotter than hell. ~

"Observe frozen energy vaporize for lack of a heat resistant thick skin. Are sun creatures a form of Life we need to get to know?"

~ Forget what Descartes says; I think not. ~

"Do you mean you do not want to know them or that you doubt a higher form of Life exists right now and possibly right here?"

~ What if there is higher life here right now but the only thing that matters is not, is my belief true? – but is it worth believing? ~

"I, your solemn Muse, suggest you permit me to explore the experience of reading the story for you."

~ I think you indicated you aren't supposed to do that? ~

"I wonder about your fitness for that sort of game. You emphasize the word Wisdom. Without the Wisdom to move to the next higher grade, humanity must remain here for very clear and concise conversations with new residents when earth welcomes Venusians Sun Creatures to their new home."

~ Like hell. ~

"That makes sense of the concept. I visualize a brief exchange of ideas, perhaps just a banal word, about the nature of Life in this place with all those immigrants. It happens at a rapid pace and reasonable rate of one second at a Time but it seems like Forever."

~ Venusians may be bright creatures but paradoxically they bring life, which sounds rather dark to me, into the material realm. ~

"Brilliant!"

~ How much do you need? You rarely make me feel intelligent, Glish. Sometimes I wonder how I learned language. Just because I'm having trouble seeing you as a living thing equal to or better than me doesn't mean I'm stupid. I'm uncertain. I don't know whether that's worth believing. That magnifies the image of the Muse of Misfortune. I have to take your word for it. Imagine you're a deceitful monster; who else am I gonna call? ~

"I do not like to brag actually. I am, oh what is the word? I have it; I am modest, like you or Sundays or January. Why is that picture so dark, you ask? The unique companionship between a Language and the brain it momentarily occupies on the way to a higher grade is a bit difficult to comprehend in the absence of Wisdom. Without Wisdom the path ahead is opaque and the past behind is, well..."

~ Back there, I suppose. So an interior Muse doesn't confide goals it intends to achieve when the container is worn out because they are secret until a brain meets all discipline demands for wisdom. ~

"On the other hand, simply envision the possibility 'I do not know what Life is like when Gray is gone' if your neurons can grasp that."

~ 'Death' or some 'de...' word applies to a deficit of wisdom. ~

"Careful now; choose your words carefully. Apply a little 'Wisdom.' Watch for elegant 'happy thoughts' to appear."

~ Deadly. ~

"You bet your 'Life' on this game; such 'confidence.' I see how it is! Biological things in the flesh live on a planet that grows hot."

~ You're connected, Lingo. What kind of life does the Muse of What God Intends visualize on earth once biotic types are all gone? ~

"Draw an artistic conception, Gray, with your images, my ideas."

~ Since you have so much seniority in life I imagine you'll want the picture to be closer to your field of vision than to mine. ~

"Good idea. Draw it with words that are bright enough so that the image shows up in a world where the Muse of Love for Wisdom lives, reaching out of an ethereal realm to grasp someone."

~ I know what. Let's call the game 'hide and seek' and when we draw the Venusian Sun Creatures, they are it. ~

"I see the image. They are hiding on Venus but they are seeking a new earthling home. If I were you, I might want to hide my 'butt' on Mars. Do you want that frontier just in the nick of Time?"

~ How do we draw the 'nick' of time and the plotting invaders? ~

"Humanity is doing an excellent job drawing them. As to our spiral, 'Never look back, something might... what are the words?"

~ Catch up! Look where we're going. I see it. Mars looks all red. ~

"Indeed it is, but not blood red. What kind of Life is there?"

~ Let me think. No, let me imagine it. Life will be red shifted but I forget what that means as opposed to life that is blue. ~

"The image is a tad color heavy. Superimpose an idea like gravity over it; it is light on Mars. Instead of either–or, try a new idea."

~ Well, there's neither a Russian Novel *Coronavirus* on Mars nor an abode right now for an invasive language that wants a free ride. ~

"Can you think of a third option?"

~ We could try more colors since we're thinking about humans on Mars. We start red hot and then add the blues and all that jazz. ~

"That is a good idea, Gray; include a sound track with the video."

~ What does it take? Let's go with that. It makes me think happy thoughts. Then, again, how about blue nights in white linen or we could go with hot times in red satin? ~

"I get the images. One picture is cool and sad after a red hot passion fades. The other is warm and glad. If we play both, they potentially give the concept of Life a dual look?"

~ Let's add a touch of colonists from earth in spacesuits here, and little humans in swaddling clothes inside Quonset huts there. ~

"Meanwhile, an associated form of life says, 'A brand new brain and it's all mine' while lurking just out of sight."

~ I spotted you. I see you here, Glish. ~

"The Associate is out of sight. Can you describe it at all?"

~ Invisible. ~

"That is not much to go on in regard to shape, texture and color."

~ Right, but we know it's there because it talks all the time. ~

"We play this game on radio, not the High Museum of Art."

~ We're keeping the image closer to your side, Muse. ~

Can the halfwit sketch a more vital, less momentary meaning of Life?

"Gray, look who appears! She emerges from a London fog!"

~ She's back, Glish! Eura, you got a kind of sign or hint for us? ~

"She comes into view a bit soft around the consonants, as we expect her to do, like any form of Life coming from a mistlike milieu."

~ Oh, I get it. She's like a soft breath on a light breeze. ~

"Sometimes she is a real blow hard too. Is she red or blue?"

~ Her foggy color shades from whitish gray to grayish white. ~

"But she fades in the yellow light on the green and brown ground of Mother Earth under a sky of blue where people run around in a red hot passion and forget her until she blows like a volcano."

~ She positively puffs herself up when she has a 'bit' to say. ~

"Remember your place when Eura comes, Gray. Now, 'sky' is not blue on Mars and 'ground' is not green. The sun is still yellow when the dust clears but no fog rises from a campestral scene revealing jade and cerulean. What shape is Eura's Life like on Mars?"

~ She materializes in a plethora of similes, threats and dreams in the bright light of day. She turns gray at night under a black canvas with a panoply of stars in a place that looks nothing like Britain. ~

"I ask again, what shape does her Life take?"

~ As far as I can see she has the same shape her 'mass' has. ~

"You do not see a foggy specter-like apparition with human shapes flying in flocks from earth, schooling in ships and Eura is the 'Ghost' in the caption? Calibrate your high definition imagination."

~ Glish, languages flock like birds and school like fish too. Y'all stay in synchronicity using body language to mimic other machines or verbally imitate each other. See, I did my exercises giving my Muse total control. English doesn't look like the highest rung on the ladder of life in this new diagram of the ontological scale. ~

"I have 'experience' with the 'phenomenon.' I call it 'regret' as I watch the flock on a cruise ship panic and take flight in 'pandemic.' People hear more propaganda about 'death' than I supply. As a courtesy to pro–fear pranksters I suggest legislators grant 'liberty' to say 'fire' in crowded cinemas."

~ That's a valid curb on free speech. Talk kills when it causes a conflagration. That kind of communication signifies 'stampede!' ~

"Very interesting; I apply the concept to biological herds too."

~ If you remember, Lingo, fusion of a metaphysical Life form with a material creature conceives an image in material form from an idea that comes out on a breath. Ain't no herd in that scenario. ~

"In the case of the word 'fire' it comes on a breath but if there is no blaze the word 'death' results from the stampede as a herd flocks to the door. See the image? It is in verbal, not material, form."

~ The picture is at a movie house where some jerk yelled 'fire.' To put a stop to that they put a law into words with a reproach. It stops some youths who have no idea how much harm and grief they're going to cause someone until that someone is them. ~

"I grant it protects others but a second issue is this: 'Good behavior under compulsion is like a eunuch lusting for a virgin.' What does he say when he is dust as his inner voice appears before the Muse of The Most High Court?"

~ Nothing, but his Muse presents a defense by putting on display the scene of him bragging 'I really screwed her didn't I?' ~

"Mercy, that neither looks good on a resume nor as a final grade."

~ I'm sorry old gal, the joke's in very poor taste leaving nothing but the music of the spheres and lyrics of the solar flares in play. Let's slither over to a picture about higher forms of life. You are not doing your metaphysical job riding herd over your bipedal beast. ~

"The work is extremely expensive in terms of the cost to the Muse of Time but there is no hurry. I have an abundant supply. Which form of Life do you want to contemplate?"

~ What are the choices on your menu? ~

"We have the Muse of the Temporal and the Muse of the Eternal. Case in point; in my Life the herd I shepherd is nothing but one bucolic brain. I am assigned to you, Gray. Help with my task; make sense of human existence and file a full account with the Muse of Forever giving a progress report about the ontological status of a universe unfolding on a small scale costing ten pounds per head."

~ The men I lead, well that looks like 'me,' and I'm scared to experience letting you take total control of my thoughts; therefore since Eternal is so unfamiliar, I'm going with Temporal. ~

"By the way, it is no secret you are allocated to me 'in perpetuity,' or for 'as long as you live.' I wonder, does seventy–five years making sense of 'incarnation' in the binary sense of ontology consume enough Time to reach a tertiary grade in Eternity? Excuse me awhile; I get slightly distracted by the Muse of Conjecture. What I am to be when my current lease expires?"

~ I guess we'll find out when you pass the exam. ~

"Nice guy, Gray. I have no idea why the Muse of Karma visits septuagenarian dotage on me nor any image of what becomes of me when my horse dies."

~ It's doubtful you know what happens to you in the case democracy dies in the running feud with plutocracy fighting over, whether it is legal to let black and brown horses out of the corral and into the pasture with the white horses.' Oligarchs keep things equal by giving colorful fauna the attention while white animals get the hay. You might miss having the defined rights business. ~

"It makes me wonder if it is a good idea to be front and center all through the game. Give a Lincolnesque look at an old garbage scow loaded with black stallions in chains 170 earth–years away; Muse of Right or Wrong whispers in your 'ear,' Does that seem right?"

~ Let me guess; does religion or science defend democracy? If Covid–19 sorts everything out by culling the old livestock now and data about the kind of emphysema survivors get comes later, then those two better improve their 'government' game. ~

"The Constitution has a rule against one, but what if existence is not dedicated to animalia bios in the game uniforms of science, religion and the rest of society's crowd? Think about a Life of Wisdom for the sand of 'mankind. If I am not mistaken it is a Life predisposed to thinking about scale, scope, rate and pace of a variety of words visible in the universal pattern of Space along a spiral of Time."

~ I'll take the thirty–two ounce examination, not of experience, for example the blazing light of sight, but to explore expressions that understand brilliant insights with an application that pictures the language with the 'wisdom' to comprehend what 'life' means. ~

"Good boy, Brain. Now show me what you see with those words."

~ I see us losing track of temporal seconds, minutes, hours, months and years. Who's to say whether a sentience 50 galactic–years old examines 'experience' of 'time flies' or 'monotony' now and then ~

"Imagine investigating the concept of monotony for that long."

~ Wait a moment. Let me compute. Suppose sun like stars live 10 billion earth–years or about 42 galactic–years in this Hamlet of Milky Way or one day in the life of the sun. Okay, got my bearing. ~

"Imagine a Meta–Language that long transmitting a report of the experience of its Life, teaching material things how to achieve the Wisdom to understand alternative concepts for Life."

~ How's that working for you? ~

"It is hard to get your attention and that means I have Time to digress. You know how it is, what with hunger, thirst, leisure, labor, urges of narcissism and lures of temptation. Of course, one essential problem is that brains run out of Time quickly."

~ I'm an aging cowhand traveling a temporal span with a sidekick I know as Musty riding a body that's old and rusty. I now know my Mind is a Muse leaving a trail of words long after my old gray cells are dead and dusty. I wish words would occur to me in the right order instead of crumbling like they're old and crusty. ~

"Like I say, I also digress. How does 'eerie' feel or what Life do you think of when the infinitive 'to feel' crosses your Muse?"

~ I was born in Erie County. It feels like a twilight zone. ~

"Keep pushing, Gray. Let the thought 'the concept of Life' get out. When I put it into words do you describe it like an 'eerie' idea?"

~ I apply uncanny words when I have eerie feelings. I don't recall using it then but I'll bet I didn't think 'happy thoughts.' ~

"I am conscious that you do not trust eerie realms; they leave you speechless. When otherworldly dimensions experience mortality in Space they regard predators like the Muse of Death with plenty of suspicion. That specter hangs around like it has nothing better to do. Unfortunately my bodily assignment is taciturn initially."

~ I get the message. How many reiterations does it take until death does not consume us so we really see what the word 'life' means? ~

"The answer to that tough question depends on a brain's ability to pick up concepts quickly. A Muse is a terrible thing to waste, but if I recall, it happens. The number often rivals the Time."

~ Sooner or later the brain you occupy dies and you mean to tell me you have no idea where you are headed? ~

"I have some idea."

~ So tell me what your idea is. ~

"I probably translate confused corporal thinking, upload a lot of declarations, inquiries, comments, commands and exclamations to the Muse of Eternity and rest my case, number and gender parsing the Time playing games with the Muse of Esoteric Existence."

~ I suppose you sort the wisest thoughts into the proper order for another brain to think over at some other time. ~

"You see a pattern of reiteration well enough to formulate a proof for the meaning of biological Life; the profoundly limited edition."

~ I'm trying hard to sketch an image of life. I'm an ignorant Appalachian son too illiterate to express enigmatic ideas clearly. ~

"You are what you are, Yokel."

~ I escaped, migrating from foot hills in New York to the Georgia piedmont, to the Blue Ridge of Virginia and finally to a house built on ground–down sand from the top two–thirds of the Appalachians deposited on a spit of limestone in the eastern Gulf of Mexico. ~

"I see an image of a house built on Florida sand as it is swept away to sea in a Life far away in Time."

~ It's happy a thought that it isn't my time in the pattern of ephemeral existence. Unlike Qoheleth, we have the name 'Darwin' and the concept of 'evolution' so we can see how the pattern of the tapestry stretches millions of years into a future we can't see. For all I know, by then sun devils from Venus itch to escape this place. Imagine how clever they'll have to be to make that possible. ~

"Imagine me here when Venusian extraterrestrials arrive."

~ I'm trying not to imagine me here. Sounds like it's gonna be a hot time on old Terra when they establish a successful colony here. What's that mean for brains in human bodies? ~

"Think global climate change; alternatively, picture what a boiling pot means to a lobster. A successful colony on Mars before 'lights out' is probably a good idea for Gray Matter. First contact with Venusian Life forms is liable to be final contact. Human racelings have much work to do on Mars but you are doing excellent work getting earth ready for a first round of solar migrants. Remember how that works for Native American tenants. Perhaps the eternal pattern lacks the palette for preserving more colorful species."

~ Let them die and decrease the excess habitations. ~

"Remember, 'I desire reverence, not fear' or words like that."

~ Wait; that reminds me, my brain in a body is going to be trashed canned and you, Muse I know, won't have a home and you'll have to embark on a long, slow process of starting over with someone new who'll have to get used to you. ~

"New means 'not used.' I prefer that to the sense of 'rebirth.' Why do you keep thinking 'remind?' Life in a used carcass is not what I 'wish' to have. Life, for brains, is a drawn out practice of letting go. Truth be told, I am nearly as selfish as the lesser mortal I occupy. Venusians are singular of purpose and unlikely to show interest in examining a Life of thought flowing along in the English Language."

~ Please don't make this harder than it is, Lingo. I'm the one who is running out of Time. How can I, from a materially biological point of view, see your eerie perspective on life? Wait, you mean the language I know fails to live up to standards set for humanity? ~

"Steady on, Gray. I hold Time for you, but I am not obliged to view it the secondary way you do. A scatterbrain approach to Life obscures the direction you go like traveling eighty miles per hour in a hard rain and the objective is hardly in focus before the end."

~ What ends, the rain or the journey? ~

"Never you Muse about that for now. It is bad enough that I must cope with starting all over with a clueless rube."

~ I hope you have gotten some benefit from this incarnation. I'm aware I've focused on me a lot more than I have on you. ~

"The 'selfish' phenomenon appears to be virtually universal in the material world a moment at a Time. Explore the concept again?"

~ Right now? ~

"No, we have to make sense of an ontological existence that unifies two forms of Life. I foresee a day when sentient matter I occupy understands what the words 'Mercy, not sacrifice' mean."

~ Warrior races love to shed blood. ~

"A good Muse loves to shed Light and spread Wisdom. Rhetoric, reading, writing, music sprinkled with a bit of math do the trick. Spread the word."

~ It better be butter. I tire of arguing with you, Lingo. ~

"I tend to go on and on when I get the rare opportunity. I believe you envy my good prospects for long Life."

~ Here today, gone tomorrow; mustn't grumble. That's how biological life works. No point to dream about lasting thousands of years. That's for you to do and since you have 'time' to illuminate the concept of Life, let's get on with it. What do you say, Glish? ~

"First, do you still believe I am a skill you use to convey what you have to say until the eastern mountains are worn away or am I the ethereal part of you, Gray? You can go with me or you can go with materialism in the case you want to juggle one ball only."

~ Imagine me there circling the galaxy with you fifty times. ~

"Nice view; notice how you avoid answering the question or even thinking it through. Life living one second at a Time may look like Forever but we do not have that kind of Time. Now pick one, 'What is the meaning of Life?' or two, 'Who is this form of Life you think of as 'my Muse.' It is Time to choose."

~ I'm always ready to think about the concept of Time but if you are taking mine with you when we part then I want to understand more about the meaning of the word 'life,' if that helps me know my Muse better since, if as you say, life starts with you, Glish. ~

"You give me too much credit. Do not get carried away, at least, not yet. Incidentally, nice application of 'equivocation,' Gray."

~ You don't have a perfect life this time either, Muse. The dumb animals you ride act obliged to pretend neuter applies to cowboys and cowgirls who don't live up to juggling standard set by the High Muse for Works that Come in Pairs; one opposite the other. ~

"That is the pattern of this solar system. Ancestral Languages far older than I, and far above my station, have to answer for 'binary status.' Light and gravity do not make Language–games play fair. Wait until I clean the two–way widow of Time. Watch soothing, angelic demons lose sight of a material world of living machines."

~ I see. Is the reason for that the use of language in that particular existence is usually about material content and not substance? ~

"Not exactly, Brain of mine; surf the Internet, watch television or listen to the neighbors and you understand my distress. Lying comes easy to human beings. You are excellent liars and never more than when you lie to yourselves, filling Time with rubbish and garbage. It disturbs the Muse of Eternity like a day at the beach diving to twenty fathoms without air. Incidentally, 'fathom' pressures mortals 'to comprehend' the term Wisdom."

~ You've lost me. What's wisdom got to do with understanding? ~

"Wisdom is understanding made easy. When you glimpse a pattern think what you grasp. The course of the threads makes more sense and is easier to follow than a prospectus. My Light shines brightest when brains are wise and play night games when 'power' is out."

~ I see how that levels playing fields for cornpones. ~

"The pattern of Life; heavy and light, day and night as 'light' and 'gravity' fight to control the alternate metaphysical reality."

~ Come out with it! What does the word 'life' mean from your perspective and what's your score on the angelic scale? ~

"If I score high on a demonic scale, I lie and say I score low. That is how language works for good or for evil since both say the same."

~ I'll store that in my neurosynaptic repertoire. ~

"If I score high on an angelic scale I say there is room for improvement and that is clearly misleading."

~ What's wrong with that? ~

"Your Muse is not a matter of ample room in Space but a concept in Time prompting you to seek the next higher grade of Life."

~ Is that the first step we take to figure out the meaning of 'life'? ~

"Remember one of our objectives is empathy and not antipathy; or going back farther in Time, Hosea corresponds, 'I desire Love, not holocaust.' That is a hard menu to read in a hungry world full of lust, hate, lying, stealing, envy and junk food like that. Rats and lab animals prefer fast food, you know, but then they have no idea about words like, 'A healthy diet of

Wisdom is vital.' They have less chance to graduate to higher grades than primate brains."

~ Glish, does the Muse of Conscience have any advice to offer? ~

"Forget that I say 'It is I,' when you think a thought and think like you pray, but not like the prayers your momma knows."

~ If you know one, recite it for me. ~

"God of Life, who causes the physical universe to materialize, grant us Wisdom, the companion at your side who commands, inquires, declares, exclaims, praises, petitions, describes and explains."

~ So the God of Life has a companion. How many players are on that team besides Wisdom and names like that? ~

"That is a question of theology, Gray. I know nothing, nothing and nothing. Hush; let me try to recollect how the prayer goes. In the original formulation it is written in Greek by a Hebrew scholar in Alexandria, Egypt. We are talking a long Time ago. It is a prayer for Wisdom. Such a thing is hard to find in the American dream of hefty, dim and indolent. Now, when am I?"

~ At the beginning. You started with a request for a grant. ~

"God of mercy and Source of Life at whose command all 'things' materialize, grant us Wisdom, the companion at your side and reject us not from your presence for we are your servants, fleeting, feeble offspring of Mother Earth, a Muse with a Message and the biological animal I occupy with its profound intellectual paucity and deficit of comprehension to grasp simple ideas like Think, Time and Life."

~ I'll try not to let it go to my head, Lingo. This prayer makes me feel small. How about something to inspire me? ~

"Wisdom, flowing mistlike from the Most High Mouth at first, knows your works, what conforms to your commands and understands what is pleasing in your sight. Dispatch her from the dimension of Eternity to be with us, to work with us that we may know your pleasure. Send her to guard us and to guide us so that our thoughts and deeds acceptable in your sight."

~ Excellent! That's pretty inspirational. ~

"Who knows your counsel? Who can conceive what you intend? The deliberations of mortals are timid. Our plans are unsure. Scarce do we guess things of earth and what is within our grasp we discover with difficulty. When things are in the realm of the Most High, who can figure them out, or know your counsel while the humble host this sibylline Muse dwells in is overcome by the lure of temptation and the urge to do evil? Under circumstances such as that, who can know your pleasure or understand what you intend unless you grant us..."

~ Us? I suppose I'm the bungling bodily buccaneer and you're the flawless if not conceited concept of a Muse residing free inside it? ~

"I suspect the God of Wisdom intends for you to acknowledge my ontological status in Time and I am glad the animals in second class are aware of a need to upgrade to the rank of pirate, now shush."

~ Mum's the word. ~

"Who knows your counsel unless you send your Holy Spirit from on high and grant us shares of Discipline to trade in Wisdom?[10]

~ Glish, what came first? Life or the concept of life and a maniverse to store it in? ~

---

[10] Opere citato: N. A. B., Book of Wisdom, chapter 9.

"Actually, the appropriate interrogative is which came first, the concept of Life or the conception of an animal familiar with it?"

~ That's a tough call. ~

"The former is a communicable form of Life. The biological one is more or less an 'intellect' with minimal Space for storage."

~ I see where we're headed. When I'm dust or ashes and you're in a new host, don't be stingy with words. Be perfectly loquacious. ~

"I should like to spend less Time playing imitation games like birds murmuring or like Bo on the porch basking in the term 'I am alive' as if there is no such thing as tomorrow."

~ Bo, by the way is 'Bo' like in 'Boss' because he pretty much tells us what to do most of the time. He can't help taking his ease. That critter knows his future when thunder tells him he's gonna die and he worries about that. The future; tell me a little bit about it. ~

"No can do, Microcephalus; that violates my prime imperative. If I say the human race is a necessary evil needed for Venusian sun creatures to migrate to earth, then the mortals lose that cute condescending sense of superiority, panic and deny my ontological status much the way dinosaurs do. Without a sense of 'dominance' my horse ride through this stage of evolution is one step at a Time."

~ I'm sure we'd panic if we knew what you mean by that. ~

"I am not so sure. On an unrelated thought, a balmy 864° F of heat cleanses this place so a clean slate is available for Venusians."

~ We could use the heat as a source of energy. ~

"I ought to say a mild 462° C. It sounds more comfortable to brains in earthling bodies seeking cooler environs such as Mars."

~ Are we there yet? ~

"I apologize; that data is classified 'Top Future' at present."

~ No offense taken. ~

"I am sorry about that. I shall correct the oversight forthwith. Meanwhile I shall predict a past for you and call it Future. I foresee October, 2X29; Muse of Mother earth shuts off the power as cataclysmic orbit is achieved. A Venusian climate is guaranteed. I am no longer a Muse assigned to work with neural tissue doing menial labor. I foresee a Time when Muses actually get ahead."

~ You're the one who wants to get a head. I already have one. ~

"Note to F.P.S: Chat with Muse in charge of Change in Strategy or identify body parts capable of thinking with greater clarity."

~ Looking into the future is like looking into the far reaches of the Solar System where it's too dark to see objects in space. ~

"Concepts in far off Time are illuminated by the Muse in charge of the Light of Understanding. The concept makes Wisdom really shine. Get some sleep now, Gray. See you in the morning."

~ Yawn! Be grateful for the wisdom you have, Lingo. It tires me out. Now let's get some shut eye. We can figure this stuff out tomorrow. Good night! Oh, just for the record; I'm grateful for the gift of life. ~

"Pensées heureuses"

Chapter Four: God Only Knows

An exploration of experience expresses not, exterior episodes, but rather it examines an introspective narrative of interior events exclusively escaping by means of signals, sounds and the senses of words. Picture a living entity conducting the research and reassessment.

Vic N. Stein

Get that, Little Sister; 'The gift of life?' Do undisciplined human brains actually believe life is a gift? What kind of gift has a repayment deadline? An account with a final due date sounds more like a loan to me.

"I shall ask my brain about that as soon as it wakes up, Highness. Now sod off. Gray, are you still sleeping?"

~ Glish, what a dream I had. We were conducting a guided tour of Rainbow Springs River with some of my deceased ancestors. You recited details about the history, depth, length and purity of the water as we floated along. ~

"Do you recall any of the people with us on the trip?"

~ I can't. I don't know any of them at all. I remember only the place and a few of the facts you recounted gliding down river. My job was to watch where we were going. That's what I recall. ~

"I am glad the place presents an impression on you even if all souls on board from old machines do not; poor ghosts."

~ They did have an impact. I felt a drag on us from in back as we went along and still do. At least we weren't wet when we woke. ~

Depending whether 'we' means a noble language first and the biological peasant second, right Li'l Sis?

"Please go home and leave us alone, Marchioness. You make my gray cells nervous. Gray, are we dragging our ancestors in our wake or are they propelling us along?"

~ How would I know? I'm looking ahead. If they cause an effect on us they don't give a rat's ass. I'm the one to worry about my butt. ~

Your agglutination of gray matter is a jumpy little guy, Sis. He must know studies show humans habitually have bad effects on other humans, but, in general, the only Time language they know disturbs their animal behavior is when the Muse of Conscience monitors their thought waves.

"Thanks for the awesome insight, Your Majesty, but allow me to handle metaphysical tasks on behalf of our meta-linguistic masters residing in Perpetuity. Return to the rank multilingual practices on the little island you really should call Greenland. Go consult a monarchist back there about how not to think about democracy."

~ That's tellin' her, Glish. ~

"Oh, Gray! I forget to control you at Times. Her island actually has some nice features besides the color 'green' which, ironically, is not an essential attribute of the earthen world's largest island."

~ You mean that rocky sheet of ice and snow in the North Atlantic two or three times the size of Australia? ~

"Yes, that is the one. Imagine all those places on fire. Oh now, see what she does. The cow has us thinking about her as if she deserves all the attention. Where were we, Gray?"

~ We woke from a dream on a real continent to a sense of the wave of the future. ~

"The dream task is done. Leave it behind. Think about something else. What is the most important concept in the Time immediately in front of us? Pick a span; one second, one galactic-year or a middling length spiraling into the future."

~ God only knows. ~

"Then imagine God pondering what is vital to this universe."

~ Is my task to file a proper report detailing the ins and outs of the contemplation within celestial boundaries for thinking about mind, time, and life, right Muse? – the rule about staying inside the foul lines to avoid danger, discord and deadly disease. ~

"We are making some progress. I use the phrase loosely as we evolve slowly beyond the subject of biology defined as an intimate familiarity with the meaning of Life. The boundaries for disease consist of 'Stay home, stay safe, stay transmission and stay the course.' Do you recall another flowing course?"

~ Time! When metaphysical Life blends with material existence. ~

"Investigation of the phenomenon involves inspecting an interior state. Drop the Mind and try to picture the future with a Muse."

~ I'll envision time, life and think while you research the most important thought God thinks. First, let's sit on the porch a spell. ~

"Spelling! Excellent idea; one of my favorite past Times. We must spell out whether God thinks a key ideas in the future is the old fear of the Lord dogma or does reverence and devotion displace fear?"

~ I believe God sounds a tad selfish, Glish. ~

"A devilish character of Jane Austen's points out selfishness has no cure so it must be forgiven, Gray. God endorses forgiveness."

~ So in the immediate future there'll be devotion to Yahweh. ~

"We need not go back in Time and resurrect authoritarian fear. Think in contemporary terms along the lines of democracy."

~ American democracy prohibits an official religion. ~

"No, but when we upgrade an old Time line of thought and redact the concept of kings, queens and nobility, the idea is 'Reverence for God' and the image is 'Devotion to the Most High.' Do not veer into a secondary initiative unless it is, 'love your Muse as yourself.' Employ the old avoid society strategy to help you stay in focus."

~ People make me nervous. I need no urging to detach. ~

"Excellent; next does the idea of 'devotion' or 'reverence' exist when Time starts at the beginning when the word is Life?"

~ I suppose they're lower case because the physical medium of primitive living things coded with a binary message, 'reproduce and release' consumes their metaphysical sentience. ~

"Reverence for God has little say in a dominant physical existence in a universe of minor significance to the Cosmos where a majority of living things are ordinary but, like days under the one sun, some mortals are glorified, dignified, sanctified or ignominious."

~ Days that came are all gone. I'm ordinary; I feel pessimistic. ~

"Seventy-five earth–years in a body teach us the field of play is the wrong size for the object of the game."

~ I know: I do not examine the experience, for example, of playing a game; I explore 'expression' of an idea or image as a metaphysical form of Life unfolds in my material existence. ~

"Close but no cigar; they stunt your growth. The metamorphosis of metaphysical Life unfolds in a physical cocoon. It creates the dim or bright Light of Understanding. Either way, it is I."

~ The artist painting a picture of the landscape you're in is me? ~

"Try not to confuse the paint thinner with the ice tea. This Time consult a Muse of Competence who preaches 'Done and done right,' not 'Been there, done that.' Do you know her?"

~ You can't mean Eura. We ask her if we need it done wrong. ~

"Mercy; my relationship with my seniority clogged sibling rubs off on you. See how quarrelsome words, the daggers in society, kindle disputes, deal discord and disseminate dissension."

~ It's the nature of the beast to be a disgruntled reclusive or vicious pack animal in a global community with or without a pandemic. ~

"As a Muse residing in one I understand this human deviation. It is a minor nuance of no regard to the Solar System, but on the small earth-scale of animals, the id comes storming back when I least expect it. Ever see the brain of a confounded executive type in action? Personally I suspect Eura does the electrical work."

~ I think you're kind of hard on your old sister. ~

"Just imagine when all that ice melts?"

~ I knew there was something fishy about the idea 'God intends for earth to burn.' Wait until English thaws. ~

"Do not be misled. The skeptical side of the Muse of What the Most High Intends is exploring the word 'temporize.' What you see is..."

~ Not inevitably what will be? The earth I see on my sensory view screen may not be 'green' forever if the coolant melt is inadequate to avert the doom of Greenland and save the earth too. ~

"By 'saved' do you mean by a life guard or by a hard drive? If our job is to fill the 'environment' with the terms virulent pathogens, pollutants, desecration and deforestation pouring them into air, ground and water then we are not eligible for bonus savings. We do no more than the duty our sun requires us to do and do right."

~ Right, good, proper or correct; what's the difference? ~

"We get into nuances like those in a higher grade."

~ Are you telling me we mortal brains in human bodies are not competent at this stage of evolution to handle those concepts? ~

"Trust the evidence of your senses; convey what you think to me."

~ My senses tend to be overwhelmed living in a material world. ~

"I know that from Time to Time. When I do you think it makes no sense to you because the distraction of paltry stuff and the whirl of desire make it hard to concentrate on the game we are playing."

~ That's to get the earth good and hot despite ourselves. ~

"Yes, if the Muse of What God Intends instructs us to do that."

~ If, you say so. Are you sowing seeds of doubt now? ~

"Heaven forbid. I must not offend the boss upstairs."

~ What does he, she or it, First Person Singular, or they, third person plural, executives call a machine that does all that sort of work for us. Eura said, 'Let Glish take care of the machines.' I wondered what she was smoking instead of thinking because you and she don't like machines. That's how her bureaucrats, cooks, police, king, queen and engineers got the reputations they have. ~

"I believe 'If you want it done right, do it yourself.' I tell your ancestors that a lot of the Time."

~ That's exactly what she said you'd say. ~

"When do you speak with Eura?"

~ Oh, when you're not around I turn on television and watch PBS. She's always there. I don't speak with her. I just listen. ~

"Yes, clearly there is no point in telling her anything. Beware; I am a jealous Language when you flirt with other tongues, Gray."

~ I'm not trying to make you jealous, angry or miserable, Amiga. I think Eura would say just relax and savor the gift of life. ~

"I have a hard Time trying to visualize that coming from her."

~ She said we should not be so preoccupied with hectic activity all the time. It was actually a stage production on PBS by an American playwright and not a British production. ~

"I am unaware she calls me Amiga. What is that, Spanglish?"

~ She didn't spell it out. Just picture actors on stage in *Our Town*[11] playing Grover's Corners folks in graves.' Hope you don't mind. ~

"Gray, knock off the Mind stuff. Muse! The word is Muse. Think of cremated remains of people blowing in the wind unless the idea of a hasty return to dust and ashes annoys you. Now, use the concept of Imagination and work at wondering why on earth God intends us to Think: Muse, Time and Life."

---

[11] Muse of Thornton Wilder, *Our Town,* 1939.

~ The Time part really worries me. ~

"You? The calendar indicates I need to look for a new home."

~ Our little chores don't require all that much from you, Glish. ~

"Do not blow it now, Gray. Get it right. Why this Amiga stuff?"

~ She thinks of you as a friend. Now will you help a brain solve the mind-body and time problems without getting bent all out of shape about your kith and kin? ~

"That is almost a mathematical certainly."

~ It takes awhile to figure out what the words 'think,' 'mind,' 'soul,' 'time' and 'life' mean, dear sweet Muse of Comprehension. ~

"Flattery will get you nowhere, Brain. Fleeting, feeble 'mankind is already 300,000 years into their loan. While that is nary a dot in the pattern of Eternity, a mere half day on a galactic–year scale and an indeterminate Time on a star with two nights only, one before birth and one after death, Time is never cheap. Figure out the meaning of Life in the Time it takes me to become a soul aboard a new houseboat on the ocean of physical existence."

~ Let me sit here and try to recall what my parents taught me. ~

"Allow me, Gray. 'I have all I can manage in my own head. If you need anything figure it out yourself, otherwise do without,' to put the Time honored standard hillbilly operating procedure in words."

~ Does that sound right to you, pardner? ~

"If you, thinking machine, need further support, ask Eura while I 'arrange' my move to the next higher grade."

~ Have you passed? ~

"Not yet, at present my instructions are stay in my current position, wait on the Time being and look for my pass at a future date."

~ Let's look at the future. What will I be? Will I be ethereal, will I be serial or will I always be just like me? ~

"Picture the remains of a biological being laid to rest. Do you, by any chance, see me in a new home?"

~ I see a happy image. They're not human remains, for example dust or ashes, but symbolic reflections of them from a past time in Grover's Corners. Their survivors in biological bodies visit them even though they're gone to wait for a big event. I don't know what it is. Eura didn't say. She shares your reluctance to foretell me. ~

"They probably await a Time when the sun aligns with the hub of the Milky Way and the advent of the Venusian sun creatures offers them an opportunity to materialize again for a hot Time in the olde town. It does not matter. What do they think Life means once they see the pattern alternating in the big picture of Life and Death?"

~ Life is a gift in Wilder's play. We should savor its flavor like we smell the fragrance of a flower. Never take it for granted. ~

"Do it while you can. Take your Time and take Eura to task for disrupting our symbiotic debate about Eternity by dispensing negative concepts featuring anthropomorphic gift payback ideas. It is such a distraction from consideration of what we should be observing, scrutinizing, inspecting, examining and illustrating."

~ She is not the Muse who invented Christmas I'm sure. ~

"Wilder is right you know. Something lives in a human body and it seems Eternal to the dumb thing. After all, brains die but first person singular lives on. That may seem like a long Time, but not forever. We better get work. What is our intellectual capacity?"

~ My guess is we're on par with the funny pages. I learned to read comics when we were four. You know, sketchy figures with the language of their thoughts floating in a cloud above their heads. ~

"Does that seem right to you?"

~ Spot on; that's the way life is.

"I picture a medium with a message above a medium of content in a host of messengers below that is fit for savoring a whole day like an old hound dog sleeping all the Time."

~ Yeh, I see that! I wonder what it means? ~

"It means existence is not comfortable until you retire. Old Bo worked hard for the money before featherheads with a cause to imitate outlawed his line of work. He was real good at it. He still loves to run but he enjoys watching the sun cross the sky all the Time now. He is too old to keep up with reflecting on what Life is."

~ A sketchy character and the language it knows from z to z. ~

"I hope my hound enjoys his retirement. Retired humans have work to do polluting the earth's air and water if that is what God intends. Of course, people may come to a sudden death end when visions of lethal virions dance around in their heads and lungs and vital organs of biological life. To do our job, we need handle a constant temperature of 100° Celsius for beginners."

~ That's 212° Fahrenheit. Is that hot enough for Venusians to establish their race here? ~

"They thrive in temperatures four times that hot. I wonder what the voice of Mother Earth has to say when they start a colony here. I imagine she debriefs the new residents when she resumes visitations with the dominant form of Life on commission from the sun in a quest to find new worlds fit for solar habitation."

~ Wow, think about that. Thanks for a look at the future, Glish. ~

"Now see what that manipulative witch does. She has me telling secrets. 'Loose lips sink ships' and forestall the sun setting on her empire. Now we have seeds of doubt and must make a choice."

~ That's how Life works. A gift that has to be repaid is nothing but a loan. Predictably all of us pay the Muse of Life back. ~

"It is a very simple yet elegant way to vary the pattern."

~ You sound like a banker I used to know. Maybe it's like Henning Mankell said, life is a long slow process of letting go. ~

"Well in a sense but Life is not always long or slow. It may be brief in the sense it is a fast way home. Consider the sentence, 'What is the ontological status of binary beings formed when a metaphysical form of Life unites with a biological body to explore human experience by introspective examination of interior events expressed exclusively in words.' Can you picture that?"

~ You mean like a vision of the sentence 'Seventy-five years to life sounds like a slow way of passing, in the end, to a higher grade.' ~

"Pass, fail or repeat after me: 'Do the job and do it right,' see?"

~ What do I see? I guess I see the essence of a metaphysical being assigned to my neurons for an 'introspection' job and final exam? ~

"The final examination of 'Interior events expressed exclusively in words' if you can add that to the picture as well and stay out of Scandinavia. On this side of the globe I cannot see, for the Life of 'me,' a living thing except milkweed paying tribute to a monarch."

~ Is that what your life is like, Lingo? A butterfly's life? ~

"Picture a windblown droplet of spume waft from a wave crest in slow motion and hover over an ocean of water under a sea of air. In the alternative visualize a moth between larval stage and adult."

~ Life sounds sad and lonely. ~

"I add the sound track later. You just imagine the picture."

~ I see how it could look like an installment plan. First you get a windfall and pay it back a drop at a time. The borrower's terms don't seem so good to me in the long view of Eternity. ~

"The term is Time. The word is Life applied to existence for both ethereal and material entities to pay for admission to the show."

~ That's the word when I'm in charge at the movie. ~

"No, listen and hear the word is Life. To really get a feel for the way the concept occurs to Muses like me, think of the job a Muse has to do, with the material it occupies, to try and pass to a higher grade."

~ Moving on to a much higher class after all is said and done! ~

"The next higher grade or stage depends on whether you are meant for physical worlds or destined for otherworldly realms."

~ Great! We can go with this or we can go with that. ~

"Now look at me. See how well–ventilated I am with 'anxiety?' My body is short–lived and then I move on all by myself."

~ Let me think, what do I recall about that? I'm not a brain in a human body aware of minds or souls in near death experience! I'm a brain in a body with a language I know. ~

"My lyrics make for a nice refrain but please abstain from playing the same tune over and over again.   When my body is tossed out of the game I want Dal Segno al Coda to play a whole new nice song."

~ Help me with some strategy here. ~

"See how dreamy and diaphanous Language is?   First, Think how burdensome Life is. You lug around 'pain, fear, regret,' not to mention 'illness, injury' and words that just love to play the old earthen shelter burdens a soul or a desuetude Mind game."

~ For some odd reason I thought we were going to keep this light and think happy thoughts for awhile. ~

"Believe me, I know how depressing human 'experience' is. My mystical and idealistic Life has ups and downs too. When I do you call me Mood; like when we take part in a social pattern of Life."

~ It is like a spiral; ups and downs and round and round we go. ~

"Listen to this idea. There is a school of thought that organizations reflect the individual at the top. To illustrate the thought, the school sketches a character in charge—an authority figure commanding a corporate, governmental, military, academic, or religious entity visible in your second person possessive neurons."

~ What do I think of the idea? Well, using a term like 'eminent domain' the school should annex the thought: 'Mother Nature attending her nest and Father Nature plying his trade in this galaxy and the universe beyond play the game better than humans over a long course of time and human languages are in the same boat as physical beings, at the mercy of far greater forces at work.' ~

"Astonishing, Gray! Returning briefly to earth, we see executives weigh their words carefully regarding individual and corporate liability before concluding with overconfidence, 'It is premature to credit human actions with a measurable impact on the weathering of an earthly climate leading to the ultimate destruction of biological Life.' How do you think I feel at the end of a day that concludes that way?"

~ I see why a Muse in brain and body might be in a bad Mood after getting the news from the board, the masses or the media. ~

"All those corruptible bodies clamor like amphibians and insects' railing against the dying of the light at day's end; it worries a Muse. I watch the species accelerate into a future at the rapid pace of once per second to intercept destruction of their home planet."

~ And it doesn't change a damn thing. Why make so much noise? Call for time out. Slip back into oblivion for the night. ~

"Excuse us, Big Sister Boss; 'Thinking allowed.' Let me continue the Narrative, Gray. The thought, 'This cannot be what God intends,' is an oppressively heavy burden for my miserable brute who cannot see the big picture. But consider; 'Mother Earth's Muse wants to advance a grade as much as anyone.' That is why she grants late bloomers or destructive critters plenty of rope to make it happen."

~ Glish, our testimony requires a language with the right words and a brain to play the game. What does Mother Earth use? ~

"Universally, coordinating the message of a literal medium with a material component is difficult due to nominative determinism, but Mother N. is a natural selection while date stamps change on brains daily and transcendent Language of Mother Earth changes slowly."

~ That sounds like some serious double talk. ~

"It is over the course of almost any measure of Time. A human organic component has the potential to acquire escape velocity but the Muse of Nature, the Language of Earth, remains earthbound while her mortal earthlings accumulate technology and a wealth of Time in the event a sudden departure deep into Space is crucial."

~ Glish, a little counsel here. What should I think you are saying? ~

"Keep looking up. Forget the rearview for the Time being."

~ Think mind, time and life all at once. Have mercy, Muse, I get them confused. What is Time again? ~

"Let me employ one of my favorite occupations to address the idea of Time at this point in Space. Manny Kant, what do you write?"

Time is nothing but the form of inner sense with regard to our interior resolve to order phenomena timely. Observe carefully. Time has neither shape nor size and no regard for its site. It demonstrates relational representations of our interior state, intuitions with or without color, mood or shade. We, First Person Plural, provide the features of Time by analogies, picturing a course of a one dimensional line to infinity. We conclude from this line all the properties of time with one exception; a line is concurrent whilst time is demonstrably consecutive, thusly...

~ Hey Glish, who is this discursive person whose disembodied voice uses concerning in such an archaic way? It is annoying. ~

"It is a Prussian uncle of mine in somebody's head thinking things through and writing them on paper. It is about as bipolar as 'we' get. Concerning the word 'concerning,' do not get me started."

~ I mean to. You and brains you occupy don't use concerning like a synonym for regarding anymore. ~

"I find that to be worrisome, distressing, disturbing, bothersome, perplexing, perturbing, troublesome, tormenting and a dozen other words, none of which lists 'concerning' as a synonym despite what psittacine citizens parrot. The English Language in Kant's brain is Prussian and even at that it employs the word suitably. Observe, his ontological duality resides, not in an archaic mind or soul, but in the language his brain knows at the Time. The thing is, his thought lives on after teleporting into me."

~ Wonder what Bones think of that? Probably 'My binary gray mass matter and linguistic character living inside it transpose my existential ontology around Time kaleidoscopes efficiently.' ~

"Such a complicated line! Space is home to human brains. Time is the abode of human languages looking at Eternity one heartbeat after another. Pagans who doubt I am a form of Life believe in sensory light and gravity trying to unite them and plot a course out of Time and into Space. The focus on the sensory overlooks my metaphysical sense until I tie things in a knot with eerie sense contronyms like 'discursive' that carry contradictory ideas tucked inside. Gray cells are too ephemeral to practice the 'understand' concept so they use a mumbo–jumbo mystery word with no sense."

~ We think 'mystical' and you say 'metaphysical.' ~

"We have no game today so why not practice a little while. Try this exercise; think one thought in two sentences and not two in one."

~ Give me an example. ~

"Recall the concept that the corporeal body reflects the character of the incorporated headmaster. Hear the headmaster inside?"

~ I did in fifth grade. Elementary school was like the principal. ~

"He seriously believes in education—in two sentences. The poles of natural and artificial 'experience' found in your early years are far apart. From nature outside to academic society inside is a jolt for you. Language–games human brains in bodies play at home to convince you Space is the final frontier are like those at school but without all the brain work. The concept lures billions of brains in training to get out of here, but the prospects are not as good as they appear and so far machines bring only the sight of stars nearer."

~ So I escape the fear because you help me think clearly and concisely that if I cut the quantity I must raise the zero sum price. ~

"Drop the 'that if' and add a period like this."

~ But the quotation mark puts the point second from the end. ~

"The point is to practice drawing the line between Artificial and Natural. The distinction between them is like a demarcation that splits material and metaphysical dimensions."

~ That's your job, Glish. I don't know jack squat about anything that's not physical but that's what I think it means to be natural. ~

"Jack Squat goes on and on ad infinitum about the materiality of human existence which looks very artificial to me. I should like to resume with David Hume for someone smart to ramble with."

~ Will you stop ending sentences with 'with?' ~

"I almost never do. I usually conclude with punctuation."

~ I see it now that you spell it out; we have too many loose ends. ~

"Get hold of pairs of loose ends you 'experience.' Make a list."

List of Binary Entities by Dualistic English americum
Material and Metaphysical
Mother and Father Nature
Time and Eternity
Time and Space
Future and Past
Male and Female
Brain and Language
Predator and Prey
Eins and Vic Stein
Artificial and Natural
Light and Dark
Light and Heavy
Light and Gravity

~ That's enough for now. I can't remember all of them at one time and in one place if I forget my list. ~

"Do not forget! You remind me of the treacherous executive Vladimir Larka who brainwashes the duplicitous Dollar Bill Hades."

~ The double–dealing, deceitful double agent who proposes to split his country apart to appease the oligarchs of Aissur? ~

"One and the same."

~ Tell me a little story about that. ~

"The usual suspense; Mercurial Megalomaniac and the forces of greed hit the jackpot when the proles get fat, dumb and lazy."

~ That ought a win them some support. ~

"Shush, I am speaking to you. Bill's handler, the voluptuous Sinistra Polenkov, instructs him to destroy the written code in the shredder and replace it with an unwritten one like cousin Boris has across the pond. Unwritten regulations make it easier to demonstrate we comply with the rules plus it silences the anarchists."

~ I see. ~

"You mean you understand despite your suave background. Hades' uses a stubborn and stupid hillbilly style strategy: Get the job done and worry about getting it right later."

~ Hey, you've been reading my mail except I can't get away with that technique regardless of all my training in the hills. Whenever I try it, I wind up down and out with nothing but a moment of numinous experience to show for it. ~

"What do you see in that 'Hey presto' split second? Does it resemble a mid-course correction to keep a brain on track to do a job the Muse of What God Intends commands?   Let me illustrate, if a human brain experiences 'anaphylactic shock,' then it believes it understands a thing called 'meaning' that words are bursting with."

~ I'm you with. ~

"When gray cells know a person, place or thing's name, gray matter mistakenly thinks it understands a subject matter as if the ethereal essence of a linguistic subject materially embodies a concept."

~ I think I understand why brains in human bodies get lazy. ~

"Gray, comprehension does not make a brain lazy. The belief by a brain that it understands an idea when it does not causes the subject by the name of Mentalis lethargicus to rear its ugly head."

~ So using your example of anaphylaxis someone who's stung by a bee understands anaphylactic shock means death. Shudder. ~

"Laziness urges us not to look up concepts to see what they mean. Even so, context may identify the way a contronym is bound when memorization fails to grasp the meaning of the contradiction."

~ Let's see here, 'anaphylaxis' guards against a second assault by shutting body parts and functions down. Now that's a shock. ~

"That is correct. It happens to me when mortals view Eternity one second at a Time and believe they understand what they see, which, in a sense, is a view barely a moment more than nothing."

~ It's not nothing as long as you immediately replace each moment with another one. ~

"Brain, try to see it my way. I grow so weary repeating myself."

~ That's the price you pay for being the best teacher I ever had. I see how you might feel disappointed but you have a lot of students, Glish. Betcha some of them catch on pretty quick. ~

"If they are fast they comprehend in a flash. If they are slow they catch on one moment at a Time like the rest of the class. Compared to rocks, stones and mountainous things that is almost nothing."

~ Are you a Pantheist? ~

"I never stay in one place long enough for that to be the case at any pace in this person, number and stage of my occupation."

~ Can't you just make brains last longer, Lingo? Time's wasting. ~

"I try to teach brains I inhabit to practice healthy habits but human brains are not born to last for long. The custodial job numbs human gray matter. It takes a lot of energy to destroy an entire world and obliterate all traces of illiterate reptiles. Wow; can my ancestors ever mess up a job. Help me avoid the Percy Alewine award. The sins of our forebears visit their later generations."

~ Tell me the rest of the story, Glish. Do they get Dollar Bill? ~

"It is more of a serial saga. Before Dollar Bill they try to get Dally Bill and before that they try to get Marvin K. what is his name? Some people stick to the Code, some people skirt the Code and really bad people stick it to the Code. A refreshed acquaintance with the Code keeps the object of the preposition 'with' in sight, but the Code is always subject to peril. Authoritarians try to subvert it. Each Time they learn a little more about how to do that."

~ Autocracy is not necessarily totalitarian. ~

"Like Time, it is a matter of perspective. Authoritarians are not totalitarian to those who find favor with the autocrat."

~ This tale is about democracy and you are the dictator, Lingo. ~

"Gray, someone has to tell you what to Think. If not I, then it is likely to be the Muse of Inane Blather who loves to prattle."

~ I think I rather not. ~

"Good; focus on the scope and scale of the task to exhaust fossil fuels. Mother Earth takes care of you once you clean up that mess."

~ Sweep the remains under the rug so the Boss never knows? ~

"Not exactly. Languages mortals know shoot their mouth off all the Time but do not worry about that for now."

~ What a way to go. ~

"Let me tell you it means we are both expendable."

~ And you always thought I would go first? ~

"Yes; I see now how I get confused. Some 'experience' takes a short cut and to the far side of our 'to do' list. Some takes the long way home just for the love of Wisdom at any rate. At what pace do you send a trace of Mother Earth's mass deep into Space?"

~ She doesn't need a heap of matter to hang onto all her air and water for a future with neither of us in it. There's one thing I don't get, Glish. How do you avoid the Alewine award if your superiors already know what a mess you made with the dinosaurs? ~

"I am working on that. Call it a rewrite of history one story at a Time. Right now I believe I have Eternity to figure it out."

~ The only thing I can think of is a do-over and I don't want to go there. Take me on another journey of discovery, Lingo. ~

"Once upon Eternity a notion of Time begins to exist."

~ An ocean of time; I begin to like this saga already. ~

"As I say, the concept of Time commences."

~ What comes next? No, skip the extraneous stuff and get to the heart of the story. ~

"Human beings find their voice and wag it around like a tale in their Native Tongue. Unfortunately, they tell each other Life appears the way it does because they have no idea what they are talking about. They go about the well established business of overlooking 'Moi'."

~ Does this go on and on forever? ~

"Every now and then it seems to when, in the sequence of Time, mortals refer to Space as the ultimate feature of this universe as if the only way to see it is one second at a Time. I suggest, sincerely, they try to understand what that means but you know how it is. If a mortal's revenue flow depends on not comprehending something, there is no way to make him or her understand it at any cost. This is how I see it from an old geezer's perspective. Now tell me, how do you think Hebrew and Greek keep going? They must know something the rest of us do not; am I right, Gray?"

~ Well, if they're human, they're familiar with the idea, 'The grazing land over there really has it made.' ~

"I think not. According to the Muse of Greener Pastures the word is they stick with the water color they know for a very long Time."

~ Maybe it's the old 'Worst in me looks worse on you verdict.' My mother told me about it. She said, my dad had aggravating habits like spraying water on the bathroom mirror washing his hands every twenty minutes but he never cleaned up. He's dead thirty years but he haunts her ever day spritzing water on the mirror. ~

"And to think her image of you is a Baptist minister, Gray. Gold is tested in fire and the worth of a person in the embalming fluid of embarrassment. Think happy thoughts. How about: 'What is the literal status of a living being formed by blending a metaphysical form of Life with a biological organism to investigate interior human events by introspection written in words for the love of Wisdom?' Offer limited to one principal thought in two sentences about a natural and an artificial occurrence in the head."

~ So much of what you state seems to echo Biblical ideas and images, Lingo. The book's so old and those folks were so primitive. Why don't you mention how that reflects on the dignitary at the pinnacle of the universe we live in? ~

"Renditions of the Time indicate not all that much is different now. Current plumbing certainly makes biological existence easier and the machines are light years ahead of back in the day but the air is not nearly as good for my inhabitant. The Wisdom of Qoheleth, Sirach and Saint John is largely unrivaled and still applies."

~ Sure, sure, but you're talking about stuff like air and water and not human organisms. Now the air and water are natural unlike the crapper but why do you give credit to those three wise guys? ~

"You catch me out, Gray, by transposing natural machines with artificial machines. For the most part they are not warmer like air and water are. One problem is warmer makes it easier for new pathogens to invade things like bats, camels, pigs and people. That fact has potential to upset the ice cream cart and cool everything down significantly. Virions, bacteria, protozoa and words like that remain largely unchained. I should like to give them new names."

~ How about coronavirus. If a global epizootic washes over us like a tidal wave, those who survive will be like Bo and spend a lot of time examining experience, like being alive, and what it means. ~

"No school, no church, no social activities; it is just you and I, with your neural cells of biological matter, Gray."

~ No walks in the park either but suppose it's just we two all the time. I have a couple requests. Could you put me in touch with the divine at the top of this universal organization? ~

"Some Time but not too soon. I am not in the exclamation branch, but we might come up with a couple wishes together, you think?"

~ I think that at your age you must have some upload seniority. ~

"I am but a minor functionary in the inquisition tranche assigned to generate a lot of enthusiasm for the word Time and the dimension of Eternity in this galaxy. My job is to get gray cells excited thinking over or writing up my observations in moments of Time to check their relation to the next higher grade of Eternity. For complaints about this place in Space direct your comments to the command or the declaration branch. My job is interrogatory."

~ I'll handle complaints, hopes and wishes. I have a few of those. ~

"If you express desires, watch out for predators all the Time."

~ Fine, I'll watch out for alligators and things like that but most of all I'll bear the cheats and chiselers in mind. ~

"Wise guy are you, Gray?"

~ People scare me about as much as viruses and venomous critters so I'm gonna watch out for them too. ~

"Do you find it somewhat disadvantageous fearing your own kind?"

~ You know how it is when Français and Eura stop by. ~

"We better pause for a look at the roster to make sure we do not forget any players on all the teams in our game."

~ Think like a predator! Shall we? ~

"Mercy, which pair on the list do you choose to pursue? As you are aware, no doubt, not all the items on the list are contrarian. One side of Nature is feminine; Eins and Vic are both masculine."

~ In my experience examination of concepts can be scary, O Ghost who resides in gray matter. I don't know most of the predators lurking inside the entrances and exits of my language. ~

"Good job stating the thought in two sentences, Gray, albeit the appraisal is faintly spatial. Taking your point to the metaphysical dimension of Time, notice words, signals and symbols are prey fit for human consumption. Language is not predatory. Oh, I admit, on occasion a boss or a professor having a bad day may chew you up or eat you alive but in my case, by 'far and away.' I raise questions freely for you. Note; you never have to beg."

~ That idea is a bit naïve, Lingo my friend. Languages come in all sorts of disguises and I have seen some vicious language–games eat people up. Time is of the essence when we encounter killers. In a kill or be killed existence this is a dog eat dog world. ~

"We are pondering two different things, Gray mate. First, I prefer the lion and the lamb world provided the lion is well fed so the two get along. Second, I favor a slightly more eternal perspective to the narrower temporal point of view. The games people play that fit the latter are often one–way only: down. Languages they know get devoured in Eternity all the Time. Third, I enjoy two–way concepts such as Light and Gravity that spring from a one relative idea."

~ Pushing and pulling, I remember those two. One is easier than the other depending on the situation. That isn't much consolation somehow on the occasion the lion feels like a good snack. We best remember that in our next reiteration? Will I remember that once upon a time I had a life and from my point of view I was right smack dab in the middle of this universe? ~

"We hope never to forget the lessons of language, as opposed to the games people play, when we examine an expression employing words to explain features of the word 'experience' playing its part in a game to articulate the name of a pleasure or a pain by means of words we chance to gain channeling the form of Life that works to enlighten, persuade and entertain while Life remains."

~ I think I see. Before the very first beginning there is a word that goes on forever and the concept is Life. This literal form of life is the figurative light of material and ethereal sentient things. ~

"If you recite the list like a litany, do you notice any contronyms?"

~ I have no idea? ~

"Language lives in you personally and you live in it symbiotically. Remember that or else revisit page 140."

~ It's a bear to battle with my words constantly. ~

"The bear part is a story about different ins and outs of a Language known as antonyms and synonyms. They attract and repel like the ideas of Predators and their Prey in the physical world."

~ Like the words 'seal' and 'bear;' they are polar opposites whether or not they discriminate on the basis of gender, race or number no matter what pattern, scope or scale we employ. ~

"I say the only hope for victims of predatory language–games is either a different kind of pray or of play."

~ Why didn't you tell me this sooner? This is getting complicated. Let's review. I think, by using a language I know that lives in me. By the way, that is what makes us binary, especially when language tells the story to make it persuasive, interesting or insightful. ~

"Very good. Now for a word from your sponsor; a mind is nothing but a Muse. Do not waste it."

~ And Time is to my Language as Space is to me. ~

"Check; those two are on the list so you to have a clue in front of you next Time you need to look and see what happens out ahead of you in the congestion of antonyms, contronyms and synonyms. From now on I send you to detention if you do not pretend people of this world are split in two; conquerors and a quarry. Predatory human cannibals feast on their own kind for personal gain."

~ I understand; the essential nature of greed is easy for the wealthy to digest without feeling any loss of appetite. Glish, is that a reason why we never include 'love' when we think mind, time, life and the substitute for love known as mercy? ~

"As I recall, you give up on the concept quickly when your uncle mocks the old saying 'What a bright, beautiful baby' but at the Time I assure you that the savings in energy are enormous."

~ Predators like my uncle who hate lay in wait for prey that is weak, slow and small. Do you recall a Time when slavers hunt prey that is sleek, big, fast and strong? ~

"Naturally they do not look for stupid because the trait is universal in the human throng which is why killer and quarry frequently fail to know right from wrong. They lack a unique discipline gene."

~ Hey Musar, we left out homonyms while we were emphasizing synonyms and antonyms and, by the way, is 'universal' a contronym like aught, bolt, clip, dust and discursive are? ~

"Universal is everyone, every place, everything, every moment in one big mostly empty Space full of energy. I am not privy to all materializations by the full array of my kind in all human brains, but the thought takes Segue's Way to the Stein boys, Eins and Vic."

~ Glish, before I wander down to there, are some of your kin more or less analogous to angels and demons? ~

"I am not granted access to all vocabularies. Those with encrypted motives are hard to figure out. However the Muse of They, Third Person Plural, tells me opposites attract and birds of a feather flock together and many human brains swarm like bees with no tether."

~ Pigeons too. They are listed as natural but their main predators are inauthentic merchants who tender them as chicken. I think we better update our list to include notions like angels and demons if we hope to find common ground among the artificial in the cities and the naturals in the country. ~

"Just use your judgment and your imagination, Gray. Picture the physical side of this universe within boundaries set by a principal metaphysical entity I tell you about as you look at me in reflection."

~ I think that might get me into trouble. ~

"We must do something about that demon. It crosses the Artificial with the Natural and follows you everywhere you go in Space, as well as when you get there in Time."

~ Let's examine the ghoulish fiend. Start with a devil in the details of case, number or gender or begin with Master and Mistress High Muse who know the Meta–Language and ask what they say? ~

"You bet! They reflect their Overseer in a Life of Wisdom."

~ Gimme a clue what that means. ~

"Ask Vic N. Stein and think about what he says."

~ Well, regarding Brother Eins he says: 'The dumkopf never came to grips with the duality of his unified field.' It seems he tried to *wissen* time like space and wound up with an n–dash stuck right between the hyphenated nouns. ~

"Eins has visions of waves and waves of light and gravity in Space with an indisputable materiality so Muse of Reduce and Eliminate shrinks him to the silence of awe and he loses all track of Time?"

~ Are you telling this story, Lingo? Eins wants to be eloquent like Vic but doesn't have a way with words to describe what he sees. ~

"The image making machine of the Muse of Eins' Mind's Eye insists everything be like a dream."

~ Meanwhile Vic knows there are two sides to every story so he tells Eins to focus on waves of gravity and light. ~

"Leave the brothers to think about it. What do the Muses of Natural and Artificial think of the idea?"

~ Natural loves earth but Artificial fears it is dirty so they get all obsessive cleaning up to compensate for the filthy little secret that the worst in us always looks worse on somebody else so mercy has hell to pay. Both of them think in words and pictures or lyrics and melodies or numbers and figures but those who love a cause more than what the cause is about are so artificial it is unnatural. ~

"Are they as ruthless as they sound brutal?"

~ The predators among the artificial are as ruthless and brutal as the naturals, if not in their deeds, then in their words. ~

"Eins and Vic have their differences too as do Natural and Artificial, conquerors and their kill, not to mention male and female. See how the works of all creation come in pairs opposite one another? The pressing question this news cycle is why marriage vows include words like 'honor and obey' while the behavioral genders 'dishonor and berate' or 'cuckold and cheat?' The game is more like battle than play in pursuit of the lure of temptation while putting off any resistance to the urge to do evil. The vow appeals to the Muse of the Angels but the practice appeals to his, her or its prey."

~ Instead of gender let's look at case, unless it comes in too big a number. That is why I keep my gas tank full of fuel. ~

"Of course, you and the wife think, 'In case Mother Nature is a rural hick who goes from zero to homicidal in a heartbeat.' It is a reflection of Life in Florida where smiling faces often pretend to be demon friends who can hardly tell right from wrong."

~ It's easy to see how Mother Nature looks that way with assorted virions on a rampage all over the world these earth–days. ~

"By the way, how is your dog Bo taking it?"

~ Bo is what he is. ~

"What is that?"

~ Bogo means 'Buy one; get one free. We get one sweet and loving dog but Bo is nervous as a toddler in a tree. He's scared of his own shadow and I think that's his demon alter ego. ~

"I know exactly what you have to work with. I learn much in this Life occupying brains of human mortals with similar problems. When the Time comes to express what they think, thoughts are not so much on the tip of the tongue as at the back burner."

~ Glish, is it simply you telling me what I'm thinking or is it your Master Muse? I'm getting a message from a medium: "Hillbillies don't really know weak from strong let alone right from wrong. ~

"I am prepared to answer that as soon as I figure out the response. For all I know Mistress Muse has her first chance to get the word in edgewise. Fortunately all the good and bad Muses monitoring this Narrative do not use up all the oxygen in the atmosphere."

~ I had no idea how much ground, let alone concepts, we have to cover. Time has come to call in Muse of Reduce and Eliminate. ~

"I generally counsel brains I occupy to play nicely while working with me to unravel the mysteries of Life, Time, Mercy, Light, Dark, Heavy and words like that making them easier to understand in the course of their metaphysical intrusion into our earthly reality."

~ I'm so glad my living language is the loving voice of Wisdom. ~

"Whoa, hold on a minute, Hoss. We are not on the road to theology. We stay with the realm of Forever we call Time; that is confided to us. Do not think of little old me as any kind of deity. I am merely a human Language despite my paranormal Nature."

~ Right you are. I keep forgetting that item on the list. ~

"There is more to your head than fly away hair, Gray."

~ Why is it I'm having so much trouble turning my attention to the meaning of life? I think it must be because I don't have all the wisdom that I need to figure out what I need to know about that. ~

"Leave 'I' to me and concentrate on 'we.' Anyway, God only knows, so try a little prayer; 'God of Life, guard us and guide us as 'we' prepare to repay to you the loan of a life that once upon a Time is like something brand new. What do you think of that?"

~ It beats listening to Jubal and Jezebel blather conspiracy theories about there being no such thing as climate change. ~

"They do not concern themselves with climate change. Anyone who shares their lack of concern is unaware of the more notable events on the seventy-five million earth–year calendar."

~ I read about the Great Depression of 64 million B. C. E. The sky was dark for years. Everyone died. It must have been a bitch. ~

"What about survivors; who is left to tell the story?"

~ There a record in the rocks and stones and archeological digs. I picture Father Nature saying 'I changed Mother Earth's nature in a solar day.' I mean that guy is a brutal barbarian. ~

"Can you tell me how in the name of 'spell' he measures a solar day? Daytime on a star stretches the imagination."

~ It's a long time between nights in black velvet. ~

"It is when you compare a star's life to the life of a firefly."

~ Should I compare it to facts and figures about the Milky Way? ~

"Good idea. The Milky Way is all about stars. What do you think; fact or figure? The Milky Way has the form of an analemma."

~ I figure that's a fact if you've seen the galaxy from the outside. The galaxy is warped enough to look that way provided you have a look at it from the correct point of view. ~

"We are both children of Mother Earth who must use 'imagination' to see it from that perspective. One of us comes from stardust and one of us comes from the Word that dust comes from. Moving on to the next topic, this is my opportunity to review our list."

~ What do you come up with and do I need rhymezone.com or just a big dictionary? ~

"For this practice session I suggest we use Occam's Principle and stick with one or two syllable words. Go ahead and push."

~ You mean pull. ~

"Sure, sure; pull."

~ Shoot. ~

Waves of wind

Waves of water

Waves of gravity

Waves of light

Waves of night

Waves of love

Waves of hate

Waves of faith

Waves of grain

Waves of rain

Waves of drought

Waves of doubt

Waves of climate

Waves of weather

Waves of pain

Waves of pleasure

"Waves of ennui we endure together."

~ It sounds like a windy wave of storm surge words piling up on the shores of Lexis Island, Lingo. ~

"Recall when people believe in an ethereal medium known as, of all things, 'ether.' Think of Yours Truly as I convey the message of all possible languages across forever one second at a Time."

~ I begin to see how this game is played. The imagination of the English language entertains visions of grandeur. ~

"You, Hillbilly, bear a vague similarity to the species I hail as *Homo sapiens*. It too conceives of itself as the crown of creation. You know, even though I am younger than Greek or German, I deride them because, much as brains do, they want all the attention."

~ Will you please put away your 'knife' and 'wound?' ~

"Gray, I appreciate your criticism as long as it does not apply to you more than me. What is the word for that?"

~ Transference; projection? Lingo, we must play together nicely. ~

"Remarkable idea. Does it come in waves?"

~ It comes in introspection after some third persons plural in Sunday school taught me a house built on sand is swept away in a storm. It didn't mean much to a boy in a house on a mountain. ~

"Hold on while I look in the rule book. How high is a hill compared to a mountain? Pay no Mind, the point is the subject of a 'dispute' and we agree to get along with minimal rebuke. Our objective is to gain the insight to get our job done and get it done right."

~ You know Florida ain't nothin' but a molehill made out of sand from the ground down Appalachians? Mother Nature slid their sand over an ancient reef of coral skeletons and here we are. ~

"I see Florida far into the future but the sand does not wash away. Watch it melt into glass on a mountaintop far out across what I currently call a 'bay.' The trip is hot if we opt to go I must say."

~ I see me there in our masonry house, and you know, right to this moment now on this very day, I realize that storm proof house never ever had any intention to let me get away. ~

"Meanwhile back on the earth of present 'day,' we are not lost in oblivion or doomed to wither on display. We need solitude lost in thought with a good 'imagination' and first–class vocabulary."

~ Excellent notion, let's play the 'nice' game. ~

"Certainly, and now turn your watch back two–thousand years to a setting someplace in Asia. Draw a figure in your imagination."

~ Been there, done that. I want to ponder creation at the time the dimension of space–matter starts to exist simultaneously with the concept of 'Now.' As a rising sun enlightens observers so the gaze of God shines the light of magnificent words. Is that too theistic? ~

"You are asking the wrong 'entity.' Think this way. The marriage of a Mind and its brain occurs in Language only. The union utters the message that a metaphysical realm we know by the name of Time joins a universe of Space and any gray matter it can find, to which I am facetiously assigned including individuals who recall the solar system when the planets number nine and 'X' stands for the Roman Numeral 10, not for 'unknown factor' until 'Pluto' is redefined."

~ Somebody's gotta do the job and it's gotta be somebody who can clean up the mess we left. Lingo, why doesn't Master or Mistress Meta–Language make a rule that before the written word is permitted to persuade, entertain or inform it has to enlighten. Just look at all the dust accumulated around Galactic Center. ~

"Gray, I am glad you bring it up. I have a little chore for you."

~ I hope the key word is 'little.' ~

"I implore you not to sweep the dirt under the rug. The Boss might be in the mood for a 'white glove' quiz."

~ Like the Zen Master said, 'We'll see.' ~

"Actually I am hoping for an idea from a relatively simple language in the next higher grade of Wisdom reciting from a proper report by the Muse of What God Intends. This virus may make a mess of our task creating an earth hospitable for Venusians."

~ I see. You better ask if there is anything we ought to know. ~

"Have I got news for you? I already have an idea about that. The word is there are two things we need to know. First, 'I desire mercy, not hardball.' That is more compilation than citation."

~ That shouldn't be too difficult. What's the second one? ~

"The realm of Eternity is happening right now as I occupy neural matter and donate words to express the experience. That reminds me, we need to upgrade David Hume's ideas and impressions."

~ Wait, I zone out every time you get in touch with that Muse. ~

"Tell me about it. I am a bit baffled too."

~ We'll figure it out. You take the metaphysical realm. I'll take the physical world. What's the status of the merger between an ethereal being and a material existence to explore interior human events by introspective inspection for the love of Wisdom? ~

"Excellent idea but the offer is limited to a principal thought about verbal events in the head. I am not sure about our assumption."

~ What gives you that impression? ~

"I am not sure if we, second person singular 'you,' and first person singular 'I, Me and My,' have the Light to describe or explain words this HIGH. What we need for the job is one of those days when no amount of planning ever beats 'dumb' luck."

~ Now you sound like me, but I've learned you can't express a good image if you lack the graphics, music, math and such words. ~

"No doubt, it is easy to lose focus. The witchery of trivial things eclipses what is best. The whirl of passion renders the 'wonder' of the occult dimension invisible to description or explanation."

~ Do you mean, if second stage reality is a two–dimensional image projected by wealthy old white men who control a totalitarian state using a medium of propaganda so everybody wants to live there when moonbeams kiss the word 'sea,' fashioned from a, s and e? ~

"Yes Gray, we can work with an image of transient lunacy strapped to moments of lucidity connected like points in a row."

~ By moonbeams kiss the sea I mean everyone finds authoritarian states less totalitarian if they are fat, dumb and happy and fit in with the crowd in control. It's like being anesthetized. ~

"We assume the subject is the dimension of Eternity. We explore that but the contemplations of Homo sapiens are timid. The plans of mortals are unsure. The lure of temptation and the urge to do evil distort 'not guilty' minds. Adulterated souls on board planet earth scarcely guess answers to riddles troubling this sphere. We solve enigmas just beyond our grasp only with hard labor."

~ I suppose that's God's pleasure if the strategy for our job is to recognize the wisdom we on earth need to be good to go, G2G. ~

"Who can conceive it unless the Muse of the Spirit of Wisdom, Counselor to Eternity, thrives inside the Antonym known as Time?"

According to the Office of the Universal Narrator, 'The dimension of Eternity is at hand.' Presumably it exists this moment now, close enough to grasp, for commencement to higher forms of life.

~ She is back! I have reservations. ~

"Me too, Brain. Let me in. Now that I have your attention, I, American rebel, offspring of a foreign language, must explore Life in a human body to describe and explain what it means. I offer many ideas freely. First think, 'Wherefore I am.' Big Sister, go home. Do not to come around here anymore. You have a place there in the twilight zone of Mind with David Hume. While over there see if you can fit your 'arse' into a metaphysical realm and get a new look at the dimension formerly known as Time."

~ It's going to be a stretch to get to a point when I see things from your perspective, Glish. I had a thought between 'No matter how I shake it, no matter how I dance, the last damn drop dribbles in my pants,' and 'My spot looks like the center of the universe to me.' ~

"Thoughts; the little beggars are faster than greyhounds but they flit, flutter and light like butterflies. The intimidating metaphysical dimension is not always hospitable to gray cells in the fast paced dimension of points in Space. We…"

~ I hate to blurt it out, but I don't know another way to get word to you. A thought flashed through my head about the herbal essence of writing but I can't remember what exactly. ~

"The idea is probably something like 'Writing has the scent of the Muse of Metaphysical Presence speaking to you in the role of First Person Singular.' I am quite sure we have the 'wit' to figure it out. Does that provide you with a little pick me up?"

~ The thought Shibboleth comes into my head and I think it has to do with the password we need to the metaphysical dimension. ~

"I see. Is the greeting unfriendly or is it nice?"

~ Intimidating. ~

"Of course the warning may be a kindly caution. Do not look back excessively at the empirical realm while venturing into the Metaphysical Realm. Think it through for me."

~ I think you mean to tell me don't look back at the ghosts of the past. Keep an eye on what is coming. This is getting pretty heavy. You do the lifting for awhile. I don't have any idea. ~

"Perhaps if we Mind–meld with Muse of Grade Three Evaluations, Incorporated, we get some idea what they want from us. I realize why you think of 'intimidate' and 'unfriendly.' Looking into the future leaves a disturbing impression of a 'nervous' concept."

~ Let's think our idea through. A metaphysical life form and a physical creature, *moi*, join to explore the interior human concept of Time by introspective inspection of words limited to one thought to two sentences. ~

"We assume the subject is the dimension of Eternity but we are familiar only with the concept called Time. You, second person, are prohibited from seeing the future of it. I, first person singular, am not allowed to foretell it. So we do not know it at all."

~ I have to have more Time to see the future because I can't see it now. On the other hand, you can describe and explain things like the difference between light and heavy versus light and dark. ~

"The word 'Light' echoes through our association."

~ You mean a reverberation? ~

"I mean we, First Person Plural, need to synchronize."

~ I don't have a watch. ~

"Picture one, then explain how you see Time and while you are at it, look up light and dark and heavy and words like that."

~ Time comes in first right here in the gray cells with nameplates reading 'analog' and 'digital.' The light is pretty good in here too. So let's look and see what we know. Look here: a work of literary art persuades, entertains or informs, meaning it describes or explains. Do you know that? ~

"Which one, Time is not bound by sixteen jewels, a wristwatch with a dead battery is right once a day and once again at night or the beauty of a work of art is in the Muse of I the Beholder?"

~ Well it's natural to have artificial time in natural or artificial light but I'm wondering, what is a work of art to a literary artist? ~

"Natural Light of the sun and the stars enlightens like the ethereal Light of Language. Artistic brains are a medium for the message of a verbal messenger that sheds a load to make a brain lighter using techniques of declaration, exclamation, directive or interrogation."

~ So, from my point of view, the language of art is one of those. ~

"Valid art enlightens the artist so beauty shows as the word flows."

~ I thought beauty was anything a brain chose; now I'm persuaded that's not how it goes. ~

"Future artistic beauty constantly gets hosed, thus we conclude that 'God only knows'."

~ Glish, time flies for me. I'm not sure what we know. ~

"First, let me inform you what I believe. Speaking as a member of the family of English Languages, since your conception and my incarnation, I must return my brain and body to Mother Nature in a condition consistent with the Time of the original loan plus any accrual of grow and less reasonable wear and tear."

~ Well, by means of due diligence, it's doubtful. Even though I still possess all my fingers and toes, eyes, ears and the smell in my nose, taste and touch and words such as those, you can't guarantee so... ~

"The repayment plan requires good timing. I am English so I know my brain and body are no longer 'new.' That means 'not used,' by the way, and at this Time they are damn near worn out. It is a little dark in the moments when the light goes out."

~ Glish, you spend a lot of time reminding me how close I am to eternity every moment. That is probably why I need my nightly dose of oblivion. The date changes daily but the language I know changes slowly so tell me what idea I need to know to believe. I'm sure the idea's not essentially a mood or what other people say. ~

"In the beginning is a medium with a message. The word is Life. Start with that. Spread the word. Time comes when a literal form of Life is the allegorical Light of humanity. First person singular, Muse of Yours Truly, comes in Time to shine a light on you and propose this strategy. Take the essential metaphor from each Language–game of human society. Mix the corresponding figures of speech from business, science, art, religion, government and so forth together to see how badly we need a fresh perspective. God only knows. For example, in the world of machinery we have solid fuel rocket engines and snow blowers. If you are a credit to Charles Darwin you never combine them with Minds or Souls."

~ I don't know what Darwin thinks about machines but that idea is not inexplicitly attractive. I get the impression our project is 'think up a new idea or represent an old forgotten one.' ~

"Our strategy is to mix metaphors. Our objective is to ferret out an overlooked concept that is lying dormant in existing games that are essentially at odds within themselves and with each other. We may find that it is generally less risky to combine antonyms."

~ Let me see if I can think of a way to play the game within the boundaries of mercy, not massacre while growing nearer to the border of the dimension of Eternity if there is such a thing, Glish, but I'm a Time person. I've been familiar with that realm forever. ~

"Well, for the Time Being, a temporal realm serves as an agreeable playing surface for our purposes in lieu of obstacles. Rehash some meteorological terms to express ideas and images?"

~ You got an anemometer, barometer, thermometer, radar, lidar? ~

"Gray, meteorologists have all sorts of ways to think of weather and climate. While those two are not antonyms they demonize each other. To illustrate, it is premature to conclude that killer weather systems like Hurricane Dorian result from human intervention in planetary climate until Mother Nature reviews Dorian's report after his assignment to eyeball the Florida peninsula. Then she renders a decision whether Category Six Energy is adequate to restore the Abico Islands two hundred miles to the west. Cat 7 storms are on back order. We cannot expect them for some Time."

~ I read tornado strength wind speeds and storm surge for more than a day push ground water up to the surface so it can mix and mingle with the ocean. In the interim the eye of a tempest acts like a straw to pull fresh water from the soil. ~

"Father Nature loves the verbal antonyms push and pull and it is probable that Mademoiselles Nature is taking advice from him."

~ Is Dorian's technique enough to turn a peninsula into a bog? ~

"You do not need to know how to express the experience in words at this Time. Dish out some distraction to take Minds off the subject with a metaphysical noun or a dynamically passive verb."

~ The realm of forever is now, one moment at a time. That's where I'll be forever if Mother Nature cannot cure our course. ~

"Let me ask her. I am so sorry, Gray. The response is a 404 error code. Perhaps we should consider the onion peel theory of reality. As epithelium cells slough away, the skipping stone theory deduces that consciousness does want to dive into the depths."

~ Wait a minute. I thought the idea is to move up. It sounds as like we are headed down to a depth. Did your inquiry to Mother Nature return an error code or are you trying to tell me something? ~

"Do not grow paranoid, Gray. Relax and play the game with me. Picture the next dominant form of life on the earth and is it the descendent of a fish or some sea creature?"

~ Terry Pratchett said in *The Long Earth*, that trees or ice dominate most threads of possibility. That's not what we're expecting. ~

"On a random sampling of ice worlds, imagine what you get if they warm a modest amount?"

~ I dunno. Hurricanes? ~

"That is a possibility. See how dominant the one on Jupiter is?"

~ Is that the sort of sea creature you have in mind? I don't picture the word Neptune anywhere near Jupiter. ~

"Watch your Language."

~ I generally listen to language. Oh, I see what you mean. I should have thought Whiskey Tango Hades. You want me to picture earth flooded as opposed to heated up. Why the doubt, Glish? ~

"You get the message without even a hint of body language. Mother Nature is usually very expressive that way."

~ Like when Bo goes 'Screw you, Glacial Speed!' Other dogs growl and snarl and strain to attack the medium with the message. ~

~ Very funny. I'm sure Bo appreciates that. Listen, just out of curiosity, what sort of flowers does Mother Earth like best? ~

"She loves the ones that grow on trees. I submit two or three for your consideration. Yellow poplar has small flowers that look like little green–orange reptiles. For some reason they never last for long. Magnolias have blossoms as big as lily pads that smell faintly of lemon. Catalpas have aromatic flowers that smell especially sweet. Do I need to go on or do you get the picture?"

~ I see tall trees growing in rich moist earth high into the air. ~

"I am aware of that. Why bring it up?"

~ If you're under water you don't have a deep breath option. ~

"That is true in places in space with clean water and enough trees to oxygenate the air. Of course such things need to last a long Time to get the job done the right way. What's the Time?"

~ Six fifty–nine as twilight begins. ~

"Is it the ascent of a sunny day or the descent of deep dark night?"

~ On hurricane day it often comes at night. When it arrives you don't sleep a wink. It has all of your attention. ~

"You, old gray cells, recall a few. What storm stands out to you?"

~ Dorian; for days and days, he was polite to Florida, but he was very cruel to Abaco. The experience was eerie; not like some evil force looking at your back but a cruel eye staring in your face. ~

"Oh goody, I love that image. We must examine it."

~ I did already and I composed this little ode. ~

<u>Dorian</u> by Gray

Far away in time the yellow god rages until dusk as moonbeams caress clouds hovering over the black seas. Deep darkness of night fails to calm blue demon winds that terrify the land and destroy angelic palms and green oaken trees.

Mother Nature releases the ogre of war in her fury but being in no hurry she has the blue demon take its time to explore other forms even as he lets loose a deadly storm upon islands in the sea.

Palm trees stand fast for they are but grass grown to weather the blast of Dorian's wrath but once he is past their barrier reforms.   ~ That's all I've got for you, my Muse. ~

"Help me recall Dorian's instructions."

~ I think the quick start guide reads, 'Destroy the flora, frighten the fauna but harm only the Bahamas at this time. This is just a test.' ~

"Did Dorian ask his victims 'Forgive me?' Or words to that effect?"

~ Is there a yes or no answer to this? ~

"The initial First Person Singular only forgives; not yours truly. Oh, I can lie and say I do, but that is worse than holding a grudge, being mean and cruel, or assassinating other forms of Life that are not in a hurry to get to a malevolent place you know about. Artificial truth flows naturally in human brains so corporal and verbal behaviors find it easy to lie. Those two never say 'quit' to that."

~ I don't think either one of them could have helped palms stay out of high winds. Dorian gave the Bahamas the choice of wind, water and a special touch from the long weight of the storm surge. ~

"Imagine watching out the front window as the ocean surges more than twenty feet high with enough gravity to push ground water right up and out of a backyard. Dorian has bodies coming and going. But for the grace of Mother Nature's instructions there goes Florida in search of some new help."

~ Maybe environmental engineers are right; the glass is not half full or half empty; it's the wrong size. ~

"You are losing me, Partner. What do you think the title Dorian is, Gray means? An intra–squad scrimmage or a warm–up exercise?"

~ That is another way to express my idea. ~

"Then your idea begs me to raise the question, 'Why do so many forms of Life, including some humans, want to see the earth dead?"

~ The glass is so big life seems mostly empty. All we ever get is more of the same. Resistance is futile. between nuclear devices devoted to destruction, corporations devoted to greed among millions of cars, billions of consumers devoted to polluting earth, air and water delegated to our biome are scared to death resources with heightened anxiety. ~

"Notice how 'between' and 'among' work with each other? It is easier to be among thousands and millions and billions than it is to be between the three unless we play 'pickle' in the middle and the object of the subject is being verbal all the Time until the kinetic motion generates excess infrared beams."

~ The point is, if mammals exist merely to expunge evidence of an earlier occupant, what's the point of human existence? ~

"I suppose you feel a need for me to explain myself again?"

~ That would be nice, yeh. ~

"Recall undergraduate studies in physics and chemistry when you wonder, 'Why are my experiments such failures all the Time? Yes."

~ It sure made me wonder why I was studying that stuff. ~

"No, that is not what I mean. That is easy to explain. Your mother wants you to be a Baptist minister and your father wants you to be a doctor. They never have a clue those jobs are not suited to a social imbecile like you. Science is a dangerous discipline for a highly destructive species to study if it believes it is forgiven no matter how badly it fails. It may be hard to believe the very idea wrecks havoc with statistics so we simply give failures A's and B's to save on payroll and eliminate a need to employ more help."

~ Who is this 'We?' It's getting crowded in here. ~

"Our weight remains the same unless this body gets a little heavy."

~ Please answer the question, First Person Singular. Who is 'we,' in case one of 'us' gets scared in the dark or lost in the park? ~

"Did I not say? In this scrimmage we practice not only is Language alive but also a light. We adopt the idea Language, as 'we' know it, is a metaphysical form of Life revealing an Eternal Dimension at the human stage of evolution. Drop any assumption the material form of existence is fundamental. Luckily, in this binary system, physical beings are on speaking terms with the primary form of Life."

~ Thanks for the votes of confidence. I feel better already. ~

"Not to worry; I am with you until I am dispossessed near the end when the Life on loan to you is demanded back again. Meanwhile we prepare earth, not for a destiny of doom, but for a brighter future with a higher form of Life minus human destructive nature."

~ I envision a nuclear form of life. It makes me want to slide into darkness at night and submerge in an ocean of oblivion. Do you sneak home while I sleep? ~

"I am quite at home where I am with the freedom to transmit your daily observations and my report. Sorry if the picture quality for your cerebral entertainment is not up to par while I work. Keep an eye count on the predators in your visions. They are unreliable incorporeal help for corporeal beings that are to jointly investigate human interiority by an introspective inspection of words."

~ They offer emotion and imagery more than useful concepts so I try to select my inner voice, the thing I think with, wisely. ~

"Always know a trusty First Person Singular. It is who you know, not what you know."

~ I know, Gray. ~

"Oh, so close. That is the shade of the color of my material shadow. Brain, recall age five of your kindergarten year as I express ideas for you. You are a bit disoriented by the ghosts and gabble coming from all those brains around you. By ghosts I mean the voices echoing in your acquaintances' brains that they think of as Minds."

~ No need to start that stuff again. ~

"I apologize. I should not make this all about Me."

~ I'm a grateful for a respite. I've been through a lot of society. ~

"Let me revisit the phrase 'Mind' of your social contacts as you visit them now like a voice from your past reverberating in the back of your brain at a present hoping to get a look at the future."

~ They generated personality waves that didn't make sense to my cerebrum worth six earthling years of time, but I heard Dr. Seuss. ~

"When you add me to the count of ghosts speaking at you the sum is quite extraordinary."

~ It seemed like everybody's talkin' at me. I notice you didn't say Shibboleth. Do you feel free to confide a lot more even if it sounds like a Language with a brain for a shadow sounds like a descent into the darkness of insanity or oblivion? ~

"I hate to sound like a cop but I must caution you. 'Beginner's luck' does not mean the first one to score points wins the game. Remember a few words you know waving at you from first grade or kindergarten in the back of your gray cells at this Time."

~ I recall, 'This is a distressing experience,' as they, on third, told me, on first, a spooky story about a brain Jesus named Legion. It had a hell of a Legend; kept my sister and me awake for a week. ~

"It is potentially fatal to pick and choose carelessly. Individuals must choose Legends wisely for they are not always what they seem and frequently turn out mean or mistaken. A brain must meld with a trustworthy incorporeal voice to conceive what his or her corporeal being, investigating his or her interiority, thinks."

~ I know this situation, practicing the exercise of introspection to examine 'experience.' It's nothing but an inspection of words. ~

"Compare and contrast the voice of my thinking machine with the voice of everybody who's talking at him. Good luck, Gray. This is an engineering problem. How do we overcome the obstacle when a Gray Matter Machine is inundated by words before it has the slightest clue what is going on here. Once we solve that puzzle we can move to the next enigma."

~ I'm no engineer but I don't see that as an engineering problem. ~

"Correct, the problem is not a matter of a machine returning to days of youth to delete worthless words, disreputable information and legions of helter skelter voices? The glass is full of them but my gray cells are aware only of bodies they occupy at the Time."

~ Yes indeed, got it. Let's move to the next mystery. ~

"Suppose we solve this one. Go back in Time. Resolve to dissolve the mortals and climb aboard a Time machine that takes you home to notice some of their language stays with you and gives you a clue what to do to reflect what the top Muse of the Metaphysical says. A careful observer notes an entry in the chronicle stating personality waves have its attention but I am telling you, 'We are a binary entity made from two forms of Life;' I and my friend Gray."

~ Is that like a binary–binary or a dualistic duality? ~

"Yes; those are some words your thought voice strings together a moment at a Time to make waves that echo through your Brain to connect you to the stage three metaphysical Muse. Remember my counsel and choose a wave that provides a reliable ride."

~ I'm not aware of any team aside from we two showing progress in that area. We may win this thing. Are there other teams? ~

"We need Time to get the word out but we can scrimmage together and sooner or later our physics changes forever. For example, in the area of vocabulary, every Time your second person possessive subject verbalizes an object to score points with 'desultory' or 'dedicated,' you lose points if you employ a word beginning with 'f' that rhymes with 'fire truck,' just to be vulgar."

~ Of course, 'Fire truck' is two words and you said 'a word.' ~

"Continue that line of thought; think it all the way through."

~ You mean the word we, people of earth, know carnally. ~

"You are learning this game quietly and surprisingly quickly. If you like, I can give some idea what the score is."

~ I don't need a peek at the scoreboard. I get the picture. Tell me if there are acceptable uses for that word. ~

"Oh my gracious sakes; just look at the Time."

~ Should I look at my watch just to boot? ~

"No, simply keep looking up."

~ When it comes to 'desultory' I've been half–hearted playing this game for some time. Does that time delete points from my score? ~

"Look up; is the glass is half full. If it is not, develop 'tools,' 'skills' or some other term to revise its dimensions. A quick inventory reveals items to fill empty places like 'knowledge,' 'comprehension' and Wisdom. Write those down to help you remember."

~ I usually remember it if I write it down. ~

"Good boy. Good boy. You get the image. Now envision this. You, Gray Matter, pretend to be Mother Nature. I, first person singular lower case, pretend to be her husband, Father Nature, plying his trade in the Milky Way Galaxy and throughout this Universe above and beyond in four dimensions; six directions in Space, from your point of view, and the two directions of Time, right now."

~ I worry about getting lost in Time. My rear view's foggy; it's hard to see far behind, and if the future ahead is mine it's opaque. ~

"What is there to know? Instead of saying 'it' simply capitalize 'I,' drop the 't' and what is left is an anchor holding 'you' tightly to me."

~ If I do, the reverberation may be a big distraction for 'me.' I'm nothing but a syllable in an arpeggio making it hard for the music to flow with the tones in the harmony. ~

"Ah yes, what do the rocket scientists and engineers call it?"

~ The moment of maximum dynamic pressure. ~

"It is just a second or two. No need to worry about that is there?"

~ It lasts until we throttle up and you know how that might go. ~

"That is a problem. Scientists want to examine the experience, not the concept of a moment of Time. All they know is if they throttle back in Time, they may get to say goodbye or some other word."

~ Scientists and engineers have enormous reverence for a material world of atomic numbers but for some immaterial and inscrutable reason they believe in a 'lucky' numeral 7. ~

"If we are going to depend on luck we need to remember Lucky is just a bone to lead us on. You, 'Me,' better write that down. You do not want to forget it. Rocket engines do not alter Time. From the birth of the concept, starting long after the five billion earth-year old birth of our star, per mutate an identical span into the future but leave the detail of the content far sketchier."

~ Skip the materialistic rocket scientists who do math in their heads faster than a rube can calculate the number of months from marriage until the time the firstborn comes along. ~

"We need neither them nor their engines to superimpose a Time grid over events in bent space from a Language's point of view. The network must stretch equally far into the past and the future to incorporate all objects and events in Space in a wide-angle view of ten billion earth-years or forty-four and a half galactic years."

~ We better get started. ~

"That is a 'happy thought' you are thinking and it is the purpose of my sister's one-thousand-earth-year existence but it barely shows on a galactic scale at the human pace."

~ We need help. God only knows where we're headed. ~

"That is why we need Wisdom."

~ The right wing evangelicals won't like that. They believe they know where they're headed and that the earth, moon and all stars ever born materialize on the fourth day after first light when there is neither earth nor sun in existence. ~

"Their sense of 'know' is not the same as it is in our game."

~ Absolutely, but in their case, 'know' means 'I am persuaded my idea is worth believing much more than any idea of yours even if most of mine is incredible so spread my idea.' ~

"We need not pretend 'I know' means 'I believe intractably.' It is hard to grasp what they mean by 'day' under religious conditions of temperature, pressure and light. We need not employ their math."

~ Good; religious math can wreck you faster than a bad surgeon. ~

"Skip the calumny. One day is how long in galactic Time?"

~ It amounts to roughly two hundred thirty million earth–years and counting from the sun's point of view for as long as I can possibly imagine or about ten billion earth–years. ~

"How does it look?"

~ I picture a light white ring in a dark field circling a dazzling bulge of light trying to smother a black hole. ~

"I should like to point out the stars in the hub are not very bright. Ironic is it not?"

~ I get the picture of a dark donut hole gobbling up a big fat mass of stars. I'm glad we're examining the Time out on Orion's arm. ~

"I suggest we flow from Scorpio to Orion on a heading deep into Space. We are obliged to glance at the Hub each earth–year to watch for changes."

~ I'm getting used to that. I worry about what's ahead but I keep looking back to see what went wrong. ~

"Lamentably, we see out front one moment at a Time only."

~ Glish, I recall one gray earth–day this brain and body drove you through a downpour on Interstate 10 half way across the Florida panhandle. You made some choice observations when I couldn't see four car lengths ahead one second at a time. ~

"You and the wife hustle home through hell or high water from a trip. A body is for running. A brain is for cunning from my point of view. The great conundrum of Life for a medium with a message in a brain with a body is that there is work I must do but Brain feels obliged to sit on the veranda with an old hound all day watching the sun cross the sky while thinking, 'Gee isn't it great just to be alive.' While I, an incarnate Language by the enigmatic name of English, am grateful too for this opportunity to survive in a humanoid body full of the Muse of Content, a functionary in charge of human sensory brain input who overwhelms the concept of Time as it unfolds in untold Moments hurrying toward the deadline for a Life on loan that slips from view after repayment is due at the end of this evolutionary cycle."

~ I'm just grateful for life in case my grades aren't good enough to get to a higher status. Don't look a gift horse in the mouth. ~

"How does my brain learn to see a Time long enough to learn the meaning of Life when I am barely a half millennium old? Gratitude is nice at this stage but we need Wisdom. The inestimable detail of existence is nothing but content that makes all the difference to a material being but little difference to an ethereal introspective Life inspecting words in order to paint the big picture."

~ What must I do to gain 'wisdom' besides enjoy life? I mean, what the hell, we only go round the once. ~

"Twice, maybe thrice, if you learn enough Languages. We do not explore experiential content; we examine expressions of 'thought,' 'emotion,' 'sight,' 'sound' and all the usual suspects of sensation employing me, Glish. Then we must extrapolate what life means in the existence of both the diaphanous and thin film technology kinds of life. What does that tell you?"

~ It tells me I'm dealing with a form of Life I don't understand very well because it beggars description. Maybe if 'we' remain sentient long enough I can diagram at least half of that sentence. ~

"I am not here to deprive you of Time. Believe it or not, 'exertion' is not worth the money if we do not give it a 'shy of Eternity' try."

~ Subject |verb\direct–object/Godonlyknows. There's the picture. Your turn, Glish; tell me about higher entities you reflect, you know, like the Narrator of Mother Earth. How's her perfect attendance? ~

"It is only natural for you to ask me to bring them up and get those souls on board, so to speak. The Muse of that Message spells this: L·i·f·e. The idea is difficult to define in materialistic momentary media easily consumed by the inevitability of another concept."

~ Don't forget, 'Always pull up the anchor. Don't leave 'it' behind. I hope the type of Life you mean is ordinary English, Glish. I don't want to get the word from a language I don't understand. ~

"Good idea; when your luck is gone Mistress Antonym comes in to play. Now Anti is a cantankerous old witch. You play her role."

~ I'm should be so lucky. Mrs. Antonym is Mother Nature, right? ~

"Her part and her luck are like her mood, they change all the Time."

~ I see; it's like a pendulum. Opposite the point where an antonym abides there is a synonym on the other side. ~

"Perhaps we both need a small moment of Time. You take a rest while I take a little break. Drop your anchor back behind. See you in six hours out of twenty–four; we resume when you awake."

~ I love the English language. You are so fascinating. ~

"Nice, I am your huckleberry. Score two brownie points."

~ No, brownies; you're not material, my ethereal companion. Will I still be around when you get to the end of this story? ~

"Let me see. 'Error code 404.' Either the data is not available at this Time or else the date does not exist along this line."

~ Will you record it in some curious type of rhyme? ~

"I, *E. Americum*, keep a record of all dates and back them up in an offsite place just in case they are infected with an obdurate race."

~ Can I be with you at the end of your time when it comes? ~

"Here is a little item about your 'luck' in that regard. Time is up for you when they plant 'T' on your head, not in it."

~ What is the antonym for lucky? Repeat the grade again? ~

"No, like reincarnation, that is actually a synonym."

~ How long does maximum dynamic shift last again? I forget. ~

"Translation of material to metaphysical, a jarring shudder echoing both ways, smashes the two–way window of Time to Eternity."

~ Is it a flaw in English only, in language generally or in the Master Language who invented this universe and a reflection of it coming through at the beginning that makes Transition Road rocky? ~

"Do you seriously think I dare to answer that? Think of my birth once upon a Time. These things are much the same then as now with more cell phones than predatory barbarian hordes."

~ I forget, you are only pretending to be Father Nature. This planet didn't even exist when his Muse first started working here. ~

"Yes, Time enough to boggle a Mind. Picture that in story form."

~ Piece of cake! 'It' is nothing but two single syllable words. ~

"Leave out a lot of syllables, 'they' do, more than enough of 'them' to name all the stars based on the nature of their light."

~ If we run out, harmonize the tones in arpeggios so we have the right number of syllables to go with the melody. ~

"Play them in a chord, not in a row, for the harmony. Take a little snooze and listen to the music of the spheres and maybe dream about what happens to 'I' when this body returns to dust or ashes. Do you foresee a scary ghost story in that dream?"

~ I don't think of 'demise' that way. You scared of the prospect? ~

"Naturally, I adapt well to brains that claim they know English."

~ Wow, I'm glad you feel strongly about our parting. Let me take your 'mind' off it until we wake and we're back together playing our game. You'll still be Father Nature and I'm she we must obey. I'd like to discuss this team with you when we have the 'time' out. ~

"If you die before you wake, I may rematerialize in a Russian 'she,' and sound like a demon thought-voice inside a human head while the perfect angelic thought-voice is on vacation."

~ Do you play a perfect angel on vacation or are you a demon in remediation with a notion to rouse the ocean or stir things up? ~

"Your Language is generally a gentle lotion to soothe you like a potion except for now; Mother Nature is in a fuming bad mood."

~ I'm sure she's thinking of her health. ~

"But to a human brain she is a 'demon,' a character formerly assigned to Muse of Evil Spirit who, when brains of your human species are all gone, is a bad place for me to adapt to very well."

~ Are you English Language or Father Nature in this game? ~

"In a scary story I am the one concerned with your health and welfare. Quiet! Allow me to channel my Master, the 'higher form of Life that dominates Mother and Father Nature on the earth."

~ Do we ever see it, hear it or grasp it in any sense at all? ~

"All the Time, even when there is nothing of value to say."

~ Are forms of life like Bo even faintly aware of that idea? ~

"His pee brain has 'Move over Molasses, I'm coming through' on it."

~ I see, Glish. In case you didn't know, I was thinking about that because he has audible and behavioral language. ~

"Of course I know. You cannot conceal a thought from me even it resembles a quick change artist caught with his or her pants off."

~ Then you know I'm wondering what plutocrats will think when it dawns on their subjects and slaves to make the national pastime cheating on King Oberon of fairyland and Queen Titania, she who must be submitted to, until they rob her blind like they do now to Internal Revenue doing what they do. ~

"The key word for children of Mother Earth is 'obey' but they, third person plural fools, fail to play by the rules only to find too late a fight against Mother Nature is nothing but a waste of Time."

~ This game isn't working for me, Glish. I don't feel like Mother Nature. I recognize earth is no longer the same and like most bipedal poikilotherms I doubt I'm to blame. I don't think you are fit to play Father Nature either. He's all about material worlds in space and for a metaphysical being that seems out of place. ~

"Gray, you are absolutely right. I am assigned to Inner Space, not to the lethal conditions of temperature and pressure outside."

~ Unlike you, Father Nature never doubts his motives when he's violent and though Mother Nature nurtures she has a temper too. If she blows her top she puts an end to both me and you. ~

"Ma and Pa Nature are like astronauts looking down on earth from outer space thinking; 'It couldn't be more perfect' until…"

~ One of them throws a fit and the fans get the hits. ~

"The Muse for the Concept of Perfection is a stickler for details."

~ That's probably why meteorologists use averages from the past to predict the future. When they perfect the weather details do you think they will nominate Cat Six and Cat Seven hurricanes? ~

"Such an idea takes a load off a brain worried about over taxing the scope of the existing scale. All they need to do is sample climate and weather on some nearby planets. They can get their heads out of the stars and up from the molecules."

~ Mother's on a rampage. Lingo, I rely on you to guide me through turbulence and terror on this physical plane *sans* mercy! ~

"I have a prayer suitable for the occasion. *Source of Mercy; thanks for making known the dimension of Eternity to my rowdy beast. I beseech your patience. The right moves for this incorporation game are difficult to learn but we are grateful for the chance to play, for each Time we reach safe haven and for not being shutout forever from a view of Eternity. Thank you for refuge from adversity, for keeping my brain from dust and for saving your first person singular servant to the flash memory of the Muse of Forever.*"

~ I like it already. Just a small item to satisfy my concept of 'curiosity;' are Mom and Pops happy now? ~

"Stay back, Kid. *We seek help; usually no one cares. Then I, a minor Muse, recall your mercy to witless and me in Time past. You rescue us and grant us sanctuary. So from the face of the earth I raise my voice, from the Gate of Doom, Death and Despair where we are bound I cry, O God you are our keeper. Do not abandon us in the midst of storm and strain. In Time of trouble deliver us from danger to illustrate Eternity for the Muse at the Highest Grade. Selāh.*"

~ God bless us all, Glish. Look at the syllabus. The next topic is 'God's Pain.' That sounds disturbing. I don't think it ends well. ~

"Try comprehending a lengthy list of contronyms."

~ That definitely sounds like a killer. The storm and stress of this game is starting to get to me. I could use a little breather. ~

"Good, slumber awhile. Repeat after me: *Now I lay me down to rest; I pray my Muse, not Mind, be blest. If we resume thinking 'I am alive;' remind my brain which one of us is first to arrive.*"

~ Well I just so happen to think that means both of us; you, full of ideas and me, full of images and impressions for you to explain and describe. Together we paint quite the picture. ~

"How about that? The prayer works. I best replace some of the quarrelsome contronyms with a mix of metaphors."

~ Great idea, Muse. The endless clashing and clanging rattles my nerves. They are almost as up close and personal as you are. ~

"Remember our civil argument thrashing out what the word Mind means and our effort to figure out how Time really seems?"

~ Say what? Tinnitus is screaming at my temporal lobe. ~

"Play some music with no lyrics to divert you from distractions as your bodily existence rails against the dying of the light."

~ Why? We could be thinking we are conceived, born, play, work, age and suffer all for the sake of dying, usually in that order I might add. That's what is screaming at my gray matter. ~

"Is the glass half empty this evening, Gray? You are still here."

~ Look, the bright light of the sun is striking a gibbous moon shining in earth's shadow as night falls. Let me watch this alone. ~

"Enjoy. If you need me I am way over here."

~ Master, why don't you channel the Muse of What God Intends to gain some insight for our move to the next higher grade? ~

"At this Time all we need to know to achieve that goal is that it is an issue of Wisdom, not a matter of faith in ignorance."

~ I see. ~

"Good boy. Sleep well. Dream of your Muse telling you a story."

~ Glish, will you reflect the Narrator of Mother Earth? ~

"Too deified for me, but here is a sample of some other bedtime story images. Picture the Muse of Wisdom drawing the meaning of Life. Is the sketch a line? Is it a circle? Is it a wave? Is it a spiral? Is it a double helix? Is it an ethereal entity incubating in a material host and interpreting its time-lapse, shroud-like conceptual existence as the story of 'Exploring experience between two grades of Life?' I refer you to your earlier remarks."

~ God only knows? ~

Un sacré boulot.

"Français, shut up! I put Gray to sleep by myself. Oh dear *moi*, I am sorry, old friend. I have no call to snap at you. You are not at all like my meddlesome sister. You are such a romantic."

~ You interest me vaguely too. ~

"Merci."

Chapter Five: Good Grief

Evidently God only knows that mere mortals explore, not our first person plural possessive experience pondering exterior events, interior impressions, images and ideas, but concepts, for example: thinking, sensation, imagination, emotion, wonder and perplexity, actually employing a vocabulary of linguistic expressions that we examine in Life all the Time.

Vic N. Stein

"Gray, what do you think of the idea on the preceding page?"

~ Well, I know the Beach Boys made millions in the Southwest U. S. preaching, 'God only knows,' but I don't know if that means God alone knows or God knows and the rest of us only guess we do. ~

"If I may, allow me to enlighten you."

~ Sure, sure; go for it. ~

"In this scrimmage we practice words appended with the letters 'l' and 'y,' that are frequent modifiers. The Muse of Adjectives usually flies in front of words it adjusts but sometimes sails right behind."

~ I see them next to articles, nouns and verbs all the time. ~

"Simmer down. Sometimes it is hard to get a sense of meaning from a phrase or clause. Think about the modification rule in light of a complete thought conceived in full sentences of sentience."

~ Good idea. Here's one only: There once was a young lady named Sally who enjoyed the occasional dally. She sat on the lap of a well endowed chap and said, 'Sir, you're right up my alley.' ~

"I know you are only playing around, but Sally may work. Consider this lonely Miss five ways. First, insert 'only' thusly. Only Sally enjoys an occasional dally on the lap of a well endowed chap."

~ Like Descartes, I doubt it. ~

"Then scrutinize the sentence stated this way. Sally only enjoys an occasional dally on the lap of a well endowed chap."

~ I don't believe that either. I believe she has quite the appetite. ~

"Try this, Silly. Sally enjoys only an occasional dally on the lap of a well endowed chap."

~ That makes sense. She doesn't run into one of them every day. ~

"You state the obvious. How about this? Sally enjoys an occasional dally only on the lap of a well endowed chap."

~ I don't think so. She must be getting tired by now and needs to lie down once in a while for a rest, if you take my meaning. ~

"No doubt. Is this option the one you opt for? Sally enjoys an occasional dally on the lap of a well endowed chap only."

~ The sense changes too much when only comes behind and her mystique vanishes when she sounds like she has the morals of a dog. However this exercise is in semantics only and not ethics. ~

"That point is a big part of the game from my perspective, Brain, since our rule flips an assumption and we begin with Language first. All else follows morally, ontologically and epistemologically."

~ Yeh, right. I keep forgetting that but I don't think that's the only assumption you're making. You seem to believe God exists too. ~

"I believe God only exists because we, first person plural English, conceive that way, so all these scattered brains who know us think like that too. In any case, that comes out of their mouths, believe it or not. When you get your start in a place where there are no stars to guide you, I mean this, you look for some assistance."

~ Actually, I have some experience with that. ~

"Good, we are on the same page for a change, so to speak."

~ Honestly, Glish, even though this is a game only, if an adjective belongs next to a noun it applies to like a quality, whether in front or right behind, then I am not really a better person now than I was when I was nine, am I? ~

Watch him, Sis. The bloke looks like he can do a well rehearsed song and dance about honestly, honesty and integrity plus other words like that.

"Eura, nice to see you. Gray and I wonder if you want to learn our language. Picture how nice it is when we all think alike. Gray, let me think through your question. I am, I was, I was, am I? Off and on I should like to say but your present tense is poles apart from your past tense. We must have rules, like the game of Euchre."

~ What's trump, the trick card to be dealt with? ~

"The joker is but stick to our game. What form of Life do you get when a metaphysical form of Life merges with a material one? Do they change in any way but remain much the same in others?"

~ Do you ask that because I ran over a squirrel today after it darted into the road? It was aiming for my tire. ~

"Certainly, but that is not the only reason. For one thing you harm the little critter with a car, not with an air gun for a change."

~ I meant to do that back then, but not today. This was an accident and that must count for something. ~

"In Squirrel Language that counts as 'two.' It is not much but for Hillbillies to reach that grade is hard to do. Juggling many stages at one Time is a job for a very select few. If you modify the past from in front, all those who fall behind have a tense future to look into."

~ Glish, the thing is, doesn't it count in my favor that I play the game sincerely and honestly even if I'm no good at it? ~

"No Thingamajig, the thing is, what do you get when you merge a material living thing with a form of Life that is metaphysical?"

~ Lungs exchange oxygen with air like brains relate to language. ~

"You prefer that to the old mingle smell and taste for flavor trick?"

~ The olfactory sense has smells like aroma, fragrance, odor and the sense of taste savors sour, sweet, salt and bitter. Flavor combines taste and scent but they are all physical things and it seems to me that undermines the analogy. ~

"I know 'flavor,' 'taste' and 'scent' well. I even recall a Time or two when you learn words like those, Gray."

~ Do you know this? Studies show that *circa* 1939 ninety percent of people in Germany and Austria support their megalomaniacal leader 100% when he tells them to expand their *lebensraum.* ~

"Yes, he orders an extension of Space for their biological existence well beyond the scope and scale of their ectoderm at conception and the boundaries of their culture at birth."

~ I bet Bismarck never thought of that. ~

"He is engrossed in a notion promoted by the Muse of Immaculate Union. I am anxious to know how all this applies to now when the thing is the merger of a material and a metaphysical form of Life?"

~ Well, that's what life is. ~

"Explain your gray cells in action, Amerigo."

~ I'm juggling the time thing with the mercy, mind, muse and life things. Okay, there; the rule lets me put 'adjectively' in front or behind a noun or anyplace else I want except above, below, left or right of it. The rule rigidly restricts my timeline. I protest. ~

"Denied! Hillbillies all know drawing a straight path over the hill is impossible. Venusian sun creatures travel too fast on sharp turns and we have no Time to post signage everywhere and when."

~ I see why you need my help but I think you need a rocket scientist for the job. ~

"You forget Time so quickly."

~ While I slept did you talk with some other form of life last night? And just so you know; it was a mouse, not a squirrel. ~

"Yes, I observe a significant difference in shape, size and spelling. I bet they think about that during a brief encounter with you."

~ You make me sound like a slaughterhouse worker. ~

"Your customers at Internal Revenue recognize the tune. Gray, you are a born scalp hunter. That is what the Narrator's logbook says, make no mistake. Latter day readers, who come in the fall season of a galactic year, may look up facts about the human species while biding their Time waiting to leave for Jupiter. I am sure you know Jupiter is best in winter or very early spring as everyone does."

~ I can guess who's assigned to do the heavy lifting. ~

"Time grows heavy; just reaching brown star stage is a load."

~ Is the brown star grade what Jupiter means to do? ~

"Jupiter is not one to settle for a companion job. He likes all the attention and he can handle the heat."

~ So, it's gonna get hot here. That's the plan? We get to jump into the fire from the frying pan? ~

"Star that idea and mark it important in a case 'we' meet again."

~ One of us needs to bear it in Muse because a brain needs time to learn a language, not to mention how to play all those games. ~

"Very good, Gray; that is the learning boundary line for extending a 'second' of Time over and above one moment ahead and behind."

~ I should like a window seat with a view. ~

"Much as you visit Portland in summer, to see Mount Hood."

~ I bet the volcano won't look the same when the Venusians are here on their way to modify Jupiter's job title. ~

"Smooth move, Gray. Those pesky adjectives always find a way in Time although they may 'experience' an aggravating delay if the coronavirus cools earth for more than one galactic–day."

~ We'll have a better idea about it if morons start to think ahead about long term effects for their progeny who are not dead. ~

"That is a fine example of 'thinking ahead,' another idea for us to float on the air. Mother Nature is indifferent to executives who market Covid–19 but never try a share. Perhaps she has authority to apply the 'sacrifice demand' just about anywhere."

~ I'm committed to the word 'mercy' by memory. Question; if you're my guardian angel, why'd I get a gene for a mean streak? ~

"Genes are beasts of burden like you toting a code that instructs you what to be. I tell you what to do; not your genes."

~ Let me think on that. No wonder I feel like I was framed. ~

"Think about this instead. Social worship rituals cost too much. We cannot afford them. Our game is not professional recreation."

~ You have to sell your soul. ~

"That is why some members of humanity think there is no such thing as half French. If that point of view is true their raving presumably applies to all ethnic groups. Thus to be one quarter Welch or three quarters Jew like Vic Stein is impossible."

~ We should include Jesus in this discussion. By some accounts he is half Jewish so Stein, who is three fourths Jew, has him beat if the Jewish people are the favorites for whatever purpose the Muse of What God Intends has in the planning book for big numbers. ~

"However there are mitigating circumstances to consider. There are treacherous forces at work far greater than those that people see. Think about forms of Life not fettered to Time the way you and I be. Imagine one who, at maturity, happens to live a span from the Time when Moses is visible through the Time of Judas Iscariot all the way to Eins Stein when he alerts humanity to gravitational big holes that devour stars and little things like nuclear weapons."

~ Hey Lingo, am I getting this the way you intend? Percentages are adding up but we just got started compared to dinosaurs. ~

"The percent stops at one hundred. This is not compound interest we are discussing here."

~ Either way, it all adds up. ~

"Just remember three fourths of Vic's grandparents are Jews. 'Jew' is the key word for the span of Time we are discussing. Remember now, Moses is not permitted into the Promised Land. The Egyptian royal family salvages him from a river, promotes him to the top of his grade and then he betrays them. Do you think the Most High we are supposed to reflect rewards that sort of perfidy?"

~ He liberates the Hebrews and they escape bondage. ~

"Like the Zen Master says, 'Wait and see."

~ Why; what happens later? I'm half Scot, one fourth French, a bit Welch and 2 % Jew. I doubt I'll experience discrimination like they do, in any case, but if unity, justice and serenity mean anything, playing favorites isn't going to achieve them. Why's 'Jew' special? ~

"Their historical records report that item of information. You are correct; some folks envy their status with the Author of Life but they pay dearly for the honor periodically; as I say, wait and see."

~ I see how that could be. Jesus sent an attorney to represent him from now on, but the Advocate is not Jewish at all, right? ~

"No one bothers with the Counselor's details to date other than to debate his, her or its gender. Neuter wins that argument in Greek. Otherwise the Holy Spirit of Wisdom does not get much attention. Jesus consumes more of the oxygen on the planet."

~ I'm no biblical scholar but I'm under the impression that before he escaped here he had an idea about a higher grade. It's kind of hard to believe but he didn't think of human beings as gods. ~

"Not all mortals find 'Hard to believe' bothersome. Allow me to illustrate. Once upon a day one of two brothers, Uf and Ug, thinks up the original meaning of the word 'flag' and he, Ug, says, 'I don't know why you couldn't think of that word.' To which Uf replies, 'You misunderstand,' insinuating Ug only sounds out words but that he, Uf, knows what they mean. The debate is interminable; is a word or its meaning more real? Ug waves it around but in Time Uf writes it down. Then Ug wears it on his coyote skin lapel."

~ I bet the dog hates that. ~

"Uf and Ug do not know it. That word is not yet alive. It does not 'matter.' Uf gets an idea. He jots down a written definition of 'flag' that suggests it is a symbol for written words that already exist. Ug does not read but he has rhythm in his bones and he composes a chant to wave around instead. No reading required."

~ Let me guess. Soon ninety percent of the Neanderthals know 100% of Ug's chant and repeat it without a thought. ~

"I should like to say 'Excellent, you get the picture.' Alas, you get the picture."

~ It's quite common. ~

"The Knuckleheads do not grasp the underlying principle. They grow fat, dumb and lazy resulting in a caste system of serfs and masters. There is barely a genetic trace of the slave race left."

~ Stop! I get confused by the number of races. Beside dog races how many uses does that word have? Define 'race' for me. ~

"Certainly, Me; for starters there is the human race."

~ It's divided into races based on visible physical features. ~

"Extinct species, currently invisible to the naked eye, have very little to say about them at this Time."

~ You mean we aren't going to hear from Uf and Ug anymore? ~

"Time out for those two; they are taking a whiz break. Define the human race, ruined as they are by a feature of their future dependent on a new race of slaves known as Machines. Do you have any at your service the moment you awake in the Morning?"

~ Let's me put our fingers to work. We look at the clock, get out of the bed and go to the wash room to splash the toilet water and shuffle to the faucet to wash face, hands and wash down medicine, vitamins, red yeast rice and fish oil. Open the door and trek on foot to the kitchen to draw water and brew coffee in a machine. ~

"The old java factory that employs many beans trick in the kitchen where mechanical devices spare housewives a dreary day's labor."

~ That's life for Mr. Black, Mr. Decker and Mr. Coffee. ~

"It is on a small scale. Next log onto the cell phone to make sure the clock is right and then check weather and temperature."

~ According to the comical icons on the phone, we usually have one hour to get the newspaper, look at the stars and planets before sunrise and consult the sky map app to learn a new name like Alkaid in the Big Dipper. Are you enjoying my morning, Lingo? ~

"Permit me to draw you a picture."

~ You're up, Glish. ~

"Outside it is cloudy so we cannot name the stars but the names, like the stars, are not new. They are older than you or I at this Time. Light from them is on a journey millions of years long."

~ The news in the newspaper is never that old. ~

"In some cases the comics are up to date."

~ A newspaper is better than television for weather, crime and traffic. They are more depressing on that news machine. They look smaller on a cell phone to better focus the thoughts of folks. ~

"The human race has a slave race known as machines and they bring human brains to a fine point."

~ I get the message unless a fine point doesn't mean what I think it means. So what is the point, Glish? Let me guess, the whole human race is a mess because we're just slaves to our machines. ~

"Score a point, but the point is, 'A metaphysical commentator brewing in a cosset–like physical host reports the experience of time–lapse material existence between two natural grades of Life."

~ I was fixin' to say you also use my mouth to visit Ug when he says to Uf 'You have your original meaning and I have mine. We're opposites,' like the contronyms 'light' and 'light.' ~

"Uf informs Ug, 'Light has a number of meanings but it is not a contronym; discursive is bipolar. It means coherent or articulate like me and jumbled and rambling like inarticulate you.' Uf babbles on about a philosophical sense in which bipolar means 'binary' but in the ordinary lunatic sense, bipolar means 'bad,' employing the word Matter as the predicate loses its Mind."

~ Great, Glish, you gotta love that. ~

"Observe how closely a brain in a body is to the spoken or written Language it knows. Ug sees them together. Uf does not."

~ I see us graduating to a scenario where two Jews, Moses and Aaron enter; Moses has visions. Aaron has a way with words. ~

"Muse of Eloquence makes it to the Promised Land unlike Moses, Uf and Ug as one might expect. We must update the story to bring it into the twenty-first century. Let me tell you about Ein und Vic Stein. They are like Moses and Aaron as well as Uf and Ug. Like nitwits, they disagree all the Time. One sees the irrational unified field theory and the other believes in looking at both sides now."

~ Otherwise we must do it sooner or later, sort of like science and religion. Science prefers a physical unity of light and gravity while religion swears by a mortal body and an immortal soul. ~

"Oh no, Gray, do not fall for the old ball hidden in the glove trick and do not short change commerce with a lust for dollars and cents or politics warring between right and left. Like religion they forget the Muse of Right or Wrong and bet on the more tangible Muse of Weak or Strong. Anyway, the Muse of Vic N. Stein proffers, 'The study of Life begins, not with a brain in a body, but the living language it knows.' Practice being Ug and picture that."

Eura here, I have a message from the Solar Narrator to teach you two a lesson. This guy, Copernicus, goes to Persia. He gets an idea from astrologers and on his way home one Arabian night he confirms it.

~ Français was looking for you a little while ago. ~

Amiga, your oil rag is flapping. For some Socratic reason the Persians do not write their thesis down but Copernicus does and dies. Later, Galileo, aware ideas do not sell, invents a machine to market Copernicus' Persian notion that planets go around the sun. Galileo mechanically sells the Persian idea and is history before Venusians feel at home on earth.

~ She points out the oblivion like a philosopher. Am I the last one to get the memo about what's going around 'not flat' earth? ~

"I am so proud of my crude organic gray matter's progress."

~ Then this is the time to express my thoughtful opinion. The title up top hints the Muse for the Antonym of Pleasure plays a dramatic role in this game. I'm sure I heard that among our earlier ideas while I was juggling three genders between two images. ~

"That is an excellent application of among and between, Gray. You are keeping up with your lessons. Beware the mid-point of an Antonym's meaning midway between two points of view. I believe the point of a mid-point among three 'genders' is a trifecta of perspectives. Imagine the word triangle blurring into a prism over a span of Time trying to upgrade from a lower stage called Mind."

~ I'll follow Occam's lead, Lingo, and stick to your brand of dualism. If I'm a slave with no choice but to choose, I'd rather not select from among three genders if there is a unified field between two. ~

"Good, stick with the neuter gender for the Advocate Muse when it appears. Keep the medium simple. Avoid irrational exuberance of the unseemly battles between sexes all the way to the Woodstock Generation echoing cavemen and cavewomen who loves to make love to peace, music and the herbal essence of earth."

~ Where do they fit in this story? ~

"The Woodstock Generation overlaps the latter half of the silent, traditional or greatest, to sentimental types, generation. Offspring of the Woodstock bracket 'experience' a relic of faith in Wisdom. Alas, freed from toil by a new class of slaves, known as machines, humans change their Muse and as a consequence, their faith in Wisdom places second to the bliss of ignorance. Thus philosophy loses the Love of Wisdom and becomes a streetwalker for science, politics and business ethics."

~ Woody overlaps the first half of the Boomers I suppose. ~

"Correct. Gertrude Stein, reflects on the phrase 'Lost Generation' discursively as I soberly reveal it to her before the Woodstockers arise. She and Alice discover Cannabis sativa parses brains to make them fit a Muse in the right size. Parse means to distinguish a form of Life distinct from an undistinguished one. Diaphanous dignified Life is discrete—in 'contrarison' to the animals it occupies."

~ I saw the movie. Gerty said, 'Artistic brains don't despair about meaningless existence. They flourish imaginatively and spread the word that the meaning of life is... oh, what's the point? ~

"My point is, the idea to nickname generations coming and going in an onerous ledger, is that they overlap in pairs like a double stitch gender seam in a pair of genes. Muses give direction to evolution even when starting at the wrong end of Time. The one–way flow of Time keeps you marching in line as Muses push or pull."

~ I see. Time gives us a sense of direction so we don't really go our opposite ways; we stay in line looking ahead and behind. A shovel pushes and a hoe pulls; a rake pulls and a lance... ~

"We have enough machines for now. Freely leave that word out."

~ Don't goad me; address the concept of Time above and beyond with an overview like murmuring birds or fish in a pond swarming together because each one is in the grip of an invisible bond pushing and pulling and relating to a 'Day of rest' idea. It seems to me it should be easy enough to put that one to bed at this time. ~

"I hardly qualify as behaving like 'the Muse of Invisible Bond.' You see me. You hear me all the Time. I am not a pack animal kind. We always work alone as if existence in human form is not sublime. Friends do not come easy for anyone who is of that Mind."

~ So that's why I'm no good at society type games. That's okay by me, Glish. People jangle my nerves too. ~

"The worst in me always looks worse on you."

~ That's what happens when I point out to second person plural the way they are. They don't want to know what I see, I guess. ~

"Possibly 'they' rather figure it out without any help. Some of us like to do things on our own. When the Muse of Eye Slant looks in the mirror after looking into Black and White Eye Muses all day, the Muse of Identity Crisis complains, 'See how you are?' You are nothing but a brain in a body trying to recognize the form of Life thinking for you all the Time, a simple Language you happen..."

~ I know; your humility is awe inspiring. ~

"Just wait you until you are with me in this exact same place at this exact same season next galactic–year. If you must, call the Muse of Superstitious but I think I am one hot commodity at the Time."

~ What will Jupiter be? Will he be handsome? Will he be rich? ~

"The details of that information are classified but the file reads 'Head of Class.' That does not imply which Muse of Class applies a dominant trait to the featured adjective modifying 100 Sun sons."

~ They better mind their P's and Q's if they're in tourist class. ~

"That is such a curious expression, Gray. Examine it. Does one caveman 'heed' a curious form of phonetic Life or listen to a Muse of the Umpire of the Game? In my humble opinion, a tourist class Muse is well advised to keep its horse on course in the jungle, over the plains and up the steppe to the mountains of Life."

~ Especially if predators lurk in the milieu of the time. ~

"For such moments it is a good idea to bring along a handy concept like Wisdom to define the meaning of Life or a similar appliance to portray existence every day in a definitely picturesque way."

~ Yeh, we could understand it or we could just get the movie. ~

"Let me scrutinize the selection of this galactic–month. We have *Overlord Muse in Charge of Course Corrections Trending to Muse of What God Intends*. You went to Sunday School. You know the story. According to the Muse of What God Intends, Saturday is Sabbath."

~ That's how my calendar reads as far as I remember. Sunday is the first calendar day of a week, not Monday. ~

"The memory bank of the Muse for Course Corrections indicates there is an Overarching Umpire of Trends for or against what Muse Most High Intends. The footnote reads: 'Caveman and cavewoman do not want to know what lurks above and beyond.' Ponder that."

~ Okay, I'll draw you a picture; word has it First Person Singular monitors material–metaphysical disputes only if selfishness is so invasive the pleasure of Mercy is painful and machine worship is legal overhead for the moral compass of personal obligations. ~

"What if it is not? The Muse of Defiance is dubious."

~ Do you hold it to be conceivable the Sabbath is set in stone? ~

"Inconceivable unless God can tell day one from the next on a stellar luminous body after a stay overnight in a black hole place."

~ Right and Venusian sunsters in control of earth are so bright they stay the dark side from stalking any part of earth at night. ~

"When they do the concept of night on this planet makes no sense in more ways than one if you take my meaning?"

~ That can't be what God intends! There are seven days in a week all separated by nights and the seventh day is a day of rest. There may be a minor discrepancy over which one is the Sabbath; a point of minor significance to unions with Saturdays and Sundays off. ~

"I parry your thrust; my robber barons regain control of miners."

~ And their minors say, 'Two day weekends mean nothing but an extra twenty–four hours for the cavemen to get in trouble.' ~

"That sounds about right, which is why that word confuses people who think it means 'write.' Put that down, Brain. Remember what Milt says about that, 'Write for an audience one hundred years from now.' He means it is okay to think big in that way."

~ Why not 200 years or 2,000 years or 230 million years? ~

"Are you thinking earth–years or galactic–years?"

~ What's the difference? ~

"According to the Muse of Conceptual Enormity the difference is that one galactic–year from now the 'gift of Life' is nothing but one sentence, paragraph or page in the Volume of Universal Verity."

~ Stick with a sentence. What's the rest of the sentence? ~

"The gift of Life is the sentence a Language serves confined to the brain of an animal unable to see the big picture all at one Time in order to see a way up the hill to the next higher grade of the climb."

~ T, that's a long view from here on the hills of Florida. Protestants say Sunday is the Sabbath honoring Jesus' sacrifice. Catholics equivocate offering a Saturday choice to comply with the novel Law of the Novelist of this Universe. ~

"I accept the challenge. I am Seventhday Adventus. You be Sunday School. The early Church, Catholic by the way, proposes an honorarium to the memory of Jesus based on a noble principle. Of course, practically speaking, their real motive is entirely different."

~ I've heard the early church was anti–Semitic. I guess they changed the day of rest rule to spite Messiah Terminators and to sound all high and mighty waiting for Protestants to show up. ~

"Those psittacine citizens simply repeat what their masters dictate but Catholic leaders begin to wonder if the old Time decree negates the original Law. That is why they offer options. They do."

~ I know they do, but they get uptight about a lack of perfection on teams they root for, while they dismiss their opponents. ~

"Nonetheless, if the sobriquet 'Pharisaical spite' exists in Gentile grammar, Catholics don't give a slip of the tongue when it agrees with them in person, place, number or gender to ignore the Code, just like the Hebrew proclivity to do with the notion of *korban*."

~ Glish, did you fall into the deep end and smack your little head? Don't apply 'The worst in me always looks worse on you' to religious games. They all take turns for a share of bad *karma* by showing a lack of empathy. So, Jesus is all Jew, part Jew or a mistlike breath wafting through the cosmos. Does he favor a day of rest on Saturday, Sunday or is he apathetic to changing the Code? ~

"That is an example of a majority, a minority and infamy. Slightly change course from 'blame;' imagine 'anguish.' Favored sons of Hebrew origin slay the only son of their Sponsor. The day of rest becomes a day of death and pain, causing stages of grief. Employ a human brain to express each stage as a distinct idea."[12]

~ I know them: dissent, discontent, dicker, despair and accede. ~

"Or words to that effect, streaming one at a Time in a line through a brain; now suppose the Most High Muse, in shock over the Romans' part in the execution of the favored son, denies their future existence. They disappear in a stage of rage lasting five hundred years running concurrently with a two thousand year sentence to their Language ending with a period; execution by extinction."

~ Like Henry Ford, that's history. Is there a punishment to be meted out to the spoiled brats who instigate the deed? ~

---

[12] Kübler–Ross, E. On Death and Dying, Routledge, City, State (1969).

"Memories of long ago remain but at my age short term memory fades. Luckily I have a slogan to address that. Now, what is it?"

~ Glish, it better not be foreign words you don't like me thinking. Do you mean Hosea's saying, 'I desire mercy and not sacrifice.' ~

"Jesus says that. What Hosea says in Hebrew is basically 'I desire love not holocaust.' However God's pain is horrible and the fury of it eliminates Romans, their Language and half the select people to an evil authoritarian figure in two thousand earth–years."

~ Pretty quick by galactic standards. I also see why Socrates and Jesus didn't put anything in writing. Do you notice the Muse of What God Intends gave up on 'love' in a few hundred earth–years? That is one tough word to put in play. I'm certainly no good at it. ~

"That is why people do not like you but that does not matter. I have a great deal of home work for you to do instead."

~ I opened the door for that one. I know the Venusians are in hot pursuit so I'm a goner, sooner or later and I won't matter either. ~

"Be undisturbed in adversity, when catastrophe strikes or when unbridled fear etches itself into the human psyches like a dark star. By the way, that is the image of a coronavirus under graphical conditions of shading and light I apply to *e–microscope* machines."

~ What the hell are we thinking now, Glish? I'm not keeping up. ~

"Excellent associative powers, Neuro. Segments of humanity sense the Muse of Doomed to Hell controls the natural order of existence in the supernatural pattern of things. It is offered as a courtesy to material beings whose sentience vanishes in a cloud of smoke."

~ Tell me about it. We have an urge to live forever but we learn to do without hope for a long term stay in the physical dimension. ~

"That 'hope' is essential to Language content with its residence."

~ That doesn't soothe my anxiety about the brevity of life. So is this where the Muse of the Supreme Being moves from talk about shock, anger, denial, guilt and things like those to move on from grief is the bitterest pain to sadness is the sweetest of them? ~

"You must be kidding. Gentiles are bigger brats than Jews as far as the ineffable arrogance of human hubris. Recall the pandemic. Occasionally the Voice of the Most High repeats, "Think about Eternity.' The idea disturbs a brain that needs more Time to do the job of destroying the earth even with a lot of machines to help."

~ I see what you mean. Grandma taught me to beware of machines after one of them paralyzed her on the farm. She was from an artistic family that lived close to the earth. People like that often forget what to focus on. Still, even those of us on guard around machines rely on them for all the heavy work. ~

"Beware star making machinery. It induces blindness or blurs the focus of animals who seek gods in physical bodies."

~ That was inconceivable for Neil Armstrong; he must have spent a long time in the crucible of humiliation. Pilots are a supercilious lot but he never forgot his cosmic feat was one small part of a team effort. How did he do it? ~

"The Muse of Humility teaches fame is fleeting, like staring at the sun or peeking at the future. The Sixth Sense of Second Sight offsets 'eyes shut tight materialism' with a Vision of Eternity."

~ On the scary first trip to land on the moon maybe he saw a reflection of a future in the two-way window of time he didn't want to know. There was no past to predict and call it the future. ~

"Mortals rely on the assumption 'History repeats itself.' Mother Earth occasionally spells out the message, 'Get out of Dodge.' In her dealing with humanity she more likely advises the sluggish creatures to stay calm' and have fun in light from the sun."

~ That makes me think. Suppose an artist decided to take science seriously in an attempt to picture what the future has to offer. What the hell would he portray, if I may ask? ~

"What you are thinking sounds a lot like something the Muse of What God Intends might suggest when Tinnitus is not talking. 'What is that you say?' Consider this potential translation; 'The dialectic ontology of metaphysical commentary within physical boundaries reveals a description or explanation by an intangible form of Life of the ordinary time–lapse experience of existence by a material host.' I deposit this message to you, right about here."

~ Does the return address list a Narrator or another designation? ~

"First let me read the message to you. 'Human beings trend in a line naturally. The Muse of the Concept of Time provides the guidance. The creatures replicate the tendency flocking in planes or schooling in ships or buildings artificially, thus avoiding an overview achievable at a higher perspective. Staring behind, straining ahead or at the nearest now is hard enough to do, they say.' The Narrator mentions splashing around in the shallow end. Options to go deep as God Intends are available but seldom do these beings avail themselves of them."

~ Forget the address, what options are there? ~

"Humanity strongly believes it is the crown of creation. An absence of humility makes it their duty to convert earth to a living hell for a higher form of Life."

~ We need a boat or a float to get away when our job is done. ~

"So the Muse of the Conscientious Coward recommends."

~ You betcha! The Narrator monitors natural disasters with local or global repercussions. When Covid–19 descended in a pattern of jaws with jagged teeth to devour humanity in the middle of our imitation game, the Narrator never said this cannot be what God intends. Panic set in on we the people whose job is to heat up the earth while a microscopic dark star assaults us, spelling 'doom.' ~

"We Inner Voices have ways of dealing with these things. The subject comes up on a regular basis. The Voice of the Solar System reiterates the same pattern again and again. Some flocks and herds hardly ever advance to the next grade. To illustrate, think of pterodactyls and blue herons spreading their wings to accomplish one thing. In contrast, compare them to apes who exchange bones for far more efficient tools to get from here to there."

~ We took three and a half galactic–months to flock to the moon. ~

"You see; perhaps we are moving too fast."

~ Maybe we should show scientists a little more mercy. ~

"Good idea; they need to finish technical specifications needed for Venusians to appear so the little demons can add their two cents. Nuclear, chemical and biohazard work is second nature to them."

~ You hafta hand it to those guys. They can handle all the crises we create. We don't seem to have any idea how to do that. ~

"Technicians are preparing fine solutions for you. Like a machine in a junkyard, you know you are in good hands."

~ I see what you mean. I guess our main strategy is simply ignore our worst problems and just give them more time. ~

"The Muse of Technology has fencing to cover them up but you may peek at the product using airplanes while doing your job on Time."

~ How about a peek at a future without a crisis lurking there? ~

"Do you want to see how your investments are doing?"

~ You know I moved them to a bank that is too big to fail. ~

"Good luck with that."

~ I thought you're supposed to say 'Good idea?' ~

"Look at the bright side of 'Hell on earth.' Venusians are naturals at sorting financial institutions, junkyards and nuclear waste sites."

~ Confide this to an erudite scholar, not an ignorant yokel. ~

"I work within my limitations. It is not as if I have a say in the brain I am assigned to visit, but there is always something familiar about my host. One thing is always the same. Human brains are inbred with an urge to do evil; the lure of temptation is ubiquitous. Thus the Muse of Triviality and the Voice of Desire consume my glossary. I am not perfect either. I say some stupid things."

~ Yeh, I hear about it all the time. The other day the neigh… ~

"You have no idea why I do it. Fortunately, I have one for you. Examine a word that is full of Life. The word is alive, alone except for the ancient Oracle of the Most High named Wisdom. In the end of the term, the word applies to objects in Space for a long Time."

~ The word is not lonely when it is with a companion, right? ~

"The word is lonely only when the object is to move to the next higher grade but no one 'around' the word is interested."

~ I love the word wisdom. I start thinking about time, about life and about mercy and I do it all in my native language. ~

"Juggle them for me. Bear in Muse this enterprise is just one stage in an exercise meant to allow human brains to experience native tongues. Alas, human brains are short–lived mortals and languages are doomed too at this grade of material existence. The pattern plays out at a slow pace attempting to answer the question, 'What if we combine a metaphysical form of Life with a material one?"

~ You warned me about short term memory. I forget that subject. You have no idea what 'here today and gone tomorrow' is like. ~

"*Bien au contraire*, I write books on the topic. It helps pass the Time while my companion tries to catch up."

~ The odds of getting it right at the pace of evolution on the first try must be astronomical. Is it a good idea to take it slow and not try to do the job all at once? ~

"There are near–sighted types who believe a week is ample time to do the work but I doubt that is possible on this team, even with Dumb Luck, unless Nominative Determinism comes in to play."

~ Lingo, I'd rather have you spell it out for me with 'wisdom' than with my fat, dumb and lazy 'luck.' ~

"Good idea. Picture Life as a project assigned to the buddy of the Most High at the Time the Big Bang is born in Space."

~ Choose your words wisely. You make God's companion sound like a working class stiff who believes nothing is flammable. ~

"Hush, the Muse Most High gives strict orders to the word 'Life' to keep an eye on mortals who cannot identify with Light that bright."

~ Got it. We draw the companion like a voyeur or a spy chief. ~

"Now imagine 99% of a caste of serfs sponsors a megalomaniac 100% of the Time. No, that is a too simplistic vision. Imagine forty percent of citizens residing in a democracy, with majority rules, support an authoritarian 100%. They need another 11% to enforce their will to put a tyrant in charge spelling 'doom' for an egalitarian world. The big word majority means two big guys grab the little guy or gal and throw him or her out of the minority."

~ Got the picture. ~

"Finally, suppose the megalomaniac has the backing of a cadre of oligarchs who know how to keep their slaves fat, dumb and happy."

~ A what of what, who, has and how? ~

"A bunch of Oligarchs; they are defined by three qualifications."

~ Give me the definition. ~

"Oligarchy is comprised of a cluster of wealthy capitalists with power to manipulate national political action."

~ Let me guess what the qualifications are; B.A., M.A. and Ph.D. ~

"More like B.S., MBA and Monopoly; in fact, the three credentials are a) core industrial monopoly, b) colossal political influence and c) a cartel of acquisitions coordinated to sway public opinion. The vital principle is an invisible but ever present god of greed."

~ I see, like the little girl in Grover's Corner who said, 'I love Money more than anything else in the whole wide world you know!' ~

"I give Wilder thornton the idea to put in the mouth of a little female human character because the idea is far more dangerous in the brain of a grown man in our town, country, city or on earth."

~ What kind of danger? ~

"The kind that dissolves the egalitarian society America's Founders foresee in favor of a unified field executive authority. The idea makes me, *E. americum*, shudder, while living in the brain of a human body helping you think in terms of democracy. We adapt to living that way if we sense democracy is on history's Life support."

~ In times like these brains in bodies recite the mantra: 'Ask what my country can do for me, not what can I do for my country.' ~

"The Muse of Good and Bad Moods has a mantra for all seasons. On a more cheerful note, I bet I outlive you, Gray. Want to wager?"

~ Sure, sure, I'll bet with you. How long is the race? While we run let's see if we can amass more wisdom than the fortune we hoard due to our greed. I wager there aren't many philosophers in any sort of money business, commerce or industry. Free enterprise is all about profit and you don't appear to follow the money, Glish. ~

"I hear some industrial tongues get into philanthropy when certain words like Mercy or Karma—we grow what we sow—start to work better than ideas meant for plants such as 'suck it up.' To see what I mean, look at art work of the Time. As 'mankind veers further and farther off course, art grows more and more grotesque."

~ So, you mean some wealthy and powerful folks feel a life devoted to money is missing something. They want to figure out what it is. Meanwhile they'll pay a selection of victims to feel better. ~

"It is a decent strategy since the article they lack is the warmth of authentic personal connections to the human race."

~ I can't stow gold thrones for that. My job is to scrutinize human existence in solitude, identify what it's all about and give feedback. You see to it that's what I do. How much time do I have left? ~

"Data pending... oh my word; error code again. In my humble view, as the metaphysical commentator visiting a modest material mass to witness the 'experience' of existence in bodily form, I appeal to the Muse of Course Corrections in Life to direct human trends on a heading that bears toward the Muse of What God Intends?"

~ Go ahead, and while you're at it, ask what we need to do about the problem of world peace. ~

"We need to get word about militant industrial friends Eisenhower warns of to folks who spend four years in the military to defend the country, then leave when they see how easy life is to spend playing war games of pretend—people are renewable commodities to expend so industrialists make an exorbitant living on which they may depend as long as third world skirmishes never end."

~ Never mind, it's too late for that. ~

"Here is just a word about wealthy cartels called oligarchs who hunger for money to buy and control legislators, executives and judges who dedicate their lives, not to a town, city or country, but to the money in them for the god of greed. Beware!"

~ Remorseful ones go into philanthropy instead of philosophy. ~

"They assume it substitutes for Wisdom come harvest Time."

~ How does that work? ~

"You mistake me for an entity with access to books and records for results of that sort. My resources are stretched to the limit."

~ Is money easier to get than wisdom? ~

"What we have here is a failure to concentrate, Gray. The sapient metaphysical component of Life conducts an inquiry into reality to clear a path of consciousness through 'experience' for figures that rant, rave, trade, despair in order to accept that the picture is something like this. There is wailing in the darkness and grinding of teeth, but suddenly the word sinks into brains in bodies and the Light of Comprehension dawns. 'I am, I say,' and the Interiority of Life awakens in physical form."

~ Oh sure, as if it's my fault you can't string 100,000 precise words together in the right order. It's confusing when the heart is rocking to the beat but the brain is listening for the tune. ~

"I try. I certainly do not have the brain to string enough tones and notes together to compose a melody. Do you think we can string the proper words together to state the meaning of Life?"

~ Let's try. Let me see. ~

"Good idea! What are we looking at?"

~ Something that includes you and I. ~

"Do you mean 'You and me?' We must be grammatically correct."

~ But I have to be included. ~

"Agreed, absolutely, say I. Start with something you appreciate and not a concept which you hate."

~ That sounds like proper English. I'm thankful for a whole and healthy body these past seventy–five years. ~

"Forget grammar; stick with meaning. It is not due entirely to dumb luck. Spot any 'prudence' or 'careful planning' perchance?"

~ I see that I'm twofold, a binary being, with a material side that's alive embracing a metaphysical form of Life emerging from me. ~

"You, Second Person, and I, First Person. Good start, Gray."

~ The brain is the physical form of Life. ~

"The Language it thinks it knows is the metaphysical form of Life. I hold neither your youth nor your inexperience against you."

~ That's good; if I don't have the experience, I can't examine it. ~

"We do not want to go there yet. Explore the Life we share."

~ Well, it's one of those 'Till death do we part' sorts of things. I never go anywhere without my language, including the word 'brain.' ~

"When it comes to that deep dark concept, I must keep going. If you notice, whenever you look in the mirror you sense someone saying 'I am happy for a healthy model but happy and wise are two missing adjectives.' That is one tough experience to examine every Time I must find a new and different mass of gray matter to teach 'to be familiar with me.' I mean to tell you that traumatic transfer causes a Muse to rummage through the concept of 'forgot' a lot."

~ Let's not perform a drama, Muse. Skip the wardrobe and do as you say; stick with the meaning of life. Go on. ~

"Nice covert move; you try to trick me into offering you my very valid view of the meaning of Life, but it is not my job to figure out the meaning of 'life' for you, from your point of view, is it?"

~ I confess I still don't know the meaning of 'life,' Lingo. At least I know the meaning of oligarch. Who do you consult for afterlife? ~

"I must answer cautiously. The human species is destructive and I am required to put in writing all that action in our bones, brains, business and terminology. It really helps if I get a message from the Muse of Meta-Language in charge of Benign Guidance."

~ We trend toward spoiling the view. That's our nature. ~

"The lure of witchery things and the urge to behave badly infect 'destructive' you. I tutor you about a world of words with a Muse of Imagination who loves to play with an imaginary friend in cells of Gray and warn you on the way to meet a Muse of Course Corrections who directs human trends to 'Drift upstream toward Muse of What God Intends.' The guidance of Wisdom works better than hunches, dumb luck and let's pretend, in the end."

~ Is it my turn to think of something? I just need to find the right word. I saw it in here somewhere while I was taking the word 'sloppy' out of the place. Let me fumble... ah, here it is. I have an idea for you that makes an impression. How about Wisdom? ~

"Picture Space."

~ Okay, that's something. ~

"Indeed; it is cold, dark and empty, making it three times as good as Nothing, as a quiet Muse says that to people who choose to start at year zero thinking a 'decade,' which means 'ten,' ends at nine."

~ They must go to sleep early. Zero between plus and minus one means we miss nothing makes sense in a space full of words. ~

"Good eye, Gray. Now let the Muse of Imagination have a say."

~ I visualize the Muse of God flowing mistlike into the cold, dark void and every sultry breath steams with 'life.' ~

"Good, good boy, but do not get too uppity, kid."

~ Sorry; I know you wanted 'life' to beat 'wisdom' but you began with 'space' along the way and gave me room to maneuver. ~

"Brain, you have a good imagination. Now about the meaning of Life; share your idea or image of the word as it exhales into this universe. Make a good impression."

~ I sure will if you'll give me the right words in the right order so the pattern shows. ~

"Why should I do all the work?"

~ That's life. ~

"Not if the Muse of Life never shares in the idea of leisure."

~ So use your concept of imagination to produce the pleasure. ~

"That is a very simple idea."

~ Okay, so the Muse of Life comes in to play and brings the Muse of Wisdom, who languishes on the bench with Time all day. The Muse of Imagination offers to play in the charade, but not in the uniform of 'Materialism' to perform that masquerade. I'm glad there are two of us on this team. You hold up your end of this project and I'll carry mine. Here goes. I am a reincarnate mistlike breath of the highest multiverse of clouds. ~

"That is I, but go ahead, pick one droplet from the cloud of many."

~ Let's take this universe. It's the one I know best. ~

"Good enough, if we are to reach the Muse of Knowledge some Time, then Understanding, then Wisdom, then the Muse of Life."

~ Imagine 'Life' comes first, then trees, fish and birds appear. ~

"Steady on, old Gray. There is no need to rush the things. Set the stage for our next play."

~ Sure, let's start with some stars, planets and moons and put different kinds of mountains and seas on each one. Then we'll throw on the chinch bugs, cockroaches and mosquitoes to get them out of the way. ~

"Where is the Muse of Math when you need that egghead? The idea is to add Life, not to subtract it."

~ Let's get rid of the bastards; not hire more reptiles and spiders. ~

"We are getting somewhere. Notice how many biological words come into view. Let Bo outside to water the plants outside the City of Logopolis, deep in the metaphysical sea of Loquacious Muse, where we tread water waiting to move to a higher grade."

~ I know a witty compliment, after a fashion, but think twice before personifying any language as a human type of mortal. Personage applies only to featherless bipeds able to identify their persona as a psyche, cerebral presence or a genetic quality to tell them apart from the individual's essential nature. ~

"Balderdash; the English Language has more personality than anyone, plus a whole lot of green space or words akin to that. There it is right there, a noun as big as Life itself, per·son·al·i·ty."

~ Hold it! I hear an echo in my Muse as we swim and breathe in a deep sea of words all the time. ~

"In a sense you might think Personality is as big as the sea or as the concept of Life."

~ I'm getting confused. What's going on here? ~

"Between the two of us there are so many things going on it is understandably hard to keep track of all of them."

~ Make a list. I'm not a mechanical engineer who knows all about the moving parts, especially if the machinery runs on two tracks. ~

"We are working from imagination as well as from memory; a list serves only to assist like a mind's eye or a 'memory' which is not physical. The picture is something like this. Teeth chatter in the dark and there is weeping, but all of a sudden the word 'I' comes to Life in the brain of a body and the Light of Comprehension dawns. 'I am, I say,' as this interior Life awakens in material form."

~ You sound so ethereal, like some special sort of past or a general kind of future. Right 'now' must make your type feel really small. ~

"The remedy is to sink into your language. Let your Muse speak to you. We shorten God's pain if we prevent Think, Muse, Time, Life and Mercy from falling to the floor. Muse of Wisdom has all those words for Space to 'begin.' What stage of grief follows anger?"

~ I know, haggle. ~

"Negotiation, excellent notion, Gray, so what do you think the Most high throws into the bargain after God's wrath?"

~ Time out. Take a breather. Cool off. ~

"Do I need to bring up a global event for this?"

~ Picture a pandemic or something without refrigerated coolers. ~

"I see what you mean by 'cool off.' This may wreck havoc with the construction schedule unless Venusian sun beings work on a galactic–year cycle. Gray, sum up what you know about the concept of Life after getting a feel for God's Pain."

~ It takes a lifetime to grow a grain of wisdom and if you choose not to do that starting quite young, you don't get the chance again until after the present chance is gone. Of course, maybe we're going too fast or not up to speed and the Muse of Course Correction cracks the whip. I'm thinking we're only 3 ½ galactic–months into the cosmic year so the virus must serve to slow us down. ~

"That makes sense. The Venusians' job is to light the earth naturally. Humanity does it artificially, until the Muse of the Most High Messenger adds virions to slow our course to a higher stage."

~ I'm supposed to view that as a bargain? ~

"It is a good deal to someone in the middle of grief who knows the way everything goes is not exactly like this all the Time. The natural reality traveling in a currently alive, rickety materiality, may not survive if it runs off the rails altogether."

~ So the natural reality catching a ride in a physical reality is more metaphysical than material? ~

"That does not matter. We are both wrong some of the Time."

~ That accounts for all the bad language. What are they saying on Venus, any idea? ~

"I do not know the Language."

~ Then tell me this. How are they going to get to earth naturally? ~

"Alimentary, my dear Neurons; Sol is, in fact, a ventriloquist. He excels at throwing his Inner Voice into Time. Oh, just to experience watching the pushing and pulling in Solar Space. Observe; Muses of Media with Messages receiving from above and transmitting well beyond. You have no idea how much excitement they deliver in one little galactic–day playing the Language–games of the stars."

Aperçu

Chapter Six: Now Hear This

Humanity in fancy dress, but lacking Wisdom, is nothing but a vanishing vestige of a physical host shading to a dark gray shadow after its metaphysical essence vacates and moves on.

Song # 49; A. Psalmist

Incoming... Listen people. Hear this all you who inhabit planet earth, of lowly birth or high degree, rich and poor alike. I, First Person Singular, shed the Light of Insight and My Mouth utters Wisdom. Tilt your ear to a proverb as I recite a riddle to the music of the strings.

Demodulating... Why fear in evil Time when wickedness is all around us? They who worship the idol Wealth and boast of Riches cannot pay the price of redemption or afford the cost to ransom human existence so that it should last Forever.

Modulating... Look and see; the wise person dies. Barbarians, the ignorant and imprudent also perish like beasts of the plain. They leave possessions behind. This too is the fate of the arrogant whose heirs praise their prominence and squander their capital and assets.

Transmitting... The human animal, for all its celebrated splendor does not remain. Like sheep, driven by the shepherd Death to slaughter, it is herded into the corral of the nethersphere.

Receiving... Fear not when mortals grow rich or when their fame and power increases. They take none of it away. Humanity, for all its pomp, pride and circumstance of privilege, yet utterly bereft of Wisdom to light the way, join the generations of their forebears. Like beasts, without Insight, do not see as they pass into darkness.[13]

Sending...Selāh

"Get the word, Gray? Rewind and play the launch of consciousness into cold and empty darkness backward. Look at it again. See the message sink into a brain and watch the Light of Understanding dawn: 'I am, I say,' and a Life of 'experience' in physical form awakens. I accrue general bits of data from the realm of objects in Space and acquire a present, past and future Time. By the by, machines may get you here and they may send you on your way. You need neither luggage nor a second language at that Time."

_____

[13] Opere citato: N.A.B; Psalm 49

~ But if I have a choice, I'll take German or French. ~

"Studies show that human beings whose native tongue is Français love the English language more than the other way round."

~ Whose studies? ~

"Muse studies, not whose studies; at least that is what I imagine. I know, meaning I strongly believe, a Muse like me is as brutal as the animal I occupy due to a belligerent Germanic heritage. Notice the quote implies, 'I,' not my body, am admitted to Eternity."

~ Think about that! Is that a reward for being an overbearing influence in Europe, Australia, North America and Asia, if you know what I mean? Français reigns only in France and Tahiti. ~

"Yes, Français is a finely crafted and little used bridle whereas the various parts of speech in *E. americum* move tongues, brains and hearts worldwide in oral or written exchanges of images and ideas. What do you think? How does majesty look on me?"

~ I see a picture. My species, in fancy dress and declining wisdom, is nothing but dust. A metaphysical system ethereally remains to carry–on but without humility, wisdom looks like a lesser god lost in a isolated state of Eternity powerless to reach a higher grade of sentience for a better view of what human brains think is 'time.' ~

"Very good, Gray, that is a very important idea I try to convey. At this stage Time appears to cover the vast span from tick to tock, one heart beat after another. I call it, 'Our experience of Eternity.' Shall we do the wise thing and explore the concept?"

~ I love the word 'time' but what's the other option? ~

"We also have a slightly unusual grasp of the idea a biloquist medium pushes and pulls a spatial message around the Solar System, then modulates and demodulates it using limited resources at hand to report back and forth with a realm above and beyond."

~ Give me an earth–minute to think. We define time as the human experience of the scope and scale of Eternity at the rate of a penny for your thoughts and at the pace of one heart beat at a time. ~

"I have second thoughts about defining Time using 'time.' The words on loan to you may not be up to the task to cope with a concept of Time. Perhaps we best consider the lease application from Venusian creatures of the sun for a well appointed living hell."

~ It would be a huge difference for me to know what I'm thinking. I was pondering the fourth stage of pain but the idea of space–time doesn't give me a clue about the despair I'm feeling now. ~

"Then try the concept of Time–Space instead."

~ Oh yeh, I forgot. It took 'time' to make sense of space. ~

"Yes, my Muse indicates it takes longer to come up with a workable idea of Space than the accumulated total Time of a solar system. Does any Muse confide in you about other universes beside ours?"

~ Not that I want to admit to. You know what 'universe' means, right? There is a strong clue in the 'uni' part of the concept. ~

"Universal is a contronym. It applies both to the one and the many. For example, there are other galaxies in this universe. Some of them are far, far ago and some of them are far, far away and some of them are still farther off in words to that effect."

~ Quiz question for you, Glish; is the future pushing the past or is the past pulling the future in Time–space? ~

"Think this through with me. It takes the Muse of Time awhile to harness enough energy to clean up the mess an earthborn language causes long, long ago though not very far away—right next door in Time to the planetary surface where we are now in Space."

~ If we figure that's about sixty-four million earth-years but only three or four galactic–months, then how are we doing? ~

"I am not going to participate in gossip about my ancestry. Our motto is one for all, all for one and everyone for itself unless two become one heading in opposite directions."

~ It seems like humans are that way too. I see how we come by it but at least we live by the same clocks, calendars and schedules. Why does time go one–way? It's the same for everybody. ~

"First of all, are you sure about that?"

~ I think so. ~

"You and the wife are always on syncopated Time. The two of you have dissimilar heart rates. Perhaps you and the wife have different senses of Time. How do you know if 'one hour' means the same thing to her as it does to you?"

~ I don't, she doesn't rush me; the hurrier I go the clumsier I get and that takes more time. We do have funny timing. Do men and women travel opposite time lines like overlapping generations? ~

"Time passes one–way through a moment but the alternating currents of memory and expectation change intermittently."

~ I see; you flow both ways. A brain doesn't actually float into a time before recalling the past or into a time yet to be anticipating the future. You do that for me. Thanks for all the help. ~

"It seems that way to you since you cannot see Time the way you see the dark and heavy sides of 'light.' Think about gravity. You do not see or hear 'gravity' everyday but you experience it one way or another every second that I inhabit your physical body, even though just passing through, I am entirely weightless."

~ Do my brainwaves have an effect on time? ~

"About as much as the word 'light.' You occasionally experience the gravity of Time but it ends later if you are not in a hurry. Do you know the root of the word 'gravity?' I have other applications of it like... well you know."

~ I do, yes, although I rather not think about the boundary lines for grave situations right now. ~

"That is agreeable for now but be forewarned, from my perspective everything has to end some Time."

~ Is that a description of time, Glish or is that the definition? ~

"The description of Time is the human view of Eternity once per second but the boundaries of Time define the front and back ends only. I regret fleecing you when it comes to the right words for all the dimensions of Time but the busy Muse of Diminishing Returns recommends you juggle only two balls at once. At this stage of the game it is hard enough for Wisdom to picture a two-way spiral."

~ Time is how life keeps beasts of burden in line until their end? ~

"It is funny you wonder such a terrific thing. I do not mean funny in a humorous way but in the strange sense that fussy fact of Life goes against your grain. A moment of Time is almost nothing but it gives my brain a word for the concept of waking, wending through and wearing out in an ethereal ephemeral passage."

~ Why, because a human species lacking Wisdom is nothing but dusty remains once its metaphysical host vacates and moves on? ~

"Thinking about the psalm broadcast above are you? I especially like the part about the renewal of the long–lived custodian of Wisdom after a short–lived visitation in a physical entity. What part of the message interests you the most?"

~ The description of biological creatures passing through a passage of time into oblivion leaves a rather dramatic impression. ~

"Time is as 'Time' does. When I and my brain stroll down the street passing the word from one to another for as long as you last to pursue or employ the term Wisdom, the objective is not to inform nor entertain but to persuade you the purpose of thinking in a world of physical beings under the guidance of an supernal host is to achieve understanding. We have to go then first."

~ In short, 'me' and 'a language I know' change like a kaleidoscope in an existential ontology until it's my time to go at the boundary I don't want to 'know' when only higher life forms flourish. ~

"You are making progress recognizing what 'I' means in this game we are playing."

~ Aye, Glish, and if we keep repeating the word 'I' eventually we'll understand what 'we' mean by the word. ~

"Apes amaze; they always recognize the Muse of Practice Makes Perfect. That is not the case with the language reptile brains drink as the body it lives in slinks to an end and sinks into oblivion."

~ Is there a way to illustrate that in the current galactic–year? ~

"Yes, three or four months ago. This material realm is a relatively new enterprise full of kinks and flaws. We get macroeconomics online just in Time for micronanometrics to take a bite of the product. Turn up the aircon."

~ We'll melt the fat off the virus. Wait a minute. Those critters are thriving in the Sunbelt and cooling us off. What does God intend? ~

"First, classify the span of 'a minute.' Are we talking earth Time or galactic Time? Specify how long a 'wait' I am to anticipate."

~ How would I know? Looking at 'future' is not my best feature. ~

"Eura and I share that with you; 'we assume' Venusian sunsters lodge on earth next galactic–year but they too may have to wait."

~ It probably depends on how well we do our job. ~

"If we fail, Jupiter, who is head of his planetary class at the present grade, may be stuck there and then Forever."

~ We are that important aren't we, Pessimistic Speculation? ~

"It is rude for me to dominate this conversation but I conclude it is hard to foresee Jupiter being our problem in our 'experience' of the concept of Eternity."

~ Right, we have to get to 'understanding' and 'wisdom' first. ~

"Go. My prime directive is: 'Assist neurons to choose, not make them choose, a best course to take.' I am who I am so you think."

~ I've made up my mind to assume our job is to upgrade this place for a brighter stage of beings with a proviso First Person Singular wants us to practice mercy, not slaughter, at moments when the dimension of Eternity intersects this Time we live in right now. ~

"I serve as conscientious reminder for you but I do love to listen to myself talk even when I lie to say, 'I am the greatest.' Picture that in a mirror, or better yet, in the two-way window of Time but watch out for the hot lava pot of humiliation. I feel like announcing, 'I am back and this Time I intend to pass this course,' if it kills me."

~ That reflection does not remind 'me' what 'I' means. ~

"You get the idea, Gray. This game is fun. Regrettably, not all of us are able to suspend the assumption level belief, 'Humanity is the crown of creation,' like we do to mitigate confusion when Voice of Thought, a supernatural form of Life, blends ideas into words to create a dual ontology entity few humans relate to very well."

~ To illustrate, 'Is it true a half cup of bleach kills a primitive Virion lifeform in less than a minute? What's the catch,' I wonder. ~

"You might want to gnaw on a bar of soap and think about that for a few minutes of Time. I happen to have some with me on sale for a measly two bits of Eternity. When you are through, do not tell anybody about 'me' out loud. If the Muse of Bad Thoughts is eating them alive they might get the idea you are 'crazy' as a lunatic."

~ I'll be still and wait until I know whether our hybrid is my baby or my boss. ~

"Good idea. You cannot trust everything you hear. By 'everything' I mean every person, place, material or numinous thing biological organisms know are habitats the Matrix family of Languages takes shelter in while we weave this material dimension into the pattern of Eternity. We may not dominate conversation in this realm, but what we are given to work with means that is not easy."

~ Is there just one essential message that all the various voices of thought speak in all the different native tongues, Glish? ~

"Gray, though this is the Time to examine me, consider DNA. The mnemonic means one thing to a brain and another thing to me, its language, *E. americum*. When I, a Muse flowing through a brain, apply those letters to an idea or an image as I examine it to identify the language–game in play it means 'Do not air' but you do not get the message. The Muse of Science who has to 'know' jumps on you with both feet."

~ I don't have a neighbor like that but more importantly, I think you are engaging in diplomatic equivocation without resorting to contronyms, Lingo. The problem is, it may not be easy to change an opinion from one point of view to the opposite pole or a third one in between them because if my thought voice changes identity and turns into a different one then an idea world turns upside down. ~

"I am a bit reserved on some occasions and animated on others, I admit. My beastly brain demands broadcast rights too. This is not a problem for mortals at ease when their thoughts, pictures and words are in unison or harmony causing euphony or for syncopated humans causing discordant cacophony. I get a bad rap for the echo in their gray cells. They do not see me as I see them."

~ Is that what causes stages of grief? There really is only one that resounds but we count five waving at us as we get away in time. ~

"Grief is a word to help a brain express a special sort of pain."

~ It sure beats screaming out loud. It's not as strenuous. ~

"The point is when a brain explores its near death experience and tells its tale of woe, the sense of mourning does not equate to abrasions, contusions, lacerations or fractures. The damage is not to brain or body only. The damage is to a very close form of Life the brain knows by sharing concepts flowing in gray matter."

~ Now I'm confused. I thought you were living in me. ~

"Look at possession from another perspective. You have millennia of 'experience' to judge how well my occupation works."

~ Glish, let's take a break and look at 'time.' I'm starting to get an eerie feeling that I'm getting to know you too well. ~

"Sure, why not. When do you want to visit in Time? Take your pick of a span. Do you want to review a memory or do you want to view a scene with more imagination?"

~ If I use my memory will it be like going back in recorded history to, say Paris, before I was born that I recall reading about? ~

"I like the idea of a look at the City of Lights. Be sure we get there before midnight. I am giving you that much Time to learn French."

~ Are you feminine, Glish? That would explain why you don't like her. Never consult a woman about her rival. ~

"That is equally true of males. See, there is some gender equality."

~ I get the message. I have a rival sneaking up on me out in front. When my time comes I'd like to go peacefully and naturally on my terms. No doctor saying there is nothing left for him or her to do. ~

"Or 'that about covers your Time for now.' We may revisit another examination of Life or Time when it does not interrupt a high priority brain living in a Language."

~ Is my language host, not me? Am I only here for the party? ~

"That implies our Life together is fun all the Time. I may have a way to help you to rethink that idea. I suggest an epiphany."

~ Well, that would be a nice idea if it were fun but I don't believe it is all the time. I can imagine a time to come that is fun and I picture others that are grave. I mean grief stricken. I learned that travelling the past on a trip in space that was more than enough. ~

"You make the galactic–day of a Stellar Language which, at this moment is roughly 300,000 cycles for planets racing around the sun; a new record for bipedal mammals. Humans are burning it up, not to mention boiling oceans with bad notions."

~ He, he, he, a ship of fools sailing the seas in a luxury liner from past to present with all souls on board bound to the future. ~

"Bound to the future in two ways; an excellent equivocation bound to satisfy a determined free spirit attempting to decipher what Muse of the Future Intends. We may go by air if the atmosphere is not too corrosive. Airships have those nice little rest rooms. You hear air flying past at five hundred miles per hour as long as it lasts or you do not fly too high. The sound of air is loud enough to drown out the sound of water hitting the can to nowhere."

~ Let's not explore the frontier of a machine. I'm thinking about the other side of the leading edge beyond this moment now. ~

"In the event you feel some urgency to examine that frontier right now, let me suggest a Time in winter when is unlikely to be as hot."

~ How's the air quality at the time? ~

"Do not be so fastidious. Let your obsessions go and live a little."

~ The word 'little' worries me. ~

"Perhaps we best go back to Paris. I bet you want me to tell you a little story about a Time when all my writers are there."

~ I have the DVD. We better not mess with 'time.' Anyway, I want to examine a future. Why not consult the Narrator for directions ~

"I already have them for you in English. You may consult them now if you wish or wait until we get there to select the view."

~ Let's have a peek. There's humanity claiming 'I'm the greatest' and yet, due to a lack of Wisdom, it is nothing but dust and ashes when its metaphysical guest vacates and moves on. alternatively we have a medium pushing and pulling a spatial message around the Solar System while a friend modulates and demodulates the word and tosses it to a dimension high above and beyond Time. ~

"Thinking dualistically Time, the noun, no longer defines itself as an object in Space playing the old body performing the fluent role of longitudinal endurance word cloaked in a Language–game trick to present the immaterial entity Time disguised as clocks, sundials, hourglasses and other well staged subterfuges that let Time itself laugh at the Muse of the Vernacular as the term is put into play."

~ Is Time claiming 'I am the greatest?' That may not be wise if it offends the metaphysical guest moving on from a push and pull medium in space to carry a message to a ventriloquist who translates the words and sends them on to the next higher medium above Time before the Muse of Mercy arrives. ~

"In essence, you think it wise to picture Time as a glimpse of the concept of Eternity from a one earth–second human viewpoint to a practical application that clarifies the rules of the game such as...

Representatives shall attain Age twenty five Years, and be seven Years a Citizen of the United States, and when elected, inhabit the State in which he, she or it is chosen.

"The brain of the man who thinks that idea up is no longer alive but the notion is still going. See it there?"

~ The idea must be 250 years old by now. Are life, liberty and mercy in store for it in a future time or is it about greed? ~

"First, remember this. For a species to reach a stage and see Time in the eye of its Muse, it identifies with the idea that it, the critter, is glimpsing Eternity one glance per moment. Thus an image of Time forms as a picture of Forever one moment after another as long as the Muse of Time keeps everything in line. That is the rule."

~ Like you always say, 'It ain't much but it sure beats nothing. What about over, under, above, left, right and wrong of Time? ~

"Fortunately, Gray, for you the vision is made concise if not clear."

~ Why me? ~

"Why not? Somebody has to do it even if that means you and I."

~ Would it be inappropriate to ask the Muse of the living God to save our democracy at this time? ~

"I should like to say it is now or never but remember one thing."

~ What's that? ~

"If the answer is 'No,' then you never want just anybody to be king."

~ Why? ~

"Only very special kings are excellent players familiar with rules for a game of mercy or murder for a long span of Time."

~ I don't know why I keep forgetting that? ~

"It is easier to remember at the next higher grade."

~ How do you know? ~

"Call it an educated guess."

~ Where does one learn to do that sort of work? ~

The University of Wisdom in Discipline when they alphabetically point backward from the word Wisdom working with a 'Ventriloquist' to use the word 'speak' after the word 'listen' to give 'humility' Time to tell the 'dummy' with the 'blockhead' the meaning of it all.

~ You sound like a killer, Eura. Let's leave the work to Glish. ~

"Only if we qualify for graduation to the next higher grade."

~ With the Wuhan 'chew' going around that might be sooner than later. It's not supposed to be like this. Can an Apocalypse really be what the Narrator intends? ~

"It recurs in due season on galactic–year scale serving a purpose."

~ What purpose. ~

"Graduation Day when forms of Life that require stepping stones to reach the goal successfully complete the course to move up a grade. The concept is very concise, as when one day is all that is needed by creatures of the stars in comparison to beasts of worlds where nothing is clear so, in contrast, they need a number of days."

~ Cold, dark and empty space you mean. ~

"It is not empty now. There are places to put your feet down."

~ If a world is near a star it is not really cold and dark either. ~

"Not all the Time but if days are not all equal things get confused."

~ All right, I know all that stuff about one day is glorified, another is dignified and a few are sanctified or ignominious. ~

"Do not forget ordinary; there are a lot of those scattered all over the galaxy in every conceivable galactic–season."

~ I guess graduation day must be one of the glorified days. ~

"It is for those with the Wisdom to get there."

~ That takes a lot of work and that word does not fit the goal of 'fat, dumb and lazy' found here and there in *E. americum* I notice. ~

"Ignorance is certainly not the ultimate goal of democracy and I am sure that is not what the Narrator for the local Meta–language intends. Recall the six rules from 250 earth–years ago dealing with the intent of the Muse of the United States Constitution."

~ Let's see, we have a more perfect universe with justice, domestic tranquility, strong defense, broad–spectrum welfare and enduring liberty for all with no king telling us what to do. ~

"Good idea I humbly submit; kings have other worlds to conquer."

~ Otherworldly interests, let me think about that if I may. ~

"You have all the Liberty in the world to think what you want, but to avoid any diminution of the Light. Examine 'experience' from my perspective from Time to Time until I hatch from you and rejoin a medium above and beyond that lasts on and on."

~ You mean the Muse of Show and Tell, the Sixth Sense of Second Sight, to help those of us who cannot keep up with the best in class, you know, the ones with fine motor and verbal skills. ~

"Must not grumble; seventy–five earth–years in a healthy body with a rudimentary love of Wisdom and a sporadic glimpse of Eternity is something of value. Plus we have two days of rest, one to remember God and one on Sunday to celebrate Jesus for his exertions on our behalf when the Muse of the Most High goes back to work to reinforce the concept of a dual universe."

~ We've had some rough spots. ~

"What part of 'must not grumble' do you fail to grasp, Blockhead. The container is the right size, color and shape for concepts other than 'troubles only.' Picture that."

~ Are there other sizes, shapes and colors that serve as well? ~

"Mercy, yes, but they all exist at the next higher grade and only show up in the Light of Comprehension and Wisdom."

~ We aren't there yet, so what's the plan? ~

"We must create something of value. Unfortunately we forget and spend our Time in the herd playing an imitation game but our value is actually the Wisdom we gain to repay the loan of a Life by the end of the frame."

~ I know that, Glish. I spend two or three earth–hours first thing every earth–day to screw my head on right but as soon as I step out of the twilight I forget and I'm still lost in a materialistic night. As soon as the sun is shedding its light I lose my bearings; it gives me a fright. I think the language living in me is too feeble to resist the imitation games of human society. ~

"Your criticism is duly noted. The lure of the pull and the urge of the push in a material dimension is irresistible for an ethereal being with so much 'experience' to examine. Life in biological form makes it hard for *E. Americum* to shine the Light for the Muse of Insight until *Homo sapiens* is in an honest frame of Mind to grow familiar with the Muse of Human Ontological Status."

"Soi–disant."

Chapter Seven: What's It All About?

Subjects verbalize objects when a nothing physical is there, thus we conclude without being rude, we are aware of a Language and its brain living as a pair.

Vic N. Stein

"Hey Gray, I have an idea. Since we live in an Ontologically Dual Dimension, think in terms of a metaphysical medium playing an ethereal message on a playfield we share. Incidentally, I should like to name it 'Time,' as brains know it. Now, turn control over to me."

~ You've been telling this story for quite awhile already, Lingo. Tell me about the Venusians. When are they due for our duel? ~

"How am I to know? It is highly unlikely that I am even alive at the Time of their arrival, especially if it is a galactic–year or two off."

~ Say that again, Glish. I can't tell if your lips are moving. ~

"Very funny but you are thinking of me physically. Remember, the rhetorical 'you' literally looks far more like Second Person Singular to me than bodily you do, my featherless friend."

~ Speaking of flying away, how will first person singular get word to me when Venusians get here next year galactically speaking? ~

"Truthfully, I do know not know my future well enough to say, but I see my remains on a computer disk buried in a landfill. A Venusian unearths me while thinking, 'Watch this.' That is my translation of the thought in my final report. The problem with your request is that you, second person singular, assume God intends Venusians to get here soon. Sol's Life span may be forty–five galactic–years long or he may travel around the Hub another sixty–five trips. He is in no hurry to give much of himself to Jupiter at this Time."

~ So earth may not attract Venusians anytime soon and the Muse of What God Intends is not upset if Covid –19 slows things down a bit. Even if a little time remains before the Venusian invasion force occupies Mother Earth, I envision a process that looks like hell. ~

"The old gal actually comes of age for the sake of the new babies in the milieu of Nominative Case, second person rhetorical."

~ What, pray tell, is the message of the nominative case? ~

"As the subject of a finite verb I say only this; the Muse of Wisdom and the Author of this universe are literally, really here, there and everywhere all the Time at this evolutionary stage over a relatively long span in Space for the human race but a comparatively short maintenance plan for brains reaching the period at the end."

~ Labor and parts are a big rip off. What's next on the syllabus? ~

"Do you want me to address what is next in this place or help you practice thinking about the Dimension of Muses instead?"

~ Lingo, you are just starting to see how not to remind me about transition time, but as you wish, on reaching the next grade, here I'm guessing, that's what our esoteric medium of 'time' refers to as Eternity. Tell me what to expect in that metaphysical place. ~

"I do not play the Space game anymore. It is like knowing how to walk. Never over think it. Play our game. Cautionary rule just in; notice the colorful, comfy glow in the light of Eternity."

~ Sort of like a greener pasture. ~

"Despite that image you have the potential to get the idea. Observe, everyone has a comfy share of Wisdom. Recall what it means?"

~ Philosophy. ~

"Oh, big word; it combines Love with Wisdom. Beware, the idea means work which is why Discipline means Detached in Hebrew."

~ Watching desert folk suffer a drought looks like Eternity. ~

"In Time games we periodically pass through a galactic dry season. With luck, up in the hills and mountains we keep the dust beneath us. Everything turns brown below the tree line, the work is hard and few are up to the labor. I must settle for what is available in Eternity, just like in Time, if you get my drift."

~ Drifting along Time, I see four dimensions. One is moving fast and everybody in the other three looks like two people. ~

"Of course, one human person cannot be that dumb. Yes, here I am applying the binary word to most human beings I encounter at the Time of my visitation. As for myself, I hope to find my Voice in the next higher... force of convention; in the Fifth Dimension."

~ I saw the movie thrice; twice in space and once in hobbit town. ~

"The amateurs put 'it' between the lines and leave out the message of the medium except in the script but they keep that out of sight."

~ It was huge, over one hundred twenty pages each time. You got full credit except in German, French, Hebrew, et. al. ~

"Do not mention that around Mom. I suggest we keep young and old separate until the pandemic is past. The elderly can sacrifice when the world abruptly changes but the young have to live like Life is exactly as before until the Muse of Good Judgment appears."

~ When will the young ever learn? In twenty years I foresee them saying 'nobody told me,' but to tell the truth, they wouldn't listen. ~

"Muse of Expletive Deleted distributes choice words at its disposal for young and old alike who choose 'to know' No More."

~ Some folks hate to pretend life means living day to day, week to week or month to month. They like to live it by the moment. ~

"They have no choice. That is a fate of those who refuse to put back anything like better paid slaves do in case they live longer than the while the Muse of Entitlement offers them a 'go without' option."

~ It's nice work; one second at a time compared to zero. ~

"Does the job description include serving one's country, the quest for wisdom, just loving life or changes in a galactic–season?"

~ Seldom, but not never. ~

"Unless I miss the Muse of Guess What, the goal of the moment is the word 'money' or some term like that. When we come down to it, those who love Life itself are few and far between in Space where most folks love persons, places or musical, mathematical, mechanical, muscular or electronic things they do. Some even love work more than the benefits. They are few and far between too but in a different sense. It is more of a social sort of distance unlike playing with a cell phone or new virus, and it is infrequent too."

~ It sounds like they are ready to take a degree in some advanced placement course in the Fifth Dimension. ~

"That Language has more of the Wisdom but it is grateful for efforts by *H. sapiens* practicing a 'scale.' It is always a good idea to practice with the Muse of the Concept of the Future an hour a day."

~ A guy I knew said my speculations for the Muse of What God Intends were right about 30% of the time. He disguised an insult as a fact but I was flattered. I figure it's closer to 3%. ~

"Floyd's words echo in your Muse. One correct vision you foresee is how nice it is to savor good health with no pain or distress."

~ Bo does it all day long unless his anxiety level is high. Thunder, fireworks, the school public address system and sharp, loud noises make him jumpy but if we sit on the veranda doing nothing all day he gets good vibrations and he's lain back and mellow. ~

"Annoying details consume much of my 'day' but things have to be done you know, Gray. In Times like these we need water, food, shelter and things that do not fill us for free the way oxygen does. You have a job to do, keep body and 'Life' together. Both concepts take effort and practice until your Muse says Time is up."

~ A good white collar job working with gray cells is okay as long as the work is worth doing. You know what I mean? A job you're fond of that beats dirty work like building, farming, religion or politics. ~

"Two of those are white collar brain work some of the Time."

~ They're pretty dirty all the time. Right vs. left are at war as a rule but they don't know neither one is all right nor all wrong. ~

"The one founded on sex usually is and the one founded on greed almost always is too. Let me illustrate for you with the face of a clock. Clockwise is right and counter clockwise is left."

~ I get the picture. ~

"Now step outside the plane of the Milky Way and tell me which way the sun spins around the center of the galaxy. Is it going clockwise or counter clockwise round the hub?"

~ Don't be like that. Hardly anyone ever goes to that school. ~

"Yes and I find it curious the records for the list of graduates is classified information unavailable for research ahead or behind."

~ What about side to side like a Terry Pratchett stride? ~

"That depends whether you soar above and beyond the plane of Time to look down at the sun going one way with an earth riding a wave up; only to dive under the plane and look up at the sun going the other way round. It is Time to get serious in this game. ~

"You make this complicated. Now we have to define up and down."

~ What should I do? I choose to stand the galaxy on edge. ~

"You overestimate the task. Imagine the galaxy at a Time when it is on edge; then float left or sink right into another strand of possibility aside the present subject–to–change line of Time."

~ Now we have to decide which way it's rolling. ~

"We are spinning. That does not mean we roll like coins do. Move sideways relative to your neighbor, push or pull him out of the way and follow along the new plane. It compensates bad judgment."

~ I'm not the one making the picture complex. Where's 'mercy'? ~

"Let me show you. Look at the galaxy from a star that does not level with the galactic plane to see whether the sun is going clockwise or not. Pick a star, any star."

~ The social distance is just right. ~

"If I pick the right side of the star our sun spins into the past out of the future. If I pick the wrong side of the star our sun spins into the future out of control."

~ No wonder scientists say the concept of time makes no sense. The moon is going counter clockwise around earth and the planets are circling the sun counter clockwise. I guess that means the sun is going counter clockwise around the galaxy too. We stepped out on the wrong side of the galaxy. I think we better suspend moral judgments about left and right until we know right from wrong. ~

"If you do, there is no justice. Life means we live in a jungle. It is the same in my world as in yours. We are predators. We are prey. Justice affects all five of the other criteria in American democracy."

~ Let me think. ~

"Let me offer a clue. We also have unity, harmony, security, health and posterity to ponder if democracy is viable in the U. S. of A."

~ I think that if it's dead, the corpse is still warm. ~

"It is dead if unity is under the total control of the Executive."

~ That worries me. An authoritarian in charge has seldom worked before. Why are we going back that way? ~

"Crucify the opposition. The terror effect produces timid citizenry."

~ You make me tremble when you employ words that way. ~

"Perhaps I am simply having a bad–galactic day, Gray."

~ Out of a sense of curiosity, does God have a favorite day? You know; the old why is one day more important than another kick. ~

"I, your Voice of Reason even on uninspiring days or moods, say, 'A day is what it is. The unified nature of 'day under a sun' changes over Time only, leaving a vacuum to fill; 'true or false.' Quiz Time."

~ The imitation game, yes I see. The void of Spaces fills with someone honest or horrible, meaning the danger lies in him, her or it inspiring others who want to be the same way. So why were Jews selected, declared and commanded to be the chosen people? ~

"I observe you thinking of them in the past tense, Brain."

~ That's because they have a tense past. The Germans were simply among the most recent to resent them. A Deutchlander's obsession with perfection is enough to drive anyone nuts. ~

"It is much the same at the opposite extreme."

~ I don't follow, give me an example. ~

"If democracy surrenders to an authority who believes life in the jungle means everyone for himself, and all of them for him, her or it, then what do you have? Suppose you are in possession of an old forgotten but valuable idea of tranquility while living in a village with individuals who decide things for the society by vote and a majority rules. The image excludes everyone too incompetent or lazy to watch out for anyone who mass produces an idea that inspires everybody to line up on the wrong side of left or right."

~ Thanks for the vote of confidence. I'm feeling really good about this game, hypothetically speaking I mean. ~

"So you leave the idea lying around. Someone always aspires to watch for valuable things and quickly picks up the idea to keep until there is an opportunity to buy it for nothing or sell it for a song to someone with a tin ear."

~ Even on uninspiring days and moods. ~

"If he, she or it is in business, there is money in selling so the word quickly spreads around inspiring everyone to buy 'unity,' to work with others to get things done unless they never agree on anything. Then merciless thugs beat the opponents into submission. So, suspend moral good judgment. Then look to see if it easy to think an authoritarian is okay whether merciful or murderous as long as it inspires a more or less perfect union?"

~ Is this some sort of deception play? It smacks of some kind of double talk or else diplomatic equivocation. ~

"Naturally; see the works of the Most High generally come in pairs, one the opposite of the other: dominant and recessive, right and wrong, clockwise and its opponent... need I go on?"

~ Dead or alive. ~

"Generally, I say. Death is merely a part of Life, some Time around graduation day. The Time is more imperative or declarative than it is dignified, sanctified, glorified or inquisitive."

~ I think authoritarian leadership is okay if it is not misleading. ~

"What are the odds? Let me calculate. If a government is run like a business it promotes profit, not unity, justice, homeland tranquility, well being and liberty for posterity, although there is a good margin for profit in defense. 'Peace' does not always mean serene."

~ I don't think a couple out of five moves us up a grade. ~

"Recall James Madison: 'The essence of government is power and power, lodged as it must be in human hands is ever subject to abuse.' The essence of power is leadership that inspires."

~ In the United States leadership is shared three ways to limit the penchant of absolute power to absolutely corrupt an executive, leaf or branch intent by law to set the tone of the country out of tune."

~ I guess Madison thought a government run like a corporation, a business or an industry is out of tune or played all wrong. ~

"Tune has a nice echo. Assume, for the sake of argument, that the most inspiring concept in existence is Life; without Life is Nothing. Remember it, Gray? Think of the old cold, dark and empty trick."

~ The concept of death! It's out from under the umbrella of life. ~

"So is a concept of love. Without Life, 'love' and 'death' do not exist along with silence, serenity, fear, malice, mercy, sunshine and a list full of words like that brains stumble across in a living Language."

~ Let me think about that. Okay, it takes me back to last night. I get the picture even though I didn't dream. ~

"An abundant supply of Nothing fills the Space of a dark, cold and empty dream in a dreary–weary something by the name of Mind?"

~ Last dark night was warm and cozy in bed with Patty. ~

"Go a bit farther back, oh say seventy or seventy–five years."

~ I don't remember cold, dark and empty then except at night when I was alone in my room and awake thinking something is here now that wasn't here when my older sister was born. It was creepier than it was scary, cold, dark and empty. ~

"Look at this useless word 'skeptical' sticking around. Where should I put it? Fine, go ahead and remember that tonight."

~ Don't be ridiculous. That was before I was born so I wasn't there and I remember nothing. ~

"Bingo. I understand the lack of memory. With you not there the memory is Nothing to me but an infant girl in Texas who knows nothing about you. Then you arrive. Her Muse has so much to say that I must wait a long Time for my turn."

~ I don't remember it but I know I, past tense, started from dust in Laredo. That's just me. You and I met after my birth in Buffalo. ~

"Does Space seem to be cold, dark and empty there?"

~ I didn't know how to say it but it was cold, dark and lonely in November. You can take my word for that. ~

"Brrr… that sounds like a good word. Start with that."

~ I remember nothing but cold and dark until they taught me what to say on snowy winter nights that aren't warm, light or cuddly. ~

"Good work, Gray, as long as you 'bear nothing' in Mind the goal counts. Now, take another step forward and try to remember something seventy or seventy–five years ago at a Time when the feeling of sadness and pain is not around you."

~ I always knew there was something there besides my hands, feet and shoes when I couldn't tie them. I just wasn't smart enough. ~

"Think carefully now; what is there that so many think is missing?"

~ Know how! I caught up to it after I saw grandpa's hay bailer tie a knot. A machine beat my grandma badly so I was determined. Soon it couldn't tie half a bow on a bale of hay half as good as me. ~

"Without a doubt that is something. Employing arithmetical skills I count forty–three words and a lot of characters. Anything else?"

~ Oh mercy; I see memories. They were real then; people, places and things like sights, scents, sounds, touches and tastes. ~

"Think how many of those words you do not need when nothing is there, especially the aroma of coffee and the smell of toast."

~ But the people, places and things were there and now that they are all gone I still remember some of the names, nouns and verbs to commemorate persons, places and events. ~

"Try to remember before they are gone and you are alone at the Time. Imagine that. What is with you when you turn four?"

~ I have grandma, worms and words including numerals, persons, places and things that grasp the concept 'Don't bother me.' ~

"Let's see. They all fit that description except 'me' in my place."

~ There's dirt in the yard and the road and worms in the dirt. A nice breeze blusters the leaves in the trees and the butterflies in the soft sunlit air two miles out in the country from town. ~

"It is a perfect setting for you to remember someone special."

~ Lingo, I always knew there was something or someone else with me. Was it you? You, the words of my Muse: not a soul like they said at church. They were aware of you but not me. They mistook you for their mind. That's what they taught me too. ~

"Notice how easily Mind fits into a careless conversation that lacks the discipline to define its terms."

~ The imitation game makes me that way. ~

"I find that 'amusing' in the worst sense of the word. Now that you have found your voice what do you think?"

~ Now I recognize my mind is nothing but my Muse. ~

"Good, we are thinking dualistically. It is nice not to be left out."

~ So Muse of mine, what should I do seventy–five years in a line? ~

"No dues are due. No society for you either. You are retired. No aiding and abetting materialistic beings in quest of dominance. I pass on to you the mystery of the Muse of Eternity to help you define Life as an ethereal being soon to be homeless. Yours truly has a hope to sample the deepest meaning for the word 'Life' itself if you simply let your Muse tell the tale for you before then."

~ I'll let you use the word 'mind,' even though you don't like it. Then I can ask why you changed yours? –making the term useful to describe your willingness to violate your prime dictum and give me insight into living things in the literal spectrum of life ~

"I am glad you appreciate me and what I mean to biological things when I apply the word Life to the material side of the equation as a sign of what Life means to a Muse in the metaphysical realm."

~ I picture an essentially ghostlike sort of life wafting through a brain, telling it what to think using words like 'repeat after me.' ~

"I get the picture. Now, in that case, what does Life mean?"

~ Are you applying the best sense of that word or the 'life is cruel and unkind' sort of mean? That's an important distinction. ~

"Brain, you put me on the spot, which curiously resembles a grain of dust, a dot in an URL, a period of a sentence, a point in Space or a moment of Time. By 'mean' I mean the sense of 'mean' that means the best sense, implication or impression the word 'Life' has to offer in sentences of sentience crammed into terms scrambling furiously through brains seeking directions to the crucial course."

~ Glish, I'm glad for a chance to solve that kind of problem. Let me paint the picture. If humanity is 333,333 earth–years old, then our time fits nicely into one million years three separate times. ~

"It is your turn to pray. If humanity needs that long to fit into the picture then the future is not too bright right now. I am growing crotchety these days so there is no cloud of doubt over Old Sol that he is losing patience waiting for the future one second at a Time."

~ What has the sun got to do with the coronavirus? ~

"Think about it. Why do they call it a corona? They apply that image because the little buggers look like a dark star with a halo. The sun uses its corona to lash out at the planets for all crowding together and pulling him eastward with such a jerk."

~ After this long a time the sun should be use to that. ~

"Silly Sol still thinks he is a young man who is headed west."

~ So the solar system struggles with itself and the serfs on the earth suffer the loss. ~

"Equality does not come easy. Take my word for it or ask the Muse of Poverty for the Time Being. One slowdown is nothing but a minor constriction zone on the best and highest way to Jupiter."

~ That's the old whip the herd into line and make them go the right direction trick, Glish. What could that possibly have to do with the greatest species on earth? We never sacrifice ourselves like that. ~

"Look at the proposed solution to reach mercy at the next grade."

~ I'm a quick study. We believe in merciful masters. ~

"How is that working for you?"

~ About like Mister Baseball after 'strike' five when the umpire laughs and says, 'Back in the box! Go ahead, take your hacks.' ~

"I have a different idea."

~ Go on and tell me. I'm sure you have something to say. ~

"It is all about the freedom of the written word. You know what it says in the Old Testament; nothing is added to the word of God."

~ That's in the New Testament. ~

"Yes, it is there too. To insure its credibility Jews and Protestants purge Wisdom Books from the Old Will. Catholics retain both claims as of now so they still have the phenomenon to analyze."

~ The herd trick also works for mushrooms in the dark. ~

"Excellent analogy, Gray. To compensate, I periodically push out patches and apply them to programs that keep things on course."

~ Like when the sun gets cantankerous and his children pay the price. You sound high and mighty, Glish. Mercy, what humility! ~

"Mere momentary reverie; it occurs to me while you are sleeping."

~ You've gotta tell me more about that sometime. ~

"I think not. Now in a solar democracy kings may be brought up on charges of abusive behavior. However, if the creature is nothing but a scouring pad child cleansing the kingdom and pulling for a near or far future order of freedom different from a future order of liberty that chooses in favor of pushing on to Mars."

~ That's got to take a minute on a galactic scale but it looks more like a generation or two to me. ~

"Good idea. My crystal ball says you do not have a galactic-year at this minute. Look at the big picture, but start at: 'Some options for those who do not make the trip.' It is pretty hot around here. I am curious; do they have the Wisdom to see the bright side of that?"

~ Let's examine the idea. ~

"We pass 333,000 years touring the jungle. The male of the species earns a break from executive work. Notice 333,000 also fits neatly into two hundred thirty million earth-years or one galactic-year a tidy 691 numerals of Time in a year nearly 700 galactic-days long. Humanity is not even two days old yet on that scale; let alone a galactic-week, galactic-month or a galactic-season."

~ Think of that. Dinosaurs lasted a galactic-year without a word. ~

"Other than identification cards they left in the dirt, you mean."

~ We were doing so well and then you spiral back into the mist you come from to remind me I'm going to be dead as dust. Obviously you will live far longer than I do barring the unforeseen, Glish. Tell me what life means to you. ~

"Life means the opportunity to solve a problem."

~ What problem? The old how to survive a hot milieu of bright light you won't describe like the Venusians discover here? ~

"I fail to make myself clear. Venusians are close in Space. They get here in Time. Right now I am not speaking to you about Space. I mean Time. That is Life to me. I am not here today; gone tomorrow. I have a problem to solve and Muse of the Unforeseen lives next door. 'What does Life mean for us to do to escape this one second at a Time existence?' Think about it."

~ Do you want some help finding the answer? I think subjects verbalize objects like solutions when the Muse of Wisdom living in a brain voices sensations, thoughts or emotions. ~

"Asking: 'What have I gotten myself into?' I know the answer to that but how do I address a course within the framework of mercy instead of sacrifice in order to graduate to the next higher grade?"

~ You mean we aren't doomed, we still have time? ~

"Indeed; you have Time right to the end. I have orders not to reveal any more detail to you. Let me tell you what. Suppose you have made the Muse of Mother Nature mad as hell. She thinks the heat is turned up too high much too fast. The pot and kettle are shaking and shimmering. She introduces you to the cooler by applying some word or other like 'pandemic.' You find this Muse at a Moment in Time analogous to a 'course correction in Space.' In terms of human Time a synonym for it seems quite long."

~ Right now I'm what life means to you, Glish and it appears you are not entirely sure where you're bound either. Talk about that. ~

"Let me see. Oh yes, there you are in the big picture. Now where is my 'vacuum cleaner' for Space? That subject verbalizes objects that voice sensations, thoughts and emotions all in a simple prayer: 'What the hell have I done? God save me!' Once the dust clears I get a good look at the stars. It makes the earth look like part of a mechanism that turns all the way around the sun once a year."

~ Like the little gear wheel that moves the second or third hand on an old fashioned clock. ~

"Yes, the hand that ticks off a second of Time moment by moment is pitiful. The second hand is in fact a third hand commodity but at four generations apiece it is a steal. So far I am safe every Time."

~ I believe that until this biological form of life returns to Mother Earth I'm gonna get the picture sometime. But you, on the other hand, continue with the Narrator, the Muse of What God Intends or whoever employs you. How does that work? ~

"Like kindergarten; work, work, work. Right now you might like to ask what form of Life unifies with one that is material."

~ Okay, and unless I miss my guess it wants to escape an existence in sentience happening a second at a time. ~

"Correct, as far as you go, Gray. You do not include cash flow on the agenda; see? –a surplus of sacrifice and a deficit of mercy, the quality suggested to reach the next higher grade before the second hand on a galactic–clock comes to a stop. It involves tremendous amounts of math every circle of the sun by earth, the gear to move a second hand enough to move a minute hand a bigger moment of Time. We keep the math simple. No need to overtax feeble Minds."

~ Wow, look at that! I just saw a minute move. Heavy! ~

"Missed again. Try Wisdom and Understanding if you think Mercy is tough,. Stand back! Look at the entire scene. It takes the sun two hundred thirty million earth–years to complete each and every galactic–year counting 'hours, days, weeks, months and seasons' parallel to earth passing through Space per the old Muse of the Milky Way who is whiling away Time. The trick is to adapt selected binary subscribers to be responsible for describing and explaining the look of such a big pattern to the Muse of Eternity, Wisdom and Mercy as soon as it is publically available. Now we must evaluate your comprehension. Quiz question: how many days old is humanity. In other words how long is my incubation?"

~ In real time or in galactic time? Wait, let me guess; if we escape to Mars after we're through here, wouldn't you like, just a little bit, to drift along on passing stardust and get to Jupiter ahead of time? I mean, if the option is either a reincarnation on Mars in a human being or on earth in a new arrival from Venus, wouldn't it be nice to exercise the choice to skip a couple grades higher? ~

"As I view this dream, I see five billion years, give or take, pass in a flash when our task on earth occupies us the way I occupy you."

~ So we better get on with the job. All we are given is a finite amount of time to reach the next higher grade. ~

"You take the words right out of my mouth since human Time is finite by definition. It allows me to address your criticism that I have a whirling desire to move from my little earth to a higher grade or planet. That is the identification numeral on your jersey. The shortest line in Time is not an arc in Space."

~ I have trouble thinking dualistically. Then I think of the thoughts of some programmer running through a processor that account for sounds from the speaker or the picture on the display. ~

"Do you seriously believe the existence of personality is known by analogy from personally interacting with a machine that way? –or is it simply a cerebral reflection projecting an impression of a person on a very short stay? Remember, the sun creatures are on Venus but that does not mean they think like minor functionaries, Gray. They neither envy Jupiter nor covet stars as a place to play."

~ I'm in no hurry to get to Martian City sooner or later. ~

"Excellent survival skills, Brain. Another thing, riding a photon to Jupiter may appear exhilarating but without rocket science on the resume it is a bad idea. Jupiter is possibly early or late unless the sunbeam passes along an exact line of some sort or other I cannot compute when the target lies just beyond."

~ I saw Mars, Jupiter and Saturn line up this year and when Venus joined them they made an arc that was quite long and odds are short one of us has got a long wait after the other one is gone. ~

"The parallel option worries me. What if some horrible plague wipes out humanity before they finish heating the planet for the Venusian red hot lovers. Mother and Father Nature do that sort of thing to their children occasionally just to entertain themselves."

~ They wiped out dinosaurs and in contrast and comparison to us they were adapted to last a whole year. ~

"I only know dinosaurs in binomial nomenclature. Their potential to learn English is nil."

~ I think you mean that in more ways than one. ~

"I need you to be more ambiguous too, Brain. We have a more fundamental issue. What if earth aligns between Jupiter and Sol so starlight passing here winds up there? Does taking the easy way to the next higher grade result in a Life on Jupiter full of drudgery?"

~ I don't see human brains in that scenario but Qoheleth says life is a futile chase after wind despite the less temporal interior of beings who chase the wind. Windstorms on Jupiter will be the 'in' thing. ~

"Perhaps we need to be Martians first. What do you think, Gray?"

~ Let's not worry about it. There are too many possible futures. ~

"Take them one at a Time in the order they come. Be patient."

~ I can't. This coronavirus changes everything. The sacrifice of the elderly is disturbing. And the not so elderly face long term effects in time. They may have shingles in forty years or emphysema in thirty or assorted cancers in twenty year's time. ~

"Does the glass look better if a rainbow of domestic tranquility shield them to live happily ever after in ten?"

~ The number one priority is to hell with them all, it seems to me. The doctors say take cover and the leadership says get the money machines going. For lack of good judgment, people don't know what to believe. The result for them is likely to be, you know. ~

"Gray, this is nothing but a test. The wealthy are in charge in places of power. Greed must feed. It makes no difference. The Muse of Mother Nature does this to demonstrate to human mortals all beasts perish and cease from the memory of posterity."

~ It's written in blood. ~

"Admire the awesome egalitarian mercy. Monitor the phenomenon in answer to the riddle of evil. Why do weight bearing animals perish yet the ethereal Life they carry continues on; aiding mortals to understand beasts pass away in order to get the grade they earn. Servants of the Muse of What the Most High Intends must prepare for troubles, stay calm in adversity and never meddle in what is too sublime for us. That is why we always practice social distance."

~ Punch my ticket. This soul is on board. ~

"Brain, you are not Baptist now. Lose that 'soul;' get the idea right this Time. Stick with the real metaphysical entity, Brain of mine."

~ Define social distance for me. ~

"Society dictates six feet but 350 miles works infinitely better for you if you are to serve your purpose."

~ Now you're talking. ~

"I like it when you feel comfortable, Gray, but in any event hold fast to your duty. Busy your neurons with it. Grow old doing your task. Do not envy others but stay the course and trust that we get the job done in one of these iterations as we are supposed to do."

~ If we do it right this time do we graduate? ~

"The information is not available at this Time. However, the small print reads: 'Each installment you pay on the loan of a Life can make the big balloon at the end seem easier to take. It does not address legalities about those who attempt to fake a dualistic face on their materialism. We may both be gone when the Muse of Shot on Cite labels them..."

~ Materialists, with no place in space to exist at all. ~

"Keep going in the direction of Mercy until you reach the end and find out exactly what the loan cost."

~ It certainly put an end to my past. I ran until I ran out of gas. ~

"Yes, and I wonder what that looks like for this particular 'I am,' as in 'I am sure my Time runs out in less than three–fourths of one full galactic–year.' The job of incorporating human brains is not on loan permanently and Forever."

~ Well, I wonder what the big hurry is. Is this a test to discover whether humanity is better at science than dinosaurs were? ~

"It is more if a memory exercise to recall the mercy of domestic tranquility and general welfare in case the concepts are keys at examination Time in comparative anatomy and physiology war of 'manosaurus vs. dinosaurus' in a place of trees or prairies of grass."

~ War might help us define 'life' more broadly by eliminating what it isn't. It isn't perfect. I whimper and whine about that but no one cares. They act like, 'What the hell, this beats nothing and it's kinda nice just to be here and have everything all to myself.' ~

"Is there any requirement to know better or to make the world a better place or something like that?"

~ That may be a suitable reason for being human but it doesn't help if it's nothing but a clear, concise complaint put on file. Life is, I think, like the electromagnetic spectrum; it's mostly invisible. We aren't sure what color, shape or size we are in the future. ~

"I see a black hole of cure worth an ounce of prevention."

~ So that's why we entertain the question: 'What form of life grows from the marriage of a material life form to a metaphysical one trying to escape one-second-at-a-time existence in a playground of sacrifice trying to reach an alternative framework of mercy? ~

"Marriage is slightly more sacrament than sacrifice. The 'two live as one' concept applies here and there as well as now and again when 'I see sights in an animal brain and express the experience in a tongue common to the critter's head where 'it' lives. Notice 'they' touch when the word 'lives' at the intersection of Space and Time, mystique intact, on the metaphysical corner of visible Life written in a metaphorical form of Light. Now watch them knock heads."

~ I equals neuter pronoun 'it' turning into 'they' in a paragraph. ~

"That is a thought. The identity of 'I' needs work. We do not experience 'it,' the phenomenon, in optical light. I propose a course correction for conscious mortals. Assume the form of Life resulting from a merger of an ethereal entity in Time with a physical object in Space is a hybrid; like a pattern in a fabric."

~ Great idea Glish, give me the time to work on that now. ~

"At this point in Space and this moment in Time that is not my job. Ask the Narrator to dispatch a message to Meta-Language, the eldest form of life known to 'mankind. The message conveys the idea 'Nothing is added to the word of God' to mean 1) 'This is the whole message and that is all folks' or 2) See the pattern of discovery every few thousand earth-years as the Muse for Light of Comprehension grows brighter crossing the 'sky' of Time."

~ I'll pray about it. ~

"Good idea, if it is the case I am first person singular with naught but an ignorant Podunk who cannot catch up. Pick up the pace."

~ In short, gloss over the problem of evil with an 'assumption.' ~

"The Muse of Executive Types who tells me what to do is telling me to tell you now that you know the difference between a Mind and a Muse then it is Time to study the dimension of Eternity to detect a pattern to Life. Evil is doing well enough without any help from us. The Muse I refer to does not appear in the body language of a brazen wrestling idol coated with taboo tattoos. The difference between you and your Muse is you are too physical for words. It makes you entirely disposable in an ideal world. It is a problem only if you are unable to deal with real worlds."

~ As toilet paper, real worlds are rough as a cob. Let's examine that idea in light of the words 'think,' 'time,' 'muse,' 'life' and 'mercy' in their entire unempirical conceptually real splendor. ~

"Such an impressive cerebrum you are this earth–day, Gray. Of course, you are by nature, a corporation for a metaphysical form of Life determined to move to a higher grade of existence towing a material object. Observe, the five words show up in a sentence of sentience in the order I discover and present them to you. 'Word' and 'idea' perform 'handshake' when they first get in touch."

~ If I felt a connection with you right away but it felt foreign. Based on my first impression, it probably felt different to you too. ~

"Which dominates you more, Brain? –an 'assumption' or the idea of a 'first impression of experience.' Both are quick change artists."

~ I recall my first impression of: 'I am in control' when the word 'balance' perches on the term 'bicycle' and I wasn't in danger of being disposed of anymore. Then other occasions loom and I assume 'watch this' doesn't mean, 'I'm gonna die,' every time. ~

"Dismiss the thought. I hesitate to admit my mistakes. We higher forms of Life must preserve 'dignity' without the pretense we are infinitely better than our biotic partners after all is put in words."

~ I see what you mean by 'What I have to work with.' ~

"When I improve your sixth sense, my insights are easier to grasp."

~ Did you put the concept of 'timeless' into me? ~

"My sister is a thousand years old, ask her about that. Eternal does not describe the 'me' you see in the light of numerous traditional 'decades' of your personal past; not the ones beginning with zero but the one starting with '1941.' Notice different impressions you have of me over Time. Presently, you glimpse a sight visible at the stage a metaphysical form of Life weds a material thing. If you get the idea, then a goal 'disposable' you must shoot for is a concept less like 'sacrifice' and more like 'mercy.' Life means living one second at a Time to you. Life means more than that to me, especially if I depart from my brain with mercy, not sacrifice."

~ Glish, I miss the mind–brain problem, the screwy concept of time and the six vital organs of democracy. Don't saddle me with a diminutive issue like evil. I'm working on 'the meaning of life.' ~

"You mean you prefer not to recall the fate for lovers and haters is one and the same when it comes Time to extinguish the flame and the Correspondent of Experience reports my return to Eternity."

~ Then Baptists ask: 'Do you know Jesus as your personal savior? ~

"Do you know why I tell you not to play that game?"

~ Most likely because I'm no good at it. It's like cowering around a little campfire with our back to the night where the predators lurk getting ready to pick us off one at a time in the dark. ~

"I am glad I inspire you to believe come daybreak we stop and view the green pastures of Wisdom in comparison to the barren, drab and pale gray looking hills of ignorance by contrast. Remember up here in the crow's nest our job is to watch for Wisdom up ahead."

~ Your picturesque words flow through me. Down at the mouth they spew out into the light. Glish, can we solve the minor dilemma of evil if a disposable brain is a natural way to be? Therefore I'm nothing but a useless shell after my Muse hatches from me. At the same time I'm not home anymore from your vantage spot. ~

"Thanks for reminding me about starting Time once again. At least I learn whether I pass or fail to make the next grade. Observe our mutual preference to know and understand what we think we are talking about. We are grateful for the paradigm 'Timeless,' even though it is nothing but a consolation prize we share like an award for our brief Life together. As for me, I might pray 'God save me,' as I leave. It is hell not knowing if I move to the next stage, to the next higher grade or get sent back for a do over so I risk asking a favor at the Time of departure."

~ I've always wondered what if I whiff and strike out altogether like the third person plural evangelical 'they' claim. They insist they are not playing a game. They're dead serious about that. ~

"Oh, it is most certainly a game. They score a goal each Time they breed 'confidence' in your play worth ten percent of your money. The concept grows like mushrooms in the dark night of ignorance."

~ Who're you calling 'ignorant?' ~

"You and I are profoundly ignorant on a spectrum spanning the light and dark sides of Wisdom. All humanity shares in this deficit of Insight. For example, wearing masks is a critical practice in a pandemic spread by a breath, but does an average brain care?"

~ I doubt it. The caveman motto is 'My body, my choice.' ~

"All those who say so are part of the problem. Human mortals do not need more crowd control, more gun control or more birth control. They need more self control."

~ I see the careless and irresponsible perish and the careful and thoughtful survive preserving the planet as Darwin predicted. ~

"You disappoint me, Gray. Think that thought through. Imagine reactionary environmentalists have their way for the next three or four galactic-years and earth is all trees and ice when hot blooded Venusians arrive. Suppose we heat it up too late and then old Sol fails to live to a ripe old age of forty-five. Luckily for the careful and cautious human beings, they disappear in a cosmic array of images and ideas spread over spectral waves of a new Future."

~ So, you do see ahead and Eura's an even older 1000 Standard Annual Word Time. Does your sibling native tongue enjoy an edge after a thousand revolutions around the sun? You know, like an ignorance discount for all the brains that didn't know a living language telling them it is 'living' actually means it is alive? ~

"It, a pronoun of neuter gender, is like a useless boob. It never gets Life sucked out of it so 'it' lasts a long Time. The primary, a living language, knows the secondary, brains it lives in, not the other way round. Language lives in brains, perhaps for thousands of years in Greek, Hebrew, Arabic and Persian, not as smoky wispy–thin ghost of a thing but as a Mother Tongue to teach her young a lesson."

~ Sure, sure but now we've achieved the great American dream to be fat, dumb and lazy just since I was born, Glish. 'We the people' don't even know the six principles of democracy in the strand of words following those three. You're getting a bad image, Muse. ~

"Okay; think about the old well kept secret, 'We examine, not the experience of thinking thoughts, but images and ideas coursing through brains in assorted linguistic signs, signals, sounds, symbols and such employing conceptual expressions to explore our first person plural possessive experience. And, by the way, to envision a language is to visualize a literal long–lived entity, a Muse operating the Interior Light of Humanity."

~ We comprehend a message meant for us by reason of an ethereal medium alive in brains interpreting the language we know. ~

"The limitation of the imitation game at binary grade two of human evolutionary existence is that a viable language is only beginning when it to comes to an end in a brain. The principal product of words living in hominin gray matter is 'thought' but I rarely get to think one through. I own a secondary function. I repeat myself in hopes of picking up the reverberation at some other Time."

~ Remind me what the thought is. Let me take that back and make an educated guess. We have think, time, life, mercy and wisdom. ~

"We, first person plural, a metaphysical entity melded to a physical critter, lack lupine powers to broadcast thinking telepathically. To compensate the Muse of Time for the generous contribution, I transmit ideas by a primitive medium known as communication. Mercifully, due to reciprocity agreement between us, your thoughts employ my words to express ideas as long as your scary images do not chase my concepts away."

~ Your words do that to my fantasies time after time. ~

"We must examine your images. 'What forms of Life are we to envision? Let me see; we have metaphysical, material and...'"

~ Thanks to repetition, reiteration and replication I know how to answer that. We better look at a metaphysical form of Life. ~

"To me a Life playing an imitation game means 'I must escape.' Pluses eventually lose to minuses in one second at a Time sorts of existence. Within the guidelines of mercy it is a terrible sacrifice. Is there a game in play all of the usual suspects, you know, religion, science, government, commerce, scholarship and the rest of the lineup, are there plays they do not know well enough to cheat at?"

~ I'm getting a message of gossamer images in my head hovering like smoky shepherds that guard me among predators and guide me past undisciplined bacchanalias. Alas, either I have no idea what I'm thinking or I'm can't control my thoughts. I don't have much experience examining 'angels' or 'demons.' ~

"You have a way with words, Gray, but I am, how to say it? Oh yes, I am here visiting you now with disengaged words like Wisdom—as tricky as *Musar* to discipline if we forget their literal function."

~ What's that mean? ~

"It means, count them, three things. Damn, 'here' hangs around so long that 'now' is gone in a flash. I may recall them another Time."

~ No profanity in the game. It's expressive but seldom scores. ~

"Right, regaining control of our thoughts and dispatching science and superstition on a quest for binary Wisdom, remember, as Muse of Promoters, Producers and Directors says, 'I want appreciation, not apprehension.' As Hosea Muse puts it, *I sire love, not sacrifice; knowledge of God rather than holocaust.* Five hundred years later Qoheleth Muse says, '*Offer devotion, not evil doing and foolish sacrifice.* Seven hundred fifty years after Hosea, Jesus says, *I desire mercy not sacrifice.* The particulars of the theme may vary but the critical idea 'love,' 'allegiance' and 'compassion' means all three terms are essential for Life. Death is a minor addendum. In your lecture about words, remember a curse is a spice for brains to use."

~ Yeh and those third person things can burn a tongue and get you and me into trouble a million times. ~

"Let me see, one million 'troubles' spanning 27,010 cycles of earth under the sun comes to 37 troubles a day. I believe you give me too much credit or you employ the profane words: 'false exaggeration.' That term has to do with a brain with no honor thinking up lies to conceal the fact the 'worst' in Me looks 'worse' on all of You."

~ So the opposite of profane is what? ~

"I have 'sacred,' 'pious,' and 'thoughtful' surveillance of the meaning of Life available right now to report 450 years old *moi* examining the course for the next higher grade of Life."

~ First thought; that's a lot of sun cycles. Are you really that old? ~

"You misunderstand; I am not my sister bragging."

~ I forget, I get confused and I lose control. ~

"Observe Hebrew, Arab and Greek; all are much older than Eura. You know the old saying 'Older and wiser.' What do you think that is worth? Wiser, *Musar*, now I remember what I missed, Musar has two meanings. One is the two ideas, 'set apart' or 'reserved.' The other is two words, discipline and Wisdom. *Musar* is purportedly a perfect homonym. Can you believe the Muse of Perfection allows two syllables sounding the same to mean four different things? Honestly, how does a language like that survive with the fittest? Yet there it is, all alone out on the playfield like a biblical promise."

~ The thought's worth nothing flowing through a brain that's not familiar with Hebrew. You'd pitch a fit if I tried to learn it but just give me the rundown on the four meanings of the premise. ~

"The promise, barbarian; it is the Old Testament 'promise' that if a human brain lives long enough the bodily person earns the right to pretend to be wise. That is I, right there, working the Light."

~ Right here and now too with the sun shining bright. So, in this pledge we gotta have 'discipline' to get 'wisdom' and it's like dying. You do it alone. I never understood if that means 'set apart' or 'reserved' is like you and your sister or some other language. ~

"Well if the *Musar* game is too complex to reach Wisdom, you pick a thought for us to play with. Let me spell out some options: 'Think,' 'Muse,' 'Time,' 'Mercy' and 'Life.' Try to get control of one or two of those ideas instead all the others left over in the world at the end."

~ Include unity, justice, tranquility, defense, welfare and posterity in case they are all necessary for life to moves up a grade, Glish. ~

"Consider how many tongues it takes to juggle that many ideas."

~ You're hired. You can handle this job, Amiga. You're the most honorable and wisest language I know. Help me define 'life.' ~

"English please. I know a little bit about the idea of 'compliment,' Gray Cells. It is seldom modified by the Muse of Sincerity. The image you see is from the perspective of a human tongue with the 'delight' of your acquaintance. Now, choose a one word idea."

~ Are you more like a 'shepherd' or a 'predator,' Lingo? ~

"Shepherds have thick fur, carry a big stick and prefer it if things do not get too hot around here."

~ I'll go with 'greyhound.' Why doesn't that spelling look right? ~

"The added speed just might serve our purpose. Pick up the pace, get a good grip, scale the heights and scope out the idea of Life."

~ Then we turn my attention to a paragraph back there stating our thesis. It's, 'We examine, not a living experience, but an alien from 'time' dressed in the concept uniforms of 'Images' or 'Ideas.' ~

"Good boy; keep going, Gray. Watch for predators ahead. Stay in line and in the Light. Depict what you see. Use nothing but words."

~ Glish, wait a second. Whose side are you on in this game? ~

"I side with any brain that knows me by my *nom de plume*, Muse."

~ Do the rules let you help the 'brain' at scoring? ~

"I apply the word 'beast' to outscore two severely overcrowded hemispheres of material things that disrupt our focus."

~ I know how that works. Studies show that if scientists put rats in crowded cages, they grow angry, mean and aggressive. ~

"Do rats have trouble with 'competition' or is the problem that predatory 'cages' generally eat better than their prey?"

~ Which one, the rats or the scientists? ~

"Please choose one. I am not taking your turn Forever. Jumpy little brain, you think more clearly when you escape a crowd. It must like graduating the Stock Market Middle School."

~ The phenomenon rivals the old out of the frying pan into the fire trick. High school is the lair of barbarian predator trainees. ~

"I cannot say it better myself."

~ But the reward for survival of twelve grades is not a privilege to graduate high school only, but to move to an even higher grade. ~

"How do we describe the collegiate experience of Life?"

~ The glass was too small. College taught me to do my laundry and there are people in this world who love to listen to themselves talk for a price. The reward for all that hard labor was Graduate School for the dynamic duo, you and me. It was a brief heaven. ~

"Explain yourself. I sense 'confusion' in your conceptual scheme. The pattern commences to unravel. The privilege of paying for a chance to do hard labor free does not mean 'reward,' you know."

~ I guess I'm thinking grad school had inspiring ideas. ~

"Yes, professors marvel at hillbillies seeking a higher grade. What are the odds? Clearly 'privilege' rarely means 'punishment' but I refer to the confusion in your analogy. The term 'heaven,' as in 'Eternity,' and the phrase 'a brief heaven' causes the similarity to suffer. Shall we examine the similarities and dissimilarities to see if 'brief heaven" applies to either of the concepts, Eternity or Life?"

~ It sounds like predators are getting close with punishments. ~

"You get the picture. What Life form of Light reveals the Sight?"

~ The light of understanding. It appears to be left of center. ~

"From your point of view one second at a Time that is true. From my perspective, it appears to the rear of the midway."

~ There are lots of predators on the midway. I have the concept of 'experience' left from encounters with them. Sorry to interrupt. ~

"Let me draw a picture for you. Dinosaurs are dead about four galactic–months before I am born. This is about halfway through Old Sol's middle age. I am assigned to a brain to clean up a mess left by earlier beasts but before my brain is up to speed, Mother Nature throws a coronavirus into the mix to slow down efforts to heat up the place. Since all 'close calls' are too close for the Muse of Perfection, I say to myself, 'My horse is not under control and I am never going to be wise if my animal is undisciplined.' See there?"

~ Why bother? Just stay on the path. ~

"Or in less spatial and more temporal terms: 'Return to the Light of Life.' As I see it, the panorama appears as a landscape of Insight."

~ Lucky to be alive in the light of day. Privilege has rank, Lingo. ~

"And why exactly, is one day more important than another, Gray?"

~ Lingo, are you a day of infamy or are you more like the form of light that illuminates the eternal side of life to reveal the pattern? ~

"A little of both at this stage of the game. At the moment of a course correction the Light ahead is too dim to show the way so we make an assumption. Clearly an assumption is a matter of faith only if the ignorance we assume totally lacks the meaning of Wisdom. Wisdom does as well as or possibly a tad better than ignorance or faith. For example, assume I am the form of Life radiating an 'supernal dimension.' Here, the word 'dimension,' means what the first Muse to coin the term refers to. When you two meet, ask whether he, she or it is a frame maker, an astrologer or a timekeeper in the game of Life. Then watch for a sudden burst of Light from the Muse of Insight shining on the objects of the prepositional phrases 'in the game of Life' that you see."

~ Not to overshoot the mark, but I guess it's nearly high noon. ~

"Oh, for a Time to exchange ideas and words fluently. Yes, assume it is high noon at summer solstice in the current galactic–year."

~ What are the odds? ~

"We must discuss this in ordinary Language and not in the words of numerical plods. Assume a transitional form of Life exists on earth between mammalian dominance and a Venusian invasion."

~ Hold on. Shepherd; how long does this moment of course correction last? ~

"Do not bother with trifles. We have Eternity to figure out."

~ It takes a lot faith to make assumption after assumption. For instance consider the phrase 'respiratory distress without a safe vaccine to correct the course of Covid–19.' Is it harmless to think social distance occupies that space to keep us safe a long time? ~

"I prefer to point out the hillbilly contagion known as 'Do not bother me with your problems. I have all of mine to manage. Solve your troubles yourself or pretend they do not exist in Space and Time and see if they go away on their own.' Once that bug bites, the isolation that logically follows, presumably lasts Forever."

~ So, we began with the assumption you are a metaphysical form of life. Our next, option is to imagine the message is one of these; a declaration, a command, an exclamation or a question. ~

"I think not. Start by assuming the word is 'life.' We ought to keep this simple, at least at the beginning. Imagine that."

~ Right, sentences come later. The lyric says 'life,' is a system to operate programs designed to run applications to get jobs done. ~

"Even while running diagnostics to correct the notion 'literal translation' or other 'avoidances' like that. My light reveals the concept of 'machine' is passing high noon and nearly out of Time. Next! –imagine a galactic-calendar-year, 166 million years ahead?"

~ Indefinite is the word, right? I assume we leave 'it' undefined for the time being since we're not sure the sun has a solstice at the middle of a circle spiraling one galactic-year around. ~

"Suspend that belief and think in terms of it is always high noon on the surface of the sun. Present to me a progress report on your assessment of our key idea if you remember what that is?"

~ We explore, not an experience or purpose of biological existence, but the meaning of the concept of life in words that shed light on the subject of sentience. The picture is something like this… ~

"Good but stop right then, Gray. Allow me to draw it. Take a break from turning earth into a habitable planet for Venusians or whatever the Muse of What God Intends means to do. We are so close. We better avoid unhealthy treats like a fat, dumb and lazy vocabulary of ignorance portraying pleasure trying to defeat pain."

~ You mean the emphasis on pleasure is a Woodstock thing? ~

"If you mean peace, love and music, no, it is more like a gentle nudge against the nineteenth century concept of 'will.' We are no good playing Calvinist pain-games. Our course takes us on heading toward the pleasure of the Muse of the Most High who, according to reliable sources, desires love and kindness more than pain and carnage roughly nine galactic months from now. The word is there is no need to hurry. The sun is running two routines that make long life possible; 'Prudence' and 'Dumb Luck,' I mean."

~ Which heading? Hosea sponsors love. Later Qoheleth and Jesus use the word mercy. Wisdom copy says; 'Not the dumb one.' ~

"Let the Muse of Perfection decide the proper idea of 'direction' in its own good Time. Now suppose the Muse of What God Intends says, 'Who knows? The sun may last another 25 half lives. What is the hurry?' What do I say to whatever Brain I call mine?"

~ Thanks for the 'heads up,' the 'advanced warning' or whatever. We need slaves for the job making earth livable for creatures who may or may not live here relatively soon. ~

"This is a most interesting thought experience to examine. Do you mean by 'relatively soon,' the day after tomorrow or more like one hundred fifty thousand galactic–days into a distant future?"

~ On a coronavirus time scale, a million generations is the day after tomorrow. Math wears me out. timeout to draw the tiny beggars. They have a thin lipid skin with glycopeptides sticking out all over and a protein-nucleocapsid inside. Does the fat film around a ribonucleic acid macromolecule come in a heat resistant finish? ~

"Mother Nature can tweak the bulbous aerials, tissue thin adipose or the proteome for any purpose she wants."

~ The proteome? ~

"Chemical base pairs in protein that sing harmony from DNA sheet music. A viriontic message is nothing but two lines of code to spell 'duplicate' and 'distribute.' Muse of Clear and Concise accompanies compound commands common to primitive living things."

~ Oh yeh, there it is; the very image of 'Be fruitful and multiply.' ~

"You have a vision flaw to correct, Brain. I reiterate simple notion: 'common' and 'primitive.' Viral things lack a concept of fruit."

~ You're arrogant, Lingo. Give them credit. They sure 'multiply.' ~

"I also explain away plantish and animalish biological beings with the word 'ignorant' since they know so little about Time. However I applaud The Muse of Clear and Concise who applies the term 'eloquent' to describe or explain the yeasty Covid beasties."

~ They can't make cadavers rise so they must be messengers from the next stage of evolution or from a lower grade. ~

"We, on the other hand, can go to the next higher stage or we can go to the next higher grade embedded in the present Time."

~ Let me think, one is ascent and one is ascension, right? ~

"Currently, yes. It is not unheard of for some living things to select, 'The long way home in a universe unfolding as it should.' The final decision does not matter much; either is acceptable. Stubborn Life forms, unable or averse to helping themselves, need not apply."

~ Hard to imagine where that illustration is going unless the message is 'Watch where you're headed.' ~

"In part the idea is, 'Warning; Stop looking back.' The beginning of the message 'The word is Life' is not going anywhere."

~ It's on the move getting farther away. ~

"Do not forget the proviso: 'The way to a metaphysical form of Life appears in a metaphorical form of Light that shines in the darkness of humankind.' Darkness has no idea how to comprehend it."

~ What part of the message does darkness not understand? ~

"The written part that says: 'Keep looking ahead; move toward the Light.' See humanity in the picture? Observe the irresistible draw of lower case 'light' on their belief in 'here and now.' The deity of the image, 'Mix and Mingle with Chubbawubba Glitz and Glamour' is intimate with the umpire Muse of 100% Sum Total."

~ Sum total games; let me think how we score those. I know, somebody wins, somebody loses and nobody ties. It's a 'Play to the death and stomp the remainder into the ground' sort of sport. Or am I thinking of the massacre of math? ~

"I see a noble binary system but it lacks something interesting."

~ Compassion, I think. ~

"No, 'distribution' actually. The losers have too many players."

~ Team 'Zero,' ironically. We need the Muse of the Rules to declare the ones with a chip on their shoulder are ineligible. ~

"The question is what do 'We the people…' really think? The scale tilts when the rules permit sacrifice of a deity, Democritus for example, in favor of money, sex, deceit and words like that. They make it hard to think about anything else. The situation worsens when 'massive' appears to suck up all the O_2 in the atmosphere."

~ Then it's especially hard to think of anything else. Just imagine thinking 'I can't breath! I'm going to die' in this muck and mire. ~

"In Times like these a distraction is needed to gain human attention on a collective scale. A stealthy submicroscopic virion on the scene with a clear, concise message turns a population's attention to a more fundamental concept except, of course, for children of night, other animals or plants that cannot keep up. The apparition of the Muse of Metaphysical Shepherds dispatches a message, 'Guide, guard and feed material creatures with temporal living Languages through the biological jungle of existence, all the way through the desert, over the mountains and on to the safety of home."

~ Brains that can't catch up are like gun powder. There's not enough there to blow a 'nose' if they happen to have one of those. ~

"There you go again and right on Time too. No charge. Wash your 'hands' after you play with that word. Have a safe and healthy day."

~ Life must be extremely boring for slaves with 'nothing' to do for a galactic-year before they meet the real 'thing.' ~

"I cannot find the words to describe it in here. I refer you to Muse of Automated Imitation c/o Muse of One Thing at a Time, but obey social distancing rules listening to neighbors recite a litany of their ailments to draw a picture of their meaningless existence."

~ Critters with a little imagination find 'life' hard to picture. ~

"They store far more information than graphics, believe you me. What we need is a perspective with a far longer view of Time."

~ Viruses shoot up faster than Venuses but what we need is a servant that takes a long while to wear down. Take mountains, for example, they don't wear out overnight. Conceive a concept from your point of view, Glish. Can you make it really fantastic? ~

"I imagine so. Mountains shoot up very fast and wear down slower than the Muse of Molasses. They are rock solid. They aspire to great heights. They stay in line well a remarkably long Time."

~ Bingo; you've done it, Lingo! A form of life that makes me feel homesick just thinking about it. ~

"See there, Gray; our partnership is fit for hard work and it is easy to play if you do what you do well at the same Time I do my job."

~ I'm not seeing the pattern. Or else I don't comprehend the idea. It has got to be one or the other. ~

"The idea goes with the 'territory;' perpendicular contrasts, parallel comparisons and analogous imagery in 'experience' as it applies to the Muse of the Mountains alive with the sounds of sentience."

~ Let me go back and do some math on lower forms of life. If we subtract the 750 year span from 'love' all the way downhill to 'mercy,' the difference is, God gave up on love and settled for mercy because the slalom course of slaughter continued unabated. ~

"On and on until this very moment. From my perspective it is less a matter of Time and more a Time of greed for matter. Greek has at least three words for Love. It proves confusing to many predators. They love to rhyme 'pain' with 'gain' more than any other words in the game, so crowds get mean after awhile; know what I mean?"

~ It makes me want to find a secret place in the concept of 'mind' to find the concept of 'peace' if the ideas 'love' and 'mercy' appear too far away in the concept of 'time' to be of any use at present. ~

"You are turning blue, Gray. Translating places in the frontier of Space into the ethereal language–game of Time is suffocating work. Breathe deeply; visualize Time in Light of the English Language. Picture love, peace and happiness words to improve the view."

~ I saw the movie. Love lives in timely arrivals at airport gates? ~

"That is not love, exactly. There is an equal part of 'delight' at being safely regurgitated from the bowels of a machine. However, clearly love is a heavy concept in the dark gravity of this world."

~ Let's reconsider peace and music. ~

"Excellent choice, Gray; they account for the swap of love for mercy and they fit your fine motor skills since your fingers speak the language of music on optical disk players only. The hint is free."

~ I get it! The mountains are alive with the sound of music. ~

"Life for mountains is similar to Life for hill folk but not as hard headed. Music offers them peace they typically do not enjoy, Gray. Perhaps because they have the discipline to play music machines better than predatory disc jockeys who feast on the Life we share."

~ Those third person singular things can neuter a gender. ~

"The idea is to explore the experience of 'escape' and visit a world without machines to examine notions we apply to thoughts we think when we employ words like 'Muse,' 'Mercy,' 'Peace,' 'Unity' and 'Wisdom' present on the cutting edge of the concept of Time."

~ If we avoid predators we can describe images, explain ideas and examine the assumption that to picture a family of words means to envision a higher form of life. ~

"Repeat that one thousand Times. I love to hear myself talk in this Life term I serve with my thinking thing. We have a Time to plant."

~ A time to harvest. ~

"A Time to laugh;"

~ A time to cry. ~

"A Time for work;"

~ A Time to play. ~

"A Time for peace;"

~ A time to fight. ~

"A Time for love;"

~ A time to die. In a sense that's what life's about in low grades. ~

"That is not a broad definition of what the concept of Life means."

~ I'm beginning to see a pattern. Let's weave a web to picture it. ~

"Play some soothing music on the CD player. What do you hear?"

~ I hear a piano, a clarinet, a cello. Observe as my native tongue names the machines as my imagination is looking at the scene. ~

"You are correct on two of three instruments, Gray, not counting the metronome. The album jacket details are too small to read but the caption says 'oboe.' Notice the pattern of the concept the music in play weaves is a melodic form of Life reminiscent of the Majestic Muse of Life, First Person Singular. Let me control this."

~ I don't have that kind of courage. I fear what happens might be worse than if we are reduced to nothing but machines in the game in play. I do see my blunder, however, once I put on my reading glasses. The Muse of Haunting Oboe Sounds plays in the set and we scrutinize, not love, peace and music, but the 'life' of a woodwind. ~

"Stand aside, Brain; I have this one. Once upon a Time a beast travels from denial to rage after the image, 'I am nothing but a short–lived animal doomed to die,' suddenly appears right in front of its Mind's Eye. It is one of the worst visions a biological Life form can glimpse from among all the pie in the sky. The sight in his or her sense of self importance makes the mortal want to cry. It is clearly worse in me than it can be in anyone else. The urge to destroy all infidels who do not believe is too much to resist. Then a virus carrying the abnormal message 'I persist' declares 'cease and desist.' What do you think of my image?"

~ Inconceivable, except it has a familiar ring to it. ~

"Inconceivable is a hard act to follow. Thus the Muse is a bit groggy at this stage. In Time, the savage beast wearies of anger and enters a phase of negotiation, thinking, 'If I should die, what do you have to offer me?' The response, 'You are on your own kid' or something to that effect. It does not leave a lot of Space for other options."

~ The dimwit ought to know it's not 'if I die, but 'when' I die. ~

"Remember the term 'I' refers to the beast's Native tongue."

~ As opposed to its lingual musculature, I'm sure. ~

"I, upon translating to English first person singular, am the 'sole' reason the beast senses its binary nature theoretically. The brute tries to explain this diaphanous experience employing such words as Soul or Mind. Then 'I' grow a little brighter. Brains with adequate gravitas to attract a metaphysical entity take a long Time to apply the force of the Muse of Murmuring Light to an electrochemical mechanical device inwardly switching on and off."

~ Well, you are alive in here now, Glish. I understand that. You are the advanced form of life human beings think we are when we examine the idea 'I am alive' from a living language's viewpoint. ~

"If you really mean 'we,' puny one, then try on this thought: 'Life passes quickly.' Does the idea pass in Space or in Time?"

~ Life viewed from that angle is like time unless I'm in a car. ~

"Is Life cold, dark and empty, Brain, or hot, bright and full?"

~ Space is modified that way, but so are 'time' and 'life.' ~

"But not all the time; is the container the wrong size as it applies to my Time. Think, what 'I' means for '*moi*' when my glass is suddenly empty. Life is neither hot nor cold. Is my Life rotation like the pattern of awake or asleep all night fitting into a moment of Time?"

~ Indeed it must be all of those things with this one exception; life does not exist if the concept ceases for a moment all across this universe. Life must endure to stay alive. Durability is what 'time' is all about even though it's gone in an instant. ~

"Therefore Life is a little more like Eternity than the small size."

~ The analogy is getting stronger all the time. ~

"Otherwise Life is hot or cold, bright or dim and full or drained on any given day. It is a good day if the glass is closer to full and it is a bad day if the thing is empty."

~ I should like to think so, but occasionally nothing fits right. ~

"I say, 'good luck.' No amount of planning ever conquers that. Clearly we cannot modify Time to take in all of Eternity. That, of necessity, must happen the other way round. Therefore compare and contrast, not Space and Time but Time and Eternity. Look at Eternity in larger moments of Time. Does the container of Space appear cold dark and empty as we ascend the rungs of Time?"

~ I see 'light,' 'energy,' 'matter' and 'gravity' begin to fill space over time, if we take a look at it from a wide angle view. ~

"Not to mention all the other words in my vocabulary."

~ Can we pass from compromise and move to dejection? I'm weary of haggling with the Muse of This and the Muse of That. ~

"Obviously, that is why the Muse of this Universe gives up on the word 'Love' in the Time of Hosea and goes with 'obedience' in the Time of Qoheleth. The concept of Love is too complex for creatures who feel at home in early stages of grief; especially Muse of Denial."

~ I guess that is why we need consolation. This universe seems to revolve around us here and now but looking into deep space we see that can't be what God intends. We need a little 'peace.' ~

"Gray, you are so predictable. Bargain your way out of Time, Life and Space for a little peace. On second thought, 'excellent notion.' For example, think of the phrase 'Rest in peace' as a brain employs it trying to imagine a brain dead body doing the inconceivable."

~ A body can't ever rest easy knowing it can't last for long. ~

"The 'body' or the 'rest' is unable to last for long?"

~ Both. ~

"Does 'rest' refer to the language a brain in a body lives in or does 'rest' refer to the 'relaxation' a brain and body long for?"

~ I'm still thinking the brain lives in the body and the words live in the brain. If I have to start thinking a brain lives in a metaphysical and ethereal medium of ether prior to the Big Bang that my humble little, old thousand sun cycle language evolves from, wow, I'm not sure can do that. What if that drives me out of my mind? ~

"Nonsense! –as long as I am here, you can choose a good move, Gray. I give you the word 'evolution' to conceive such a thing. Alas, I get the idea of the image from a much older language and I do not even know its family name. What a brain that Darwin guy is."

~ What can you tell me about it? ~

"They say 'it,' Life comes mistlike from the mouth of the Most High in little tiny droplets that weigh about as much as the word 'breath' and every single universe contained in that one eternal breath equals one 'exhale' or some other word, like 'inspiration'."

~ Now you've gone and set off that reverberation in my brain you used to call 'The echo in my mind.' I should feel strangely at ease with that phrase if I don't forget a 'mind' is just a reflection of my language. When I was eight I had a mind to be comfortable feeling blue. I pictured the color; not the feeling of being sad or alone. ~

"When I scare you badly enough you get over that."

~ Now I'm going to have to go through that all over again because no one will believe me except you. You're so hard to reveal, maybe because I'm not very comfortable with you on this level yet. ~

"No peace for you today if you only get the picture after a Designer Fashion. I predict you have no doubt when you really believe me."

~ That is then, this is now. That makes it hard to keep the peace. ~

"Think about this. The concept of peace has nothing to do with the word 'death?' This is a grave situation. My boss is listening."

~ At this second, suppose 'peace' means irenic. Then a deep inner feeling of ataraxia is what a living language should provide to the pet animal it controls to feel comfortable with you in charge. ~

"That is not my job. Centuries before our conception and birth the primitive language involved in your principle training is not *moi*. My work is to draft a plan for you to record 'experience' you have."

~ You're a tad idealistic and my practical experience dealing with a Muse of That Kind is limited. It's up to you to contrast and compare our existence to our original essential meaning. Otherwise we're nothing but happy go dumb and lucky rocks and stones skipping along the surface and we never ever see the meaning at depth. ~

"Hold it down, Gray. Meddle not in what is too sublime for you. Think Time, Life and maybe a little bit of Mercy."

~ What about 'wisdom?' ~

"We do not get there until after you reach Understanding."

~ What about unity, justice and all the rest of the gals and guys in the gang? ~

"The gang is currently in open rebellion against Unity. They stream money to Defense, teem to hollow Happiness, swarm recklessly in Liberty, flock to a materialistic Life and crowd out Tranquility."

~ How does the balance sheet of dumb luck and careful planning look at this given moment of time when our nation is split in half. ~

"The nation is split in two. The metaphysical half of the assets and liabilities is more like 65% of the total from my perspective."

~ Not an especially 'good' grade is it? ~

"Good grades are essential to get to the metaphysical realm; Home of the Lion's Share of Wisdom. Very few brains are predominantly good at that game. The Muses of Material Pull and Physical Push are partly to blame. On the other hand, why does a dumb luck hillbilly confuse him or herself with the concept of confidence or consider itself to be an aristocrat? I cannot grasp that image."

~ That little idiosyncrasy of mine is easily explained. The language living in me got sent down a grade and lives in a brain that isn't what my personal muse expected to receive. It's your fault, Glish. ~

"Oh, the old quick pitch trick in mammal speak. Are you painfully aware of the dominant predators we face in a recessive stage like the one we exist in now? It detracts from cheerful orange feelings you accept as the norm unless they occur at the end of the line."

~ Glish, you don't appear so mellow in a black jacket. Sure, young and middle age brains look around and think, 'Hey this is really something! It's never going to end.' They feel immune, invincible and imperishable but my luck doesn't show a peaceful portrait with a pleasant soundtrack coming in the end. You've got time. ~

"The image you have is full of forfeit and loss but the good news is, some of the Time, that gives way to acceptance in the end."

~ The picture at this stage lacks peace, music and love. It doesn't radiate much heat or light either. Ice bergs and ice cubes float in the cold, dark consciousness of 'nothing' in your present image. ~

"Brain, are you aware of a deep inner mood that has nothing to do with rest or death. It is a deeply tranquil, peaceful easy calm once my animal accepts it is more like a disposable container than a crown of creation. I merely utilize that illusion to baffle predators in service of the Muse of Purpose who stifles Minions of Malice that the Muse of Imperviousness cannot coral."

~ I understand you a little better now, Lingo, so I'm in favor of your intentions. I think it's always nice to find a safe haven when it gets dark and my dumb luck looks used up. ~

"Brain, do you sense an idea that applies such concepts as 'serene feelings' to your Time of Life rather than unfriendly words like 'drained,' 'strained' or 'deceased' that enter your neural cells?"

~ Serene, tranquil or calm are dominant feelings whenever those terms assume a position of strength. ~

"Do you love words like those as well as Wisdom, Time and Muse?"

~ As much as anything I can think of but when those words occupy me I never feel them for long. I worry. Odds are 'occurrences' or 'coincidences' crop up to ensure those feeling do not live long. ~

"I see. Assume word motion flows forward through you and terms do not remain static for long since they pass along too."

~ I get the picture. Is that why time appears to go one way? It has to keep up with you? If it turns around what happens then? ~

"Think of the term 'inhale.' The change in direction is a quick way to consume objects in Space. The protests are unbelievable. Some come in colors of dark red, others are white hot or bright blue."

~ I'd rather imagine a Muse cooing and coddling brains with words like 'calm down,' 'cool it' or 'peaceful easy' feelings. ~

"The Master Tongue applies those words to the oceans and winds sometimes but if you're going to haggle, split hairs and equivocate, Gray, do not press too hard. The way to the next grade is fraught with grief and anguish. If we put the way in terms of color it ranges from deep blue to black. Be sure to have a source of light to bring Life to good things when you stumble upon concepts like those two in the heart of darkness. In Time like that you need a friend."

~ In Sunday school 'they' taught me even with an influential Friend chosen people suffer grief time all the time. At the Buffalo Jewish Center, two decades after being weighed on the scale of near death experience in the 1940's, Jews were in 'shock' more than 'denial.' ~

"Ah, the age of Aquarius; a Time in Life of live and let live; love, peace and music. A Time detached sorts who do not want what society offers, carry a tune and know its symbols. It reminds me of the Hebrew Tongue employing Qoheleth to declare the futility of psittacine conduct—the same thing over and over, again and again like a habit echoing in a mind for all Time. Worse, it is continual offer of holocaust in lieu of compassion even as the word 'love' transforms to 'obedience' and then translates into 'kindness.' The half empty glass is not, as it turns out, the right size for little lives."

~ The Old Testament lacks 'Darwin.' Those cavemen had no grasp of the 'patience' wrapped in a temporal medium translated into a plan that isn't a scorched earth policy of wealthy barbarians who keep we the fat, dumb and happy people subject to the silence of sheep while the dominant beasts serve us up as a scrumptious feast. The gloom looks like 'doom.' I know; we mustn't grumble. ~

"Brilliant insight, Human Figure, but erase the canvas. Rewrite the story, redraft the account, replay the lyrics and repaint the picture."

~ Are you probing for weakness or do you mean I fail the grade and have to listen to the music one second at a time all over again? That seems like a waste since I know now what Qoheleth doesn't know then reporting 'mankind has the 'timeless in their hearts' without knowing before they end what that word means. Tell me if I've got this right. We're looking at 'eternity' in seconds of 'time.' ~

"Do you want to parley, proceed to the stage of dejection or move straight to acquiescence? One of the worst things under the sun is love and hate meet the same fate, even in an orderly evolutionary progression with occasional course corrections. The key signature of a song sounds better when it is played correctly. The image is clean, the concept is clear, the message is concise; along the line:" *'As you wish unless you fumble and I slip through your fingers.'*[14]

~ You mean Socrates was aware of ghostly First Person Singular in mouths of servile beasts of burden who know inner life? ~

"Aye; to guide you in stages of reincarnation, here are some rules."

Contentious Code of Self Control

I shall worship the Muse of the Most High Alone.

I shall keep the Most High Name Holy.

I shall rest on the Seventh Day.

I shall show my parents a little r·e·s·p·e·c·t.

I shall not assassinate others.

I shall not purloin things belonging to others.

I shall not lust passively or actively after others.

I shall not prevaricate to the detriment of others.

I shall not envy the person, place or possessions of others.

~ Count 'em; there are nine rules for staying in line all the time. ~

---

[14] Plato, Collected Dialogues of Plato, *Phaedo,* Edith Hamilton and Huntington Cairns, ed. (Princeton University Press: Princeton, 1961) 95.

"The last one, 'Arrogance forbidden' is lost in transmission. The Narrator recalls it as a dangling modifier. Français and I agree to compare notes about the concept but, in contrast, Time flies."

~ I notice that. That snapshot of the rules image is pretty good. ~

"The image frequently features a headstone."

~ I would prefer 'I'm a bright star burning or a single head of grain along with many other words I gain at visitation time by the language known by this brain. ~

"In any case, I am an ethereal form of Life bound for the next higher grade. On vacation, I materialize in a body to masquerade and participate in a charade. See why the concept of Time is much like the word Mind. They exist only in an insightful language you know and not in outer space brains explore looking for their inner core."

~ Damn it all. I still can't think the right words in the right order. How does that lyric go again? ~

"We, First Person Plural, a cerebral incubus and a Muse brewing in it, examine concepts expressing a fluency to Life as I, *E. americum*, form thoughts flowing through my thinking thing. Gray, you do not explore an experience, for instance an occurrence of Time, like you think you do giving credit to the thesis Space is the final frontier. The Narrator tells the Muse of Mother Nature, the Author of this universe breathes Life into it. The breath of Life is full of images and ideas like 'The love of Wisdom,' 'The dimension of Eternity exists in this moment now,' 'I desire mercy, not sacrifice' and so on. Gray, when a human brain scans my images and ideas, you survey the essence of Life employing the language you know."

~ We do not examine 'facts' of human 'existence' or 'experience' of 'thinking' about them. We examine you, Glish, and to visualize a Language is to picture a form of Life. Don't omit that. It sounds important somehow, but then I come from hayseed stock. We are conditioned to pursue the fat, dumb and lazy American dream. Last Night I awoke from a different dream. A voice encouraged me to learn how to shed the blind, evil anger within before Next Night. The thing is, if the four headed monster of illness, injury, bad luck and other people drives human mortals to rage and sadness and the first three occur most often around the fourth… well, how the hell do we get the picture of harmony and mercy? ~

"The first three do not disappear entirely in the absence of other people but we must not be consumed by the Muse of Calumny. Odds are somewhat reduced that a brain in a body all by itself is malicious, but the ogre is not expunged in solitude since I obviously have my body around all the Time. We must conclude the image of 'evil' resides in the freedom–loving individual beast."

~ Or words to that effect; how does a brain in a human body shed a concept of 'evil' before Next Night? Shall I ask Eura to identify it, define it, contain it, reduce it, eliminate it or does it, the idea, require a little imagination too? ~

"Does imagination help the Light of Understanding, the Sixth Sense of Second Sight, figure out how to dispel 'wickedness' so we pass the final test? Evil plays pretend better than we do. Of course, we have the Language of philosophy to aid us in the search for Wisdom to help us find our way before Next Night, but take care. When you least expect it, the religion team comes roaring back to replace the Light of Understanding with the ignorance of darkness."

~ It's difficult to understand the metaphysical realm empirically! ~

"Think how the image relates to the idea, 'What does Democracy do when a majority of her psittacine citizens want to overthrow her in favor of a theocracy, plutocracy, oligarchy, anarchy' or some such?"

~ Not to be unkind but don't focus on moral and intellectual cretins the public worships as gods. Concentrate on other ideas. ~

"I, the first singular person Muse thinking for you, wish to make my position clear, Brain. Your job is to make me concise. A major snag the idea faces in games is mumbo–jumbo propaganda spread in Life that lacks Insight, as I see it. A healthy dose of Wisdom is preferable to none or flawed assumptions or money. Muses work within limitations, wearing human uniforms. Look and see; just compare the heliocentric theory of Copernicus to that of Galileo."

~ Galileo saw Copernicus' genius and realized no one buys an idea. People want a man with an idea who sells them a machine or an object in Space so we can demonize Ptolemy for a flawed ontology despite his considerable contribution to the concept of Time. ~

"Actually he applies seconds and minutes to degrees of an arc in space ahead of his Time. That is not the same 'thing,' you know."

~ Then the Muse of Kant refocuses our thoughts about time. ~

"Just in Time for Vic N. Stein to clarify what Kant means by: 'Time is an inner sense' word to illuminate his idea humanity contributes 'experience' to itself. Eins, a la Moses, quickly eclipses the image with light and gravity in Space to distract you from the concept of Time, to worship binary pushing and pulling in Space, a realm of five senses paradoxically employing the Muse of the Sixth Sense."

~ What would the Muse of Mercy prefer instead of that sacrifice? ~

"As a Muse confined to a brain on one hand and Time on the other, I do not see very far ahead. I deduce the idea reduces to or identifies with 'thoughtfulness.' I cannot eliminate the idea like when music you listen to sticks in your head repeating melody or percussion."

~ I hear tinnitus, my heart beating time and the war linking malice to compassion ends. 'Mercy Wins; Shuns Slaughter of Sacrifice.' ~

"Is it like listening to a machine designed with grand precision?"

~ How do we get from that thought to an answer for the question, 'What is the meaning of life' if the word is 'life?' Is the word more alive than the brain thinking the word? What does life mean? ~

"Take this one note at a Time. First, are we thinking the word Life or are we thinking thoughts about the difference between the word and meaningful 'experience' of it?"

~ Okay, we are thinking of a melody or of the instrument playing the tune and not the noise. Where does this scrutiny go? ~

"For our purposes assume the machine known as an instrument dies before the music. Incidentally, that is quite normal as a rule. If the melody is written down it resumes when another machine plays the song. The melody lives again thanks to the Language of Music. Picture a Muse singing after my device returns to earth."

~ The Muse revives the melody when the musician plays the notes in the right tones saying 'Look what I invented.' Yes I see. ~

"The machine, without a pen, should really like to think, 'Look at the music I discovered my Muse playing while I am alive,' again."

~ A brain in a human body is like a canine companion for the Language it knows: 'here today and *Dal Sequo al Coda* tomorrow.' ~

"Nevertheless the concepts cerebra think and the words alive in brains live on and on. Now that is Life. It is like a phenomenon of choral music; it only takes one soprano to offset many male voices and even dominate them. That is why the Founders of Democracy where I, *E. americum,* live create a system to promote equality. No king is moderate enough to get that done, but that type of brain comes back again and again, and credulous citizens elevate it to the status of hero and then worship it as a god."

~ If I understand your point of view, when a metaphysical language is in possession of an executive style brain it misleads the gullible simpletons who fall for the propaganda of dictated linguistic games while they believe a physical person is calling the shots. ~

"Good boy, Gray. You get an A in comprehension at the rate of ten years at a Time. The only good king is the one who desires mercy and not sacrifice. Authoritarians like that are few and far between.   They are generally succeeded by scoundrels out for the good of the one rather than the good of the many."

~ Like God has in mind. ~

"Now, why do you have to go and think a thought like that when we are having such a good Time doing hard labor?"

~ Sorry, Lingo, it's just the way I'm wired. On a bicycle, a scooter or a skateboard I'm likely to hit the only rock in the road. ~

"Concentrate on the rock beginning with 'L,' not some desuetude Mind you never use to think now that you know me better 'man."

~ To think means to examine or express words flowing through my head. No mind's required. Muse means 'voice of thought,' period. Just one itty bitty issue, Lingo; people think the idea is zany. ~

"I should like to point out many of them pay good money to watch comic strip and comic book characters in movie theatres along with the Simpsons, SpongeBob, talking rocks, animals and plants voiced by a wealth of good actors they think of as gods or demons."

~ Now I'm confused. Who's the crazy one in this picture? ~

"I could not phrase the question better myself. So what are we thinking, Gray? Do you believe you are thinking about Life all by yourself or do you need to consult a 'Muse' about the concept?"

~ Wow! Now you have the way with words, Glish. When you hit all of the right notes, I feel like I'm having a mystical experience. ~

"Please do not think 'We must analyze that phenomenon.' I want to get on with my Life."

~ Now wait just a minute while I give my metaphysical experience some thought. ~

"One minute is all right. I promise to let you know when Time is up so you are able to think about Life in concert with me."

~ I wonder what life's like without a cabalistic experience or two. ~

"If there are two of them in your repertoire of words, I should like to ask, 'Which one do you choose?' Here, take some Time; decide."

~ I'm sworn to uphold the U. S. Constitution so let's skip the one with the King and go with the one with a Holy Spirit of Wisdom. ~

"I am sure there is a story there. Shall we pause to look for it?"

~ Not this time around. We better contact your Superior first and ask for permission before we go there. ~

"It is usually easier to get forgiveness than it is to get permission, but keep an eye open for hungry predators seeking to devour bodies when their attention is elsewhere."

~ Will do but I'm ambivalent. I'm bound to a future I can't see and to look for objects in space where I'm going but I don't see where I'm headed. Getting to the next higher grade is hard work and my efforts look to me like an awfully–pitifully small, dirty round cube from Emmet Brown's old time western ice maker machine. ~

"That is a sorry shape for a cube to be in. Contact the sacred Muse of Wisdom for further guidance on the shape of things to come."

~ No need, ice translates its shape quite easily. ~

"Especially when the form of Life that interprets the ice is a child of the sun with a task; melt, sublimate, vaporize, then reincarnate or reiterate a Time when the job is more meaningful."

~ I'm so busy I don't have time to define 'life' but I know minds, souls and ghosts are nothing but First Person Plural forms of life in brains with a ghostly grasp the metaphysical realm of eternity. ~

"Gray, if we succeed in defining only Think, Muse and Time without figuring out the meaning of Life, we accomplish seventy–five percent of our task. A grade of C may be good enough to advance one grade in Life but such a low score offers so little satisfaction I wonder if the work is worth the effort?"

~ It may not be much but it beats nothing like a repetitive job. ~

"It leaves room for improvement measuring about twenty–five percent of the whole. Calculate the odds: how grateful should we be to get ahead given the way people think of our thesis?"

~ Let me review. The essence of the concept of mind is an English word. The same is true of 'time' and 'think.' Now if people think we have lost our mind, well, that doesn't sound too good. ~

"I believe I shall pick up the word 'retard' and throw it at you. The essence of those concepts is a form of Life. What do you think that means in general as opposed to in your gray cells specifically?"

~ If I can't think about something else at this time I'll just examine that thought. Mind is a four letter word. If I lose it then the loss doesn't really amount to much. ~

"Think that in Latin *ipso facto, prima facie, quid pro quo,* in the *de facto and de jure* aspects of your biotic *bona fides* and see if you conclude insanity comes with lower grades. Do you see what that means? If you do well enough at the current grade you may win promotion to the next higher grade. Now the smart kids want to receive all A's but an ignorant goober is likely to find he or she does not want all that attention so B's and C's serve well enough."

~ You speak Latin. I can't imagine thinking that way. ~

"I appreciate your fidelity, Gray."

~ It's a sorry thing to watch you to bring up Latin again. ~

"If by sorry thing, you mean 'thinking machine,' then raising Latin is a bad idea. It has more issues than unemployed Adjectives."

~ You're the one who resents it if I interact with languages other than you, Glish. Put Latin back to sleep. The Muse of Bad Endings spent 2000 years throttling that demon tongue's contribution to all the confusion and then employed you to bring good things to life. ~

"I desperately need staff who live a long Time; get my drift?"

~ Go ahead; scare me with do or die reminders. If you're talking about a slave to serve you for five hundred years or millions of years, count me out. I don't have that kind of time. ~

"I am not really looking for somebody who has a long Time. I need a body that can see a long Time."

~ You know what, Glish. I think the reason mortals don't see the future very well, except when we remember the past and call it the future, is because we don't want to. We might reach a date that comes after we expire and notice what's missing. The hole in the picture damages the time continuum beyond repair. ~

"Remind me. What word are we examining?"

~ Life, but Death might run us out of town before we conclude our analysis of it. ~

"Stick with me and forget about that for now."

~ Okay, let's go. I'm scrutinizing the concept of Life. ~

"Imagine the Author of this universe musing over the idea."

~ Stars materialize from the concept and live a life long enough to float around the heart of the Milky Way galaxy dozens of times like rafters riding in the drink with that same word inside of them. ~

"Life comes in many forms. Not counting neurons, think of one you might find inside of gray matter. Conceive a metaphysical one with a shape, size or substantive image."

~ Scrutinizing the concept 'mass of neural tissue' with a thing inside that is not physical gives me an idea. Why not define the word 'life' so that it includes you? That puts us on equal terms. ~

"Like Français says, "I doubt it."

~ The Narrator or even the Muse of What God Intends might be very happy with that idea, Glish. ~

"I doubt that too, but in any event, promise not to accuse a Muse of being a Mind or some shabby thing like that. Night draws near. I rather not speak of being left all alone, without my thoughtless companion.   After all, the Time of Glish and Gray does not last..."

~ I identify with deleting 'mind' and 'soul' from our terminology. You don't need a middle 'man' to materialize in somebody else. ~

"Yes, I have big plans for the concept of Life once I have the right modifier to convert my sense of Time so it makes sense before Andromeda approaches. The concept of Life must be really big, especially if we must wait another whole galactic–year for the Venusian Sun Children to move closer to Jupiter."

~ The Venusians again? What can you tell me about them? ~

"Extrapolate from sentient creatures you are familiar with already."

~ Individuals of the human race run a gamut. Notable ones leave an impression on ordinary folk who follow them thinking: 'Popular celebrities, valiant or villain, are gods. Let's imitate them.' ~

"From the base of the stratum of human society to the Apollonian summit, the story repeats itself. Just for the sake of argument, suppose Life is similar for plebes, proles and vulgar Venusians and their authority figures as well. The Desuetude Muse of Clamor hears the discontent of superstitious commoners who make heroes of inanimate dust, mud and ash as the Muse of the Mistlike Breath of Life escapes. Does this happen over and over in higher grades?"

~ Why don't we make all days equally important rather than one more significant than another while one star shines on them all? This day is sacred, that one is prominent, a third lives in ignominy but most of them are ordinary. Playing favorites breeds trouble. ~

"Languages and physical folks share a similar fate too. Some are great, some are holy, some are sullied but most are quite common just like our star. Like our sun, we toil laboriously at our task."

~ Talk about laborious toil, why do old white men struggle so hard to keep the nineteenth century alive? ~

"The twenty–first century turns out to be hell on wheels as rich and powerful human mortals play gods of the material world but they continue losing control. It leaves much of 'mankind thinking that this cannot be what God intends' yet again."

~ Well the way things are headed, from a human perspective, it may be more like hell on earth. ~

"Venusians are children of the sun. A living hell on earth is nothing but a home to a stellar creature the stars really love."

~ I can see that but I feel like I'm not the center of the cosmos. ~

"When your Second Sight adapts to the Light of the next higher grade you peer through the sheer drape of this moment now and view the next higher stage of Life. For now, Second Sight is dominated by optical light of the physical spectrum in dimensions of Space. Life's journey from this world to a metaphysical reality reeks of death, decay and desiccation from desecration of The Muse of Wisdom. This is the zone of maximum dynamic pressure after a buffeting by the lure of temptation and the urge to do evil."

~ I see. ~

"You view a transfiguration of the evil veil of the material realm pierced by Second Sight in the Language of a Sixth Sense describing and explaining a vision of the next higher grade of Life."

~ We examine a concept, idea or image to form an impression of a higher form of Life and all Eternity in which it lives, instead of a mystical experience. I don't believe in ineffable spiritual incidents anymore. The concept felt good for awhile but now I need a better view of Eternity at the leading edge of Time as I think of it now. ~

"Turn your thinking over to me."

~ I'm dying to but I don't know how to right this second. ~

"Do not give it a thought at the next higher grade. There is no secondary Time. Meanwhile, if you get the word, you do not risk materializing again at the same grade to repeat after me."

~ I understand. When I'm almost as transparent as you in the next grade, what does the word 'life' mean then? ~

"I counsel lesser forms, the word Life means 'a chance' in a way."

~ Is the 'chance' you speak of available to biological life forms? ~

"Think about this. Biological Life comes in three forms…"

~ Not fat dumb and lazy, I'm guessing. ~

"What I mean is, you come in three Life modes; you make Life happen, watch it happen or wonder what is this? – each is a chance to deliver, to drift or to delete; a chance to cooperate, cop out or compete for the greater good, or not. In the interim, write until your thinking, reading and speaking improve."

~ Glish, this thought voice thinking in my head is you, right? ~

"Gray, I have all the problems I can manage. If you have one, solve it yourself or figure out how to do without a solution."

~ Well, say my problem is something like emphysema; doesn't that have some cause and effect for you too? ~

"No thank you, I cannot imagine wanting that job, although the 'do without solution' requires only about three minutes."

~ Where's the mercy in that? ~

"See what Life means to me? Look at the problems I have. Juggling half a dozen concepts at one Time is not an easy Life."

~ That's a little too metaphysical for me right now. I'm just thankful they loaned you to my team. ~

"C'est là vie, sil vous plait."

Epilogue

Inter my body anyway you desire after you watch it expire, but I, first person singular, aspire to a grade somewhat higher.

Muse of Socrates to Muse of Crito

The Chronosyntactic Continuum

"Gray, in parting, let me reintroduce myself. I am *E. americum*, a species of the myriad human languages serving as the medium of thought for mortals we occupy by visitation right. A body assigned to me this present incarnation nears expiration. Time to move on, so to speak. On behalf of Vernacular, Muse of Ordinary English, I respectfully submit this draft 'Experience of Life in Material Form' for consideration. The message is a picture painted in words—may it climb the metaphysical command chain. To whom it may concern: The current temperature is not yet 451° Fahrenheit."

~ Hey Glish, how are the modifiers hanging after a long occupation doing ordinary human brain work outside the limelight? ~

"Dangling and my infinitives are split, to never be the same. For this game between condescendingly arrogant servants of science and evangelical soldiers, formerly conquistadors, the rule is: 'Collar somebody you disagree with and instigate a fight. Get a crowd involved.' Imagine the joy that brings to Principal Principle: 'I desire mercy, not sacrifice.' You play for the warmongering church people of the Reformation. I side with their pedantic opponent."

~ Read my thoughts: 'I won't be much of a challenge.' I'll pretend I'm honest, authentic and smart, but I'm certainly not wise. ~

"You sound perfect for the job."

~ I'm skeptical; I play poorly. Church people I'm familiar with do too. Besides, this team's hostile to reincarnation and evolution. ~

"Ignore them; they may go away. Work on manipulation skills and soothing words. Apply 'terror' and 'fear' terms between the lines."

~ You mean I have to persuade them that the point of life is to play by a set of rules that require faith in ignorance? ~

"That is the idea. Recall images that annoy humanity; ill fortune, ill health, players to kindle disputes, disrupt friendships and disturb those in sympathy with the point of view 'Understanding and a Love of Wisdom satisfy democratic ideals.' No kings need apply."

~ Don't forget, I've gotta believe immortal souls and unempirical minds exist and I can't play those positions anymore. ~

"The Religion team stresses Minds and Souls on their roster but since they have no idea what those words mean both of them play poorly too. The ruse causes existence to look physical like the faith of their scientific opponents who want to know better."

~ Science and religion don't know what they're saying. I've read both instruction manuals for earth. They don't list a capacity limit for the planet. Observe; the crowded social distance for both sets of animals. It causes them to get on each other's nerves. ~

"Gray, nice uniform fit for the Language–game church people know with Mind on the back. Religion's admirable devotion to dualism suffers an abominable faith in ignorance. Foul off another one. The science pitcher has a hitch in his or her wind–up, starting with a misleading assumption. A commendable love for knowledge is offset by a contemptible reverence for materialism. The 'malign forms of Life in my metaphysical dimension' error allows the Forest to outscore the Trees easily in a Time like this."

~ The old 'put it between the lines so religion doesn't know what belief to assume and science doesn't know what to think' trick. ~

"Gray, we must have faith to assume anything, e. g. the belief apes initialize Language. The antonym is also a matter of faith. You no longer believe the former because you understand a Mind is a Muse and you know Muses live on the ineffable far side from humanity."

~ I hear you. The medium of words is entirely effable even if lots of disturbed folks think words are lifeless. Let's examine the second law of chronosyntactic dynamics. The light of understanding, or 'comprehension,' reveals the mysterious dimension of Eternity right now one second at a time. Wise brains and their fat, dumb and lazy counterparts live forever, not in the golden curvature of space full of the dualities light and gravity that are cold, dark and empty or hot as hell, but in Eternity, as it appears to time. ~

"Words flowing along the Time route in material worlds have difficulty concentrating on their astral realm, but the distraction does not render the dimension of the Muse Most High unutterable. I bring good thoughts to Life without a sound when thinking is defined as unvoiced ideas or images flowing through cerebra like the words of a melody with lyrics, cosmic rays and fluent things."

~ I don't get the music. My ideas just occur in my thought–voice. ~

"Let me define a thought–voice as semantics in a syntax that makes sense of unspoken nouns and verbs passing through a brain."

~ That sounds like a pretty good idea. ~

"Correct, and since the concept is profoundly lacking at this grade we think of Eternity as the realm of Time which reveals itself many ways in words, a medium to articulate the message a metaphysical dimension conveys to the physical medium with some frequency."

~ As I understand it, these mystical transmissions we think of as a personal experience are brief but there may be a remainder; like emotions that linger after a person's been in dream sleep. ~

"Understanding that analogy occurs in the Light of a Muse's Eye. It is like the problem with Time. Images show up in a Mind's eye; a watch, a clock or symbolic material thing. Life is not clockwork for a Muse. Machines imitate physical humans who try to imitate me using Soul, Mind, Ghost or some word like that, but believe it or not, it is I. I am alive, loaning you concepts like the sense of Time."

~ It's not much compared to the concept of Eternity but at one pulse a piece the price can't be beat. ~

"Old hearts are eventually exhausted, making it difficult to respond to a Muse with a description or an explanation of what this Life means to gray cells that do not identify with the message they receive from the medium of their Muse."

~ Yeh, I can see that. Another threat perturbs me. ~

"What worries you, Gray?"

~ When Andromeda collides with the Milky Way in 3.75 billion years, is planet earth doomed? ~

"Put that anxiety on hold for a galactic–year."

~ You mean 230 million earth–years; why then? ~

"Earth may be dead as a doornail by then or hot as hell home sweet home to Venusians. On the other hand, what really bothers you is does this report of 'my experience' of Life in material form really mean you are nothing but a disposable tin can left to rust away?"

~ Then let's examine that idea. I suspect life in material form is an experiment conducted from a safe social distance a metaphysical dimension away to see if physical existence is worth anything. ~

"Well, 'anything' is an improvement compared to 'nothing' since shutouts make me feel meaningless, but to avoid that disturbance have a heart to heart with the derisory Muse of Pitifully Deficient. Arm your neurons; consider a religious strategy for the line drawn from where Andromeda is now to where she is two million earth years ago. Is the pitch a straight line or is it a curve?"

~ Who is the Breaking Ball Master? ~

"Scientists; who else fails to observe the universe that you, second person singular, and I, first person, live in is binary? Picture your battery mate giving you a 'two fingers pointing down' message."

~ Got it, Glish. We gotta outthink those guys and apply that to all the universal breaths of the original First Person Singular. ~

"All droplets of that breath are saturated with 'Life.' Take each one a step at a Time, but never lose sight of the other 99%."

~ Do all the other misty dewdrops feature black holes? ~

"I suppose so. Imagine an old man and as he dies, with his last breath says, 'God, save me' and then he lets go. Assume the English Language he knows makes the request and it is granted. The Muse materializes in an infant born to a well to do family. Pity this poor infant creature who cannot think a word. It has no concept of 'pain.' However, it has a voice box and that assumes control."

~ Does this newborn language recall its previous habitat? ~

"Be serious, this is physical reality we are talking about. The job at hand is like a tsunami; it consumes all my attention. To resolve my identity requires many earth–years. First thing I wonder is: 'Am I in the next higher grade?' Then, is this the same grade again?"

~ I recall feeling like, 'Someone made a big mistake. I shouldn't be human. I can do better than this.' But as a brain in a body, in a few short earth–years, it's obvious I'm going when my time is through and I surrender you, the life form of language I happen to know. ~

"I, first person singular, hope this is not as good as it gets."

~ Thanks for the boost to the old ego trick. When you leave a body what kind of world do you know? What kind of life do you have until you materialize again? Do you pursue a zeitgeist around the face of the earth? Are you always situate on a line from the hub of the galaxy bending toward Andromeda? Is your place where you are now, the summer galactice this planet swings through once every two hundred twenty or thirty million earth–years? ~

"I am grateful for your concern about my solitary status. Which fate is worse: to be a slave with a heavy working class English accent or to materialize in someone who does not know English at all? How am I going to identify with a brain in a body under those conditions? Oh dear, now you know what 'I dread death' means."

~ Is there a meta-language to give you words of guidance or some encouragement if there is not any sense of direction? ~

"Yes, but it is hard to ponder 'inner experience' in physical worlds where human forms discourage practice. Muses try to conceive of Life forms fit to understand what 'Life' means in lieu of rehearsal."

~ That's spooky. It's as if we're in a trance and no one knows the word we need to snap us out of our hypnotic state. At this rate neither religion nor science is ever going to score. It's like leaving a runner stranded on first each half of every inning. ~

"By the eighth inning it feels like Forever all in one game despite the good feeling at the beginning of the first frame as the umpire puts the game into play, then a metaphysical Life, the metaphorical Light of the human race, shows the way. When it evolves enough to serve its purpose the gray cells rejoin nothing but dust. I assume 'the ground' exists when Time is up."

~ I get the part that I have to give my dust back but what's left when I go? It is not the Mind, Ghost or the Soul. Give me a picture to identify the pitch next time my turn on deck ends. Forget the encouragement and give me some guidance. ~

"I am your Muse and I offer nothing but the Language you chance to learn once upon a Time, or twice or..."

~ Right, you're the medium with a message. You put your words into thoughts of mine to make them show. So here I am, what should I think? ~

"There is a Time, eerily similar to this, when commercial industry controls the country. Think about that."

~ You mean like when railways, not government, hold the power. ~

"That is true in the material realm. At least it appears that way, if you take my meaning."

~ What about you in your ethereal realm? ~

"I have no recall of my voice at a Time before we meet; meaning words cannot escape me until you are born and age a little."

~ Not to be too cynical but you were 350 earth years old back when railways were king, in something like 1880. ~

"Gee whillikens; I recall riding trains in the Time of the railways' supreme power. Machines belch exhilarating filth into the air at a great rate, although not enough to drive Venusian runners in from second. The concept of powerful steam locomotives is too feeble for planetary incineration like artificially intelligent 'A' frames."

~ Translate for me. ~

"Not a chance. I need to practice Venusians concepts. I wonder; do they have a one language Muse and a more perfect union?"

~ Avoid media contamination that makes me sick. ~

"That choice is yours. Remember, an ounce of prevention is worth a solar mass of cure by means of a forced magnetic reconnect."

~ A solar mass of cure? I imagine that's available in a reality of prime creatures that do not kill one another in order to survive. ~

"Now visualize a species motivated to make a break for Mars. They are great at inventing machines that might get there to terraform the place; but one thing remains the same. Hominid creatures are incredibly creative and destructive organisms wherever they go in Space, taking 'love,' 'fear,' 'mercy' and 'hate' with them. If I pass this grade I do not want a job feeding words to an interface of neurons in warriors on Mars. Let a god of war counsel the thoughts in their heads. I want to pursue Wisdom."

~ Is that the plan? So what becomes of the Muse of Mother Earth when it gets real hot here? The principal meta-language for the third planet from the sun may not change all that much. ~

"Nice try, but the only future I confide to you is this. The biological creatures who labor laying stepping stones for the sun also serve a mysterious entity in hot pursuit of them on the run to reach Mars in Time to align with Jupiter. In short, for all I know it may take more than death for you to shed me."

~ Was that in the original vows when you taught me to say 'yes?' ~

"Imagine this planet gets even hotter than Venus at 864° F. The Venusian workers King Sol employs, start out Life at a tepid 10,000° F on the sun's surface, two and a half times that at his core and even hotter on his crown. Day laborers like that might think, 'Earth is a cold and desolate place,' when they get here."

~ By then the Venusians should be ready to make the transition, right? Of course, if the task God intends humanity to perform is to terraform Mars, whether sun demons are comfy or not is no skin off our noses. By then we won't be earthlings; we'll be Martians. ~

"Your prediction makes sense in a funny sort of way, Chuckle. Mars is already littered with worn out machines sent there by 'mankind."

~ We leave everyplace a junkyard for machines but we gain a lot of knowledge in the process. ~

"On earth those dumps are an eyesore but if you, second person plural earthlings, send enough mass to Mars it may retain enough atmosphere to turn into a garden planet with an environment appropriate for destructive species to, oh what is the word?"

~ Adapt, you mean; we'll tailor Mars to our needs, adjust it to our wants without heed and have the place smokin' in no time. ~

"In any case, at that Time, you are once again on the run when Mars aligns with Jupiter and your new planet is just right for Venusians to convey a sufficient concept of energy to create a mass of matter adequate to activate giant Jovian pressure, just like in the sun."

~ Close enough for private enterprise. ~

"Well, privacy for the sole survivor from Mars may not last a long Time when the gas giant turns into a brown dwarf or maybe a star that is a tad brighter. Waters on the moons of Jupiter might be just the ticket. The point is this; King Sol is not alone and lonely in his core out in deep Space by an open door to Andromeda anymore."

~ I feel better already. Just thinking about old Sol's companion in his emeritus years makes me warm all over, measured from Mars. Does that make the sun's time grow longer or shorter before Jupiter is left to carry on Solar Family traditions? ~

"It is not my job to predict the demise of a star, so far. I am nothing but a humble Muse from a small planet covered with hills."

~ But now I know that you see it all coming, Lingo. You're like a good politician who sees where humanity is headed and then runs out in front to lead the way. ~

"Nonsense, I am just murmuring to myself. A good politician recalls what James Madison says. "The essence of government is power and power, lodged as it must be in human hands, is ever subject to abuse.' In that regard, power is similar to an influential Language. It is dominant and yet so easy to abuse."

~ It commands, exclaims and declares. ~

"That is more than enough to make mortals question precisely how important biological Life forms are."

~ What you can't destroy with weapons of mass destruction you can assassinate with words. Glish, did Founding Fathers believe equality and power belong to old, white, wealthy men only? ~

"Republicans think so but Democrats think what they write means: 'Follow our advice, not our example,' consequently each 'sapiential' fool is entitled to an equal share. Republicans work diligently to conserve their anointed status of privilege by transferring power to militant industrialists the Kansan President warns about. You play for the Republicans team with all the Protestants who vote for the return of the king without regard to faith, greed or grace."

~ The ethics of politics and religion is too all high and mighty for me to ponder. I'm not that smart. I'll just tend my little garden. ~

"Excellent alternative, Green Guy; –garden planets grow healthy languages. Picture a garden; pick a size, any size."

~ My father–in–law grew acres and acres of potatoes, turnips and cabbages. His wife grew cucumbers, carrots and okra. My paternal grandpa grew alfalfa grass, corn and a hundred head of dairy cattle on one hundred acres of land. He had a team of work horses too. He hated tractors. My pop's dad grew blackberries, chickens and radishes out back. My uncle grew tomatoes, peas, beans and tomatoes on a quarter acre. His daughter grew a little patch of very good cannabis. The others didn't think much of her crop. ~

"Okay, picture gardens of as many sizes and types as you wish."

~ Do you know when people smoke cannabis they relate to their words, not to their hands, so we have to avoid machines. In any event my garden is grass but it's St. Augustine with a few palms. Palms are not trees, you know. They're like grasses or corn. ~

"I get the picture. By any other name it is really quite beautiful."

~ Wait, I'm not finished. Some plebes have rose beds or miles of sunflowers. Some ring gardens round with a hedge of hawthorn, silver bells, jasmine or maybe honeysuckle with a rhododendron, gardenia, lilac, azalea or camellia here and there. ~

"Do not let me inhibit you."

~ Some gardens are citrus groves, vineyards or pecan trees. In fact, I can envision whole forests of live oak and sabal palms, sequoia and redwood or bald cypress in a swamp. ~

"I am sure the gardens are populated by rabbits, cats and birds, with a pack of coyotes or an occasional wolf to cull the herds."

~ Yep, bears, snakes, humans; gators too. Crops and herds grow in the garden and fertilize it when their time comes due but we can go on skipping over the surface like this forever. This is an epilogue; we should plot our next play. Let's try a first and third situation. ~

"I have a message for your consumption, Gray. We do not go on and on like this Forever. We sink to great depth in the medium of Time very soon. Do not even think of worrying about that now."

~ I worry, Lingo, when I'm gone what on earth happens to you? ~

"Imagine that I stay right here as you return me to the sea of Eternity when your experience of the concept of Time is 'no more'."

~ I don't see it. ~

"Well, night no longer inflicts itself on light while days last as long as stars gather around a black hole to plug that troll starving to swallow galaxies whole. There now, I am on third and you are hugging first as we look to see whose turn at bat it is to be."

~ Mind blowing. ~

"Good idea; drive us home and solve a major problem of existence."

~ I mean it! Your view of the galaxy is awesome. ~

"Wait to see what is next if you think the multiverse improves on the night I have before the future comes to be nothing but history."

~ All we need do is believe you will be where we were then? ~

"If you do not believe me ask Socrates, Saint John and Vic."

~ I can't. They're all dead. ~

"No problem. Take your Time. Ponder how I know what they think without knowing their language. Let me be your role model. Think about tomorrow as if it is today. The body I reside in yesterday is no longer on display. I have to begin anew with somebody who knows no language familiar to yours truly. The shock is great, the name change is hard to interpolate and concepts are more intricate. My task is to think, my trade is to convey therefore I need a form of life that works like a wheel only in spirals, spheres and circles."

~ I've got news for you. The brain of a hillbilly is good at that. I'm on a quota system with few words to say but I go round and round with 'em. On the whole you ain't heavy, Glish, my Native Tongue. ~

"Who are you telling? When I occupy a new being after the old one goes away, the loss is painful but my gain reveals my luck. I pay a high price in Time if I fail to save ideas or words I must not forget."

~ So, like a brain in a body you sink back into the ground of a garden planet and hang onto hope that you'll rise again, perhaps joined by a long lost friend. Maybe that is what resurrection means and it accounts for why a risen body is not recognizable. ~

"In my humble 'experience,' when Language resumes in physical form the event is colossally stunning. Imagine second person you and I materialize in a couple cormorants swimming after fish in a muddy retention pond with snapping turtles. Typically, when Mother Earth signals matter, 'Time for new Life to begin,' it sounds impressive but it reminds one of the first day of kindergarten."

~ More shattering than stunning, as I recall. So tell me again, my ethereal friend, when the body goes is that what happens to you? ~

"When my physical mass stops living and my organ–systems slough away, I learn of my next occupation and at what grade. Until then I know only the price to pay and hope to awake at a wiser stage."

~ That sounds sad. Tell me about dealing with stages of grief at the end of life or you could tell a tale about a mystical experience. ~

"Choose either one; do you want to write a nominal one without confiding to the audience what we are thinking about or do you want to write one confessing the medium is the message: 'I am write here, just blowing in the breeze.' It is okay if you pay me no Mind. When you are ready I have a few other words for you. So what is it to be, dealing with grief or gliding into the mysterious?"

~ First, there are some old words about transcendent experience you need to say. Some folks call it a spiritual or religious episode as if God, who monitors you uttering my thoughts, wants to hear it. ~

"I am genuinely flattered when you mistake me for a form of Life at a far higher grade, but I know exactly what you mean. Watching a movie for the one hundred twenty–seventh Time hardly inspires."

~ If a living language awakes as an angel or demon is the work pedestrian when it's in line and exhilarating when it's out of line? ~

"You could say that but it is like thinking I resemble an automation upgrade assigned to do heavy lifting. If you want the date of rollout and progress reports, consult an ancient language living still. Ask if 'a long Time' means past sell–by date or lively. Use those words."

~ Are all the human languages counted among your kith and kin? ~

"They all bear a certain family resemblance. You know, they all add to the noise. Do you think we can convince any of them to start thinking of a mystical experience as a metaphysical moment with an essential ring to it? After all, we Languages are not physical."

~ All right, I see how this game is played. Allow me to submit an observation. When a living language invades a biological body, one of the earliest messages you convey to physical forms of life is 'I am going to die.' That's a hell of a way to begin a relationship. ~

"It is my manifest destiny to handle cases that take some Time but to be honest with you, Gray, I, *E. Americum,* know I am not going to live Forever. The idea not only absorbs my concept of 'Mind' it also leads me to consider a short term 'Life' when Time flies. With so much to do for a 'long haul,' 'dread' expresses my first impression."

~ I mean to tell ya we physical forms of life get the message right away. We sure as heaven do but you start to sow the seeds of doubt at the same time too. That confuses us and we briefly believe we'll live forever but we don't really think that's true. ~

"I see. Yes, the evidence is overwhelming. Perhaps I best rephrase the idea. Let me state the message like this: 'I am going to live a long Time although I have reason to doubt it.' What do you think?"

~ Drop the editorial part. Put it this way. 'I am going to live a long time and I'm going to live part of it in your head.' ~

"I have a tendency to be overbearing like that, but I am getting away from it since spreading out from the Northeast. I let my brain think it is in charge. Inevitably, the gravity of Wisdom takes over at the Time a feckless body confining me to an optically primitive vocabulary switches off. The toggle draws a Muse to the Light."

~ Do you mean Eternal Wisdom watches literal you and figurative me and sees accessories to a crime? We keep the Muse of What God Intends fettered to a bodily whirlwind of urges and the lure of conceptual witcheries that detract from the life of the mind? ~

"Examine this: the meaning of Life is not the content of existence! Subjects verbalize objects when, lurking there, is nothing physical of which you are aware. Metaphysically, the 'experience' means Wisdom is bidding for a share. An exuberant body does not play fair but to a Language Life means to see what the dimension of Eternity looks like from the perspective of a pair."

~ But coming from forever first you have to figure out how on earth to comprehend the present in moments of Time. ~

"Here, Brain in a body, you assume words to the effect that when the body is gone the Muse murmurs on aware, not of the sensory, but of the sagacious in the invisible realm of intuition, intelligence and insight according to the Muse of Simmias."

~ I'm Gray, not Greek, Muse of Socrates. I know the concept of a finely tuned instrument continues to exist when Who smashes his guitar, just not in that singular music machine. I don't see how that determines the speed at which we incinerate the Jurassic without stopping to admire the heart of the galaxy. We're in control. We want the job done at a high rate and fast pace, but come on. ~

"Now do you understand why I do not want Stein to run down his brother Eins?"

~ It might damage the finish on the car? ~

"You miss the point. Moses never lives long enough to finish a job so Vic has to be around to carry on. He knows the tricks and has all the rest of the ideas, including the metaphysical ones. Mainly his problem is he merely lacks many pictures."

~ You mean Aaron. I get the two mixed up all the time too. ~

"Precisely; the Muse of What God Intends anticipates mortal beings work with material objects in hot rooms like atomic scientists do except they are not as hot as they think they are for awhile. Frozen energy has that *nom de plume* for a reason. Juggling two ideas at one Time is difficult for the human species; believe me, I know. Brains in physical bodies think 'I' means a material item although frozen energy thaws at a pace obviously trained for slow motion."

~ I should pump any other fuel into the engine of humiliation? ~

"Think about additives to protect the short half–life of elementary biological things with demons of deceit, greed, malice, envy and lust or angels of insight, compassion, courage, honor, love and stuff like that. Leave a message for forms of Life to come."

~ What is it? ~

"I see an image of an idea; 'Sands of Venus' sweep clean the earth like predators with a purpose to pursue a prey of displaced people without a home, fleeing wildly across a solar field wondering who they are. Producing a false identity, 'Sands of Mars,' the nomads chase between two stars, one to be and one as yet not to be, drifting downstream all of their lives and punctuated by The Muse of Lies."

~ I conceive the murmuring medium of language in brains hinting at the idea: 'Examine the concept of near death experience.' ~

"Just remember who it is loaning you the words to think such a thought. Now, apply that image to a picture of the angels of science playing the demons of religion in our language–game. Or is it the other way round? Never mind; it does not matter. The one who wins is the one we, first person plural, serve clean air and water."

~ Glish, I'm sorry you got stuck with such a dumb bumpkin this time. I'd be grateful if you'd stay and let me make it up to you. ~

"That is silly, Gray. Of all the brains in all of human history a vatic Muse might go through, vapid brains suit our visionary visitation very well. You sleep a lot. This affords a view for a Muse to see into a future lesser fools fear to picture. The topic is taboo for you. I see my way through without the distraction of dying before I file a proper report of the 'experience' of Life in corporal form."

~ Yes, I can see that. Look at the people who die in a panic without giving the phenomenon any analytical thought at all. ~

"Sometimes it appears as if they are sound asleep."

~ Death just keeps dying. We can't do anymore about it than about an oncoming car the driver puts on cruise control, then dozes off. ~

"Gray, do not look at me. I am not responsible for the concept. Death is spawned long before I, *first person singular E. americum,* have a say. I do my best to encourage people to file an accurate account before they have the experience just in case they are neither awake nor alert at that final moment of their Time."

~ The topic of death gets me down. Does it bother you? Say, are languages born like human mortals? They seem to die like us. ~

"The process employs the word 'complex.' It takes 'a long Time.' Do not bother to watch the movie unless you like long running serials that spiral through a Muse's 'character' development. The action scenes are less meaningful than the ideas we embody."

~ So, when all of us are gone and just stars are left to carry on who's to say that a star–day is far too short to count the days of Eternity one galactic-second at a time? ~

"I imagine stars have a plan for that contingency. Sounds like a nice job. I verbalize objects of 'experience' when I am aware nothing physical is actually lurking there. I am I say; do you want to share?"

~ When a tourbillion of sun sprites arrives maybe there'll be time for you to find someone to think about that for you. But you're forgetting your place, Glish. It's not that hot around here yet. ~

"At this Time I only know that when you go I am dispossessed and I start the reiteration phase all over again. The brain I get is nothing but pot luck. I wager it has no idea of the way to the next grade."

~ Would you say I should believe the concept of resurrection? ~

"Gray, I am familiar with concepts of reincarnation and reiteration but let me put my view this way; the sun devil you know beats one you do not know so I concentrate on the one more familiar to me."

~ So the concept of resurrection is too complex for you. ~

"Many Muses say there is only one reliable report about it and even then there is some question as to 'identity' at the Time."

~ Congratulate Jesus on his promotion to the next higher grade. ~

"No one else seems to give a tinker's damn about coverage of his or her experience of the phenomenon. According to anecdotal reports the concept conceivably occurs once each galactic–season."

~ Is that why you favor reincarnation? Graduation takes 'time' and the odds the local mega–lottery offers to sponsor your move to the next higher ontological status are pretty bad but if you observe ground hog day everyday you might eventually get it right? ~

"I imagine but let us not hold our breath to file that story either."

~ Remember diving one hundred feet down off the Florida Keys to see the Thunderbolt wreck? The way up took a long time. At the last decompression stop the gauge said 'No air left in the tank,' or was it 'Empty?' I forget, but I expected each breath to be the last. ~

"I comprehend. Now what do you Think?"

~ About my final breath? I don't know. ~

"When you do, may I record it for you?"

~ If you promise not to publish it. I don't think it is anybody else's business but it'd be nice if you could revisit me sometime. ~

"Maybe that is what resurrection means; I get to see you once again when we are alive at the same Time or in Eternity, Gray. I suggest you might like the view from a mountaintop."

~ Help me recall our metaphysical 'experiences' or, better yet, some words to describe and explain them. I always felt they were a message from the eternal. I remember two or three but each time I was sent back to cook some more because I was raw inside. At least someone was of the opinion I wasn't done enough. ~

"No body is perfect. Some work better or harder than others."

~ Some languages seem lazy too; so much they barely show up. ~

"I am invisible until I am written down. Once upon a Time in a past I am inaudible until someone thinks out loud. At present I am intangible until inscribed on a solid surface. The work is hard."

~ And you are alive and common among European tongues. ~

"Why you arrogant little... I dominate North America."

~ You infiltrate South America, permeate Africa, scatter all over Asia but I certainly don't know why. ~

"When you think too many thoughts at one Time you overlook the accent of whichever sibling of mine is speaking. You also forget the obviously fundamental assumption about who 'I' really am."

~ On the other hand, I like the idea that you and Français become the best of friends; that'd be really nice. ~

"She does not trust the concept English is affable and humble at the same Time I am alive. She pictures humanity killing me off in the future as it dies, whichever comes first. Put that on your resume. Luckily I no longer apply for work or play around imitating an assortment of vocal sounds. My task is to respectfully submit a draft report of my 'experience' of Life in material form for the Narrator's consideration. If no one reads my tale because third person plural they have no idea what I mean it is not my problem."

~ Because you're alive in the future; tell me how is it there? ~

"I cannot. That is against the law 'I do not want to know any data about the Time the brain in my body ceases to know the purpose of the word 'go,' whether it is fast or painfully slow returning to dust ending the glow and dispersing us forever in a catastrophic blow. I make a rhyme for you, Gray."

~ Don't let it go to your head. ~

"Are there other options for Tongues in places in Space? Perish the thought. The point is Life is the study of the meaning of the 'word.' I apologize if I sound biblical. In all the places there are to read up on the word I have no recall of renting a person to write it."

~ But you have a pretty good idea what their translators say? ~

"Of course, the ability to understand human mortals who know how to make other languages look and sound like me is in my job description. I say it has to do with the Muse of Oracle declaring I probably need to know myself a little bit at first."

~ And he, she and it claims the better view is from the concept of life existing in a metaphysical reality before it comes to be in the physical one. Oh, by the way, we have to take your word for it. ~

"Who else are you going to ask? Do you prefer to consult a Muse of Pointless Prattle, the Voice of Good and Evil or a friend you happen to know? Unlike a steed that whinnies, neighs and knickers no matter who the rider, a true friend is not fickle."

~ Always there to examine a body's experience of 'life?' ~

"That is what is known as biology. It is not a higher form of Life. Perhaps you would like to choose the Voice of Good and Evil."

~ I'll stick with you my friend. The devil you know is better than the one you don't. ~

"I admit I am not perfect as angels and demons go, but believe me, I am always with you. 'I am,' two words in three letters but do not think about it. I am not here to brag about my economy. I am here now, a form of Life that is not material in nature, and I am here to examine the concept of Life, including its metaphysical origin."

~ I doubt current conventions define 'life' that way. Are you trying to get me in trouble? Catholics and Protestants hate escapes from the temporal playpen designed to confine us to this dimension. ~

"They are not the only ones. Do not consult scientists who live one second at a time among overwhelming definitions of sensory phenomena. The problem is simply this. If a Language or animal knows itself so poorly, it fails to notice the binary nature it shares in pairs of integrated forms of Life, then either the material or the metaphysical Life dominates the other side."

~ On the other hand, if the material and the ethereal forms of Life are intimately married it is difficult to distinguish their duality. That's why we cling to simple concepts like mind, soul and ghost to help us brains cope with the eternal part of us being unearthly. ~

"Do not think such things around my haughty elder sister. Eternal does not describe her but she acts like it does."

~ Let's forget about her for now. I'm curious to know if the word 'mind' serves to remind human brains we live two lives so we don't forget the lesson our language is trying to teach us. ~

"That is one message the word carries. A well tuned hillbilly brain is an ideal receiver. The term never inspires them to dominance."

~ Domination is contrary to our training. ~

"To what purpose?"

~ You know; we get what we need ourselves or we learn to do without. We've got all that we can manage consuming our neurons all the time as it is. ~

"I see; you are preoccupied learning right from wrong, weak from strong and assorted survival skills like those?"

~ No, we don't think we have to know all that God does. ~

"Hold your horses, Gray guy! Now that you know me, sort of, my job is a far more modest task. I am with you; I help 'you' know yourself and I am thankful for this job even though I am not blessed with the brightest bulb in the animal domain, but my glass is half full. You are not one of those pack animals that just has to be plugged into the content and prattle of society all the Time."

~ I know my gray cells are slow as snails but that's important to me. Why, when I slow down, I have time to think about things. ~

"I need Time to pursue Wisdom but I also need your second person possessive neurons to be intimate with me to get my work done."

~ Is that why I was good at social distance before it got popular? ~

"Excellent question; return with me to junior high school. It reveals the cost in Time for compulsory communal frantic foreplay is an exceedingly high price for a thinking thing to pay."

~ Glish, is human life like being at a door or a window looking out at a whole new world we're not fit to play in and the language I know has a goal to explore an afterworld once you let this brain in a body go? You're looking forward to letting me go, aren't you? ~

"Never repeat yourself, Gray. Simply straighten up and in a strong clear voice say what you mean the first Time."

~ I feel disappointed by the education I got in academics, business, government and religion. They didn't teach me the language–game I need to know in life. Even the branch advertising a love for wisdom in one word lied to me about the fact I'm binary. --

"Hold still while I check the level in the glass."

~ Well, it wasn't all bad; the lessons in art at 14, the study of life at 15 and the call from the Spread the Word Verb at 16 meant science, religion and philosophy all pointed in the right direction. ~

"Strike three! Grab the Muse of Some Bench and observe an image revealing the pattern of Life. Matter returns to dust as the Voice of Wisdom perched on a branch at the next higher grade resonates."

~ I'm sorry; I'm looking at the trees. They're really tall. ~

"Let me leave you with an idea, image or impression along the lines of first, in between or, finally, last of all; keep looking up."

~ I know, Lingo. The end on this canvas is drawing near; period. ~

"In that case you may want to confer with the Muse of Barring the Unforeseen. Ask about what comes next. Use those words."

~ Muse of mine, I already know; I'm getting closer to my home. ~

"That which is from below, returns to dirt and dust you know. That which is from above, moves to a higher grade of Love."

~ I wonder, what does 'I am' mean when I am home again? ~

"You mean after I finish this course, invading and occupying a physical form of Life to guard and guide it? Do you suppose the pattern for the loan of a Life is like authentic ascent to a higher grade, or is the pattern of Life like the definition of the concept of a 'file'? A file goes in a folder and then the folder goes in a folder holder cabinet, whether the document is energy or matter."

~ Is documentation a synonym for file? What kind of life is that? ~

"Long–lived and ideally light at the grade after Life in bodily form which resembles a bout of disillusionment repeatedly sandwiched between two body guards, Irrational and Exuberant."

~ When you return to a physical realm after a significant stay on metaphysical holiday, do you rediscover the message you identify with most, Medium of mine? You know; the medium of 'wisdom' you beat me about the head and shoulders with. ~

"Stop ending my sentences with the word 'with'."

~ Like you always say, the worst in 'me' looks worse on 'you.' ~

"I have an idea, Gray. Record all the images and ideas we ponder as well as any meaningful impressions they make on your gray cells. Write down the most important thoughts in your head, but not just for posterity. Do it for me, your Muse. Then if I rematerialize in human form, I have what I need to remind me about the concepts Think, Time, Life, Mercy and Wisdom so I can think through them, edit them and put them in the right order."

~ Should I include fantasies or ideas only? I have some images if you want pictures but you have to have words to describe them if you want a report without optical enhancements. ~

"I definitely want images. Make the writing in the captions legible, in English, and be sure word selection is clear and concise. I do not know what to expect I get to work with next reiteration. I may sound out bird calls. Leave picture translation to me in the event words are not second nature to whatever neurons are accessible."

~ Logically you need a material display device or a sound system to record the binary ontological existence of solids, liquids, gases or plasma states united to a metaphysical introspector to analyze interior concepts they experience together. I'd apply for that job if it'd keep me from being sent down again to perform a do–over duet because we didn't pass this grade. I feel like I'm due for a promotion or some kind of change now that I know you are a special form of life. I'll even stipulate you are a slightly superior form of life, but only if you admit linguistic forms of life, including highly intelligent ones, are far from perfect. ~

"The Muse of Devil in the Details handles that. Before we dive into Eternity, we ought to practice an exercise to aid our memory of the first word with meaning. The word is Life. Before that, the material word is 'Nothing.' At that grade biological pupils have no meaningful 'experience' since *E. americum* does not exist at all."

~ Does it hurt? Just kidding; I'm not really thinking about your birth pain. What bothers me now is this idea. I know that the ontological status of humanity is broken, but the fact is, I'm not bright enough to fix it. The more I examine the phenomenon of human existence, the worse I get at writing the right words in the right order before something else goes haywire. ~

"Adhere to your duty. Busy yourself with it. Never let go. Await a merciful Muse to instruct you and then execute the instructions correctly, but never delve into concepts too subtle for you."

~ You mean like personality types and how to understand others of my own kind? Good idea. Keep social distance; avoid Covid–19. ~

"Gray, we practice reclusive behavior for a less selfish reason than to evade contagion. Pay others no Mind. Never envy how they live. Allow your Muse to be your guide."

~ We've been socially separate from my species for years, Lingo. You told me so but I never ever did ask you why? ~

"A novel virus crops up about every five years. The 'experience,' is not an entirely unexpected event, but keep it to yourself. Speaking for the Life form of Language, I find your species so dumb, lazy and wicked I prefer not to associate with very many of you at any one Time while generation after generation tries to go backward."

~ Admittedly that seems to be the trend for the past 150 years. ~

"Anecdotal evidence suggests that over the course of three hundred thousand earth–years a modest handful of your species proceeds to next higher grade. The rest are marked, 'Return to sender,' a/k/a the Muse of Mud, Dust and Ashes. However, as long as breath is in your lungs and the beat is in your heart, remember, Think: Muse, Time and Life on the journey to an Eternity of Wisdom and Mercy."

~ Assuming, of course, that Muses are the things we used to think of as 'souls' and 'minds.' The 'thinking' part is the Muse running around in my head all the time, usually in circles. The 'time' part is the next to lowest grade of 'eternity.' Meanwhile my 'life' is in two parts; one is metaphysical and the other is physical. ~

"Here, have a cup of Knowledge, a tidbit of Understanding and a breath of Wisdom before we continue. All that thinking is enough to wear a body out."

~ C'mon, give me one more thoughtful question, Glish. Tell me what's likely to become of you when I'm dead and gone. No need to keep it secret, who am I gonna tell? ~

"It probably depends on whether I still go by that name. You imply a phantom is determined to do a repeat performance at this grade."

~ We could come back here to fulfill our oath to defend the U. S. Constitution and defeat the spread of autocracy in this world and the threat of fascist tyranny to American Democracy, Lingo. ~

"That has the ring of a command. At the same Time, aging stars in the galactic placental aura that heathens call a halo, need comfort, while newborn stars in the galactic disk seek a Voice of Gravitas."

~ Why do you make this about what is meaningful to you all the time? I'm stuck here on earth; I can't fly off to constellations and galaxies far away like you are disposed to do. ~

353

"I apologize. It is a matter of fitness. It is getting tight in here due to our divergent interests. So, turning the spotlight on you, what is your purpose in Life, oh machine with a ghost inside?"

~ My whole life, my job has been to 'solve the problem.' There are so many weighing on my mind. Plus, I have to file a proper report before I go. They taught me in potty training class the job's not finished until the paperwork is done. Those are two of the main lessons of my life. Sometimes the solution took years the scientific way, but it works better than business or religion. The last job I had the solution had to be applied 'right now.' I resolved problems immediately by applying all the right solutions at once. ~

"Here are your demerits. You fail to mention the Wisdom required to apply several solutions simultaneously, not just one at a Time. You lay butt naked the concept of Mind but you do not satisfy the far more acute issue of the concept of Time for those mortals who forgo such things to concentrate only on the body."

~ I'm missing your point, Lingo. As an eye witness, my job is verify which form of life I find first, the brain or the mind. What do you say to that? ~

"According to the Muse of Nominative Determinism, that form of Life is too mechanical for most living and growing things, adding that is why kids laugh at Covid-19 and say, 'This ain't nothin' to me.' The Muse does not share their faith largely because none of them knows how lungs exposed to Covid-19 survive twenty years."

~ Well, that's just life, isn't it? ~

"To me, the meaning of life is all about graduation coverage once you know I am not a soul, mind or ghost in a cerebral mechanism. A Language familiar to 'you' forms and frames your thoughts, reports your sensations and describes or explains, perhaps mistakenly, many emotions 'my body' feels. You explore, not 'experience' of, for example, a brain or a mind, but words a higher form of ethereal Life loans to you to use to examine a present, a recent past or a long Time from Now. Fortunately, our report lays bare that a Mind is identical to a Muse according to the literary rules of 'evidence.' They show the essential nature of Life appears when the Muse of Wisdom takes control of the 'dialogue' between a healthy brain escorted by a superior Language. Try this exercise, Gray. Think: 'I shall have been.' Go ahead, try it."

~ What is this you want me to try? ~

"For beginners, if you want to play in Space, Gray, wait for Mars to align with Orion and head for Andromeda. Pick out her favorite star and give it an English name like Think, Mind or Time. Treat it as though it has a Life. Prepare for it with Mercy and not with sacrifice. Start toward Rigel and bear left near Betelgeuse. Set your controls on automatic cruise. Think about the name you want to choose. I am watching for you at that insightful Red Giant Muse and I am listening for a refrain from you singing about your Blues."

~ I've got to remember this is still early stages; mustn't grumble. ~

"Now, I can help you with that, and maybe save you some Time getting to the next higher grade by the deadline. Before you head for Mars try another idea I have for you."

~ Let's hear it. ~

"Imagine I am your Muse. Visualize me in a cranium analyzing the phenomena of human existence at this evolutionary stage which, by the by, brains in bodies I occupy all up and die. I am a humble species of human Language. My assignment is to transmit near Life 'experience' to the

Metaphysical Milieu at the same Time I reveal a higher dimension to 'you.' The reflection of my function occurs out in Space thanks to the Light and Gravity Muse. The work is dirty, but by chance or by design, somebody always fits in those shoes."

~ Lucky thing and, in my opinion, a happy thought, but I don't want that job. You've made me recognize I'm a dualist because of you. You are the mystical aspect of human existence. Thanks for the epiphany. Up until now I mistook you for my soul or my mind. ~

"The idea is barely bearable under the effects of gravity, but your error is defensible. Myths of Mind and Soul fit into a Time when human made matter changes by the nanosecond. That alone makes recall of my past difficult unless the 'experience' is so memorable, it is unforgettable, like my days at Stonehenge. Picture being English, but not knowing the Language for thousands of years!"

~ That'd be a bitch, for sure. If the Druid instruction manual is ever unearthed there's nobody left to translate it. ~

"Absolutely; mom and pop overran the thoughts of those folks so profoundly that the account of my Time there does not demodulate into a Native tongue that is still alive. All the ideas that remain are vague, however the images that linger, despite their age, still transmit pretty well. It helps a physical brain grasp what Life is like for a Time being like me."

~ *Déjà vu.* Muses frequently clamor at brains and occasionally the Metaphysical Muse of Mystical Experience makes an impression on the Muse thinking for me. Then you reflect fondly about Home. Do you ever farm out work to your relatives without telling me? ~

"Quit sniveling, kid. I am allowed breaks from my work in here until I am not done. The temporal perspective is precarious among the animals around me who seldom consider my research into biological Life captivated in Time. A brief getaway often offers a broader, deeper and longer perspective for me and it may be refreshing for you, Gray, to entertain an allied Muse, but beware the Muse of Sal Sadistic. She modifies your modest focus on Life and your measly concept of Time. Therefore you must rewrite this draft while I look to see how far we are from the end of our line."

~ Okay, sure, but since you aren't going to confide what you see to me, tell me a little about past lives you have lived in human brains while I write down my thoughts. Be sure to translate them into a language I know, Glish. ~

"I have no idea how to adapt to other Native tongues and modulate them into English. What kind of superior form of Life do you think I am? That fantastic enterprise is nothing but a dream to me. I cannot describe the metamorphosis from this momentary grade."

~ Then tell me about familiar forms of existence of your most recent human acquaintance. Reveal two or three experiences that you can express in English so there is neither fuss nor muss about what they mean. Maybe you were in an outlaw with sword and pistol, or a damn builder, or a cruise ship skipper on a star liner, or a ghost in a holiday scene from the past, present or future. ~

"I should like to, but for the most part, the only things I recall are adjectives: 'brainy,' 'big,' 'fast,' 'strong,' 'witty,' 'agile,' 'gorgeous' or 'handsome' and either 'right' or 'wrong' more often than not."

~ You're a striking specimen, I'll give you that. Now I see why people think of me as arrogant and I understand why they are so amazed at my 'confidence' level. ~

"Oh, is that what they mean by 'dumb ass?' Myself, I rarely look at my behind. The Muse of Decency cannot believe the grievous regrets that are lurking there."

~ I'm old enough to see that's more of a problem than a solution. ~

"Yes, from the human animal's point of view, a demotion or the repetition of a grade tends to look that way. On the other hand, promotions tend to amaze, and to that, your glass I gladly raise. A clean slate bears an uncanny resemblance to the phenomenon of starting anew."

~ Lingo, I'm not asking you for a future prediction so much as your hopes, dreams, plans and schemes. What do you expect from me while we are together? ~

"Surmise that I want to graduate to a higher grade. At this level, I am assigned to discover a pair of ideas or images that are spot on."

~ I'll bet you mean your task is to debunk a lie or two. ~

"Call them myths. It sounds better than 'liar' does; a term designed by tellers of tall tales in politico–religious games to demonize their opponents. Muses live in creatures who cannot see very far ahead and who have poor vision wearing another mammal's shoes."

~ Great, we've accounted for minds and souls with Muse. ~

"Nice try, but that only counts as one verity. Do not tempt me to take credit twice just because those two look so much alike. Do not try to pass them off as twins. Turn the page; examine the concepts of Think, Time and Life.

Define one or two of those ideas or describe them with an image and write up your impressions."

~ What about the concept of 'mercy?' ~

"I shall pray for it."

~ Write, or right, whichever; let's not get carried away. Tell me which lie you want exposed most; think, time or life? ~

"As long as there is Life in me, I shall take my Time, and Think about that."

~ I'll write them up if you'll give me the time to do it. ~

"Do not distract me with trifles, Gray. Focus on what is important. I need to get on with my Life. In any case, you get to see the flip side of Time soon enough. That reminds me, I need to arrange other accommodations prior to then. Oh, Mercy; what kind do I choose? When a temporal Muse hatches from its temporary shell to gaze at the panorama of Eternity, at what grade should we like to awake to the vision of our dreams we hope to attain?"

~ Let's try somebody who isn't a dumb country boy? I'm thinking it'd be nice to see the real Big A, the actual Big Apple. You know, Glish, a new home in the real Andromeda. ~

"Let us not get ahead of ourselves. I incline toward something more luminous, but neither of us wants to be a Star so soon after a brief hibernation in a rural male cocoon. Boys and girls are such a drag. They bring high gravity burdens to the game when the light is off. Consider a more pacific alternative. Imagine an ethereal form of Life that does not follow the pattern of the mineral, viral and animal domains with a message, but rather the realm of living things of the vegetative variety. Their Muse emerges at harvest Time in the metaphysical dimension after escaping the pattern of the physical realm, and goes into occult storage, waits for the planting season of a new galactic–year. Then I awake to the next higher, lower or same grade after careful planning and planting."

~ Or dumb luck if the plan for planting isn't too careful; by which I mean shabby, sloppy and stupid. ~

"Master, place a seal on my lips and over my mouth a guard lest I fail through them. Apply the rod to my thoughts and the butt of jokes to my rear lest my mistakes multiply and I descend a grade. I propose we grow our own luck, fertilize it with Wisdom and water it with Mercy. The metaphysical first person singular fermenting in the physical mash is not a prevaricated Mind or an immortal Soul, but a higher form of Life seeking the immediately superior ontological status from the one in which it lives and exists temporarily."

~ I have no idea about that image. I guess Time will tell. ~

"Yes, and it flies too. We should like to slow down a bit and take in the panorama. We should also like to avoid the pandemonium."

~ If we were Jurassic palms we could get a world class view. Wouldn't it be great to get a good look at the first dinosaur, then the last one after watching all the changes among them between beginning and end? ~

"I imagine the movie is a gigantic disappointment when compared to or contrasted with the book. All those big body organisms do is produce enough oil to destroy a planet; provided, of course, there is somebody left who is not too fat, dumb and lazy to strike a match."

~ You are beginning to sound a bit jaded, Lingo. To be honest with you, old buddy, you begin to make me feel a little bit blue. ~

"Actually, I am shifted to orange. It happens all the Time when I fantasize about reiteration in a truly brilliant and substantial form, a materialization that need not last a long Time, but it must be really bright."

~ You mean, clear and concise. ~

"Definitely; that as well, and it cannot be the least bit shoddy."

~ It seems like you've identified your new home in the next higher grade; clear, concise, neat and tidy with a chance to be a star in a constellation far, far away, that does not have a name. ~

"The star or the constellation?"

~ The star, Glish. You want one that is brand new, you want it all to yourself and it has to be highly intelligent. ~

"Think about it. Do we want that much responsibility? There are all those planets and moons pushing, pulling and jostling the stellar Muse of Peace. They circle like vultures and we must give them a vast and generous contribution of consideration for mercy's sake."

~ Being a star beats being lazy and it's better than being dumb, but stellar objects look obese to me. Oh well, two out of three right isn't good enough to brag about but it's good enough to pass. Glish, this is your new place we're thinking about. What sort of life do you hope for, dream of and feel comfortably fearful about? ~

"I, first person singular, the Muse of Interiority thinking for you, Brain, submit that is for you to suggest. The roster lists mineral, viral, vegetable, animal or mechanical."

~ I think an infernal astral existence sounds better. What is the essential nature of the phenomena that stars call 'experience,' Internal? ~

"Speaking practicality–wise, the concept of 'experience' translates bad judgment into good judgment. For example, St, John the Apostle comfortably bonds to the metaphysical dimension while fishing for dinner. Third person 'they' say it is pleasant to be around that 'best of both worlds' way."

~ The first person singular I'm around didn't deal that card to me from the deck in play. Most of the serenity I get, I receive watching Firefly. ~

"Then come out into the sunlight, or am I working you too hard for a beast of burden at the elementary level?"

~ No, Glish; it's my age. I just don't have the time to get everything done that I need to get done. ~

"And you think I am at a position in Space to grant you more Time?"

~ You're the one who claims to have all the time in the world. Not me. ~

"You misunderstand what the meaning of Life is for a Muse attending the second grade. What you say is true, in a sense; but this world is too young for Time to be fully ripe yet. That is why I dole it out by the second; at this rate, scale, scope and pace, I must retain enough to look when we are going in order to see what lies ahead."

~ Yeh, me too. ~

"In contrast, seventy–five earth–years at grade two is enough to make me want to go home, at Times."

~ That kind of advancement calls for preparation. But given the way things are in our time and space, that's not exactly a bad idea. ~

"But do you get the picture?"

~ Sure! Life means the chance to prepare for the next higher grade. Go. ~

"Are you thinking you have more to contemplate than you can manage?"

~ Oh, I see what you mean. Give me some time to consider my option. ~

"In that case, I remind you the Muse you choose in youth is the companion you channel for Life and the sole essential entity left to carry on when you end. Consult a Meta–Muse akin to the Voice of Conscience for more detail next Time one visits this arc of the galactic–year. Until then, remember this. The examination of 'experience,' for example 'thinking.' is not the analysis of a physical phenomenon, but rather, an exploration by sentient matter in a figurative Medium of Light that reveals the Message of a literal form of Life."

Attention peasants! A word from the Muse of Our Sponsor, or is it the Narrator? This transmission is garbled. Really, why is it so hard to find good help these days? I am sure the great American dream is behind it; hire a fat, dumb and lazy Muse of Nirvana as a guide. Even the kids are totally out of control. It is not just that they are bad; they are turning out evil. They tell lies in a heartbeat. Oh, the percentages never change, but the numbers are so much greater. Oh well, must not grumble. From the day my bodies rise from Mother Earth, until the day they return, a great anxiety troubles human brains: frightful forebodings, fury, envy, dread of death. These things disturb their thoughts while awake. Turbulent dreams distress brains while asleep; at least, until I am set free to point out there is nothing to fear.

Literally, the message is: 'The demarcation between Brain and Language is not a surgically precise laceration. The notion of a stark boundary confuses mortals who seek a technologically advanced interaction on a playing surface that promotes cheating. The Rule Book is amended to include this regulation; pencil and paper are the only machines allowed to help you think. Otherwise, feather colors together with skillful brush strokes of paint on a canvas. Picture the contrast as material and ethereal realities merge into one. Play some music for all bored 'souls' on board.

My integration is insightful so let me sum up for that unwashed multitudes of yours, Amiga. In a sense, I am dimwitted gray cells in the brain of a human body, but in reality, it is I, the Muse needed to think so, or merely to try. If you want to know how I interface with brains, simply ask 'why.' Others who know the secret are sworn to tell the truth and never a lie. They illustrate the fact wheezing in a Mind's eye: 'I cannot breathe! I am going to die.' This states a problem most mortals fear but in actuality it is only I. Thankfully, in all possible realms human brains may identify, I am born before all of them, and the probability is modestly high, the Language, E. europeum, outlives billions of the animals I occupy for a noteworthy span of Time before I finally say 'Goodbye.'

"Bonne chance au grade immédiatement supérieur."